IN EXTREMIS

Also by Tim Parks

Fiction

TONGUES OF FLAME
LOVING ROGER
HOME THOUGHTS
FAMILY PLANNING
GOODNESS
CARA MASSIMINA
MIMI'S GHOST
SHEAR
EUROPA
DESTINY
JUDGE SAVAGE
RAPIDS
CLEAVER
DREAMS OF RIVERS AND SEAS
SEX IS FORBIDDEN (first published as THE SERVER)
PAINTING DEATH
THOMAS AND MARY

Non-fiction

ITALIAN NEIGHBOURS
AN ITALIAN EDUCATION
ADULTERY & OTHER DIVERSIONS
TRANSLATING STYLE
HELL AND BACK
A SEASON WITH VERONA
THE FIGHTER
TEACH US TO SIT STILL
ITALIAN WAYS
WHERE I'M READING FROM

Tim Parks

IN EXTREMIS

Harvill *Secker*
LONDON

1 3 5 7 9 10 8 6 4 2

Harvill Secker, an imprint of Vintage,
20 Vauxhall Bridge Road,
London SW1V 2SA

Harvill Secker is part of the Penguin Random House group
of companies whose addresses can be found at
global.penguinrandomhouse.com

Copyright © Tim Parks 2017

Tim Parks has asserted his right to be identified as the author of this
Work in accordance with the Copyright, Designs and Patents Act 1988

First published by Harvill Secker in 2017

penguin.co.uk/vintage

A CIP catalogue record for this book is available from the British Library

ISBN 9781911215707

Typeset in India by Thomson Digital Pvt Ltd, Noida, Delhi

Printed and bound in Great Britain by Clays Ltd, St Ives PLC

Penguin Random House is committed to a sustainable future
for our business, our readers and our planet. This book is made
from Forest Stewardship Council® certified paper.

IN EXTREMIS

PART ONE

I

Mother's corpse. This is what I keep thinking about.

Should I view it?

Why can't I decide?

I was at a conference for physiotherapists in Amersfoort. There was much discussion of the pelvic floor and anal massage. For the first time, I opted to try the treatment myself. At breakfast a Portuguese paediatrician had sworn by it. It had saved his life. The physio, from California, warned me that a single massage might do no more than bring back old pains. But I was curious. Afterwards in the shower I felt an unpleasant urgency, a burning in the bladder and, with it, a shift in my state of mind: fretfulness. It was all too familiar. Then, glancing at my laptop as I towelled myself dry, I saw an email had arrived from my sister, addressed to both my brother and myself. 'Mum going downhill fast. Better come now.'

So the question was: whether to give the talk I had been invited to give, or to depart at once. It is the decisions you can't take that make you wonder who you are – despair sometimes. But this one was easy. I was only going to lose a couple of hours; I felt a certain responsibility to my hosts, who had paid for the trip and been generous. The business with the corpse is different. Actually, if I say 'corpse', I feel there can be no problem 'viewing' it. Viewing is their word, not mine, as if one were looking over a property, or the scene of a crime. And if I say 'Mother', then I really do want to see her. Tears come. But you can hardly use the word 'view' to speak of seeing your mother. It is 'viewing Mother's corpse' that is the problem.

What struck me about the massage was the man's delicacy. He came to my hotel room, knocked softly on the door. Dropping my trousers, it was impossible not to think of a homosexual assignation. He was aware of my embarrassment and wanted only to keep the situation no more or less than what it was, a physio massaging a patient. 'Stick a pillow under you, mate,' he said. He was grinning. Perhaps he thought all Englishmen called each other 'mate'. Aged forty-fiveish, chinless and pockmarked, he was not a good-looking man, yet extremely attractive to be around. A man entirely at ease with himself, I thought. He communicated ease. I was envious. What I want, I had told my shrink on our first tumultuous meeting, is to be at ease with life. She frowned as if to say, Don't go running ahead of yourself now, Señor Sanders.

If I look back I can count perhaps half a dozen other medical intrusions in this territory. All painful, one excruciating. Invariably humiliating. On all fours, up on an examination bed. Taken from behind. You an animal; they in their white coats in complete and castrating control. Why am I talking about this now? Didn't I say I couldn't stop thinking about my mother's corpse? But that's not quite right. What I am actually thinking about, or trying to decide, is whether I should view the corpse – her corpse – knowing she wouldn't want me to. She would be humiliated, though she can't be, being dead now. Instead, this physio laid me tummy-down on the cushion, legs spread, and began to massage my buttocks, much as one does with a baby. I was surprised, tensed for violation. He chatted to me about how he had got into this line of business, years ago now. Certainly it wasn't what he had meant to do when he studied physiotherapy. He chuckled. His voice was gravelly

4

and pleasant. The gentle rotation he applied to the upper part of the buttocks was exactly the massage I had given our tiny children when they couldn't sleep, years ago. Still I was tensed for violation. He chatted on about how Dr Sharp had talked him into it. He was using jelly of course, though he must have warmed it in his hands first, because I hadn't noticed the usual warning coldness of jelly squirted onto the skin. Dr Sharp was an extraordinary person, he said. He had charisma. And, extraordinarily, I realised he was already *in there*. I hadn't noticed. Presumably with a glove on. It was warm and full and undeniably pleasant.

'My job,' he laughed.

I checked what the flight situation was. I would have to forgo the flight to Madrid and book to Heathrow or Gatwick. I did some googling. My bladder was burning. The flights were expensive, but there was nothing for it at this stage. How much should one shop around, when one's mother is dying? And how, I wondered, could an event that had been as reassuring as that massage, even pleasant, have stirred up so much pain, for it was building now, not to mention this agitated state of mind? I recognised it. Yet my mother had gone out of her way to shop around for the cheapest way to die, to save the money she wanted us to have when she was gone. That was important for her. To leave us with a little money. More important for her than for us, perhaps. Even if it would be paid for with pain. I moved from KLM to easyJet and saved fifty-nine euros, though I lost an hour into the bargain. I would just have time to grab something to eat at Schiphol. Now I had to give the talk.

Of course I should have given the talk before the massage rather than after. Then I would have been in good faith when I told the physiotherapists I was pain-free and had been for years. I was a success story. It is easier to convince people when you're in good faith. On the other hand, the very fact that a mere massage had brought back the pain – only temporarily, the physio assured me – was proof that this was a condition that had to do, as they claimed, with muscles and muscular tension, not infection or cancer, and so in a way was reassuring.

But what if it wasn't temporary? What if that one gentle massage set off the nightmare again, for years to come? Where would that leave me with Elsa?

First the Portuguese paediatrician spoke. His English was poor and he wasn't used to talking about embarrassing subjects. All the physiotherapists were women. Big Dutch women. He stumbled and made mistakes. But he was handsome in a Latin way, and a good ten years younger than me. The ladies relished his timidity, his embarrassment, his poor English. He talked about pelvic pains, back pains, shooting twinges in his legs, urinary urgency, abdominal stiffness, anxiety. 'I was beginning to think I must kill myself,' he announced rather abruptly. 'I am never previously imagining this. But life is horrible. For months and months. Also I am impotent. There is no pleasure. I am complaining every time with my dear wife and children. I am becoming a bad, unhappy person. Very unhappy. You know? And every day there is misery.'

The Dutch women were attentive. I wondered why there were no men. Are all physiotherapists in Holland women? The Americans leading the seminar were men. Or are Dutch men especially averse to carrying out anal massage? The Portuguese doctor spoke for longer than he was supposed to. In particular about the experience of self-massage with Dr Sharp's famous wand. It had saved his life, he repeated. I had the impression he wasn't unaware of the seductive potential of intimate confession. Some of the women looked promising. Meantime, I had a train to catch.

'This is a muscle like any other.'

The physio who had massaged me now stepped in, to say a word between our two testimonies. This was unscheduled. On the other hand, I hadn't told him my mother was dying. Nor that I was experiencing pain and urgency, following his massage.

'Actually, it's the same kind of tissue as the shoulder muscle. Nobody is embarrassed about having their shoulder massaged, are they?'

The physio went to the back of the room and wheeled forward a life-sized plastic skeleton, its torso packed with organs in an attractively coloured three-dimensional jigsaw puzzle. Hanging from a hook on a mobile frame, inanimate Mr Plastic swung and clacked with cheerful relaxation. Everything was loose and easy, as my body will never be. Unpacking the abdomen, the physio reached in and plucked out the pelvic floor. It was made of pink silicon and shaped rather like the cups of those plungers used for clearing blockages in kitchen sinks, or an oversized tennis ball sliced in half.

'This should be elastic,' he said, squeezing the cup and letting it pop open again. He placed it on his middle finger, which passed through a hole where the anus is. 'Instead, in the men we're talking about, but many women too, it feels as stiff as an old boot.'

Again I was struck by how at ease this man was. For all his chinlessness and pockmarkedness, he gave the impression of being truly present before us, in a way the handsome Portuguese paediatrician hadn't quite. The paediatrician had been hidden somehow, even at the moments of most intimate confession. Perhaps because he was speaking a foreign language, or because of a general unease. He was brittle, withdrawn. Perhaps it's part of this condition. You could view him, but you couldn't quite see him. In contrast, the physio's immediacy, swaying easily in cheap grey tracksuit and trainers, was heartening, even beautiful. He was a healthy man.

Now it was my turn. I shifted a desk away from the wall so that I could lean back against it and half stand, half sit in front of my female audience, commanding but casual. I had been made aware from the youngest age, of course, of the importance of posture in delivering

7

a talk. Just watching my father in the pulpit had been enough. The difference between the Reverend Sanders elevated above his congregation, in the black-and-white authority of his robes, and nervy Ted Sanders sprawled in an armchair after lunch, his trousers loosened, was total. My mother too was no slouch when it came to combining body language and rhetoric. Only a month ago she had mentioned preaching to a congregation of two hundred. You could see she was pleased with herself. 'Absolutely,' Dr Sharp insisted when I had asked, just the previous week, if he really needed me to be there. Wouldn't it be enough, I had suggested – I was feeling a little tired and overstretched – to write a testimonial for them, or do a video interview perhaps? In the end I would be saying the same things.

'No, it's absolutely crucial you be there,' Dr Sharp repeated. 'There's nothing like putting flesh and blood in front of people.' He chuckled on the phone from California. 'Someone called Thomas should appreciate that.'

I was surprised he had picked up on my name.

'I hope they won't be eager to push their fingers in my wounds,' I laughed, and he said, 'I'll pay you double if they try.'

He was serious. Actually, he was already paying far more than I was used to being paid for a twenty-minute talk. But this is hardly my regular field. He was paying through the nose to put my flesh and blood in front of fifty Dutch physiotherapists. This, in the end, was why I had decided to go to Holland and do the talk despite the fact, given Mother's condition, that an urgent trip to London was always on the cards; despite a more familiar kind of conference only two days later; despite the fact that, incredible as it may seem, I was falling in love, or believed I was, and did not want to be away for a moment longer than was necessary, since it seemed to me that every day I spent away was a day lost in pleading my cause, a day in which Elsa could take the smart decision to steer well clear of an old shipwreck like Thomas Sanders.

Almost an hour behind schedule when I got up to speak, I nevertheless spent thirty silent seconds, perhaps a whole minute, wriggling myself into a comfortable position, half sitting, half standing on and against this desk, smiling at my audience, breathing easily, letting people see who I was; above all, making sure to appear relaxed and pain-free, even though, as I have said, ever since the after-lunch massage I was not pain-free at all. On the contrary, I was now in some considerable pain. All sadly reminiscent of the past. So much for curiosity.

Kicking off, I followed the outline Dr Sharp had suggested: a brief biography, what kind of person I was, my professional, mainly academic life, a sketched account of the chronic pains I had run into in my late forties, some discussion of how the medical profession had failed me, concluding with my discovery of the Sharp and Morrison approach, my email exchanges with the doctor, and finally light at the end of the tunnel, etc., though of course I had never made the trip to Sharp and Morrison's San Diego clinic, or ever been treated by a physiotherapist following the famous San Diego protocol. Until today.

'No, it's better that way,' Dr Sharp had enthused. 'It's really better.'

Dr Sharp, I was discovering, was always enthusiastic, or scandalised, a man who seduced or repelled you with his boundless evangelical energy. 'That way it doesn't seem so much like our sell,' he said, 'or like we've brainwashed you or something. You just took our model, from the book, a couple of conversations, and ran with it. On your own.'

'If I look back,' I wound up for the physiotherapists after twenty minutes of intimate and unpleasant details, 'it seems impossible to account for this illness, this recovery, this whole experience, in easy terms of cause and effect. I was wired up in all kinds of ways over many years, then I was in all kinds of pain over some years. I sought

9

rapid medical solutions, urological interventions, in vain and with growing frustration, until, dimly, I began to perceive that the problem was me. My body was me. My pain was me. I would have to work on myself – physically, mentally, without the help of conventional medicine.'

Dr Sharp, I noticed, who is not in reality a medical doctor, but a PhD in psychology, was beaming and assenting as I said all this but, rather than reassuring me, his enthusiasm, coupled perhaps with the angry smouldering in my belly, made me feel that everything I was saying was false. I was telling the truth of course – aside perhaps from not relating these new pains, consequent on a first massage of just the kind we were here to promote, but this seemed an unnecessary complication – I was telling the truth *as of a couple hours before*; the truth as it was when, following our email correspondence, Dr Sharp had invited me to put my flesh and blood before the physiotherapists, and yet it felt like it was not the truth; in fact it felt particularly misleading and false, in part perhaps because I had become so aware over recent years of the need to *perform* when giving a talk, or teaching a lesson for that matter, any kind of public discourse, and in part because, although it was the truth as of a few hours ago, it wasn't quite the whole truth. My wife had made this objection on numerous occasions and suddenly I felt very conscious of it. 'Everything you say to people about your so-called health problems,' my wife told me, 'is false. Because you never tell the whole truth.' Ex-wife, that is. What she meant of course was my unfaithfulness, my doubleness, which lay at the heart of the matter as she saw it. It made her angry, she said, that I was applauded for my candour when in fact I wasn't candid at all. 'Nothing but the whole truth is the truth,' my wife said. And she was right. But how can one tell the whole truth in just twenty minutes? And with your mother at death's door.

'I was wondering,' asked a rather matronly woman in the second row, 'how all this impacted on your marriage?'

It was question time. Dr Sharp had suggested twenty minutes talking, ten or fifteen fielding questions, then I was free to go. My train was at five-o-five. He didn't know that. He thought I was leaving later. 'If you don't mind,' he had said. This was earlier that morning, before the massage. The fact was: questions reinforced a speaker's authenticity, showed there was someone there beyond the prepared talk, open to interaction. 'Only interaction really constitutes reality,' Dr Sharp had said, 'for most people.' This was why they learned so little from books in the end. 'People read books, even the most fantastic books,' he said, 'brilliantly written and instructive and so on, but they learn very little, because they're in a passive position, they can't ask the writer questions and hear something back. They can't touch him.' There was a sense, Dr Sharp said, in which books remained for ever in the realm of the hypothetical, because the words that constituted them were silent. They never left the printed page and, as a result, people just couldn't take them on board.

So now I was facing a question that did indeed put a finger in my wounds. The impact of my condition on my marriage. Without the gel and the gentle massage.

'I don't mean the physical condition in itself,' the matronly physiotherapist elaborated, and in parenthesis one has to wonder at the level of English that people have now achieved in Holland, compared, say, to Portugal, or Spain for that matter, or Italy or France, 'but your frustrations with the doctors, your new awareness of your body, then this whole attempt to change your lifestyle that you've been describing. Did it impact on your home life?'

I leaned back against the desk and looked at the audience. A few hundred miles away my mother was sinking fast. There were now three-and-a-half hours before the flight, of which a good hour must be spent on a train that was actually leaving rather soon. I had better not miss it. But still I hesitated. It was a good question that the buxom Dutch woman had asked; in a way, it was *the* question. Then I could see from her face that it was also a sympathetic question. She meant well. This wasn't morbid curiosity. This Dutch physiotherapist, in her early fifties I would have guessed, genuinely wanted to know what was going on in the lives of the men she was treating – what they were going through, emotionally. So she could treat them better. One might object that it was also a very personal question. But wasn't the whole thrust of this seminar that the problems Dr Sharp was treating were very personal? That life in general is a highly personal affair, hence treatment for sufferers with these problems – and I had certainly been one – needed to be not only personal, but intimate? What could be more intimate than a massage through the butt? In fact while I had been with the physio in my hotel room shortly after lunch, trouserless on the bed, the fifty or so physiotherapists at the seminar had been taking turns to practise on each other the same technique that he was applying to me. Grotesque as it may sound, fifty Dutch lady physio-therapists, aged between twenty-four and sixty, of every body shape and size, had reorganised the dining tables of this conference centre in Amersfoort in order to stretch themselves out on the table tops and massage each other through the anus. Think of that, if you will. While my mother was dying in London. They had done this so that they might know what feelings were at stake, both from the giving and the receiving end, as it were, when they treated sufferers like myself. What it felt like to have a finger penetrate their butt and explore the pelvic wall, front, back and sides; and again how to accomplish this penetration and carry out this exploration in a way that did not feel like a gross violation to the person whose butt was being thus penetrated and explored. And this willingness on their part, the Dutch physiotherapists' part, I felt, to do this – to come to the aid of their patients in this unappealing way, to recognise that a person was *also*, and in some cases perhaps *above all*, his or her butt, his or her pelvic floor, which might need to be massaged, not impersonally, and certainly not automatically, as if all patients were the same patient, but intimately and with constant feedback – Is it sensitive here, and here? What about this pressure, and this? – all the time aware of the elasticity or rigidity of the muscle wall touched through the colon, the which, however scrupulously the patient has prepared himself or herself for treatment, doubtless bears its light patina of shit – such willingness on their part made any reticence on mine, handsomely paid as I was to talk about how I had escaped from the pains in question, ridiculous. It would be ridiculous not to agree to say a word about my marriage and its relation to my problems, once I had accepted the invitation to come here and talk, come in part of course because I was being well paid (I'm not stupid), but also because I genuinely believed that without Dr Sharp's book, which despite his remarks on the limitations of books and reading I had very much taken on board, very much given credit to, allowing the words to leave the page and circulate in my mind and even alter my patterns of behaviour, without that book I would still be suffering serious abdominal and perineal pains – which in fact I *was* suffering, right at this moment, thanks to that massage, but that's beside the point – and still be getting up to go to the bathroom six times a night, something that I sincerely hope does not kick in during the days and weeks ahead, otherwise I may very much regret that massage. For why would Elsa ever want to live with that?

'You don't have to answer,' the woman said gently. Apparently I was taking longer than expected to reply. Actually I had begun to smile, though no doubt there were those present who could see I didn't really feel like smiling. I was performing. My face was being made to smile when in fact I was not smiling. Or no, I *was* smiling, really smiling, but the way one does when brought up against the sheer impossibility of a task, the sheer enormity of some seemingly innocent question. You look at this task, consider this request, and shake your head, knowing you are quite unequal to it. You will never get to the bottom of this question. Never complete this task. And in your despair, or simply resignation at something quite beyond you, you smile. That was the smile I must have been smiling now, and having smiled it, I was also holding it, exaggerating it, so they would all know this was the smile one smiles in the face of impossibility, etc., though they couldn't have known of course the business of my mother approaching death's door, or the fact that despite my age I believed myself, grotesquely, in love.

'Marriage. Illness,' I smiled. 'How can one ever – to risk a pun in present circumstances – get to the bottom of such matters?'

I hesitated while one or two tittered. In terms of their English, I suppose, it was rather sorting out the men from the boys, throwing puns at them like this. Though, as I said, those present were all women. 'We have heard Salvatore talking about the impact of his condition on his family,' I said. I sighed. 'Inevitably, when a cheerful man sinks into joylessness, this impacts on his family. Inevitably, when a handsome guy like Salvatore experiences impotence, it impacts on his marriage.'

I stopped. What was I going to say? The truth is I still use the noun 'impact' as a verb with some reluctance, slipping on a rubbery metaphorical glove, as it were, as if there might be a patina of shit on the term. I can't help remembering the time when this usage was the merest Americanism, though now it has become absolutely respectable, even fashionable – as, hopefully, anal massage may one day become, if not fashionable, at least respectable. Not to mention falling in love at fifty-seven. And when shifts like this occur, shifts I've initially resisted, raising the banner of proper language use and correcting those, time and again, who come to my seminars, only to see the shift prevail, inexorably, as is the case with 'I impact this, you impact that, he impacts the other', there comes the moment when I swing round one hundred and eighty degrees and force myself to adopt the new usage as frequently and emphatically as possible, precisely to punish myself, I suppose, for ever having presumed to know what standard English might be, for ever having imagined my own professorial opinion could count for something against the overwhelming reality of what everyone else is doing and saying. Yet even as I give in and go with the flow – suddenly teaching the exact opposite of what I have taught hitherto – I still can't prevent myself from putting on that rubber glove, from feeling that actually the language was better when 'impact' was a noun and didn't impact on other words. And even as I speak, no doubt there is something in my voice that alerts people, that tells them: Professor Sanders is using this verb reluctantly, yet emphatically, with a sort of bitter, self-destructive irony. It's off-putting. He has decided to go with the flow, but he feels the flow is a sewer. 'The reason,' the physio had told me when I had pulled my trousers back on, after his massage, 'why those other doctors you mention hurt you so much was because they didn't really want to be doing what they were doing. You know? They knew they had to put a finger up there, it's a diagnostic duty, but they didn't really want to do it. And when you're conflicted, you do things badly, awkwardly, angrily. You communicate awkwardness and anger.' In general, the physio said, much of the pain that was experienced in the world was the result one way or another of people's state of conflictedness. They didn't want to be doing what they had decided, or had been told, they had to do.

'Having said that,' I continued, still addressing myself to the matronly Dutch physiotherapist whose pale, wide eyes had fastened on mine, 'one might equally well reverse the question you put and ask, not how the condition impacted on the marriage, but how the marriage impacted on the condition.' I hesitated. 'You might even wonder whether domestic unhappiness wasn't intimately linked with the genesis of the condition.' Again I hesitated and smiled the smile of impossibility. 'To cut a long story short,' I said, 'and not wishing to attribute blame to either party, we separated.'

The woman at once said she was sorry, she hadn't meant to ask a difficult question, and I said she really mustn't be sorry. There was nothing to be sorry about. It was an excellent question she had asked and I only hoped my answer had been useful. However, alas, I now had a rather better reason to be sorry – to apologise, that is – I said, because I really needed to leave rather urgently to catch a train to the airport. I had to fly to London where my mother was critically ill. I had imagined, I told the physiotherapists, from the schedule we were all given, that my contribution would be well over by this time, but since we were now running almost ninety minutes late, I was in serious danger of missing my train and then my plane and hence . . .

Hence what?

Dr Sharp jumped to his feet and shook my hand and asked the fifty physiotherapists to applaud, which they did, and for rather a long time, which obliged me to stay and accept the applause, though I kept motioning for them to stop, giving an impression that modesty wouldn't allow me to be applauded so generously, but in fact because I was in a hurry to leave. 'Wait just one moment,' Dr Sharp was saying as the clapping died down, 'and I'll join you in the taxi. Just to check that you make your train on time.' He turned to the audience. 'Thomas will now describe days one and two of the three-week protocol,' he said briskly, and I think this was the first moment I registered the fact that the physio who had massaged me was also called Thomas. Not a doubter at all, I thought. So much for names.

Two minutes later I was waiting in the conference-centre reception area with the bag I had already packed, while Dr Sharp took rather longer than expected to join me. I went outside to see if the taxi had arrived, which it hadn't, and fretted in the cold till it did, then came back into reception and fretted again because Dr Sharp still hadn't come down. This was cutting it fine, to say the least, I thought. I turned on my mobile and sent a message to Elsa, telling her the talk had gone well enough, but that now I had to fly to London where my mother's condition had worsened. Not home to Madrid. 'I miss you terribly,' I texted. Was this actually true, I wondered, before pressing the Send key, or just a formula? Certainly I wanted her to be aware of the importance I gave to the relationship that was forming, but there was really too much to be thinking about right now to miss anyone, even my mother. 'Grandmother is very ill,' I texted all four children. 'If you want to see her again, you should travel soonest.' Should I text my wife? Ex-wife? Dr Sharp still hadn't come. I decided not.

The conference-centre reception area was deserted and I began to wonder if there had been some misunderstanding. To the left of the reception desk was a bathroom, but that could wait till the train. Had Dr Sharp really said he would come to the station with me? Could the applause have distorted what he said, so that I was waiting for him in vain? He wasn't coming. I should get straight into the cab. Having seen there was a bathroom, I was now more than ever aware of an urgency to use it. And did it really matter, if one did or didn't arrive in time for the death of a loved one? What possible difference could it make? I could hear Thomas the physio's voice through the open door to the seminar room, talking about the need to familiarise patients with the geography of their pelvic floor, which, for the sake of convenience, he said, they would be speaking about like a clock face seen from above, where noon was the prostate and six the coccyx. 'Most of our work will be done between ten and two,' he said, and I smiled, imagining that someone with poor English would be bound to misunderstand and assume he was saying they mostly did their massages around lunchtime. There were now only twenty minutes before my train was supposed to leave, when I decided after all to go to the bathroom.

The pee wouldn't come. It was a perfectly ordinary bathroom with the usual recommendations, in Dutch, German and English, to wash one's hands, and a condom-dispenser by the door, which seemed a little odd in a conference centre, unless it was just an acknowledgement that conferences have all kinds of other functions besides those officially declared. The Portuguese paediatrician, I thought, was well set up, despite his affectionate talk about his wife and family. One product was called Billy Boy. Or perhaps *because* of that talk. A guy who says he's separated and suffering is hardly attractive. Who wants a fling with a sufferer? A loser. Though I hadn't said I was suffering. I don't feel like a loser. In fact this was a blissfully happy period for me. Wasn't it? I mean the last couple of months. In any event, I had no interest at all in exploring the charms of the Dutch physiotherapists. The pee still wouldn't come. It burned but wouldn't come. Things will only get worse, I thought, with the stress of catching train and plane, and Mother dying. So much for bliss. The massage had been fatal. Not to mention the finger-in-the-wound question. Shouldn't it have been Thomas, I objected to myself, who stuck his fingers in others' wounds, not they theirs in his?

'There you are!' Dr Sharp had put his head round the door. 'I was wondering where you'd got to.'

At which exact moment the pee began to flow. Since the doctor stayed standing in the doorway, I also lost a few seconds washing my hands, an expediency I might otherwise have skipped.

It really was terribly important one made it to the deathbed of one's parents, the doctor told me as soon as we were settled in the back of the car, and he said the reason he had taken a minute or two to get ready was his decision to put together a bag for the night. I would never make it to the station now, he had realised; I should have warned him beforehand if I meant to get the five-o-five, so the only thing was for us to take the cab together directly to Schiphol, after which he would ask the driver to proceed to Amsterdam where he, Dr Sharp, was to have dinner with a wealthy Swiss industrialist who was offering to sponsor the San Diego protocol.

'Surely it's only five minutes to the station,' I said. 'We can still make it, can't we?'

A taxi to Schiphol would cost a fortune.

'Our industrialist will pick up the tab,' Dr Sharp said. And he said he couldn't tell me the name or even profession of this wealthy man, although he was quite famous in his field, because he didn't want it to be widely known that he had suffered from such an embarrassing condition. He felt it might undermine his authority.

I laughed. Having a pain in the balls was harder to admit to than being gay these days, I said. And Dr Sharp agreed. In fact being gay, Dr Sharp thought, was 'becoming rather more a boast than an admission'. 'We're so heavily invested in our self-images,' he said. 'I often tell people, you'll never be completely cured until you're comfortable with having other people know who you really are.' Not that people, he conceded, actually wanted to know who you really were. Quite the contrary. They had enough on their plates without hearing about your travails. Nevertheless, it was important for you personally not to feel you had to be forever hiding something, since that would be stressful and humiliating and would aggravate your problems. Being candid was part of getting well, he said.

'Do you think,' I asked him in a moment's random mischievousness, 'that some people who are not gay pretend to be so, in order to enjoy the celebrity of "coming out"?'

Dr Sharp didn't reply.

The taxi ran into traffic on the fast roads leading out of town. I had no sense how long the ride might take, having made the outward journey on the train. My wife texted me to say she felt close to me and to ask me to give her regards to my mother. This meant the twins had spoken to her. But the twins did not text. Nor did the older children. My wife didn't reproach me for not texting her. She was reminding me she was a fine, loving person and that I had done the wrong thing when I left her. Fair enough. Perhaps I had. I tried to concentrate on what Dr Sharp was saying about a hormonal cream to treat anal sores. Why did I feel it was a matter of overwhelming importance to see my mother before she died? And if I felt like that, why had I not abandoned the talk to the physiotherapists and run at once? Was it vanity, the desire to stand up in front of the fifty female physiotherapists and tell my story? He had missed seeing his father by a whisker, Dr Sharp now said. It was sad. Whereas with his mother, it had been a long-drawn-out affair. It was not, he said, that one has anything to say to a dying parent, anything to tell, in a melodramatic Hollywood-movie sense, secrets or explanations or anything; it was more a confirmation of loyalty, solidarity. 'When you die you want to have around you the people who make you who you are. Your people. Your folk. You want to feel they are giving this time, and making this effort to be with you, as you set out on your last journey.'

I wondered, I said, whether that was really true. 'Maybe the truth is that we project that desire on to them. So that we can get a payoff from satisfying their imagined requests, when actually they're entirely taken up with their own personal dying.' Which alas was hardly a journey, I added, but an end to all journeying.

He laughed. 'You're sharp, Thomas. Doubting doubtless hones the mind!'

But he had no doubt, Dr Sharp went on, that his mother had indeed wanted him to be there, if only because he had heard her on the phone begging his sister to come 'before it is too late'.

'Your sister,' I said. 'Not you!'

'I was already there,' he laughed.

'But did your mother specifically ask you not to leave?' I asked.

'She did not,' he admitted. 'But I never said I wanted to leave.'

I was surprised by how sarcastic and unpleasant I was being. I was also surprised by how cheerfully Dr Sharp was putting up with it. Perhaps I was angry that I risked missing the flight because of him. The taxi was in a long tailback on the sliproad to the motorway.

'The truth is,' I told him, 'there is something I want to tell my mother that I have never told her. I don't want to miss this last chance.'

And what was that, he asked?

I sighed. I wasn't really sure, I said. 'I just have that impression – that there is something that has to be said. I'll know when I get there. It will come out.'

'Interesting,' Dr Sharp thought. Or maybe he thought I was bullshitting him.

The taxi driver turned the radio on. There was some merry discussion in Dutch. Perhaps it was a quiz show. Raising my voice, I said I really needed to be at the airport in an hour and five. Would we make it? The driver turned on the navigator, which gave our estimated arrival time in present traffic conditions as seventy minutes. 'As you see,' he said, 'there's not much I can do.'

'Try to relax,' Dr Sharp told me.

Then I told Dr Sharp that one of the reasons why I was so wired up was that the massage his physio Thomas had given me after lunch had on the one hand convinced me beyond all doubt that the pelvic floor really was the source of my sufferings – my erstwhile sufferings – but at the same time just touching it had reactivated those sufferings. They were no longer erstwhile. What was I to do? The idea of plunging back into months of chronic pain was so depressing.

Dr Sharp was thoughtful. He was a jovial, generous, fleshy man, very much taken up with his own projects, but more than willing to focus on you for the few moments it took to assess your needs.

'Everything you have told me about yourself,' he said, 'convinces me that you have managed to control your problem by making a big investment in relaxation techniques, yoga, breathing exercises, whatever. Essentially, you have learned to chill a little, to turn down the stress temperature, and that has got you out of gaol. Stress comes from ourselves as much as anything else. But when things get out of hand, when you're out of your normal environment or crisis strikes, you lose control and soon enough you find yourself in pain again.'

His conclusion was that I should come to San Diego, follow his protocol for a month and have the problem massaged out of me, once and for all. It would be painful at first, but beyond pain lay comfort and freedom. 'Above all,' he said, 'you should learn to use the self-massage wand, which would empower you to take control of your own destiny.'

'Empower', like 'impact', is a word I have trouble with.

Then as we sat in heavy traffic on the autobahn between Amersfoort and Schiphol, and my mother lay dying in London, Dr Sharp lifted his bag from the floor, clicked it open and pulled out one of three or four plastic bags. Through the transparent plastic you could see a yellow-and-amber tube shaped rather like a short snorkel, except that the U was more open than with a snorkel, and instead of a mouthpiece there was a white ball the size of a large marble and at the other end a handle running perpendicular to the tube, as if at the top of a small spade, a children's beach spade perhaps. Beneath the handle, the straight shaft of the instrument was enclosed for perhaps three inches in a rubbery yellow sheath, from within which a grey wire emerged that then connected to a small box, also yellow and featuring a liquid-crystal display. First the ball was inserted in the anus, Dr Sharp explained, and he leaned back and lifted his knees onto the seat of the taxi to show how the sufferer slipped the curved end of the wand – the mouthpiece of the snorkel, if you like – covered with a rubber glove of course, well-lubed needless to say, between his thighs, beneath his scrotum and into the anus. After which you operated the handle – 'Joystick, we call it!' he laughed – to steer the ball, now deep inside the colon, to the point on the pelvic wall that triggered your pain, and then pushed forward, sideways or backwards on the wand to apply pressure and massage that point. Gently! The display on the gauge responded to the tension generated in the flexing tube as you forced the U open, and hence indicated how much pressure you were applying to the muscle, internally, so that this could be monitored and gradually increased over a period of months.

'We've had it patented,' he said. 'It has passed all the stringent US standards for medical equipment. This will do it.'

The doctor's enthusiasm was contagious. He was convinced he had the solution to a problem that plagued millions of men. And many women. If only they had been willing to listen to him on the subject of anal massage. The taxi began to move as the jam on the motorway freed up. For my mother, who would never have dreamed of inserting items in her anus, no matter what kind of pain she was in, time was slipping away.

'Could you give me one, please,' I asked Dr Sharp. 'I'd like to try.'

II

The corpse-viewing dilemma did not come whole. It crept up. The first whiff arrived with an email from my sister listing expenses incurred as a result of my mother's death – money that she, my sister, had taken from my mother's bank account in the hours immediately after the death, but before it was registered and the account consequently blocked. Mother had given my sister her bank card and PIN number, it seemed, for precisely this purpose. These items of expenditure I barely glanced at, knowing as I did that my sister would behave scrupulously when it came to money, and that anyway the very small amounts my mother was leaving were hardly of a kind to turn around the precarious financial circumstances my separation from my wife had left me in. But my eye did stop on the word 'embalming'. Embalming: £98. 'Mother would never have wanted to be embalmed,' I immediately wrote in reply to my sister, 'and if she had, she would definitely have included the service in the funeral package that she herself chose and paid for years ago.'

As soon as I had fired off this email to my sister, I felt rather foolish, for of course my sister would know all this far better than I did. At the same time, I felt a sort of concern for my mother, as if, now dead, she needed protecting from the things she would have considered a violation, not so much of her body, which she always insisted was a matter of no importance, but of her sense of propriety, and above all her strict belief in the absolute separation of flesh and soul, such that any money or effort spent on aesthetic appearance beyond the requirements of respectability or the merely practical needs of the body was a waste. Mother hated waste.

My sister, without taking offence, but rather as if I had simply queried, out of curiosity, some unexpected purchase, responded that since Mother had asked for cremation, the law required that two doctors certify the cause of death, and a third certify the certification, so to speak. Only then could the cremation date be booked. This took time. After which there was a waiting list for the cremation itself, such that at least two weeks would pass between decease and funeral. The nice lady at the undertaker's, whom my sister hadn't actually met but had spoken to on various occasions over the telephone, had suggested that since these days people liked to view the body (for 'closure', she had explained) in the week preceding the funeral, it might be an idea to have a relatively inexpensive temporary embalming performed in order to allow this to happen, in order to get the corpse, as it were, through to the funeral in a respectable state. Uncle Harry, my sister wrote, had already been along to see the results and pronounced them excellent; Mum looked, or at least so Uncle Harry had said, very much her old self, in the pale-blue tailleur she used for special occasions with matching bonnet. 'Not that I have any intention of going to see her myself,' my sister went on. 'I prefer to remember Mum as she was. But that's just me. You're welcome to, if you want.' And she explained that the undertaker's in question was the one directly opposite Hounslow railway station.

Again I responded to my sister's email immediately, which is a bad habit I have, since my immediate response almost never coincides with my more settled opinion of a day or two, or even just a few hours, later. In this case, a few minutes. 'I am sure you are right,' I answered. There was a 'certain appropriateness', I joked, rather flippantly, in Mother's going to her funeral in her Sunday best, obsessed as she always had been that one should be 'properly spruced up for church'. I was glad, I dashed off – not foreseeing as yet the area of dilemma I was entering, and I think one of the reasons one responds so immediately to emails is that if you don't, there is a good chance you'll never respond at all, with all the messages the world throws at you these days; plus of course, having been pompous and abrasive in my previous email, I was now eager to reassure my sister, who after all in the absence of her two brothers was taking on herself all the responsibilities surrounding my mother's death – I was glad, I wrote, that Uncle Harry had been cheered by his viewing of the body, rather than the opposite, since with his age and his cancer, the thought most present in his mind must have been that all too soon he would be in the same position as Mum, on his back in a box.

This was the gist of my immediate response. Reassuring and flippant. But only moments after sending it, from Berlin it must have been, I was remembering how uncannily precise and sure of herself my mother had been, when she had first spoken to me of her funeral arrangements. It was a memory that took me back some four years to a summer spent in her tiny house off Hounslow High Street. I was there, needless to say, because my wife and I now seemed unable or unwilling to go on holiday together, or indeed to spend time together in any way. I had invited my then lover to come on holiday with me to the UK but she had refused. If I wasn't going to leave my wife, she said, the last thing she needed was to start building up happy memories that could have no future. She wouldn't come. On the other hand, she hadn't left me outright. Presumably, then, she was putting pressure on me. Presumably my wife too was putting pressure on me, or I was putting pressure on her. Or on both. In any event, we had a stand-off which amounted to the worst of all worlds and there I was, a man theoretically with two women but actually with none, staying at my mother's house for the summer, ostensibly because this elderly Christian lady needed, or at least would be grateful for, my presence, being ill and having recently been operated on – mutilated might be a better description – but in reality because I had no idea what to do with myself, no idea what to do with my marriage, no idea what to do with my lover, no idea even whether I wanted to stay in my job in Edinburgh or make some major move abroad: disappear, as it were, and as I eventually did, from the family radar.

In any event, it was while I was at my mother's house that summer in a state of maximum psychological precariousness, like a man about to take not one plunge but several, or perhaps none – and loathing myself into the bargain, yet at the same time not entirely unhappy, if only from the relief of being away from my wife; this without intending any criticism in her regard, the problem was mine, not hers – it was while I was there, towards the end of my stay, that my mother, who as I said had recently been operated on and was no longer her old self, in fact had clearly begun a phase of terminal decline, and you could see she wasn't her old self by the way she so determinedly 'acted' her old self, performed her old Christian cheerfulness, calling 'cooee' up the stairs and baking apple pies and cherry cakes, but also her old Christian severity, frowning if I ever mentioned yoga or meditation, which were works of the devil, not to mention separation or divorce (her nice neighbour had been abandoned for a younger woman and this was ungodly cruelty on the husband's part) – it was while I was at her house, possibly the evening before I was due to depart, that my mother first spoke to me of the funeral arrangements she had made.

'I just want you to know, Thomas,' she had said, 'that I have made arrangements for my funeral so that you children will not have to pay.'

It was an act of generosity. She had got a distasteful practical duty out of the way to save others, we children, the trouble. I must be grateful. And I was grateful. I distinctly remember feeling, Great, that is one thing that won't need to be done.

'You will find all the papers in the first drawer under the bookshelf,' she said.

But of course it was something more than an act of generosity, I reflected now, probably in the hotel in Berlin, on the Görlitzerstrasse as I recall, having dashed off that jocular and reassuring response to my sister over the question of the embalming. It was also a bid for control. She, my mother, would be the one to decide what happened to her body, what kind of funeral she would have. Not her children. 'It will be very simple,' she explained that evening from the big recliner she had recently bought, because by this time she found it uncomfortable to sit for long in ordinary armchairs, though the bind with the recliner was how difficult it could be to get out of, once you were in it, precisely because it tipped you back in a reclining position, so that when sometimes, on returning to the house without my key, I was obliged to ring the bell, I would see my mother through the frosted glass of the front door, which opened directly into the tiny sitting room, a blurred dark form rocking herself back and forth in an attempt to launch herself out of her comfortable recliner and onto her feet to answer the door. Sometimes it could take three or four minutes. Then when at last she opened up for me, it would be with a beam of generously performed cheerfulness that denied all difficulty and prohibited any mention of illness – she never complained about my forgetting my key – though her manner might well be transformed into a frown of puritan severity if it then became clear that I had been drinking, or if there was a smell of smoke on my untidy clothes.

'Thomas,' she would sigh.

And in general, looking back now, I am reminded that standing outside the frosted door of Mother's house, watching Mother struggle to climb out of her recliner, or even in the years before that, simply waiting at the door for Mother to appear, blurred in the cheap glass as she moved towards me, often pulling a shawl about her shoulders, or fixing her hair with her hands, I always experienced, in those few seconds before meeting, an extremely strong and peculiarly mixed cocktail of emotion, which had to do simultaneously with guilt and tenderness and impatience and indecision. The truth is that when visiting my mother I never knew whether I really wanted to be visiting my mother or not. Visiting my mother was a moment of maximum confusion as to who I am. I both wanted and did not want to visit her, simultaneously.

The funeral would be simple, she repeated. No more than what was strictly required, and no fuss. She had paid for the coffin and for the cars to take everybody to church. It was only a few hundred yards. The funeral ceremony too, she said, had already been written; that is, she had written it, and chosen the hymns, and it would be extremely simple. Rather than flowers, people were to make an equivalent donation to charity. In this way her death would be of benefit to others, though not of course to the florists, who I suppose rely pretty heavily on funerals to make a living in these hard times. Quite likely she said all this while the BBC boomed out the news in background, since Mum had been losing her hearing for some years now and kept the volume turned way up, and perhaps as we were enjoying our pre-dinner sherry, which, along with a rare glass of white wine at lunch, was the only alcohol my mother ever allowed herself. Sherry with dry-roasted peanuts.

After the funeral, she said, she was to be cremated as Father had been and, as with Father, there must be no memorial. No urn. No rose tree. No plaque with words. The ashes were to be scattered, she said. Where, she did not mind. 'That's up to you,' she finished.

She looked at me softly, but also with the satisfaction of someone who has acted with admirable resolve and for the best. She knew what was right. 'That can be your decision,' she said. She leaned forward to take a sip of her sherry, and the BBC flashed in her glasses. Perhaps from the kitchen the cuckoo clock cuckooed. I heard a 'you' plural at the time. You children. But later, thinking back, it would come to me that she actually meant you, Thomas. You, Thomas, will decide where to scatter my ashes. In which case the sense was, as would ultimately emerge: And that, dear Thomas, will be your one and only decision with regard to me and my decease. For otherwise you have no part to play. You are excluded.

However, what struck me now, recalling, in Berlin I think, in the hotel on Görlitzerstrasse, this quietly compelling conversation in which my mother had explained her decisions regarding her earthly remains, was this: that on going to the undertaker's to choose and purchase her funeral package and having explained, as a starting point, her preference for cremation, my mother would doubtless have been reminded by the kind lady my sister had spoken to, or by her predecessor if things had changed in the intervening years, some other kind lady or kind gentleman undertaker – and they are all kind when you are ordering and paying for expensive services years before they are required – that this preference for cremation would mean quite an interval between the moment of expiry and the funeral, and that since the prevailing custom was to view the body prior to the funeral, the day before, say, or even the same morning if possible, decorously laid out in polished wood (of much finer quality, it has to be said, than any of the mail-order furniture in my mother's Hounslow sitting room), it would be only wise to include some basic temporary embalming in the package, at what was actually a very reasonable price.

But my mother had said no. She had no wish to be embalmed. It was unthinkable, I realised now, having only moments ago re-assured my sister that she had taken the right decision in assenting to the embalming, that embalming had not been proposed to my mother when she ordered her funeral package, precisely because it was now a standard service and very much the fashion. At the very least there would have been a box to tick – Embalming – and my mother had not ticked it. My mother was against embalming. She did not want to be injected with formaldehyde and have her various intimate orifices stoppered against seepage and her jaw and teeth wired together to prevent her mouth from falling open and her face creamed and powdered and so on, all by hands unknown to her, all in the aid of reconstructing the false impression that body and soul were still cheek and jowl when they very definitely were not, when the real Martha Sanders had already flown up to heaven. Mother had said no. Which also meant, perhaps, that she was against the viewing of the corpse in general, though this did not follow 100 per cent. Perhaps Mother wouldn't have minded people seeing her naturally decaying body. Perhaps she might even find salutary that confrontation with crude reality. I doubted it. But I couldn't know.

In any event, thinking all this over, still completely unaware of the terrific and inane dilemma that was being prepared for me, I now recalled that of course my father had *not* been embalmed when he died thirty and more years ago at an age, as it happens, that I was now approaching. In three years' time, incredible as it may seem, I will be my father's age at his death. Sixty. It does seem incredible. But he too had found it incredible, that he was dying I mean, would be dead shortly after his sixtieth birthday. Then too, in the days immediately before my father's funeral and consequent cremation, which came at least a week, though perhaps not two, after his decease, I had been seized by a powerful desire to see my father's body one last time. I had rushed out of the vicarage and up Cricklewood High Street to the undertaker's – actually it was barely a hundred yards away – and pushed the door, determined to carry through my resolve before my mind changed. I felt coura-geous. I felt I was inside an important drama, the drama of seeing my father's corpse, and I suppose by the corpse one really means the face, the beloved face, for I did love him, despite all our disagreements, before it was committed to the flames and destroyed for ever. I rushed up the busy High Road and still remember my surprise, pushing open the door of the undertaker's, at hearing a bell ding in a back room as in any sweet shop or newsagent's, as if to alert the dead there was someone come to see them. And sure enough the elderly man who presently appeared from a back room did have a curious complexion to him, dark, but dully polished, immediately inviting analogies with mahogany or mummies.

'Good morning, sir,' he said, with a slight Dickensian bow.

'I have come to see my father,' I told him, 'the Reverend Edward Sanders. The funeral is tomorrow and I wanted to see him one last time.'

Tall and stiff, the undertaker looked down on me with evident sympathy for my youth and agitated state. Then, clearing his throat, he said, 'Mr Sanders, you do not want to see your father.' There was a pause. 'Death is not kind to the body, sir. Better the Reverend Edward as he was.' At which, without even answering, so far as I can recall, I turned and walked out.

Later I regretted this retreat. In particular I regretted having accepted someone else's telling me, without any discussion, what I did or did not want to do. It was fair enough advising me that my father was not a pretty sight. But in the end I knew that. I had seen him die. I had seen the nose rise from the grey cheeks and the eyes sink into the waiting skull. I wasn't so stupid at twenty-five years of age as to imagine that a week's being dead had improved my father's appearance. Certainly there had been no talk of his benefiting from embalming. So I knew perfectly well what I was going towards and there must have been some powerful instinct pushing me that way, pushing me towards seeing my father's decaying corpse, however shocking the sight might be, until the tall and doubtless kind man who seemed to have been embalmed alive, and in a permanent rather than temporary fashion, simply said, 'You do not want to see your father' and said it in such an authoritative, even peremptory way, as if it was a self-evident truth, that I at once turned on my heels and walked out of the place. 'It seems to me, Señor Sanders,' my shrink drily remarked towards the end of perhaps our fourth or fifth meeting, 'that other people are always telling you who you really are, or are not, and what you do, or do not, really want.' I had mentioned, I suppose, what my wife had said: that it simply wasn't *me* to leave her; that I was acting out some role that wasn't mine. And the shrink had immediately connected this remark to a previous session when I had explained how my mother would repeatedly complain during my adolescence, whenever I behaved badly, that I was merely aping my rebellious brother: I was essentially a good boy, my mother was sure, but I was allowing myself to be dragged down to perdition by my brother, who, sad to say, had turned resolutely away from the Christian path. I suppose this is what one pays one's shrink for, to make these kinds of disturbing connections: my mother, my wife, each in their different ways telling me who I was.

Do I really want to see my mother's body, then, I wonder? Or don't I? Or am I simply waiting for a wife or mother to tell me whether I want to? But I have no mother now and to all practical purposes no wife, either. Certainly the undertaker is unlikely to tell me not to see her, or view her, having gone to the effort of embalming the lady to make it easy for me. So if I do darken the threshold of the undertaker's there will be no further advice. As for Elsa, I feel I should keep her out of this.

In the taxi to Schiphol, Dr Sharp removed his anal wand from its transparent plastic bag and began to talk about its various components. He shouldn't really be giving me a wand in this way, he

33

said, since a patient needed to learn how to use the wand from a qualified physiotherapist over two or three practical sessions, otherwise he was in danger of doing himself damage. Or herself, because there were female users. However, along with the wand and the gauge, there was also a pen-drive on which I would find a series of videos where my namesake Thomas, the physio, explained how to use it. 'With great care,' Dr Sharp said, 'and, above all, slowly.' For example, the first time you used the wand, or perhaps the first two or three times, you really must do no more than insert and remove it. Just to get used to that action, insert and remove, to become familiar with a part of your anatomy you had never touched and a sensation you had never known before. The transparent plastic ring, he explained, which could be slid along the U of the wand and then fixed with the Allen key provided, was to prevent you from pushing the tip of the instrument in too far. You pushed the wand into the anus up to the plastic ring, which was too wide to pass the sphincter. Recommended distance between the tip of the wand and the plastic ring was your middle finger plus half an inch. This to start with, after which you could fine-tune with use and experimentation. Once set, the fixed point represented by the ring guaranteed that having found the sensitive points at the source of your pains, you could be sure of finding them again easily and always massaging the same spot. I would know where I was, as it were, up my arse.

Why I was listening to Dr Sharp talking over the niceties of prophylactic internal pelvic-wall massage, for which I sincerely hoped I had no real need, while the taxi struggled through heavy traffic to Schiphol whence I was to fly to my mother's deathbed, I have no idea. The good doctor was persuasive, I thought. Evangelical even. He was spreading the word. About anal massage. Then of course I was still feeling the aftermath of the massage that I had rather stupidly asked for some hours earlier. Perhaps I was worried I might need the wand and wanted to have one, just in case. Already I knew

I did not want to use it and most likely never would. 'Eventually you reach a point,' Dr Sharp was reassuring me, 'where massaging the pelvic floor through the anus becomes as routine, even pleasurable, as flossing your teeth or paring your toenails.' He laughed. If only, he said, people could overcome their irrational repulsion when it came to engaging with the more intimate parts of their bodies, then an awful lot of pain could be put behind us. 'No pun intended!' He laughed again.

'They have no qualms about masturbating,' I remarked.

I had suddenly realised, on the back seat of the Dutch taxi inching forward through heavy traffic, that Dr Sharp reminded me of my father. My father too was always excited by the message he was trying to get across to people, always believed he had the unique solution to their problems. There had been something attractively innocent about my father's sermonising, in a way that wasn't altogether true of my mother's. You forgave my father for preaching because he was so genuinely excited to tell you what he believed, even if you couldn't follow him there. Mother, on the other hand, inculcated more guilt than enthusiasm. But now a message buzzed on my old Nokia. My sister needed to know my ETA.

'You're dead right about masturbation,' Dr Sharp was chuckling. People masturbated far too often, he thought. Many men, he was sure, masturbated compulsively, forcing pleasure on themselves, as if it were a duty almost. Daily, even hourly, men masturbated, some men, to prove they were in control of their bodies. With the aid of Internet porn, of course. Then quite possibly they saw their pelvic pain as a punishment for the masturbation. They tied themselves in knots. Nor did they hesitate, and again the Californian doctor seemed to find this funny, to stick all kinds of sex toys up their butts, precisely as part of this process of forcing pleasure on themselves. They had to feel they were getting regular pleasure, extreme pleasure, and that they were in total control of that pleasure. It was part of their vision of themselves as successful human beings. Hence they would buy the craziest of objects to assist them in this task, because the creation and control of sexual pleasure did eventually become a kind of task, something you had to do. Screwing up your pelvic floor in the process, of course. He hadn't really realised the full extent of the phenomenon, Dr Sharp said, until he, Tommy the physio and Dr Morrison, his now-ageing mentor, had decided to develop a self-massage tool. 'We are not designers and didn't have much money to invest,' he explained. 'We were like any ordinary folks thinking how on earth they are going to produce an object that has never been produced before.' So the first thing they had done was go to a sex emporium to see if there was any pre-existing sex toy that could be adapted for the goal of pelvic-floor massage. It would save a lot of time if there was. In the event, they had bought and tried out every anal plug and every vibrator on the market, to see if there was something that would do the trick. As it were! Offer an effective massage of the pelvic floor. Dr Sharp was laughing out loud now and rubbing his hands. 'We tried them all!' But there was nothing. 'They were never quite long enough, you know, or easy enough to manipulate, you couldn't quite press them in the right places. There was no leverage. What a movie that would make,' he went on, laughing. 'Three doctors going through the sex-toy shop.'

'Not sure yet,' I texted my sister. 'I'll let you know from the airport.' And as I did so, another message arrived. 'Go to your mother, Tom. That's the important thing. Don't worry about me.'

Elsa.

The fact was, Dr Sharp was saying, that people were all too ready to touch their own and each other's intimate parts when in the throes of erotic excitement, and in particular transgressive erotic excitement, but not in order to improve their health. A woman was perfectly willing to put a finger up a man's anus while making love, or vice versa, but when you suggested he needed a pelvic-floor

36

massage to relieve pain, she suddenly found the area dirty, smelly and repulsive. The same being true the other way round of course, of men with women. The repulsion and the transgressive attraction were part of the same taboo-driven mindset, he said, and both equally unhelpful. They found it sexy one moment *because* it was repulsive the next. Modern Western eroticism, in fact, Dr Sharp insisted, was nothing other than the overcoming of repulsion, of taboo; hence, logically, the more repulsion, the greater the excitement overcoming it. Which was why people got into so-called water sports and the like. 'I love you and love you and love you,' I texted back to Elsa, and I told Dr Sharp that my mother's cancer had been so far advanced when they finally operated on her because, being in the breast, she had been reluctant to go and show it to a doctor. She had only gone when the situation became unbearable and the tumour, or so at least my sister had told me, grotesque. For years my mother had been conscious of this lump growing in her breast and must have been aware of the dangers, but all the same, or perhaps precisely because of the dangers, because of the thought of the medical Via Crucis that awaited her, she hadn't wanted to show it to a doctor. The thought of exposing her body, and in particular her breasts, to medical professionals was too depressing.

Dr Sharp nodded excitedly and said that this was absolutely standard behaviour for every pathology that had remotely to do with the body's sexual or secretory functions. By the time people came to him, for example, they were absolutely crippled with pain and had been for years. But because it was urinary pain, testicular pain, perineal pain, they didn't want to discuss it. And still they baulked at anal massage. 'They would rather have open-heart surgery or a hip replacement,' Dr Sharp laughed, 'than anal massage. But I'm beginning to worry you won't make your plane,' he added. He returned the wand to its plastic bag. 'Remember never to use it without putting a surgical glove over the ball,' he said. 'And plenty of lube.' I looked at my watch and in fact the boarding gate was due to close in just four minutes. 'They never close it when they say they're going to,' the taxi driver offered. He spoke as if I might have been intending to blame him for missing the flight. I sat back and stared at the traffic. How had I allowed this to happen?

'Do you have a long way to go from the airport at the other end?' Dr Sharp asked.

'Change of trains to Hounslow,' I said. 'An hour or so.'

'Try not to be too anxious,' he said. 'Especially over the things you can't control.' He gestured to the motorway traffic advancing like a lava flow in the cold evening gloom, brake lights flaring and fading, flaring and fading.

Then I said the fact was that I was agitated because I had never actually told my mother that I had left my wife. I wished I had told her, but I hadn't. I would like to tell my mother this now, I felt that to tell her this would constitute becoming adult in some way. She would see me as I really am for the first time. 'But I don't know if I should.'

'Why didn't you tell her?' Dr Sharp asked.

'Because it would have hurt her,' I sighed. 'Because I knew she didn't want to hear it. Because, living abroad for the last few years, it was easy for me not to tell her. Easy to keep the two worlds well apart. I have a long track record in keeping worlds apart,' I said.

If she hadn't wanted to hear it in the past, Dr Sharp reflected, she was hardly going to want to hear it now, was she? She would have other things on her mind at this point. 'Let it go,' he said.

'It seems important,' I told him.

At last the car stopped and I said goodbye to Dr Sharp, who insisted on embracing and touching cheeks in the modern, rather sentimental way, and despite my haste and agitation I found myself appreciating this, I appreciated the momentary warmth of his body and the contact with his closely shaven skin and the shine of his evangelical eyes, so like my father's, as once again he thanked me for being so generous as to go ahead with the talk, despite my anxiety over my mother.

Freeing myself at last from the powerful magnetism that hung around Dr Sharp, wishing him good luck for his meeting with the anonymous benefactor, I began to run towards the sliding doors of the foyer and immediately had to stop. I had forgotten that I had released my belt and the top of my trousers in the car, to ease a sense of constriction. Suddenly, my trousers were down around my thighs. I put my bag on the ground, sorted myself out and started to run again. Yet even as I hurried into the vast atrium of Schiphol Airport, anxious above all to see the departure board and find out whether there was still a chance of making the easyJet flight that had been fifty-nine euros cheaper than the KLM, I simultaneously wondered whether it was really worth all this enormous effort to go and see my dying mother. Did I really want to tell my mother that I had left my wife two years ago? I was stressing myself out. Or that I had fallen in love at fifty-seven. With a woman thirty years younger than myself. Did I? It was ridiculous. It wasn't *me*.

I stopped in the atrium, noting as I always do that Schiphol is bigger than you would expect for such a small country as Holland. My eye went to the top left of the departure board. Bigger and glossier. Was my flight still up there? The floor in particular seemed extremely glossy. A Lufthansa to Frankfurt had a three-hour delay. Did my mother really want, I asked myself, still searching for my flight, to hear these things from me on her deathbed? She did not. Had she ever wanted to hear them? No. But yes, the flight was there. Delayed for fifty minutes. What luck! Go to Gate 27. My mother knew my marriage was in crisis, she had known for years, but she had never asked me what I was going to do about it. Those whom God hath joined together, let no man put asunder. 'If you don't tell people what they don't want to hear,' the shrink had said, 'it's hardly surprising that you are forced to appear what you are not.' Even as I rejoiced over the delay, the 'Now boarding' light began to flash.

'Sir, we need to open your bag.'

Pleading a last-minute booking because my mother was ill, I had pushed my way to the front of the queue at Security, only to be pulled out for inspection on the other side of the X-ray machines. It was a woman in her late twenties, Elsa's age; she was brusque and practical, understandably tired at the end of her working day, irritated with the stupidity of people who, despite all the warnings and lists of forbidden items, still put things they shouldn't in their hand luggage. I too have often felt irritated with such people and indeed was sure that I had removed all liquids from the bag, not to mention my computer, my Kindle, etc. So what was up? Around us there was quite a buzz of people threading belts back on and fastening watches. I unzipped the bag.

'What is this?' the woman asked. Wearing black gloves, she fished out the transparent plastic bag with its yellow tubing, grey wires, electronic gauge and rather fat pen-drive.

'What is it?'

The young official raised an eyebrow, in genuine puzzlement. At last something she had never seen before.

'It is not an explosive device,' I told her.

'Just tell me what it is, please.'

'Medical equipment.'

She turned the bag over and over in her gloves.

'Of what kind, sir?'

'Do I have to explain?'

This annoyed her. 'Just tell me what this equipment is for, sir.'

It's hard not to notice, as one grows older, how much young officials enjoy exercising power over someone who in other circumstances might be considered hierarchically superior. But I was more angry with myself than with her. Why had I suddenly wanted to possess this embarrassing object that, until today, I had never remotely thought of possessing, never mind using? Was I genuinely afraid that the pains brought on by the otherwise soothing lunchtime massage might signal the beginning of a new era of suffering, and that the only way to tackle them would be more and deeper massage, more suffering? Or was there, obscurely but more likely, some connection with the news of my mother's decline, some feeling that if only my mother had been more frank about her body, she need not have left the world in the way she was leaving it? That said, at ninety one had to go one way or another, did one not? The truth is I really didn't know why I had asked for it. Perhaps because Dr Sharp, like my father, was such a hard sell.

'It's a massage tool,' I told her. 'For pelvic pain.'

The woman was examining the small yellow box with the liquid-crystal display. She wore a uniform that flattened but emphasised her breasts, almost forced you, that is, to think of her breasts being flattened. By officialdom. Absurdly, and it has to be said that when my mind starts racing it really does race, I remembered that during her three pregnancies, in the 1940s and '50s, my mother had worn a tight girdle to prevent the belly from showing. This was one of the things that had somehow come up in conversation in the long limbo of that summer in her house four years ago. And Mother had laughed, shaking her head and saying those were different times and it was just not respectable to show a pregnant belly in church, with all the implications.

'If you could just wait one moment, sir,' the young official said.

The implications!

'My flight is boarding,' I told her. 'I can't miss it.'

'I am afraid I shall have to ask you to wait just a moment longer, sir.'

People say that the problem with my relationship with Elsa is that it is hierarchically entirely in my favour – I am older and more powerful than she is. More powerful because older. How can a good relationship be built on such an asymmetrical basis? Here, on the other hand, a woman of the same age as Elsa was getting evident pleasure from giving me abrupt commands. If I told her, I thought, that my mother was dying and that I wished to see her one last time, this might actually make the woman more determined to keep me in line. She wouldn't believe me. It would be a ruse to escape with my suspect device.

'I'd rather you just kept it than that I missed my plane,' I now said.

But she had already turned her back to take the anal wand to her scanning colleague, so that now, as he turned from his machine to consider the device that Dr Sharp believed could spare men and women the world over oceans of unnecessary misery, I was holding up the entire line at Security, including an impatient young man beside me, also waiting to have his suitcase examined. The two officials came over.

'How exactly is it used?' the man asked.

It occurred to me then that had the object in my bag been a sex toy, the two would have had no problem recognising it and waving it by. Sex toys must be two-a-penny in the luggage of people making weekend trips to Amsterdam. This was more embarrassing than a sex toy.

'This is a last call,' came over the PA, 'for easyJet 570 to London Gatwick. Would travellers for London Gatwick on easyJet 570 please go directly to Gate 27, where this aircraft is waiting to depart.'

'Please show us how it is used?' the man repeated.

For a moment it seemed awfully appropriate, or ironic, or just *connected* somehow, that I should be missing the chance to get to my mother, barred from speaking to her one last time, because

42

of my decision to acquire an object that ran absolutely contrary to that squeamishness, fastidiousness, prudishness about the body that Mother had always maintained and always wanted her children to share. In asking for the wand, I had been rebuking my mother.

But these were crazy thoughts. I took the bag from the woman, removed the wand, squatted down on the glossy tiles of the airport floor and pushed the U with its off-white spherical extremity between my thighs. 'You pull this up into your anus,' I said, over-enunciating the words as if these good Dutch people spoke English as poorly as the Portuguese, 'then toggle it back and forth to massage any tender areas inside.'

Five minutes later, breathless and ragged, I boarded easyJet flight 570 after a severe scolding from an orange-clad official with an earring. He might well have been in his teens, as far as I could see. Disturbing an elderly woman to get into the middle seat of a row of three, I felt at once that I needed to go to the bathroom again.

III

The dilemma that has blocked my mind for some days now and that has had me orbiting pathetically around the undertaker's opposite Hounslow railway station, or more precisely oscillating between the Costa Coffee across the street and the Barclays cash dispenser on the next corner, would not have gripped me in the way it has, I don't think, had the circumstances surrounding my mother's death – that is, my visit to her deathbed – not been so unsettling, and in particular had I not received immediately on my arrival at Gatwick an SOS from my old friend Deborah Seymour, recently Deborah Pool.

I had spent the flight in a state of some misery, having gone to the bathroom as soon as the safety-belt sign was turned off and having got trapped for ten minutes behind the drinks trolley on my way back to my seat. Barely had I sat down, with the elderly lady in the aisle seat clearly having difficulty struggling out of it to make way for me, something that could not fail to recall my mother's struggles to get out of her recliner, than I felt I needed to go again. Not urgently, but perceptibly. And perceiving it, I began to dwell on it and on the embarrassment that would inevitably ensue, were I obliged to ask my elderly neighbour to struggle to her feet once more; obliged to meet, which was probably worse, on returning to my seat, the gaze of the rather athletic man by the window to my left who had begun to watch an action film on his iPad, so that I was now vaguely aware of explosions and plumes of smoke and figures running for their lives, and of course the slight twitches and smiles on his face as, turning his pad this way and that like a steering wheel, presumably for the pleasure of seeing the image rotate on the screen, he himself seemed ready to burst into athletic action at any moment, his neck bulging beneath a collar and tie and his body constantly shifting from side to side, threatening to cross the armrest dividing our seats. He was young, meaty and confident. And hostile somehow. I felt that. Maybe I was wrong, but I felt it. Or, if not hostile, intolerant. Youth does tend to be intolerant.

The elderly lady to my right now produced a pair of knitting needles held together precariously by loops of pale-blue wool and as she struggled to organise herself and find the right place for her ball of wool, so that it wouldn't roll away to the floor beneath the seat but at the same time wouldn't be so trapped it couldn't untwine as she worked, I realised that this knitting presented another obstacle to my heading for the bathroom. Not only would the old dear have to struggle from her seat, but the needles and the wool and the small square of pale-blue knitting would have to be carefully folded away, then carefully brought out and reorganised again after I returned. And what if, on return, I quickly felt I needed to go yet again? Already I could see the meaty contempt of the man to my left, who chuckled every time an explosion lit up his field of vision or whenever gunfire crackled in his headphones. It would have been appropriate, I thought, to think of more serious, even solemn things at this moment, on my way to my mother's deathbed, and instead my body was forcing me to think of the bathroom, to worry about my neighbours' reactions to my bathroom habits. It seemed cruel. Then how could this behaviour right beside me – the explosions, the gunfire, the little grunts and chuckles – not conjure the image of my eldest son, who spent his last years at home, or so it seemed to me, from age fourteen onwards, say, with headphones on his ears. What was the point of having children, I remember asking myself more than once, if they were forever wearing headphones? Or at least what was the point of my staying at home to spend time with them, as my wife insisted I must, if they were always in thrall to explosions and gunfire booming and crackling from their tablets and game consoles – gadgets I had given them myself of course, since, when it came to Christmas and birthdays, there was simply nothing else they wanted, nothing but the sophisticated electronics that would prevent any communication with their father when he stayed at home on certain evenings, as their mother more or less ordered him to, more perhaps because of her worries over what he got up to away from home than out of any real desire for a dialogue between father and offspring, let alone man and wife, something so improbable at this point as to have shifted into the realm of the surreal.

But had my mother's knitting needles, years ago, promoted any more or better communication? For, sure enough, the unusual sight of a woman knitting on a plane – and I noticed now that her needles were of bright-yellow plastic, no doubt to avoid the danger of confiscation at Security – the sight of this woman tucking her ball of blue wool under her right elbow, the yellow needles drawing the blue thread looped around her fingers, jerk by tiny jerk, into what looked like the ribbed shoulders of a child's tiny sweater, her jaw clenching and unclenching, her left elbow very slightly jogging my right with every pale-blue stitch she made, could not but remind me of my mother who had knitted and purled away most of our childhood. One neighbour to remind me of my son and one of my mother. Myself squashed in the middle seat, with both sides threatening my space. 'But isn't it true,' the shrink had said during one recent session, 'that everyone you meet, Señor Sanders, is potentially a close relative with the right to criticise you? Wherever you are, you imprison yourself in a world of familiar gaolers. Isn't that the case?'

No, Mother's knitting had not promoted communication at all. Knitting through the 1960s and '70s, Mother withdrew into a world of woolly enchantment, a thick, ribbed sweater entirely impermeable to the explosions and crackling gunfire of those dangerous times, and uncannily resistant too to the questions of her growing children. Often you would go to the sitting room to ask my mother a question as she sat in an armchair, varicose ankles raised on a footstool, knitting a Christmas present for Father, a chunky cardigan perhaps, or for one of us children, a woolly cap for winter walks maybe, and she would not even register that a voice had been raised and a question asked. Likewise my father, his head bowed over a biblical commentary, his thick reading glasses glinting in the light of the twee lamp they had brought back from a holiday in Bad Ems – or sometimes he would make use of a huge magnifying glass on an adjustable stand, with its own built-in fluorescent illumination – likewise my father might well not register that one of his children was in the room and had asked him a question. Then my mother would begin to hum. It was an automatic reaction to the question, perhaps, or to being questioned in general, an automatic intensification of the protective enchantment her rhythmical knitting had already induced – *To God be the Glory*, Mother would hum, *great things He hath done*. Or, *And can it be that I should gain an interest in the Saviour's blood?* You asked Mother a question, perhaps a perfectly innocent question – Had she remembered to buy pellets for the rabbits? – or a more contentious question – Would it be okay if I skipped Bible Study this Wednesday to go to White Hart Lane? – or a question deliberately designed to engage your parents' special interest in matters of religion and liturgy – What should I do at school prayers when everybody turned to the east to say the Apostles' Creed? – and the clickety-click of her knitting would proceed unperturbed and a faint smile would light up on her face as she began to hum, *Surely goodness and mercy shall follow me all the days of my life.* It was a deflector shield, raised against an alien spaceship. Meantime, the frown on my father's face would intensify as he laboured over his biblical commentaries, scribbling notes in the margin in sudden predatory bursts, as if the speed and sharpness of his nib – because he always used a Sheaffer fountain pen with pale-blue Quink ink – had skewered an elusive thought that might otherwise have escaped for ever. Ha, he would mutter in a low tone and then more loudly, Hah!, his pen suddenly stabbing the page in the yellow lamplight, or under that huge magnifying glass with its circle of fluorescence, while my mother hummed in her strange, whiny way, at once smiling but full of pathos – *When I survey the wondrous cross on which the Prince of Glory died* – as if happy to be sad, or sad to be happy, engrossed in her knitting and her devotion, quite unaware of the child in stockinged feet, the adolescent with the ugly corduroy jacket and the boil on his neck, trying perhaps to ask a difficult question: Why do I always feel sick when I have to go to school? Why do I always feel guilty when I turn out the light and lie alone in the dark?

The woman to my right now, I realised – and her hair was permed into a silvery helmet that had the faintest reflections of green in it – was not humming but muttering to herself as she worked, or at least moving her lips in a way that somehow connected with the move-ment of the needles and the rapid rise and fall of her fingers as she dropped loop after loop of blue wool over the yellow needle and, in so doing, formed a protection against the world outside. She worked in a protected space, like a spider in its web, so that I could already foresee and even feel her irritation, but also pity no doubt, when I snapped the spider's threads and asked her to struggle up out of her seat again so that I could go to the bathroom, barely twenty minutes after going the first time. 'Bathroom', I should say, like 'impact' is one of those Americanisms I resisted for years, determined to go on using the ugly but somehow more correct, I felt, 'toilet' – for how can one speak of a bath on an aeroplane? – then eventually caved in, as I always do, and began to use 'bathroom', and use it emphatically, so that now I hardly say 'toilet' at all. Where's the *bath*room, I say, over-enunciating the ridiculous 'bath'. I'm almost tempted to pronounce it with an American 'a'. Yes, I could already see my elderly neighbour's pity, and it would be very similar to my mother's pity when she had eventually realised – it was inevitable, during that long summer we spent together in her tiny house with just the one bathroom ('restroom' I swear I will never stoop to) at the top of narrow, steep stairs – that her fifty-something-year-old son had problems in that department. He went too often.

Not that my mother would ever have spoken out loud of those problems, of course. For heaven's sake! Mother would never have said, 'Thomas, you do seem to be going to the bathroom rather frequently.' But her eyes showed she had seen. Which was worse. 'Have you slept well?' she would ask, meaning she had heard me go to the bathroom any number of times during the night and wished to express her sympathy, even pity, but without actually broaching an embarrassing subject, not realising that pity was worse than straightforward observation, than open discussion. Or perhaps she did realise but couldn't think of any way round it.

And I could foresee too the young man's contempt, as he raised his eyes for one split second from his treasured screen. Or if not actually contempt – I exaggerate – his distaste, repugnance, at the mere thought of age, at the thought of this male weakness of mine, a 'weak bladder', one says; it is weakness to go to the bathroom twice in twenty minutes, and it was also my son's distaste, my son's repugnance, looking up briefly from his game console, years ago, very briefly, but long enough to register distaste, repugnance, in the face of a father's age, and weakness, a father surely beyond any sexual interest in the world, surely beyond any dealings with a woman thirty years his junior, a woman as charming as Elsa. How will I ever explain my new relationship to my children? Although this was not unlike the impatience with which I viewed my own ageing father when he bent over the biblical commentaries with his fluorescent-lit magnifying glass. Weak bladder, weak eyesight.

In any event, this anticipated embarrassment at my neighbours' response to an eventual second trip to the bathroom, on what was after all only a one-hour flight from Schiphol to Gatwick, somehow managed to fuse itself with the growing pain in my belly; pain and embarrassment embraced each other, as it were, in a decidedly uneasy clutch. Then suddenly, from out of this unhappy mix, came anger: anger with the athletic youngster engrossed in his idiotic film, anger with the elderly woman who seemed oblivious to the fact that her elbow was nudging mine every two seconds, anger above all with myself for having so presumptuously insisted on trying that massage even when I had been warned it might cause pain, even when I had been feeling perfectly well for some years and really had no need of any therapy at all, and hence could have given my talk to the Dutch physiotherapists – how I had cured myself from chronic pelvic pain with years of deep-relaxation techniques – in perfectly good faith. I had presumed that after several years' remission of my unpleasant symptoms, years of yoga and breathing exercises, I was cured. I was in the clear. I had imagined that being thus in the clear, I was free to savour the technique of anal massage that I had hitherto renounced, not having had the cash to go to Dr Sharp's San Diego clinic at the critical moment. Or perhaps I had simply been too squeamish. Too afraid. I had cured myself without resorting to anal massage and now, years later when California had come to Europe to teach Europe anal massage, I had imagined I could seize this opportunity (offered free of charge) and sample the intervention when I no longer needed it – assess it, so to speak, or *ass*ess it if you like, weigh it up, from a position of power, virile in my very openness to what most virile men would not want to admit, proud of the ease with which I dropped my trousers for the Californian physio, two grown men chatting in the most relaxed fashion about things that most folks can't even begin to contemplate: anal massage.

Result? I now had the full array of symptoms all over again: the pains, the urgency and the racing mind that was somehow one with pain and urgency.

How could this not affect my relationship with Elsa? Wasn't the age difference enough, without a condition like this? I would have to hide it from her. And if there was one thing I did not want to do, it was to start hiding things from Elsa. Was I, or was I not, going to ask the elderly lady to put aside her knitting and struggle out of her aisle seat so I could go to the bathroom? Because I really needed to go.

And all this, I thought, on the very day my mother chooses to die. Mother from whom everything had always been hidden. Mother who had always been complicit in having things hidden from her, whose eyes pleaded with you to have things remain hidden. In that sense not unlike my wife. Women to whom things ought to have been said, and from whom some response should have been elicited.

I am in one hell of a state, I realised, then realised also that the elderly lady was talking to me.

'I'm sorry, is my elbow bothering you? I'm afraid I can't seem to tuck it in tight enough.'

As she spoke I appreciated she must be asking the question for the second time, or maybe even the third. I had been so wrapped up in myself, something my children always accused me of, just as I had always accused my parents of being far too wrapped up in themselves and their religion.

'It's no problem at all,' I told her. 'Actually, I was rather enjoying watching your fingers. You're so fast.'

She smiled and her previously severe face creased with friendly wrinkles.

'My mother used to knit,' I said.

She nodded. 'Knitting was more popular in the past.' From her accent, I thought she must be German. 'I suppose it was a cheap way of providing quality clothes. Especially for children. Now the wool is so expensive, it costs more than buying a sweater in the shops.'

'She even taught me to knit once.'

I had forgotten this until the moment the words came out. But it was true. When I was about eight or nine my mother had taught me to knit.

'That *is* unusual,' she smiled, 'in a boy.'

'Perhaps I was playing at being good,' I explained, 'or trying to get myself forgiven for something I'd done wrong.'

The German woman looked puzzled.

'It didn't last. I don't suppose in the end I knitted more than a few dozen squares for refugee blankets. No fancy patterns or anything. Later Mum had to stop when her rheumatism got too bad.'

Or was it arthritis?

'Yes,' the lady nodded. 'The hands get stiff.' She flexed her fingers as if checking all was okay, then added, 'I do it, for fear of flying. I always knit on planes.' She nodded to the window beyond our beefy neighbour. 'It stops me from thinking we are in the air.'

Almost at once, as if just mentioning flight had frightened her, she dropped her head to go back to her work and the fingers began to move again and the left elbow very slightly to touch my right elbow. My mother loved flying, I remembered. She was always delighted when there was some reason to travel. So it must have been something else that she was afraid of when she disappeared into her knitting. Staying on the ground, maybe.

I was struck then, watching the German woman's hands as she took up her needles again, by how many muscles and movements were involved in this homely act of knitting. She had quite small, dry white hands, the skin only faintly mottled around the knuckles with one thick gold ring on her wedding finger and, as she worked, literally scores of tiny muscles and tendons clicked in and out, back and forth, rose and fell, to keep the blue wool feeding into the pattern around the shiny points of the yellow needles, to keep her mind from thinking of her precarious physical position thousands of feet above the ground. The hands formed, as it were, a neat machine in constant internal motion but fixed in space, never shifting from their place on the lap of her olive-green skirt except, every two or three minutes, when she reached the end of one row and raised her right hand in the air for a moment to finish off and start another. It was astonishing to think that, as a boy of eight or nine years old, I too had known how to do this. Forty-eight years ago. I had been so eager to get close to my mother, I suppose, as she sat there in her knitting enchantment, so fascinated, or perhaps so bored, that I had demanded she teach me to knit too, begged her to draw me into the spell of her knit-one-purl-one. And though I have not the slightest idea now how to hold a knitting needle or tie off even the first stitch, so that you might think there really is no continuity in our lives at all and the past simply non-existent, all the same I do vaguely recall sitting for hours at a time beside my mother, needles in hand, seeking to join her in her raptness, her rapture.

Seeking and failing. For if I enjoyed fiddling with the needles and the hairy touch of the wool and the smell of the wool – and the way these repeated actions focused the mind and brought an easy sense of accomplishment as the repetitive clickety-click became a woolly form, and also an act of charity, a soft thick blanket for someone infinitely worse off than myself – if I enjoyed this simple, practical, generous task, at the same time Mother's constant humming drove me mad. The wondrous cross drove me mad. The great things He hath done drove me mad, the Saviour's blood drove me absolutely insane. And far worse than the words, which actually she barely mouthed, but which unfortunately I already knew and so couldn't help hearing in my head even when they weren't clearly pronounced, far worse than the words was the whiny sadness of her humming, its raptured resignation. This drove me wild. The whole mood of complacent sadness communicated by that whiny, self-denying hum was a torture for me, and very soon I gave up the knitting because of it. But without ever being able to tell my mother why. All my life I was never able to tell my mother that her constant humming of sad, somehow sticky hymns, something she did from my earliest memories of her right on into extreme old age, while cooking, or cleaning, or climbing the stairs or simply relaxing in her recliner, drove me quite berserk. *Rock of Ages, cleft for me, let me hide myself in Thee.* I hated the intense pleasure she took in this sticky pathos, this surrender of herself to a ghoulish story of sacrifice and salvation – *let the water and the blood, from Thy riven side which flowed* – I wanted to grab one of her knitting needles and stab it right through her, like the spear in Christ's ribs, the wounds my biblical namesake thrust his fingers in. Life need not be like this! I wanted to scream. I do not need to be washed in blood. Soon enough, I gave up knitting and headed for White Hart Lane.

'May I ask you a question?' I said.

The elderly woman beside me did not appear to have heard. The fingers and thumbs continued their mesmerising motions on her lap.

'Excuse me?'

She turned, 'Yes?'

'May I ask you a question?'

She smiled with a sudden warmth, as if in the space of a few minutes we had become old friends.

'I was observing, while you knit, I hope you don't mind . . .'

She waited.

'I was noticing that when you knit your lips move. Are you actually saying anything?'

She frowned, then sighed.

'I should tell you,' she said rather formally, her accent sounding stronger now, 'that I am not aware of it at all, while I'm knitting. I might even think you were making it up, except that my husband always complained about the same thing.' She hesitated. 'He told me he couldn't bear being around me when I was knitting, because he was always wondering what my lips were saying. It irritated him.'

'Prayers?' I suggested. 'For a safe journey?'

'Oh, I'm not religious at all,' she smiled. She reflected. 'For a while, to please him, I did try to knit with my lips clamped shut, but I found I couldn't do it. It made me feel most uncomfortable. Strange, isn't it? My lips have to move when I knit.'

'So how did you resolve the question?' I asked. 'With your husband, I mean', and I knew already that this business of my neighbour's knitting would prove my salvation on this flight, for the bathroom urgency that had been tormenting me until just a few moments ago had now receded to a dull ache; then even if I did have to ask her to get up to let me make my way along the aisle, I wouldn't now feel embarrassed at all. We liked each other. We were friends. As for my other neighbour, I didn't give a damn.

'I'm afraid the problem solved itself,' she sighed. 'He was killed in a car accident.'

'I'm sorry,' I said.

'It was many years ago.'

She sat in thought for a moment or two, then again looked down at her hands and began to draw the wool to her needles. Watching, I had the impression her mouth was moving more rapidly than before.

Came a loud ding and the safety-belt sign lit up. The athletic man turned off his drama, but still stared at his mirror image in the iPad screen. Through the window beyond him the cloud was impenetrable. We were flying on our instruments, I thought, entirely dependent on computer technology. And I thought if the plane crashed on its Gatwick approach and I was killed, what were the things I wouldn't like people ever to find out about me from my papers and computer files? It's a game I often play in aeroplanes, at moments of turbulence, for example, when you get those sudden wobbles and drops in altitude; to ward off bad luck, or to quell my fears, I say to myself, Okay, if you died now, Thomas, what sins would they find on your laptop? Then I tick them off in my mind. I did this now on easyJet 570, approaching Gatwick through heavy raincloud. And the list was growing longer and longer and the smile on my face broader and broader, thinking of the things I had done that I wouldn't like other people to know I had done, thinking that one of the great pleasures of age is the growing list of rules you have had the courage at some point or other to break, when the plane touched down with a contact as light and smooth as the caress of the Californian physio as his fingers slipped into my butt.

'It is such a help,' the lady beside me confided, visibly more at ease now, 'to have a calm, cheerful fellow passenger as a neighbour. Thank you so much.'

Fifteen minutes later, firing up my laptop in the passport queue to take advantage of the airport Wi-Fi, I opened my email and found Deborah's SOS.

IV

It was dark in England. As soon as I boarded the train at Gatwick I removed the SIM card in my phone and replaced it with an English SIM. I was aware that this SIM-switching was out of date and that the logical thing to do nowadays is to get a smartphone with a contract that will allow it to roam everywhere. But I knew I was not going to do this. I suppose I resent the constant pressure to update and be every minute connected in every way. It seems an important part of my identity to resist such things, at least for a while. On the other hand, nothing would have been more useful to me at the present moment, moving as I was between countries and with a whole series of conversations on the go, private and work-related alike, than a single gadget that gathered phone calls and emails from wherever they came to wherever I was. Had I had an iPhone, for example, I would have seen emails from my brother, my wife, my daughter and Deborah Pool, not to mention numerous work emails and a lovely message from Elsa, *before* I got on the plane at Schiphol, something that would no doubt have changed and certainly complicated my mood on the flight and allowed me to be better prepared for what awaited me in England, though it might also have altered, if not entirely obliterated, my taxi conversation with Dr Sharp, which for some reason I was now thinking of as an important conversation, one I must return to when I had some time, though quite why I wasn't sure. Certainly not for any precise content. Perhaps for the train of reflection it had set in motion with regard to my father. Dr Sharp's similarity to my father, that is. With my mother's imminent death, I had started thinking of my father, whom I hadn't thought about for many years. The fact is there were things I would have liked to ask my mother about my father, a vague theory I had that I would have liked to verify. But if these were questions I hadn't had the courage to ask in the past, when she was crying 'cooee' up the stairs and cooking plum crumbles to be served with thick yellow custard, was it likely I would be able to ask them now? I must see, I supposed, what state my mother was actually in.

'I am sure,' was the burden of my brother's email, opened on my laptop while standing in the passport queue at Gatwick, 'that the dear old bird will bury us all. I called her the day before yesterday and I assure you she was extremely chirpy.' In short, it was a typical email from my brother. I had read it shuffling along in the queue, pushing my small bag across the floor with my toe, so as to have my arms free to cradle my laptop on my left arm and protect it from other shuffling passengers with my right. Mother was made of tougher stuff than people like us, my brother wrote. His daughter, he said – my niece, that is – had been passing through London on business just three weeks ago and had found her grandmother 'in fine shape'. They had gone to Marble Hill Park together. They had walked by the river and had tea and cakes. In any event, he was a bit surprised – my brother, that is – to learn that I had jumped on a plane at the first cry of alarm from my alarmist sister. He himself, he wrote, couldn't easily envisage crossing half the globe in the next few weeks, which were packed with institutional obligations. He had had a nice visit with Mother in the summer. He had good memories of that and wasn't sure they needed adding to. The rest of what was really a generously long and chatty email encouraged me to read a new book on evolution, seen from a chemist's point of view, a book he had found particularly impressive both for the clarity of the style and the illuminating nature of the information provided. 'More and more,' my brother concluded, 'it does seem we are just a predetermined fizz of chemical reactions set in motion millennia ago. Including our most intimate thoughts. Hardly worth struggling against the tide. Heigh-ho, Tommy! Have a good trip and let me know how you find the old dear.'

A trolley now arrived selling sandwiches and, having paid for tea and ham-and-cheddar with a card, because I had no British currency, it occurred to me that perhaps it was what Dr Sharp had said about masturbation that had really impressed me. People impose pleasure on their bodies even when they don't really need it or want it, Dr Sharp had said. An act of will. People had convinced themselves they must have pleasure. All the time. Pleasure coming more from the mind, really, than the flesh. That was an interesting idea. Was my aversion to the iPhone and the iPad partly to do with the fear of having Internet porn constantly and alluringly available, so that one would always be tempted to impose pleasure on one's body? Mental sex. Though it did seem that Elsa had ended that phase of my life. Since I had decided to stake everything on Elsa I had noticed, to my surprise, that I was suddenly and entirely free from that kind of compulsion. The truth is, one day you will have to get an iPhone, I thought now, because the world will become so integrated with this new gadget, there will be so many apps one can't do without – to book a theatre ticket, to find a restaurant, to check street directions – that you will have to get one merely to function in society like other human beings, the way everyone has to wear clothes, like it or not, live under a roof, get an income, pass a driving test, take care of their teeth and open a bank account. All like it or not. Civilisation imposes these things. You cannot live simply as the animal you are, even if you might like to, or might like at least to try, or to have tried. All the same, I didn't want to buy a smartphone right now. I would wait until the last possible moment, as my mother had waited until the last possible moment before calling for help after her fall down the stairs three weeks ago, perhaps the day after the visit from her granddaughter, my brother's child, or perhaps that very same evening, for nobody knew exactly when Mother had fallen down the stairs, even though this accident was something we had been expecting for twenty years and more. She hadn't been able to say. And presumably she waited till the last possible moment before calling for assistance because she knew in her heart that when they took her away from her home she would not be coming back.

Sitting on the train from Gatwick – not the Gatwick Express but Southern, for my immediate destination was Clapham Junction – I was about to call my old friend Deborah, in response to her emailed SOS, when a message arrived from my sister. 'Please call as soon as you arrive.' Then the phone rang and it was my son in Bristol. 'You're in the UK already?' My son was evidently surprised that my UK number had responded. 'Yes,' I said. 'As of half an hour ago. How are things?' He would gladly come to see his grandmother, my son said, my eldest child, but he would need to beg a day off work. Was I absolutely sure she was dying? I had no idea, I told him. I had merely responded to an email from my sister. 'You're the doctor,' I said. He laughed. He was indeed a doctor, my son agreed, but he hadn't seen his grandmother for some time. A doctor wasn't a diviner. I was surprised the boy knew the word. 'Call me after you've seen her this evening,' he said. 'I don't suppose you'll find a doctor at this hour, but speak to the nurses. These things can be deceptive.'

I now started to call my sister, but as I did so Clapham Junction was announced and I cancelled the call to gather my bits and pieces and be ready to get off. It would be absolutely typical of me to leave some crucial piece of luggage or clothing or technology on the train. Then, having found the platform for Hounslow at Clapham, and Clapham is never easy, the person I actually called was Deborah, though all the while aware that I ought to be focusing on my mother, my sister. There were only five minutes to wait, the illuminated indicator told me, for the Hounslow train, which was a stroke of luck. I had taken it for granted, initially, that Mother really was about to die, but what if she wasn't? These things can be deceptive, my son said. He was a doctor. What if my sister was being melodramatic, exaggerating? Alarmist, my brother had said. One effect of my brother's unwavering conviction that my mother will live for ever is a desire, on my part, to demonstrate to him once and for all that she is now in serious trouble; she is mortal; people do die. Drum that into his head. Above all, parents die. They really do. To wilful denial one reacts with wilful exaggeration. Mum's sick. She's dying. Exasperated, perhaps, by some comment my brother had made – the dear old bird will bury us all – my sister had upped the stakes, to get through his thick skull – officially, it should be said, my brother is the genius of the family – that something really was happening. 'She's going downhill fast,' my sister – officially the family dunce – had emailed. This to have my brother face facts, even if the facts weren't perhaps quite as extreme as she was intimating. Or at least my son had put this idea into my head. And I realised now that I really ought to have thought of the implications of my sister's including my brother in that email. It wasn't an email exclusively for me. And I should be phoning her now to find out more. I should be trying to figure out how long I would stay in the UK, if my mother was not dying. Should I cancel the conference in Berlin? The 27th annual gathering of European linguists. My diary was teeming with appointments. *Uses of Archaism in Contemporary Communication Strategies* was the title. I had a flight to Berlin from Madrid tomorrow evening. But I wouldn't be in Madrid. What should I tell Elsa?

Vaguely I was aware that 'teeming' was a word my mother always used and that I never did. For rain particularly. It's teeming down, she would say. As I approached London and London weather, I was using Mother's words. On the other hand, Deborah's SOS had been so interestingly alarming, and had to do with people who had been so much closer to me over recent years than my family had been, how could I not phone her with some urgency? To be honest, I had hardly seen anyone from the family in an age now. With the exception of my mother, that is, whenever I passed through London, and then only because she was ill, because it was a duty to visit a mother who is ill when it's not too difficult to do so. Though never, since that long summer together, for more than a lunch or a dinner. Then surely, I thought, there would be time enough to focus on Mother and what needed to be said to Mother, and whether and when I should book a flight to Berlin or to Madrid and so on, while I was sitting at her bedside. She would hardly want to be sitting up talking all night. There would be plenty of time.

'Tom!' Deborah cried. 'At last!'

It was the same posh and squeaky voice of old. It never changed. Though she did sound flustered.

'Hi, Deborah.'

'At last,' she repeated.

I explained I hadn't seen her email for some hours because I was travelling. I didn't have a smartphone. Then in the silence that she should have been speaking into, nothing. I heard some sighing. She had begun to cry.

'Deborah?' I said, gluing the phone to my ears as the train for Hounslow via Richmond rattled along the platform. 'I'm so sorry.'

'Are you in England? This is an English number, isn't it? How wonderful. Are you in London?'

'It is,' I said, boarding the train behind a man with a stick, 'and I am, but I'm tied up right now. I have to see my mother.'

I had to go to the bathroom again too, but the fact that I wouldn't have to disturb anyone to do so, just walk along the South West Trains carriage to where my eye had already located the illuminated sign, made this infinitely less painful than it had seemed on the plane. Hence it could wait. My bladder would soon be back to normal, I decided. Today was a glitch. A little flare-up after the massage. And I didn't tell Deborah my mother was at death's door because it seemed to me she had enough on her plate. Who had used that expression already today? Charlie had attacked David with a chair, Deborah's email had said. David had been taken to hospital. She wondered if I would talk to Charlie, her youngest son. 'You're the only person I can imagine knowing what to say to him,' she had written. 'Like you did before, remember?'

I didn't.

'Perhaps you could come over later,' she said. 'Could you?' No doubt my mother went to bed fairly early, she thought. It was only half an hour from Hounslow to Kingston. And such a stroke of luck I was in London.

This was difficult. Deborah's voice had an edge of hysteria. Apparently she was just back from hospital, where David was under observation. I had no idea what shape I would find my mother in or what exactly was expected of me. Until just a few moments ago I had been convinced I was in a race against time to make it to her deathbed. But perhaps not.

'What on earth happened, Deborah?' I asked. I started walking along the carriage to the bathroom. 'Why would Charlie do that?'

But she said, No, Tom, she really couldn't even begin to talk about it on the phone. 'Rosie is listening,' she whispered sharply. Every word she spoke reminded me how posh Deborah was. In the train there were bags to be stepped over. She just couldn't, she said. And she burst into tears again. Rosie was the daughter. 'All I'll say is it's a fucking disaster. I'm going fucking crazy.' Now her voice was suddenly loud and harsh. Rosie must surely have heard, I thought, if she really was there. And I was taken aback because Deborah never swore. Deborah was a churchgoer, a high-churchgoer, one of those people who always warn you not to swear when you have a meal together with their kids. She got quite indignant when people swore. My mother was low-church, of course. Proudly low. And I swear far too much.

I had buzzed myself into the South West Trains bathroom now and was pressing the phone against my shoulder to free my right hand to unzip. I can't unzip with my left alone. Still, the last thing I needed was for the phone to fall into the loo. More calmly, Deborah said, 'The fact is poor Charlie is likely to be charged with assault and battery. The police have told him to come to the station tomorrow morning. And he's saying he doesn't care and if his dad doesn't shape up, he'll do it again. He'll kill him. Please come and talk to him, Tom. He'll listen to you. I know he will. I'm going mad.'

As we spoke, the phone beeped to warn me someone else was trying to call. The pee was slow in coming, the hi-tech South West Trains bathroom most impressive.

'David's going to be okay, though?' I asked cautiously. 'Isn't he? Is he badly hurt?'

The truth is, I would far rather have seen David than his son, Charlie. Or Deborah, for that matter. I had already been planning to call David at some point to meet for beers and to crow to him about Elsa. It was something I had been looking forward to. Now it seemed that wouldn't happen.

'Can I call him in hospital?' I asked.

'He'll be fine,' Deborah said rather drily; but no, he couldn't answer calls. He was under sedation.

'God! I'll see what I can do and call later,' I said, wondering why designers preferred expensive, push-button electric sliding doors to simple handles and latch locks. Surely it only increased the possibility of something going wrong.

Deborah told me she was counting on me. It sounded unpleasantly demanding, but there was no time to think about this because now the phone rang again and it was my sister. I was still staring into the bowl.

'Hi, Bro!' she cried, 'how you doing?'

She was so breezy! As if I'd come home for Christmas. I was taken aback. The fact is my sister and I hadn't spoken to each other for at least six months, perhaps a year. In our family my brother and I spoke to, or at least emailed, each other pretty regularly, but not my sister. Or rather, my sister always spoke to the parents, but not to us. Only my mother's illness had forced this recent exchange of emails.

'Hi, Sis.'

'Sorry, listen,' she said. 'I'm afraid things are a bit complicated, Bro.' Her voice seemed jokily conspiratorial. She was the only person I knew who called a brother 'Bro'. 'Where are you, by the way?'

'On the train to Hounslow.'

'Ah. You see, she's not in Hounslow. As of two days ago. That's why I was trying to get in touch. I'd forgotten you wouldn't know.'

My sister now began a long explanation of my mother's recent movements, while I zipped up and pushed the button to move out of the bathroom, well aware that I hadn't peed all there was to pee and hence would very soon have to go again. 'After her fall on the stairs, you see, they couldn't work out whether the deterioration was due to the impact on her back or an acceleration of the cancer. I mean, these awful pains she's getting. Obviously, if they are due specifically to the fall, then the situation might not be terminal. More orthopaedic.'

'But where is she now? If I'm going to get to her this evening . . .'

'Claygate.'

'Come again?'

'It's to the south,' she said. 'Check on your phone.'

When I explained once again that I didn't have a smartphone, she called out, 'How does Tommy get here from a train between Putney and Richmond? He'll check,' she said. Meaning her husband presumably. 'He's a whizz at these things.'

'You're there, then?' I said. 'Now.'

'With Mum? Yes. Or rather, not exactly. We've just come outside for a few minutes' break. It's heavy going. But we have to leave soon.'

'And how is she?'

'All over the place, to be honest.'

Again I was surprised by my sister's tone of voice, which didn't seem melodramatic or anguished at all. Almost offhand. What did she mean: all over the place? Again it occurred to me I might have completely misjudged her email. After all, it had popped up exactly as I was feeling the first effects of the fatal massage. I had only read it once. One thing colours another.

'Yesterday she managed a few steps with the Zimmer frame. They are eager to get her up on her feet again. You know how they are. But today she looks like it's all over, bar the counting.' She paused and began more seriously, 'What you have to do, though, Tom, when you see the doctors tomorrow morning—'

Now her husband interrupted. I should get off at Richmond, he was saying, assuming I hadn't already passed Richmond, and take a taxi or a bus, depending on my finances. If a bus, it was the 65 to Esher. 'Get off at St Leonard's Road,' my sister said. 'You see, she was in the hospice in Hounslow, where she'd always meant to go, after being with us, I mean, but then they sent her to the hospital for a scan, to see if there was spinal damage. That meant a trip to the West Middlesex. Wednesday. The scan took hours and, when it was over, the bed in Hounslow had gone because of some emergency that had come up. I thought it was pretty disgraceful, to be honest. They'd just bundled her stuff into her bag. Anyway, at that point, thank God, they found her the place in Claygate, otherwise she'd have been in a regular hospital ward with a dozen others. They even threatened to send her back to us, if you please.'

'If you please' was another expression my mother always used, but which I don't think I or my brother ever did. Like 'whizz', for that matter. In fact, as this conversation with my sister unfolded – the first conversation, as I said, that we had had for at least six months, perhaps a year – I was acutely aware that not only had our family long been split into the religious side and the non-religious side, but we even spoke different languages. Or we spoke the same language in different ways, if you please.

'Anyway, what you've got to do,' she was saying, 'when you see the doctor tomorrow morning . . .'

'What time?'

'They come round around eight. I think it's a woman. Is demand that they . . .'

The train was arriving in Richmond. I had to move, I said.

'Okay. Text me when you get on the bus and we'll meet you at the stop and say hello, before we drive home. St Leonard's Road. See you soon, Bro.'

My sister, I should have said, lives in Swanage and has a handicapped daughter to return to. Severely handicapped. In her thirties now.

Getting off the train, I wondered if I should phone Deborah again and tell her it was definitely off, I couldn't possibly come. Then I thought I would wait at least until I had seen what the situation at the hospice was. David, far more than Deborah, had been an important part of my life and though I had rather lost contact in the last couple of years with moving abroad, I was curious to know what was going on between them. Extremely curious. In particular, why on earth would their charming son Charlie have attacked his father with a chair? What had David done? Charlie, unlike his brother Robin, had always been a good boy. As I too, unlike my brother, had always been a good boy.

At the same time, looking around in the foyer of Richmond Station for some information as to where I might catch the 65 to Esher via Claygate, I was struck by the thought of the ordeal my poor mother was going through and the relaxed, sometimes flippant tone of my sister's voice. Not that I meant any criticism of my sister. Who, after all, had been on hand to look after my mother when she had finally sent out her plea for help, days after the famous fall, if not my sister? And looking after my mother in those days meant carrying her to the bathroom, or the toilet as my sister still said, or simply letting her do it in bed. And who could have carried a big-boned woman like my mother to the bathroom, the toilet, the loo, if not my sister's huge-boned husband? Who would have done the unpleasant cleaning, if not, again, my generous sister, herself in her sixties and seriously worn out by thirty years of looking after a disastrously handicapped child.

So I wasn't criticising my sister's tone of voice at all. I was just surprised by the thought that this is what life is actually like. Your mother is going through every kind of hell, in excruciating pain, not knowing what bed she will die in, your sister sounds relaxed and jokey, and you are thinking of your old friend Dave and the precariously double life he always led. David would have done anything not to hurt Deborah. He had told me that a million times. He admired Deborah. In a way he *adored* Deborah, he truly did; certainly he prized the whole family thing that he and Deborah had put together: their lovely children, their fantastic home – homes, rather – their circle of friends, and so on. But he had never really felt, Dave had told me on one memorable occasion, that Deborah was *his woman*.

Once again I wasn't thinking of my mother. But I had found the 65 bus stop. So I should be with her soon enough. There would be time enough for Mother, I thought. I didn't want to take a taxi, because I couldn't see the point of spending ten times as much to save: what? Just five or ten or fifteen minutes. This was a thriftiness, a habit, I had learned in childhood, no doubt from my mother who, as we have seen, was determined now to die in the thriftiest possible way. That was one of the reasons why she was going through this miserable ordeal, shifted back and forth from hospital to hospice.

Thrift or not, though, the truth is I hate that feeling of being trapped in a taxi having to watch the meter creep up at every traffic light. No, let's be more specific. Whenever I'm in a taxi I feel guilty: guilty of throwing money away, guilty of treating myself like a king when I should be with ordinary people on the bus. And who had instilled this guilt in me, if not the woman determined to die cheaply in order to pass on the money to me, so that I could feel guilty whenever I spent it on a cab? This is the money your mother is earning for you now, I thought, if you want to see it that way, dying so cheaply as she is, and you spend it on a cab. But because I'm no sooner feeling this taxi guilt than I realise that it is stupid, it is nothing more than a hangover from childhood conditioning of an emphatically low-church variety, an instinctive resistance kicks in and I start to mock myself for feeling guilty and to wish I was taking taxis all day long, with classy women and fat cigars and bottles of champagne on the back seat. I wish I was spending lavishly, scandalously, above all carelessly, unwisely, living it up in every possible way, and at the same time I loathe the sight of the meter creeping up to form the scandalous figure I am actually going to have to shell out when the journey ends. I feel like a sheep gripped tight for the fleecing. And since riding in a taxi inevitably provokes this conflicted state of mind in me, I have started to hate taxis most of all because of what they tell me about myself. Even when travelling on expenses I hate taxis. The emotions click in even when I'm not paying. Perhaps that partly explains my anxiety in the long taxi ride to Schiphol.

Still, at least this taxi decision had started me thinking of my mother again. My mother's absolutely central role in everything I am. No doubt my father's too, truth be told. Or the combination, Mum and Dad. They made me who I am. Suddenly, unhappily, I was now electrically aware there would be an awful lot of thinking coming my way in the next few days. Assuming Mother died. But even if she didn't. Perhaps especially if she didn't. An awful lot of very difficult thinking and very difficult emotion, to the point that I felt exhausted just thinking of the thinking I would soon have to be doing. Not to mention the emotions I would be feeling. Presumably. How would they impact on my bladder? Impact actually seemed an appropriate verb in this particular circumstance. If only Elsa were here, I thought. Elsa calms me down. On the other hand, if anyone's life had run parallel to mine over these last two decades, or at least until my separation, it was David's, and David came from a completely different background from my own and had been conditioned in completely different ways. So where was the determinism of one's parents' genes and cultural conditioning? And if any phrase has ever sunk into my skull over the years, with the purpose and urgency of a gunshot announcing a long-delayed revolution, it was when David said that evening, over beers no doubt, since David never said anything personal without a beer in his fist, 'Despite the family, Tom,' he said, 'despite admiring Debbie so much, despite not wanting to hurt her, and so on, ever, I just feel really she is *not my woman*. Not the woman for me. Never has been, never was.' And then he added with a sigh, as if admitting a major defeat, 'I suppose it must be a thing of the flesh.'

A thing of the flesh. As if David, or indeed any of us, would have given anything to have been spared *things of the flesh*, to be spared imperatives we could not control. This from a serial adulterer of the most resolute ilk. Which reminded me again of something my mother had said that summer in her house while playing Scrabble together. She said, 'I'm not afraid of the actual dying, Tom, since I'll be going home to glory of course, but cancer just smells so bad.' And we were both thinking obviously of Father. Because he had smelled. There was no denying it. 'Pounding flesh,' David used to say when he was 'out on a mission'. As I climbed onto the 65 I was acutely aware of a sharp, stabbing pain in my belly.

'This is the sixty-five to Esher Central Station,' a disembodied but definitely female voice was announcing. It's interesting how frequently disembodied voices are female. I climbed on the bus with my bag and pulled out my wallet, only to realise I had no English cash to pay the fare; they would hardly take foreign credit cards on a red bus. 'I'm sorry, sir,' the driver said. Sir! I got off the bus, crossed the road to go back to the railway station and walked straight to the taxi rank.

'You take cards?' I asked the driver. A woman.

'Reluctantly,' she said.

'Not as reluctantly as I take cabs.'

Coming out with this sharp response immediately made me feel better. Combative. The pain eased. It was odd. You feel better when you get into some kind of rapport, I realised. As when you talked to the knitter with the dyed hair on the plane. When you engage with people. I need Elsa here. That is the truth. Elsa is my woman, I thought. 'I'm going to Claygate,' I told the driver. And to my sister I texted, 'Send hospice address. In a cab. Don't want to arrive late.' Then I made a pact with myself not to look at the meter for the whole duration of the ride, not even to register the sum, mentally, when the driver finally pressed the button that stopped the figures creeping up; I would just hand her the credit card and tell her to add three quid for a tip. It would be fun discussing this detail with

71

my shrink. The tip, I mean. No, *five* quid, I decided. Let's give a stupidly large tip, against the grain, against the boy who is his mother's thrifty son.

I sat in the back of the cab suddenly drained of energy, staring emptily out of the window, and after some minutes realised that we were driving through Kingston. I knew because I saw the John Lewis I had been to with Mother one day that summer of four years ago, when she had wanted to buy me a teapot to take home as a gift for my wife. In the end, Mother was always more of a Kingston person than a Hounslow person. She should never have been living in Hounslow. And she always hoped that these small social rituals of gift-giving and birthday-card-sending would keep our marriage on the rails, despite the glaring evidence that the conjugal carriages had come uncoupled years ago. 'What do I want with another teapot,' my wife said, 'when the only person drinking tea around here is you?'

And why hadn't it occurred to me that going south instead of north from Richmond, I was going closer to Dave and Deborah's, not further from them? So if I didn't spend all night with my mother, which seemed unlikely, I might as well make the effort and go and see Deborah and young Charlie, if it would help. Perhaps I could even sleep there. I had eaten with them in their Kingston home just once, as I recalled, something over a year ago, when the conversation over lunch in the garden – they had only recently moved into a truly magnificent house – had gravitated towards the delicate question of Charlie's sexual orientation. The garden backed onto the river. Was this what Deborah was referring to when she spoke of my having once talked to him? Though I hadn't actually *spoken* to Charlie at all. Deborah and David had waited until the children drifted away from the table to ask me was it true that Charlie had sent me some stories he had written, for me to read? One says children, but they were all in their twenties now. I had immediately been on my guard. I said it was true, yes – two stories, to be precise, in an email. He had mistakenly imagined, I said, meaning Charlie, that since I sometimes work for publishers I might be able to help him publish them.

'But I actually *am* a publisher,' David observed. 'And one that publishes stories, not academic monographs.'

'So you know how naïve he was being,' I laughed.

'And are they any good?' Deborah enquired.

I remember shrugging and saying that although I really wasn't an expert on short stories, it was hardly my field, I tend to get hung up with syntax and lexical choices, they *had* seemed to me to be rather good, actually, yes. Certainly I had read them with interest. To the end. Which was rare. 'But a bit sad,' I added, hoping that this small extra scrap might be enough to round off and conclude a conversation that had caught me by surprise. Why Charlie had sent these stories to me, out of the blue, I really wasn't sure. I didn't even know how he had got my email address. And why, having sent them to me, he had then wanted to tell his parents he had sent them was even stranger. I certainly wouldn't have mentioned it to them if they hadn't brought the matter up. Or perhaps he had told his sister, and his sister had told his parents, which would make things even more delicate for me. But I couldn't know that and certainly couldn't ask.

'Well, I'm rather intrigued,' David said. 'It's great you think the boy can write. What are they about?'

I took a deep breath and sighed. We had had a glass or two. It was a Sunday lunch, as I recall. There were bottles on the table. David and Deborah do drink. The house was wonderful. Their houses are always wonderful. Looking up, I guessed from something in her eyes that Deborah knew the truth. She was the boy's mother, after all. Or at least she was afraid it might be that. While David was oblivious. David thought we were simply talking literary performance. He was a book man. And for a moment I was able to savour the irony of Deborah's being largely unaware of her husband's endless sexual adventures, but cottoning on fairly rapidly about her son, or so it seemed, and David's living a life of extraordinary deviousness while remaining absolutely oblivious to Charlie's identity crisis, a crisis intensified perhaps precisely by this lack of awareness on his father's part. Perhaps deviousness obliges a man to be so focused on his own performance that he really doesn't have the mental space for anyone else's. In the end you can hardly expect a tightrope walker to help you with your bags.

'He seems a bit shy of telling us what he writes,' David prodded, smiling at me.

David and I hadn't spoken in a while, not since my separation anyway, and although in the past there had been times of exhilarating intimacy, these days we barely communicated at all.

'Kids and their fathers,' I said offhand. It must have been obvious I was hiding something.

'Oh, come on.' David poured himself more wine.

'Love,' I told him. 'They're stories about love.' This was true. 'Who would want their parents to read their love stories?'

'Oh, romance!' he exclaimed. 'Wonderful! Sells books.'

'Quite.'

'Excellent,' David filled his glass. 'Funny,' he chuckled, 'he keeps his women well hidden.'

There was a moment's silence. What was I supposed to say? Charlie hadn't suggested that sending the stories to me – and they were as passionate and explicit as ever stories could be – was a way of coming out to his parents. He had simply asked me for a literary opinion. We had spoken about literature a few times in the past when I had stopped by at their house. We were all bookish people. And once, when my family visited theirs, we had played tennis together. Presumably Charlie had imagined I would be a sympathetic ear within his parents' circle. I was the kind of low-church guy who swore at a high-church table. In particular, I was the close friend of a father who was jovially, insatiably heterosexual and never swore at table. And Charlie was right. I *was* a sympathetic ear. I really could not care if the boy was homosexual or not. I feel a deep sympathy for anyone pushed by fleshly imperatives to take decisions his nearest and dearest are not easy with. But then I wasn't his father. He wasn't my son. And he hadn't actually told me whether or not to say anything to his parents. He hadn't asked me to tell and he hadn't asked for discretion. I was simply sent two highly erotic, touchingly lyrical stories about adolescent homosexual love. However, there was the complication that while one of the stories finished happily, the other, which was by far the longer and more ambitious of the two, ended with an accident that might well have been construed as a suicide, a double suicide, perhaps even a death pact. At the end of the family holidays on which the two adolescents discover their sexuality, the evening before their parents are due to return to their strait-laced city lives, the two young men dive from a cliff into a tormented and rocky sea. What coast this was wasn't clear, but their deaths were, as it were, taken for granted. That was the catastrophic tone of the final lines of an otherwise blissful story. It didn't bode well for a coming out.

'I guess if you want the details,' I said, 'you should ask him for a copy. I mean, I wouldn't like to give away the end and spoil it for you.'

'Damn, you've got me curious!' David said. 'Don't tease, Tommy. Tell!'

He filled my glass again. I sat smiling.

Then Deborah said, 'By the way, Tom, speaking of romance, Dave and I have a story of our own.'

David pressed his hands on the table and rolled his eyes.

'Do we have to?'

Deborah was suddenly beaming. 'Can you believe this old bear has agreed to marry me on my sixtieth birthday? Think of that!' She actually clapped her hands. At once I realised she had been dying to tell me this all lunchtime.

The truth was David had always refused to marry Deborah. They had lived together and had children together unmarried, in sin, despite her high-churchness. It had been hard for her. Officially, Dave's refusal was ideological. Child of '68, he was against all conservative institutions, he said. But unofficially I felt it was because, beyond the evident social and economic advantages of marrying a smart woman from a wealthy, well-connected family, who incidentally was five years older than he was and had always looked after him in every way, David's flesh nevertheless warned him that Deborah was not, as he put it, his woman. However long they lived together, at the deepest level they would never truly be married, ceremony or not. He knew that. Except that now, rather surprisingly, he had agreed to marry her on her sixtieth birthday.

'Better late than never! Congratulations.'

'More attrition than romance,' David commented. He was laughing, but it was cruel all the same. 'Do we have to?' he repeated when Deborah began to talk of the wedding-reception arrangements. Again it seemed cruel, but a cruelty born of unease. And now it was Deborah who, by ignoring his unease and cruelty, seemed determined to be cruel herself. The party would be on a boat on the Thames, she explained; which had the advantage of restricting the number of people who could come. Otherwise, marrying at sixty, there was simply no end to the people they might have to invite. 'Even grandchildren,' she giggled. Their eldest daughter was producing a second.

'*I* won't be sixty,' David said, filling his glass yet again.

'I suppose,' Deborah laughed, 'given what you said about the stories, Tom, we should ask Charlie if he has a partner to bring.'

Why did she say that, I wondered, when it had seemed to me she had guessed why I hadn't wanted to talk about them? Or was I wrong? Perhaps she just liked to throw out knowing glances from time to time.

'Even two,' David joked. 'A few charming chicks would give us the excuse to exclude an old hen or two.'

Deborah laughed with him. But I was unsettled. All at once I felt a powerful rush of impatience; no doubt it came in the wake of that tidal wave of emotions that had so recently swept away my own family life. I was fed up with charades.

'I'm afraid they'll be cocks,' I said. 'Not chicks.'

'Where exactly in Claygate, sir?' the driver asked.

Thirty minutes in heavy traffic and I hadn't thought of my mother at all. But nor had I thought of anal massage or bladder pains. I checked the phone, to find that my sister hadn't answered my message.

'It's a hospice,' I said. 'In the Claygate area.'

'Sorry?'

'A hospice. Those homes for people who are dying.'

The taxi driver shook her head. She had a straight-backed, rather military look to her.

'Near St Leonard's Road.'

'Do you want me to take you there?' She began keying the name into her navigator.

'I'll see if I can get the address.'

I phoned my sister now and, as I waited for the call to connect, wondered if my impetuous, perhaps unwise disclosure at Sunday lunch more than a year before – my telling my friend, albeit not in so many words, that his beloved younger son was gay – had perhaps set off whatever chain of events led to Charlie's smashing a chair over his father's head sometime in the early hours of this morning. The phone rang but wouldn't answer. On the second attempt the call was rejected.

'Okay, St Leonard's Road,' I said.

The taxi stopped. When we'd finished sorting the money, the driver turned and flashed me a smile, a five-pound smile, I suppose.

'Thank you, sir. Glad I overcame my reluctance.'

'My pleasure,' I told her. In other days I might have asked for her phone number. There was something about the woman. Perhaps a sense that she was doing a job she didn't really want to do. Conflictedness can be attractive. As it was, I climbed out of the car to find myself in a long and leafy suburban street, the kind of place someone like myself should be living in – would be living in, I thought – had I played all my cards in the conventional fashion.

Where was Mother?

V

Climbing out of the cab onto the lamplit pavement in St Leonard's Road, I phoned Elsa. This wasn't so much a decision as a compulsion. The events of the last few hours had disoriented me. I needed to remember I was a happy man who had made the right decisions in life.

Then, waiting for the call to connect, looking up and down the pavement for someone to ask where the hospice was, and it seemed rather strange to me that there was no one out and about here, in the kind of pleasant suburban street so many people would kill to live in, I suddenly found myself muttering the words, That a love should be. 'That a love should be,' I said out loud in St Leonard's Road, my voice drowned out by passing cars, passing cabs. Even the number 65 now. The big red bus came thundering by. I had gained nothing with my taxi fare.

People were in their houses, of course, where else? It was after nine. Fine semi-detached structures set well back from the brisk traffic, looming darkly behind winter branches and glossy shrubs. Perhaps I should knock and ask, I thought. There were chinks of light behind the curtains. Excuse me, where is the local hospice? The local place to die. They were the kind of properties professional couples slave to bring up A-grade children in, as my wife and I had slaved many years for a beautiful property to house our happiness and ambitious children. We weren't happy. Ambitions are a torment. The line was taking longer than seemed possible to connect. Elsa, I muttered. Much of what we pass on to our children is torment. Probably I should check how much credit I had. I started to walk towards the bus stop, where three or four people had got off. Somebody must know where the hospice was.

'That a love should be,' I told the shrink. They were the first words finally spoken through a storm of tears on that initial, historic encounter with this small, unremarkable woman. In St Leonard's Road I walked, Nokia at my ear, towards the alighting passengers, who had all set out in the opposite direction. It had come on to drizzle. Would the hospice have some kind of sign, I wondered, in wrought iron or neon? Abandon all hope, ye who . . .

'What do you mean by that exactly?' the shrink asked.

A man in his fifties wearing respectable city clothes had stumbled into her office in central Madrid, tried to explain his problems and burst into tears. Then every time this solid, middle-aged Englishman – perhaps his jacket was a little the worse for wear – appeared to be calming down, every time he tried once again to articulate, in Spanish, some explanation for his urgent request for an appointment, once again he burst into tears. Whenever I wonder if I could have stayed with my wife, if I could have stayed in our beautiful house where we worked so hard to have our children become what we thought children ought to be, my mind returns to this historic first encounter with the shrink: a meltdown.

'Tell me why you've come,' the woman repeated evenly.

In her late sixties, if not older, the shrink lit a cigarette, a long slim menthol thing. Retrospectively, I would be surprised that in a so-called caring situation a health professional, so-called, would smoke cigarettes. It was a place of work after all. At the time I barely registered the fact. For years I had wondered if I should go to see a shrink. For years the answer had been no. You can handle this on your own. What on earth do you need a shrink for? Because you are unhappy? Because you have chronic stomach pains? Isn't it the rule to be unhappy? Aren't there medicines for stomach pains? Scalpels, if need be? 'Part of the modern malaise,' my mother had frowned, when I confessed to her during that long summer in her tiny house that sometimes I did think perhaps I ought to see a shrink – no, 'analyst' would have been the word I used with her; it was quite possible my mother did not know the word 'shrink', had not registered it, as she would say. This was some time before the memorable evening when she spoke to me so confidently of her funeral arrangements. Psychoanalysis was part of the modern malaise, she said. People were too proud to look into their hearts and confess their sins and receive the comfort their saviour so generously offered. Instead they went to so-called analysts to seek justification for some evil they were doing that made them unhappy. If one was unhappy, it was because one was doing some evil that contradicted God's plan. Or to find someone else to lay the blame on. Their mothers, most likely. 'I never would on you, Mum,' I laughed, 'with the quality of your apple crumbles these days.' She laughed too. She said she was always ready to pray with me, if only I would say the word. Imagine how odd, then, and oddly exciting, when I heard a couple of years later, from my brother, that in his early fifties my father of all people, the Reverend Edward Sanders, had been to see a shrink. 'But he stopped after two or three sessions.' Where my brother got this information, I have no idea. Who would have told him? 'Complete waste of time,' my brother added. He too had given up on his shrink after just a few sessions. 'You wonder what on earth you are paying them for,' he said.

'Tell me why you've come here,' this shabby elderly lady asked, lighting a menthol cigarette. She spoke matter-of-factly, quietly. I was still blubbering. I would never have imagined I could break down so completely. It wasn't me. '*Que haya un amor*,' I eventually got out. In Spain the analysts speak Spanish. 'That a love should be.' Those were the words. I was shaking my head rhythmically from side to side, 'like a man possessed', my mother would have said, a man who has surrendered all his dignity. My mother would never have given my father her consent to see a shrink. Low-church folks don't do analysis. There was the expense, aside from anything else. 'That a love should be,' I repeated. Did my brother know something about my father that my mother didn't? The Reverend Sanders had gone to a shrink without telling her. Was that possible? He had stopped because she found out, perhaps?

'And what exactly do you mean by that,' the shrink pressed, '*Que haya un amor*?'

In her mouth the words sounded arcane, some atrophied formula, a mantra. She was a small, stout elderly woman in a sack of a dress and bedroom slippers, smoking.

I took a deep breath. Perhaps I was snivelling. The shrink proffered a box of tissues. Not a cigarette, though. Shrinks are used to weepers, I suppose. They have their tissues ready. I wiped my eyes. I took a few moments over it, trying to pull myself together. 'It means,' I said, 'that after all these years' – I sighed, what was I saying? – 'after all these miserable years, just one time in my life, there should be love.'

Never once, when phoning for the appointment, when catching the tram to go to the shrink's studio, had I imagined saying anything remotely like this. It was not me. To speak of love. Perhaps only the Spanish made it possible. I would never have gone to a shrink in Edinburgh.

The phone had finally begun to ring in Madrid. After hurrying a few steps in pursuit of the dispersing passengers, I had stopped, on the damp pavement of St Leonard's Road, very conscious that this was ridiculous. I would never catch up with them. I was losing my grip. I had set out on this journey at the drop of a hat.

A taxi, a flight, two train journeys and now another taxi. I who never take taxis. Now here I was, in Claygate, something after nine in the evening, presumably within a few hundred yards of where my mother lay dying, and I couldn't find her. What's more, until I spoke to my sister, I had no way of finding her. No one else would know where she was. And instead of calling my sister again, I was calling Elsa. In another country. Another life. The phone was ringing now. Glued to my ear. In Madrid. *That a love should be.* That is the moment I go back to when panic grabs me, when I begin to think I have screwed up big time, I should never have left home, I should be back in our handsome semi-detached Edinburgh property, protected by the winter branches and the evergreen shrubs and the carefully drawn curtains. *Que haya un amor.* My eyes met the shrink's and she understood. It came as a shock. I had said words I never meant to say, in Spanish to boot, and a woman I had never met before understood those words. She understood, and I knew she understood. She knew I knew. A foreign woman. And something shifted. Something felt different. Change was possible. Whenever I think I have made the wrong decisions, I go back to that watershed, that tear-shed, in the shrink's drab office, the moment when our eyes first met and I understood I had an ally. That a love should be. Our modern malaise, Mother said. In Madrid the phone rang four times before the call was rejected.

Nothing unusual in that. Elsa is a busy woman. She was with someone, no doubt. In a restaurant perhaps. It wasn't a convenient moment. I had to find out where the hospice was. Actually it was better this way. I would have wasted precious time chatting to Elsa. About what? Nothing. Maybe the thing to do really was to knock on one of these doors, assuming people would open to a stranger on a drizzly evening. You're at home on a drizzly evening, stockinged feet cosily snuggled on the sofa with TV or iPad, or getting dinner for the children, do you really want to open the door to a stranger with a battered bag? Do you really want to hear him ask where people go to die in your part of town?

'Excuse me!'

Someone was passing me from behind. I turned to take advantage. It was an Indian woman with a raincoat over a sari.

'Excuse me?'

She was hurrying through the drizzle.

'Yes?'

She stopped. Was it takeaway pizza she was carrying?

'Could you . . .'

My phone was ringing again.

'Yes?'

The Indian woman waited, cocking her head to one side in the rain.

I flustered with the phone. It must be my sister.

'I'm sorry, it doesn't matter,' I said. 'This call will solve it.'

'Thomas?'

It was Elsa.

'I didn't want you to pay,' she said. 'I still have free minutes on this deal.'

Having desperately wanted to speak to Elsa a moment ago, I now felt frustrated. I couldn't respond as I should have. The Indian woman was already a few paces away. I needed to speak to my sister.

'Elsa.'

'What's up?'

I hesitated, watching the Indian woman walking away in the rain. 'I just wanted to tell you I loved you.'

'Again?' she laughed. 'How's your mother?'

'It's crazy,' I said and explained I hadn't seen her yet. I didn't know where she was. My sister had gone incommunicado at the crucial moment, leaving me stranded in the English drizzle. I was reduced to asking people in the street.

Even as I spoke, a beep told me someone else was trying to phone. I should put down at once and call my sister. But having sounded unconvincing when I said I love you, disappointed even when I heard Elsa's voice, I didn't want to hang up now. The last thing I needed was to feel things weren't well with Elsa.

'What's the name of the street you're in?' Elsa asked. 'I'll google it.'

'St Leonard's Road. I spelled it for her. Her English wasn't perfect. 'In Claygate. That's clay as in earth, and gate as in departure gate.'

Ominous.

'And they're called hospices?' she asked.

'With a "c". Like ho-spice. Not hoss piss.'

Elsa chuckled. 'Okay. I have it. Wait me. Okay. There are two.'

'Damn. Which is nearest?'

'St Leonard's Road is long.' She went back to Spanish. 'It goes right down the screen. Give me the name of a cross-street?'

I began to trot through the drizzle, bag in one hand, phone in the other. The beep came a second time.

'Hang on. Nearly there.'

'I can wait.'

'Stoughton Street.

Elsa cursed the English spelling.

'Like fought or brought or bought. Not caught or short or wart.'

'Okay, okay! So, the nearest is on . . . There's no name. I'll have to zoom. Okay. Grange Street. It's quite close. Which direction have you just moved, to get to Stoughton Street?'

I thought of a line from Richmond to Esher. 'South. From north to south.'

'Okay . . . so, continue in the same direction. It's the second on the left. Go a bit of the way down that road, Grange Road, not sure how far. Two hundred metres. Three. It looks like the ho-spice is on the right.'

'You're fantastic. I love you.'

'Go to your mother, Tommy.'

Elsa closed the call.

Suddenly feeling immensely cheerful, I set off with more purpose. At last I knew where I was going. I had a wonderful woman on my side, if not quite at my side. My hair was damp now, my shoulders too. Was there any point in phoning my sister? Probably yes. Because there were two hospices. I stopped to make the call, but my sister's phone was busy.

Grange Road was a little further than I expected and the rain had begun to fall more steadily. My bag felt heavier and was banging against my left leg. I was carrying it on the left to keep my right hand free for the phone. It is an extraordinary thing that I need my right hand to use the phone. The actions involved are so few and so simple, pushing a couple of buttons, but I just can't do them with my left. Or not easily. But now I shifted the bag to my right hand, which was also rather better than the left at stopping the bag from banging against my leg. The fact is I don't use trolley bags. I have tried but I can't get on with them. It's not a question of my resisting change and innovation. I think I was one of the first to buy a small trolley bag, when they came in big time in the 1980s. The kind you can carry on as in-flight luggage. Immediately I knew it was not for me. I disliked the rumble of the wheels on the pavement. I felt it must bother people in quiet streets, or crossing the courtyard of my apartment block to catch an early-morning flight. I hate to bother people. In this I'm like my mother. And I disliked the position of the body, one arm pulled back as one walks. It felt unnatural. I intensely disliked the way the wheels bounced from side to side on uneven paving, if one tried to hurry. I am always hurrying. Or if they hit a bump or caught some litter between the wheels. I hated the fussy business, whenever you face a flight of stairs, up or down, of having to telescope the handle down into its frame, so that you can then pick it up from another handle attached to the bag itself. I know this hardly takes two seconds, but that's time enough to have the people behind you curse and push as they hurry to board a departing train. I understand their impatience. I don't want to be in their way. Mother again. So I went back to my old Samsonite. Or rather, I tried to buy a new piece of non-trolley hand luggage and found it impossible. Samsonite didn't make them any more. 'No one wants them, sir.' Now you *had* to buy a trolley bag. As later you would have to have an iPhone. Production of all hand-carried luggage had ceased the world over. That can't be true, but it felt that way. In any event, I am now stuck with something twenty years old and, to tell the truth, disintegrating. Or on the verge. Something totally out of line with my social status. Ladies and gentlemen, I would like to welcome Emeritus Professor Thomas Sanders, who has come to talk to us on the subject of syntactical shifts in global English and always uses a twenty-year-old bag with a sticky zip and a piece of stiff wire that protrudes from one of the bottom corners.

Turning the corner of Grange Road, I broke into a run, extending my right arm a little to keep the wet bag from banging against my trousers. It had better not disintegrate now, I thought. With the famous anal wand inside. Then the phone rang again. This must surely be my sister. But I was almost there. Did I really want to stop in the rain, shift my bag from right to left and fuss with the phone, when it was only a matter of a minute or two? I knew from long experience that it is impossible to extract a phone from a right-hand pocket with your left hand. What if it was Deborah?

I kept running and realised that this purposeful movement and my new cheerfulness had completely sorted out the pain in my belly. Could such a poor urinary flow – a blockage almost, it had seemed – really be entirely and merely psychosomatic? I very much hoped so. Then this whole business of right and left hands and urinary flow reminded me, running down Grange Road, of the endless debate

I'd had with my mother that summer four years ago in her tiny house about the relationship, so called, between mind and body, or as my mother chose to frame it, between body and soul. One says 'mind and body', but then 'body and soul', inverting the position of body in the two expressions. Heaven knows why.

These thoughts flashed through my mind as I trotted bag in hand down another breezy, well-to-do south-west London street, slightly downhill now, always in the rain. The English rain has always seemed to me to have a different quality from the rain in other countries, a special freshness and rawness. I was almost enjoying myself. Or my body was. The simple fact of the different functions of our two hands, I had said to my mother that summer over our long games of Scrabble, our shepherd's pies and apple crumbles, all the automatisms and immediacies behind their manipulations – tying shoelaces, for example, playing the piano, eating with chopsticks – indicated very clearly that mind and body were entirely integrated. We *were* our hands. Not to mention our facial expressions across the Scrabble board, the communication of our eyes when one of us hit a triple-word score or another managed to play a Q or a Z. We *were* our eyes, our smiles. This simply was us, hands face feet, doing whatever we were doing. In the end, mind and body, I said to my mother, were just words referring to different areas of the same single entity, me. No, not even different areas – different aspects, apprehensions. The mind was in the hand. The hand was in the mind. I felt that more and more, I told my mother that summer. Probably it was the first time I had spoken to her so fervently since adolescence. It was the revelation my chronic pains had brought me to. We were our bodies, and our bodies were our minds. Pain is identity.

But my mother couldn't, or wouldn't, see this at all. What did left and right hands have to do with it, she protested? She could lose either or both and still be herself, Martha Sanders. Couldn't she? Would she have a different name if she lost her hands? No, she would not. She grew older, she said, and fell ill, but she was still herself, her Christian, church-going self. She wasn't her body, she wasn't her cancer. She was a soul, faceless and handless. She was going to meet her Maker. So I suppose what Mother meant when she told me that psychoanalysis was part of a modern malaise was that I mustn't go looking for excuses for the soul I irrevocably was, or asking other people to take control of my life and find justifications for decisions that were my responsibility and mine alone, like having married my wife, for better or worse, till death us do part; and when my mother talked so calmly of the disposal of her earthly remains, I think the very evening before my return to my decaying marriage, it was partly to show her confidence that these were not her essential self that she was disposing of, but the merest fleshly receptacle, a skin she could shed when the time came, with barely a change of mood. Here is my right hand, here is my left. I surrender them to you. And my nose, and my mouth. Shall we bury them or cremate them? Even my eyes. Out, vile jelly. All this when it was abundantly clear to anyone who knew my mother that she was already no longer her old self and had not been so for some long time. She was performing her old self, and doing it against the grain of a body pleading for rest, pleading to be spared the shepherd's pies and apple crumbles, the gardening and the cleaning and the cuckoo clock that had to be wound up twice a day, pleading repose, pleading the end. And if anyone thinks that a man running in the rain with a moderately heavy bag, looking out for the sign that would indicate a hospice rather than another well-appointed semi-detached house, could not think all this over a distance of – what? – four hundred yards, well, they have another think coming. Because I thought all that and more. Above all I thought how unwise, how cruel, how criminally stupid even, I had been that summer to suggest, repeatedly, that the mind could not exist separately from the body, when my mother must already have understood that sooner or later, sooner rather than later, this cancer would be her undoing. She wasn't long for this world. Her body would be a corpse. I also thought that I had only insisted on this idea, despite its cruelty or, rather, oblivious of its cruelty, because, with a view finally to warning my mother of the imminent break-up with my wife – or was it that I needed her *consent*? – I was actually trying to suggest to her that there was no point in my mind's, my reason's, my will's insisting on my staying with my wife, insisting on remaining loyal to old promises and principles, when my body was increasingly telling me in every possible way that it was not happy with the arrangement. It did not want to be married to my wife. Worse than that, my body was telling me it would wilt and die if I stayed with my wife a moment longer. It would wilt and die. You have no choice but divorce or death, my body was saying, or murder perhaps, and I was trying to let my mother know this, so that she would consent to what I had begun to feel at some point I would have to do: leave home. Something she would see as a terrible sin. *Que haya un amor*, I told the shrink. But perhaps all this had merely been suggested by my friend David's celebrated remark that Deborah was not and never could be, despite twenty and more years of cohabitation, *his woman*. That was why he hadn't actually married her. The politics and ideology were just an alibi. She never had been, and never would be, the woman for him. Even if he had spent his life with her. Why? Perhaps this whole new line of thought I had been developing, mind and body, etc., this *excuse*, as my mother would no doubt have seen it, for my leaving my wife – that my body would wilt, etc., etc., or at least require anal massage, and so on and so forth, if I didn't leave – had merely been suggested to me by David, by my old friend, the way my bad behaviour in adolescence was supposedly the result of the merest suggestion from my wicked, atheist brother. Thomas Sanders had no self at all, just a shoddy vocation for mimicry. And Mother would no more have consented to the break-up of a marriage than she would have to my father seeing a shrink.

But whatever the case, I thought, slowing to a stop on Grange Road, out of breath now, my body simply refusing to push itself any harder, and to hell with worrying about my jacket getting wet, whatever the truth of the matter, I absolutely mustn't allow these corrosive thoughts to get in the way of a serene last exchange with my poor mother, a proper closure to our long story. The idea of telling Mother anything new and important, like my having left my wife two years ago, like having recently fallen in love with a woman thirty years my junior, was nonsense. It would kill her. All we could do now was share some quiet time together.

Not only did I think all this, resuming my rapid walk down Grange Road, remarking a cat hiding from the rain under a dripping SUV and a street lamp straining to light up properly, straining to pass from red to yellow, as if urgently striving to do something that ought to be possible but for some reason had ceased to be so – not only did I think all this, but I also gave some attention to the phone in my right-hand jacket pocket; because once again it had started to ring. I had put the ringtone on loud, since otherwise I never hear it when I'm out on the street. I didn't want to miss an important call. I had thought about this ringing phone as I ran and even after I stopped running, and decided not to respond, because I would surely be at the hospice any second now, and I simultaneously thought that I would very much regret not answering it, if this turned out not to be the case, or if the hospice turned out to be the wrong hospice. Hadn't enough things gone wrong this afternoon not to risk another? I had just changed my mind and decided I would after all answer the phone when it stopped ringing, and again I was just preparing for the inevitable onslaught of self-criticism for having failed to answer it when the prosaic sign, 'Claygate Hospice: No Parking', appeared on my right, exactly as dear Elsa had said it would, and at once I felt justified. I had got everything absolutely right. I had a splendid girlfriend. I felt immensely pleased with myself.

I hurried to a glass door giving onto a soberly lit reception area and, finding it locked, rang at once. There was no immediate reply and no shelter from the rain, either. I pulled the phone from my pocket and found I had been called by no fewer than four people. It seemed impossible. While covering a few hundred yards and thinking a few scattered thoughts, four people had called me. My sister. My daughter. Deborah. My wife. Not the twins, though. Imagine if I had answered my wife, without knowing whom I was about to speak to! A buzzer unlocked the door and once again I congratulated myself that I had got everything right. As I stepped in, a woman in nurse's uniform put her head round a corner. 'I'm afraid we don't have a receptionist at this time of evening,' she said, 'but you should sign the book. Who are you here for?'

'Mrs Sanders,' I said.

'Sign in,' she told me, pointing to a book that was open on the reception desk, 'while I go and see where she is. Sanders, right? Not Saunders? There have been a lot of admissions this week. I'm afraid I don't know all the names yet.'

'Sanders.'

It was as I was signing in, my head bowed over the visitors' book, wondering if I really needed to write my complicated Spanish address in full, that my sister appeared.

'Tommy Bro,' she cried. 'You made it!' Then she said, 'Mum's been vomiting blood.'

At least I had come to the right hospice.

VI

Towards 3 a.m. that night, or the following morning rather, finding myself quite unable to sleep, quite unable to take advantage of the rather narrow bed I was in, I decided – but perhaps it was more like 5 a.m. – to recall so far as was possible all the occasions I had been to the bathroom to pee that day and how much had been peed on each visit, and likewise all the times and places I had taken on fluid and how much exactly had been drunk. Partly it was anxious curiosity, to see if there was anything really the matter with me – the way when I still used a car regularly I would always check miles against petrol consumption to see if there were anomalies. And partly, I suppose, it was a way of counting sheep, though no doubt the whole point of counting sheep is that one isn't at all curious how many sheep there are. Or anxious. One just counts, and counts sheep because sheep have nothing to do with your life. You are not a shepherd. Which is probably why I have never been able to count sheep. My mind only engages where there is curiosity or anxiety, and in my case there is rarely one without the other.

Never mind. It was something to focus on. Peeing. So, I began: one pee on waking shortly after six and before going through Dr Sharp's breathing relaxation exercises. That had been in the hotel in Amersfoort, whose huge four-star bathroom mirror offered me a chance to see myself in polished profile pretty much from head to toe as I performed. There is no doubt that mirrors heighten self-consciousness, and equally there is very little doubt that self-consciousness inhibits urinary flow. It would be as well not to put mirrors near lavatories – there should be some kind of building regulation – and where there are such mirrors, it would be as well for the pee-er – I nearly wrote peer – not to look at them. Certainly I did everything I could not to look at my ageing body peeing in the Amersfoort hotel bathroom, for fear this would impede my flow. Yet twenty-one hours later in the Claygate Hospice guest room, thinking back to this first pee of the day in Holland, perhaps more to block out the unhappy events of the evening than anything else, I do in fact see myself in the bathroom mirror – I see my body in profile, peeing, waiting to pee – and I do recall thinking that this body of mine is always thicker in reality, or at least in mirrors, than the slimmer image of a younger Thomas that clings on inside my head. Inside my head I am always other than what I am in mirrors. Above all slimmer, though you could hardly call me fat, I don't think, even going on the mirror image. But enough vanity. And even if, thinking back on that pee, I don't see my face in the mirror, don't remember meeting my eyes there, I nevertheless recall that disturbing awareness of the nearness of my mirrored presence as I peed, much the way one is aware of another person's presence in the room; even when you are not watching them, you assume they must be watching you. I was aware of being threatened by the imminence of self-awareness. It was not a great pee.

I thought nothing of it. When is the first pee of the day ever a great pee? Unlike cigarettes, where the first is the best. One needs to move about a bit before peeing well, and I stopped smoking years ago. Or *I* need to move about. I made myself some tea, using the kettle available in the hotel room – fortunately there was camomile – and settled down to practise my relaxation exercises.

So, one pee, one tea. Given that this was a hotel teacup rather than one of the big mugs I use at home, I would say the volumes in and out were pretty well matched at this point.

Then another two cups of tea at breakfast, which I took early to avoid the crowd, bringing my laptop with me so I could read the papers while eating. It was the usual hotel fare, and of course the usual newspaper fare, though there was one interesting story about an old murder brought back to life, as it were, by DNA profiling. That is the kind of thing I like to read about these days, the past somehow changed and made possible thanks to changes in the present. Then the Portuguese paediatrician arrived, asked if he could share my table (we had met briefly the evening before) and began to explain, over scrambled eggs and ham, a choice I found surprising for a Portuguese, that anal massage had saved his life. He had been in utter despair, this friendly Latin doctor said, folding his toast over his scrambled eggs, when he had heard about Dr Sharp's clinic, dropped everything and caught the plane. Maybe I would try it myself sometime, I laughed. In the hospice, it occurred to me that if I hadn't heard the Portuguese doctor's confession over breakfast, the entire day would have gone quite differently.

After which, on returning to my room there was now a second pee with bowel movement. I am never sure about peeing volumes with bowel movements. I suspect they are somewhat less than the normal peeing volume. Who knows? Certainly I looked away from the mirror. Nevertheless, once again I find a ready memory of myself mirrored on the pot. At this point, then, I would say the intake with all that tea at breakfast was significantly up on the output, something rectified during the morning by a further pee, this time in the bathroom at the back of the conference room, thankfully mirrorless.

Water intake at lunch, of course. But only one glass. All normal so far, then, until the disastrous post-lunch massage, thanks to the Portuguese, after which the deluge, or rather, the over-frequent dribbles – a deluge would have been a delight – all afternoon, time and again, an endless need to go, and nothing to go with. Immediately before my talk I had gone to the conference-hall bathroom and failed to pee anything at all. How to count an experience like that? Perhaps it's appropriate; the word 'bathroom' was obviously preferred for its removal of the idea of urination, its suggestion of perfumed ablution rather than malodorous excretion. Not peeing in the bathroom, I was right in line with this vocation for euphemism and things virtual rather than real. Except I felt I needed to go.

Next came the pee snatched in the reception bathroom before fleeing for the airport, gazing at the condom-dispenser with its Banana Boy and Cucumber Kid advertisements; then another immediately on board the plane, this time reading the warning that if you smoke you will be arrested and charged on arrival at your destination. Then another immediately on disembarking at Gatwick. And yet another on South West Trains with their impressive space for wheelchair users, and here again there was an inhibiting mirror, this time to my left. I can imagine a major research study where urinary flow is measured in bathrooms with mirrors and in bathrooms without. I have no doubt this would be a valuable contribution.

Such was the state of play, then – six pees in fewer than seven hours and with zero liquid taken on, which speaks volumes for the lack of volume, I suppose – when my sister came to greet me in the reception area of Claygate Hospice and said, 'Mum's been vomiting blood', and I said, 'I'll just grab a pee, then I'm with you. I don't want to go in to see her and then have to go right out again. She might think I was upset.'

'No hurry,' my sister said. 'You can't go in now anyway. They're cleaning her up and then they'll be getting her ready for the night. We can take a rain check for at least half an hour.'

I was astonished, honestly, to hear my very English sister use the expression 'rain check'. Had the nurse said it to her and she was just repeating it for me? That would be understandable. But if so, where was the nurse from? Quite recently at a conference in Frankfurt I had listed 'rain check' as one of the idioms that still distinguished American English from English English. And no one is more English than my sister. I felt let down. I had let the Frankfurters down.

'We don't want to be stuck waiting here,' my sister's husband cut in. 'It's too depressing.'

This imposing, expansive, determinedly friendly man, my brother-in-law – he always seems to loom slightly, as if outside the conversation, but pressing to be inside – now suggested we hurry out for a quick bite, in Claygate, after which he and my sister would drive home to Swanage and I could take over 'the night shift'. Fifteen minutes later, in the tiny bathroom of an Indian restaurant that we had reached in my sister's van, a vehicle that positively stank of dog, I reflected on this ominous expression: night shift. This was the van my sister and her husband had bought to accommodate the wheelchair of their severely handicapped child, who was now a child no longer, and yet in a way would never be other than a child, lacking as she did the resources for even the most limited independence. Today the belts used for anchoring the wheelchair were tying up the three family dogs. Had my brother-in-law, I wondered, meant 'night shift' as a joke? The Indian restaurant loo was unbelievably small. He was a man who did like to joke. My left thigh was brushing the washbasin as I performed; my forehead was almost touching the frame of the open window. Perhaps not. Perhaps I really would be awake beside my mother all night. Thinking about it, I rather liked the idea. I phoned Deborah over what was now the seventh post-massage pee and told her that since my sister was unexpectedly home with my mother for dinner, I could hardly come out this evening. We could speak tomorrow. I hadn't seen my sister in a year and more, I said.

But Deborah wouldn't hear of it; this was an *emergency*, she insisted. It was life or death. Her son had beaten her husband over the head. Now Charlie was threatened with a criminal charge for assault and battery, while David was in hospital facing scans for brain damage. 'The boy needs counselling, urgently,' she said, and she said she had a hunch that, given what there had been between us in the past – myself and Charlie, not to mention myself and her husband – I was the right person to do it. The very fact that I was in town when she needed me was a sign. It was providence.

There had actually been very little between us, Charlie and myself. An exchange of emails, nothing else. Hence I had a hunch that the person who needed counselling, or just company, was Deborah. How quickly she had learned to toss out the word 'husband', I thought, when they had barely been married six months. Looking back, my reluctance to explain to her that my mother was dying, and that hence it was impossible for me to come, bewilders me now. Why didn't I? I had spared Deborah a mention of my mother's condition earlier because it seemed she had quite enough to worry about. And perhaps I didn't want to bring Mother in now, here in the tiny bathroom of the Indian restaurant where no bath would ever fit, because I didn't want to use her as an excuse. Or rather, to be suspected of using her as an excuse. It's odd because in the past I had used the gravity of my mother's illness on numerous occasions to excuse sudden withdrawals from work appointments, including, on one occasion, the cancellation of a conference – on phrasal verbs, as I recall – in Tokyo, and again, way back before our separation, I had used it to explain at least two otherwise inexplicable absences to my wife. 'My mother is very ill,' I had said. 'I have to fly to London.' I suppose the point is that on those occasions no one suspected me of using her illness as an excuse at all. On the contrary, they were extremely accommodating and sympathetic. Which made it okay, in a way. And I had often smiled to myself, thinking, If only Mum knew the shenanigans her cancer is facilitating, one of them appearing very high on the list of pleasing transgressions I tick off at dicey moments in aeroplanes.

But this evening, with Mum vomiting blood, I didn't say a word to Deborah, who was now suggesting she drive over from Kingston with Charlie to speak to me. She could say hello to my mother, she said. They had met decades ago at my wedding. Perhaps I had already reached the point where you can't tell someone something because, if you do, they'll think it pathologically weird that you didn't tell them earlier. As when I didn't tell a certain person I had left my wife until a year after I had, causing a significant change in her attitude to me when she discovered this.

'I'll call again when I see how the evening's going,' I said.

We ate biryani. Or at least ordered it. For the moment there were only poppadoms on the table, plus the usual sauces. My sister and her husband were in surprisingly good spirits. Her husband, who was allowing himself just one beer before driving, pulled out his iPad to show me photos of the dogs I had already seen in the van. Two big, heavy-breathing creatures and one exotically miniature fluff-ball. He told me their breeds, which I have forgotten; he told me their names, which I have forgotten; he told me anecdotes about them, which I can't remember at all, but which invariably had to do with their outwitting and outrunning, or just generally outdogging, other dogs. These were finer dogs than other people's dogs, my brother-in-law was eager to convince me, more interesting and more characterful. He really was in excellent spirits. The white downy dog, he said, in particular was a sublimely bossy little bitch, so convinced of her frothy specialness as to be quite unintimidated by animals of a far larger size, even pit bulls. The long, sleek, almost hairless animal that I had erroneously supposed must be a greyhound had the most playful, boundless energy you could possibly imagine, running rings round the other animals, literally, on the heath behind their Swanage bungalow. Wide rings. Concentric rings.

As my brother-in-law spoke, his long middle finger stroked image after image across the iPad screen. I also noticed a thick gold, time-worn wedding ring, something I am slowly getting used to wearing no more. Dogs fighting over a ball – he flicked his finger – dogs on their backs with their paws in the air – his finger again – pink tongues panting at the lens. 'Isn't she a scream?' my sister giggled. But this black lump of a beast, my brother-in-law was explaining now, the oldest of the three, was simply the grumpiest creature that had ever crossed the face of the earth. And not photogenic at all. Or entirely continent, alas. 'But he *adores* Suzy,' my sister cut in indulgently, and there, sure enough, was a photo of this sad old dog complacently licking the dazed but happy face of an evidently retarded young woman slumped in a wheelchair.

I felt chastened.

'How is Mum, then?' I asked.

'Pretty much ready to see Dad again,' my sister's husband promptly answered. He was still flicking through the dog photos as he spoke. 'Do you want to see her room?' His big finger poked the screen to find a different folder.

'She's such a survivor, though,' my sister said, 'Anyone else would have given up the ghost, yonks back.'

'Yonks' was an old friend I hadn't come across in a while. Yonks in fact. Not the sort of term that turns up in conferences in Frankfurt and Tokyo. I had also forgotten my brother-in-law's habit of refer-ring to my father as Dad, as if he hadn't had one himself.

'Here,' he said.

He pushed the iPad towards me and I saw a pleasant enough room with a large window to the left giving onto a patio; to the right, my mother was sitting up in bed eating from a tray and trying to be her cheerful self for the camera. Through the window, on the patio, you could clearly see a pink concrete birdbath.

The Indians were being unconscionably slow with the biryani.

'I told her,' my brother-in-law laughed, 'to take him our greetings.'

'But this vomiting blood . . .' I started to ask. I raised my hand to get the waiter's attention but he was focused on a point far outside the bounds of the restaurant. Uttar Pradesh, the place was called.

'Horrible,' my sister said. She had been on the phone – Mother, that is – to our brother, who had called from LA, when— 'But before I forget,' she interrupted herself. 'Tomorrow morning.'

'Right. You have to be tough on the doctors,' my brother-in-law chipped in. He had found another picture of my mother, this time by the large window, a French window I saw now. She was leaning on a Zimmer frame, clinging onto it for dear life, you would have said, slumped, beaten, and yet the face had lifted towards the camera and bitten off a wan smile for posterity. As recently as a month ago Mum was still refusing to use a walking stick, because, she said, sticks made people look old.

'Takes a good snap, doesn't it?' my brother-in-law said.

'You have to make sure they don't try to move her again,' my sister said. It was her lower, conspiratorial voice now, something I remembered from adolescence. 'She mustn't be moved.'

'Most of all, that they don't try to send her back to us,' her husband said.

'Since his op he just can't lift her any more,' my sister explained.

I had forgotten for the moment exactly what op my brother-in-law had had, but I sympathised 100 per cent. I could never have picked up my mother.

'She's happy here and she desperately wants to stay, because the nurses are kind and they know how to deal with the pain. They have all the gizmos.'

But why, I asked – I hate the word 'gizmo' – would they want to move her, given the state she was in? 'Didn't you say she was near the end? Isn't that what hospices are for?'

'In theory.' But my sister insisted that health professionals were like that; they kept thinking there was something that could be done, when clearly there wasn't. 'Although, heaven knows, she's such a fighter, perhaps she could battle on for weeks and even months.' She frowned. Anyway, they had moved her two days ago when she was in the other hospice, in Hounslow, and was finally getting relief after weeks of atrocious pain, and if they'd done it once, they were perfectly capable of doing it again. 'Mum is terrified of being moved,' my sister repeated. If she herself, she said, could be on hand 24/7 to prevent this from happening, she would. But she couldn't. What with Suzy, and so on. Fortunately, since I was now here, this could be my job, at least for the next few days.

I wondered then, ungenerously, whether my sister hadn't per-haps exaggerated the gravity of my mother's condition so as to have me on hand to deal with the doctors and keep my mother in the hospice. It looked like I would have to cancel the conference in Berlin. Which was disappointing because for once I had the inaug-ural spot, the place of honour.

'We're really relying on you,' my brother-in-law said, 'to be firm. Give them some of your Queen's English.'

I wasn't sure if this was a reference to my job or my notorious swearing.

'Just tell them you won't let them, over your dead body,' my sister said.

I smiled and made a mental note.

No pun intended, my brother-in-law joked.

At last the biryani arrived. But now I desperately needed to go to the bathroom again. How long was this going to go on? 'Damn,' I said, 'I need to make a call. Give me a minute', and I got up and went to the bathroom again – that made eight – where there was just sufficient elbow room to read a text message from Deborah. 'Please,' she had written, 'for old times' sake.' Which meant, I supposed, the one time we had made love together and immediately wished we hadn't. Was she threatening to tell Dave about that? Surely not.

Our beloved brother, my sister said when I returned to the table, had phoned Mother from LA. This was around the time when I had been peeing on South West Trains. Mother had made a huge effort, my sister said, to sound in good spirits on the phone. 'You know how she is. It's heroic.' Our brother had explained that unfortunately he couldn't get away in the next few days. There were important meetings lined up. Mother had said not to worry and put the phone down, sighed once or twice, then had suddenly thrown up a great gush of blood.

'Black blood,' my brother-in-law added.

For a few moments we ate in silence. The biryani was excellent.

'I told her,' he added, 'soon you'll be dancing with Dad in Paradise.'

My sister sent me a sad, knowing smile; she is dyeing her hair a light-violet colour these days. It suits her.

'Poor Mum,' she said softly. 'She's waited so long.'

VII

With the biryani finished, I had expected we would get up to go, but now my brother-in-law asked for the menu to order a sweet. Not an Indian sweet, though. The Indians were good at savoury, he thought, but not at sweet. He had never managed to finish an Indian sweet, my-brother-in-law said. 'Which, coming from Mr Hunk, is pretty damning,' my sister laughed, prodding her husband's muscles to show how solid he was. And he really was. A giant of a man. In remarkable form too, given his age. With a psyche to match. It was impossible, in fact, to imagine my brother-in-law in any other mani-festation than this huge and solid form, because he behaved in every way with the confidence of a huge and solid man. Perhaps I should have brought him into the body/soul debate with my mother. Try to imagine your son-in-law, I should have suggested, without his huge body. It's impossible, isn't it? Snapping the menu shut, the big man sighed and said, 'Ice-cream.' There was nothing else. Nothing substantial, he meant. He grinned. And some minutes later, while we both watched him tuck into his green, white and pink ice-cream, served by a minute Indian girl, it occurred to me to ask my sister had she told my mother that I was coming? I was on my way. My sister turned from admiring her husband's appetite, frowned and said no. No, she hadn't, actually.

'So, she doesn't know I'm coming?'

Again my sister frowned, as if she needed to think about this, then said, no, actually, she didn't.

I stared at her, trying to take this in. Then I was suddenly beside myself with the thought that my mother must be assuming I had abandoned her. On her deathbed. My brother had at least phoned, hadn't he? I hadn't even done that. Why? Honestly, I hadn't even thought of phoning. I had imagined, after my sister's email, that Mother would be too ill to answer the phone. She's sinking fast, my sister had written. Words to that effect. While my brother, still supposing Mother would live for ever, had phoned as a matter of course. It had never occurred to him not to phone. And my mother, or so it seemed from my sister's account, despite her critical condition, had done everything to sound cheerful and reassure him. Was that why my sister had said Mum was all over the place? My mother's determination to be above and other than her illness, and even her body, albeit only for the few moments of a phone call, and my brother's stubbornness in denying that she was seriously ill at all, were in triumphant cahoots, I thought; they made a perfect team. My mother had performed well, protected by the dubious and fleeting intimacy of a transatlantic phone line, and my brother was relieved that things were not after all as bad as my sister's email had suggested, and hence that he need not embark on the trip that I had undertaken so hastily without even phoning. I was always too hasty. Yet no sooner was the phone down than my mother had vomited blood. Black blood, my brother-in-law had specified. I didn't think I had ever seen black blood. Nor did I understand what blackness in blood might mean. These things can be deceptive, my son had said. He was an ambitious young doctor. My brother meantime didn't know about this development. He hadn't been updated. I should tell him. And my mother didn't know I was coming to visit her, even though it had never even crossed my mind not to come, when the end was near. I would have dropped anything – absolutely anything – to go to my mother's deathbed. Why did I realise this only now? That I had been waiting for this moment for years? All my life perhaps. Mother's death.

'Why didn't you tell her?' I demanded of my sister. I was a little aggressive now. Perhaps a note of alarm crept into my voice. My brother-in-law was savouring his pistachio. My sister seemed put on the spot. For the first time her face showed some confusion. 'Because,' she said, and still she hesitated. She was fingering her wedding ring. 'Because when you arrive, Tom, she will know it's the end.' She sighed. 'What other reason would you come for? Out of the blue.'

Apparently, then, I was a sort of gravedigger, a bird of ill omen. Plummeting from a blue sky. Whereas my brother, calling to say he wasn't planning to come, or not in the near future, was business as usual. Life would go on for ever while my brother didn't come. His not coming would keep my mother alive. His transcontinental phone calls. What is life in the end, or marriage for that matter, if not a form of prolonged denial? Truth kills. Certainly, I thought, the truth had killed my marriage.

I stood up and hurried to the till at the back of the restaurant, where the proprietor invited me to return to my seat, promising he would bring the bill shortly. I refused. We were in a hurry, I said. My mother was in the hospice on Grange Road, I told him. She was dying. Tonight, very likely. I slapped my Visa on the counter and simultaneously my phone began to ring. I didn't answer.

'Grange Road?' the man repeated. He seemed irritated that I was leaving my phone to ring in his restaurant. Had he understood about the hospice? Perhaps because I'd left the ringtone on loud. The noxious Nokia tone. When the payment terminal invited me to tip, I didn't. Which more or less balanced out the five quid for the taxi driver.

'Tom!' my brother-in-law exclaimed, 'thank you so much!' He screwed up his napkin. He seemed genuinely surprised, even moved, that I had paid for our meal. It's not the done thing in the Sanders family to throw money around. Settling into the front seat of the van, the dogs scratching and yelping in the back, he asked me how my wife was and whether she would be coming over.

'We've separated,' I said.

If silence is imaginable in a diesel van starting up, with three dogs barking in the back and heavy rain clattering on the roof, not to mention a windscreen wiper that squeaked dramatically, there was silence after I made this announcement – deep silence. All three of us were squeezed onto the van's front seat.

'I beg your pardon,' my sister finally said. After a moment she added. 'Well, that was a well-kept secret.'

You could actually feel my sister struggling to decide whether to be critical or not. People no more divorce in the Sanders family than they pay for other people's meals. It's just not us.

'You really separated?' my brother-in-law asked. 'Legally?' He seemed concerned. 'Are you managing okay?' He pulled the van out into the road.

'Guilty on both counts,' I told him.

'But that's amazing,' my sister breathed, still absolutely uncertain how to react. Marriage was sacrosanct, but I was her brother. My wife had never been a big hit with the family. But then I had never wanted her to be. It was one of the things that made our relationship more solid. My wife and I had been a couple against the world; above all, against our families, mine and hers. We had always felt superior to both. My sister shook her head. 'But when?'

'You can always come to stay with us,' my brother-in-law changed gear, 'if you need a refuge from the storm.'

'Two years ago,' I said. 'There is no storm.'

'Your phone's ringing,' my brother-in-law said. He had to dive in between parked vehicles to let a similar van by, the other way. With the fall in the engine noise, the wipers squeaked louder.

'But why didn't you tell us?' my sister said.

Why had I told them now, I wondered?

I pulled out the phone and rejected the call without checking to see who it was. My brother-in-law said the new bungalow they had, on the outskirts of Swanage, was near a beautiful coastal walk. We could go running, with the dogs.

Because I hadn't wanted to upset Mother, I said. With her being ill and so on, and the kind of significance she gave to marriage. I hesitated. 'Then you two have quite enough on your plates, with Suzy.'

How many times was I going to use that ugly idiom in one day? As if life was all about avoiding indigestion. The truth was that anything I had told my sister would automatically have been passed on to my mother. She knew this, of course. That's why I hadn't told her. Because of Mother. My brother, meantime, had been my email confidant throughout the whole sad story, but would never have dreamed of passing this information on to either of them.

'Mum was always saying she was surprised you two hadn't separated,' my sister said quietly.

We were buckled into seats in the front of the van. My sister in the middle. Already my brother-in-law was looking for a parking space near the hospice. It was only half a mile. Not finding one, he simply pulled in the hospice driveway beside the gate with its No Parking sign. The van shuddered with the diesel ticking over and the wipers smearing rain across the windscreen.

'Did she?' I found this extremely hard to believe.

'Well, you know Mum. Marriage is sacred, and so on. But for a few years now she's been saying she hoped you'd find the courage.'

'The courage?'

My sister shrugged. 'She thought you were sitting on the fence.'

'She never said anything to me.'

One of the dogs began to paw the partition behind us.

'Never come between a man and his wife,' my sister said off pat, and at once I recognised something my father used to say when parishioners came to him with their marriage woes. It was a rule of my father's never to advise troubled couples to separate, however much, afterwards, talking it over with my mother, he'd say separation seemed the only solution. Hearing the expression again after all these years – 'Never come between', etc. – I was struck by the order of the words and the use of the possessive pronoun in 'a man and his wife'. One wouldn't say, Never come between a woman and her husband.

'How have the children reacted?' my brother-in-law wanted to know.

I had unbuckled my seatbelt, but we were still sitting in the van in heavy rain. An hour ago they'd been in a hurry to get home.

'The children are all grown-up,' I said. 'They're fine with it.'

If this wasn't altogether true, I very much hoped it was.

'Do you have someone else?' my sister asked. 'Where are you living?'

It was getting on for eleven now.

'Let's talk about it another time,' I said. 'I really ought to get in to see Mum. I don't want her to imagine I'm not coming.'

'Where are you going to sleep?' my brother-in-law asked.

My sister now informed me that there were two guest rooms in the hospice, but she didn't know if they were already occupied or not. At a pinch, there was the armchair in my mother's room, which was pretty comfortable, she said. A recliner. On the other hand, Mother had doubtless been cleaned up and prepared for the night now. They had a drug pump in her arm and gave her the maximum dose of morphine in the evenings. To get her off.

'The last thing you want to do is wake her up,' my sister said. Actually, if there was a hotel nearby, she thought, the thing would be to check in there and see Mum tomorrow. But it had to be near enough to be back at the hospice for the doctors at 8 a.m. or even earlier, to make absolutely sure Mother wasn't moved.

'I'll check,' my brother-in-law said and had already produced his iPad. It was a pleasure for the big man to find me a hotel on his iPad. But I said no. I was determined to see Mother tonight. Otherwise, why had I dropped everything in Holland and flown over directly? I was perfectly happy, I said, to spend the night in the armchair, if it came to that, and of course I wouldn't wake Mum up if she was already asleep, but I did want to be there when she woke.

'Then she will know,' my sister said.

We sat in silence. Despite my refusal to consider a hotel, my brother-in-law was nevertheless stroking information back and forth across his iPad, tongue between his lips, brow furrowed in the glow of the screen.

'But surely she already knows,' I said. 'After all, she planned her funeral four years ago.'

'Oh, she loves arranging her funeral,' my sister laughed. 'She must have changed it a dozen times. It's different when the moment really comes.'

'But weren't you just telling her she'd soon be waltzing through the Pearly Gates?'

There are moments when it seems impossible not to sound unpleasant. My sister took the point in good spirits.

'It was always her dream to be with Dad again,' she said. There was almost a catch in her voice now, as if the person who really wanted to be with Dad again was her. My sister had been Daddy's girl.

Still dragging things around his screen, my brother-in-law said, 'She'll be going home to glory very soon now.'

His voice was solemn. What was I to make of it, I wondered? My mother knew she was dying, in the dimension where one fore-sees a rosy afterlife with loved ones who passed on before, but she definitely didn't know and didn't want to know, in the dimension where a son arrives to say goodbye just before the final rattle. Instead of screaming, I asked, 'Do you think I should tell her?'

'What?' my sister said. 'That she's dying?'

'No,' I almost laughed. 'About separating.'

She frowned. In the odd light from the rainy street her violet hair was bathed in yellow. She looked a good ten years younger than her age.

'Who actually left who?' my brother-in-law cut in.

I had given a conference in Johannesburg the previous spring entitled 'Whom? The Case of the Missing Pronoun.'

Chuckling, he added, 'I mean, did the missus kick you out, or did you run?'

'I walked,' I said. 'Of my own accord.'

Staggered more like.

'How did she take it?' my sister asked.

As she spoke, the light in the reception area of the Claygate Hospice went out. At once I was afraid there was something definitive about this. As if a door that had been open had now been locked and bolted and I wouldn't be able to see Mother in time. Suddenly I could feel a bonfire of impatience sizzling across my skin, tensing my fingers and toes. It was worse than the urgency to pee. Why on earth had I told them about separating?

'I've no idea how she took it,' I said sharply. 'In the end I can't know, can I, what's in my wife's head? It's not my problem. My problem is how I've taken it. That's what separation is about. Being separate. From now on, I think about me.'

My sister said quietly, 'All Mum – or any of us – wants is that you be happy, Tom.'

'That's right,' my brother-in-law agreed.

'Well, if there's one thing you can all feel assured about,' I laughed, 'that's it. I'm happy as Larry these days.'

Even as I spoke the words I knew they would convince no one.

'Maybe Mum would be relieved to know you're with someone else,' my brother-in-law said. 'Not wilting on your own, I mean.'

He actually used that word, wilting. 'I will wilt and die,' I had told the shrink. I opened the door of the van. The rain was teeming.

'Let me give you an umbrella,' my sister said and twisted round to search on top of the seats behind her. Then, waiting for her to pull out the umbrella, which would be precious of course, if I was kept hanging around at the now-darkened hospice door, and feeling irritated that my crass claim to be happy had only convinced everybody of the opposite, I said the truth was that I had a wonderful new girlfriend with whom I believed I was in love; just that I wasn't sure whether this was the kind of thing I should be saying to Mother, in the state she was in. 'On Jordan's banks,' I added.

My sister put a small telescopic umbrella into my hand. 'How old is she?' she asked.

Whenever a man over fifty says he has a girlfriend, the first thing people ask is, How old is she? It's not a stupid question.

'Thirty,' I lied.

'Bro!' My sister shook her head, but then suddenly she was laughing. It was as if another side of her had managed to grab the driving wheel. 'Jeepers,' she was almost giggling.

'Perhaps better if you don't mention that to the kids when they come,' I said.

My sister was still shaking her head in disbelief. My brother-in-law said, 'I know you don't believe these things, Tom, but when you're with Mum, why don't you just let the Lord Jesus be your guide? He is looking after her. He will tell you what to say. And what's best left unsaid.'

I was out of the door, opening the umbrella.

'Phone me after you've spoken to the doctors,' my sister called. 'Maybe she'll live for ever!'

I negotiated a puddle. As they turned in the road, the van's headlights swung across me, catching my reflection in the rainy glass. Here to see his mother die, I thought. Every time I see my reflection, I want to call Elsa and tell her to find a more suitable man. No, I don't. Hitting the bell, I just had time to register a ferocious burning feeling beneath the navel, then the lock buzzed sharply and the reception light came on. I was still trying to get the umbrella to close, when the same head appeared around the corner of the corridor with its same story that there was no receptionist after five, but all the same I had to sign the book on the desk.

'Ah, it's you,' the nurse said. 'Who were you for again?'

'Mrs Sanders.'

'Right.' She hesitated. 'I'm afraid Mrs Sanders has been rather poorly.'

'Can I see her?'

The nurse had come forward now. She was a sturdy woman in her forties, face frank and knowing, firm full lips, hair permed flat under her cap. A no-nonsense woman.

'Of course. Close family have twenty-four-hour access.'

'I'm her son,' I said.

'I know.' She seemed to think for a moment. 'Thomas?'

'That's right.'

'She's been asking after you.'

But when I started moving towards her, the nurse said, 'Let me just pop in first and see how she's getting on.'

She retreated. It seemed odd, as if she was trying to come between us, or to check that my mother really did want to see me, or that I wouldn't go in and find something that upset me. In any event, I had the impression that someone was mediating between myself and my mother, that I needed the nurse's permission to see her.

I stood with the reception behind, and to my right a long corridor stretching away into a row of soft red night lights. The nurse disappeared into a door towards the end on the left. The ninth door, the tenth? Perhaps there were more. I waited. Then my eye fell on a notice on the wall just inside the corridor.

CHRISTMAS PARTY.

I moved closer. All those bereaved in 2014 were invited to a Christmas party at 5 p.m. on December 22nd, to share their memories of loved ones who had died in the Claygate Hospice.

It was interesting, I thought, that one automatically classed dead relatives as loved ones. You would never do the same with live relatives. And what Christmas party was there for those whose loved ones had departed this world, this hospice, between the previous party just before Christmas 2013 and the following New Year? Why does my mind pick nits like this?

I stared down the long, empty corridor trying to get used to the idea of a place where, if everything is running according to plan, every room is an agony, every bed yields its monthly corpse. Or weekly. A sort of factory of death. But benevolent. Dying fields, not killing fields. Isn't life itself a factory of death? The hospice was the last section of a production line that began in the maternity ward. Conception the culprit. Carbon and water the raw materials. And what kind of Christmas party would this be, I wondered, where one turned up to swap stories of the recently defunct? Or was the party, in actual fact, a rather blatant invitation to make donations to the hospice, which no doubt was an expensive operation only partially funded by the State? It can't be cheap to provide thrifty citizens with a pain-free death.

'Thomas,' a voice called. I had not seen the nurse beckoning me. As I walked along the corridor I felt the vibration of a message arriving in my pocket.

VIII

Counting my bathroom trips through the night, I eventually raised the post-massage tally to eleven. As for input, after biryani and beer in the Indian restaurant, there was still a tea to go, a coffee and a can of Coke. I would also smoke a cigarette before the night was out, but that's by the by. The can of Coke came from the hospice's automatic dispenser in the visitors' lounge to the left of reception, a Wi-Fi hotspot. Where exactly that left me on input and output at the end of the day, I had no idea. Whether my bladder was bursting, but unable to pass water, because hopelessly silted up, or whether, to the contrary, it was squeezed quite dry, but still urgently determined to pass water that wasn't there, perhaps due to some sad overproduction of adrenalin, I have no idea. The sums are beyond me. You have a body and you can't even say whether there's more going out than coming in, or vice versa. Never mind the stuff that goes in and out of your brain, one way or another. In any event, of all the visits to the bathroom that day, the tenth definitely took the biscuit for the most frantically miserable.

Arriving at my mother's door, which the nurse had quickly pulled closed behind her to speak to me, I was surprised to see there was a nameplate on it. The effect was strangely formal, as if this were a managerial office in some corporate corridor. MRS MARTHA SANDERS, the plate said. My mother had at last been recognised as an important person.

'She is sleeping,' the nurse announced. Her robust figure seemed to be guarding the way. She still hadn't decided whether I was worthy to enter. 'If you need to call us, there's a buzzer by the bedside table.'

Still she stood.

I waited, trying to convey to the nurse my awareness of the solemnity of the situation, as if eager to pass muster.

'If she should bring something up – you know, if she's sick – there is a stack of disposable basins. On the trolley. And call us at once. There are always two of us on duty.'

Now that she was stepping aside at last, I stopped her and asked if I could spend the night beside my mother in the armchair, since I had nowhere to stay and it was already late and I would like to be close to my mother at this difficult moment, and she said of course I could. Perhaps she thought this was noble of me, because now she smiled. It was a wan, grown-up smile. It said, We all have to go through this, Thomas Sanders. You're right to stay with your poor mother through the night.

'I'll bring you a blanket,' she offered. 'On my next round.'

'I suppose you'd better tell me where the bathroom is, then,' I said.

She pointed to the door at the end of the corridor on the right.

'Thank you.'

Some ten hours, then, after receiving my sister's urgent email – Mum's sinking fast – I now stepped into the room where my mother had recently been asking after me.

The light was dim. Dark curtains were drawn over the patio. The armchair was there on the far side of the bed, as seen in my brother-in-law's iPad photo. On the near side was an ordinary chair. I put my bag down by the wall and sat. What light there was came from a sort of big glass saucer high on the wall to my left. The warm air was heavy and sickly-sweet. Entering, I was immediately aware that

I had passed into a completely separate world, as though stepping into a dark church from bright sunshine, or finding a deep cave along a sunny seashore. This was a different dimension. I sat and contemplated the figure on the bed.

To say my mother had aged, enormously, would not be enough. She was transformed. She had adapted, been adapted, to this other world. One with its darkness and heaviness. The bed had two guardrails. Painted pale yellow. She was flat on her back, head and shoulders propped up a little. The blanket, tucked tight as a strait-jacket, was a thick felty mauve and came up almost to her neck, where it was folded over with a starched white sheet. The arms, in a pale nightdress, lay leaden on top. The right arm, further from me, was tubed up to a drip; the left, grossly swollen, clutched the buzzer at the end of its wire, as if ready, even in sleep, to call the nurse. Her face was not white, or drained of colour. It was a bruise of mottled blues and greys, but pleated with wrinkles so fine as hardly to seem skin at all; more like a shrivelled fruit fallen from a tree. Her mouth was open and slack and, with her false teeth out, the lips had fallen in; they were gone, as though darkness inside were dragging the flesh down into itself. Her thin grey hair had turned oddly yellow and gave the impression someone had tugged it back hard, stretch-ing the forehead and forcing the skull up and out. But most of all, Mum looked larger than I remembered her. The head was bigger, the neck thicker, the body bulkier and heavier. She was swelling up. As I sat down, the open mouth sucked in air with a sharp snoring shudder that shook the shoulders and was followed by a distinct gurgling sound.

At once I felt I had to wake her. I had to speak to her. At the very least, exchange a glance of recognition. What was the point, really – and my impatience, rather than subsiding now that I was beside her, actually increased – what was the point of my coming so urgently to see my mother, if she were to die the moment I sat down beside her? To become mere material, before anything was said. Because on seeing her, I was convinced she must die at once. Already she seemed nothing but numbed and bruised flesh. Why else had they put the plaque on the door? Did they use the same plaque, I wondered, on the box that would carry her out of here? A sensible economy. You got the plaque when they knew you were going. You swelled up to be ready for death. To split open like a pod. And she had been asking for me. The nurse had said so. Still compos mentis, she had wanted me to come. If she woke, some simple greeting and farewell could be spoken, even if she then went straight back to sleep. Even if she died before waking again. Some contact would have been made. She would know I had come. I hadn't abandoned her.

Sitting by her side in the dim emergency light opposite the dark curtains drawn across the patio and the pink birdbath that, thanks to my brother-in-law's iPad, I knew were out there in the rain, I slipped my hands between the yellow bedrails and took my mother's hand. The position of the upper rail forced me to lower my wrist rather unnaturally, so as to come to the bed and her hand from underneath it. Alternatively I could have dropped my hand over the rail. I tried. But this was unnatural too, forcing the hand vertically down on the bed. It was hard to find a comfortable position in which to hold my mother's hand. So let there be discomfort, I thought.

'I'm here, Mum,' I said.

Then I remembered the text message that had just arrived on my phone. Text messages are no respecters of time or place, or different dimensions. Who was it from? One of the children, perhaps, needing the hospice address, or Elsa. Or Deborah again. Or even David. We always spoke when I was in the UK. I withdrew my hand and checked the phone. It was a message from Orange to tell me my credit was low. 'Top Up now and win two tickets to the Premier League game of your choice.' Then, exactly as I was returning the phone to my pocket, it began to ring. Its trill sounded obscenely loud, and somehow altered, in the dark room. Everything was altered here. Deborah Seymour. She still has that name on my mobile. I declined the call, but did not want to turn the phone off in case my children tried to get in touch. Or Elsa. I texted Deborah: 'Mother taken urgently to hospital. Can't meet tonight.'

The phone back in my pocket, I slipped my hand through the bars again, took Mother's hand in both mine and squeezed gently. My mother always had rough, raw, rather large hands. If I think of them now, I see their redness plunged in cake mix or bread dough, or chopping carrots, or pulling weeds. Doing things, anyway. But that night they were cold and swollen and, when I squeezed, it was as though they had been filled with air or some liquid that couldn't escape but moved around as I pressed. They felt wrong. This was the woman, I thought, to whom you once said, 'You and your body are one, Mum, you are your body, your body is you.' What would it mean to be this body now? She snored again, sharply, abruptly, and the cheeks seemed to be sucked even more deeply into the sunken mouth. A faint, sweet, cloying smell hung in the air. It was the smell she knew awaited her when we had spoken together four years ago.

'Mum.'

I squeezed her hand and this time got a faint response, a faint returning squeeze.

'Mum, it's Thomas. I've come.'

Only my mother calls me by my full name, Thomas.

'I'm glad to be here beside you, Mum.'

I pulled a hand out from under the bedrail and reached towards her face, smoothing hair that was already in fact too flat and smooth against the skin. Her forehead was damp and cold, but when I pressed ever so slightly there was a faint hum in the skin, a living-ness still. I let my hand rest there and stared. I felt deeply sorry for my mother, sorry for her face, sorry for her eyes, her head, her skin, her body, sorry that all this had happened to her and now must go on happening until the final calamity; and at the same time I felt repelled, as if I really did not want to be touching the sick forehead and lank hair, I did not feel comfortable with my wrist so near the sunken toothless mouth, the strangely flabby neck. Doctors knew they had to put a finger up your butt, the Californian physio had told me, but at the same time they didn't want to. They were repelled. I had no diagnostic duty to caress my mother's face, but with all my heart I wanted to. I wanted to care for her, somehow, in some way. It seemed important. And I didn't want to. I really didn't. This wasn't my mother of old. Hence perhaps it wasn't 'with all my heart'. There had never been many caresses in the Sanders family; that is the truth. Or not that I could recall. Can one trust one's memory on these matters? 'Mum,' I whispered. 'Mum?' And I thought it hardly mattered whether I did or didn't caress her face because she wasn't awake anyway and wouldn't sense either the affection or the repulsion. At least I wasn't hurting her, I hoped. At least that. Unless these things can be sensed in your sleep. Unless the interpretation we normally put on the word 'sensed' is far too narrow and even in sleep one's well-being, or unease, can be shifted by a touch or a soft word. We know so little about these things. I squeezed her hand again, this time with my left hand alone, and again had the impression, but perhaps it was only an impression, that the hand squeezed faintly back.

'Mum,' I said in a louder voice, but still soft. The silence in the room, or rather the soft electronic hum from some appliance or other, made my voice sound very harsh, even in its would-be softness. 'The last thing you want to do is wake her,' my sister had said.

'Can you hear me, Mum? If you can, give two quick squeezes for yes.' Immediately there was a little squeeze, much clearer this time. But only one.

I withdrew my hand from her face and sat watching her, trying to get used to this terrible transformation that had overcome her, the strangeness of my suddenly being in this dim, over-heated room beside this broken body. At the same time, the silly business of trying to communicate by asking her to squeeze my hand, when she was so evidently asleep, reminded me of a moment in Beckett's novel *Molloy*, where Molloy says he communicates with his mother by knocking on her head, with different numbers of knocks for different requests. I had given Mother my copy of *Molloy* to read sometime in my teens. She would have been in her late forties then. Like the knitting and years later the Scrabble, it must have been an attempt on my part to find some common ground that Mother and I might meet on, some territory that was not the Wondrous cross or our Saviour's blood. Or perhaps what I was asking for was some acknowledgement on her part of the legitimacy of my different interests, the different path I was choosing. Language. Books. I wanted my mother's consent, I suppose, for not being the person she had always wanted me to be, as years later I had sought her consent for an eventual separation from my wife, without ever having the courage to mention the word 'separation', and indeed had sought my wife's consent for a separation she did not want; yes, I had secretly, shamefully encouraged my wife to kick me out of the house, so as not to have to take this decision myself. As I had encouraged my mother to suggest that separation was the only solution, without ever saying, I want to separate. 'Let this cup pass from me' was one of the few prayers in the Bible I have ever really prayed in earnest. 'How many people have to say it's okay, before you will allow yourself to leave your wife?' my shrink had enquired on perhaps our third or fourth encounter.

I had given my mother a copy of *Molloy*, I recalled now, sitting beside her bed, watching for signs of life, because I found the book hilarious and captivating. I wanted my mother to be captivated too, to be taken captive, by Beckett. This was my father's habit of impulsively sharing his enthusiasms, impulsively wanting others to be captivated as he was, to fall thrall to the same spell. I didn't even reflect that I was asking my mother to read a story about a man who sets out to find a mother who lives he knows not where, and with whom he can only communicate by knocking on her skull. In the darkened, overly warm room in Claygate Hospice I smiled and shook my head. How was it possible that I realised this only now? Only now, aged fifty-seven, sitting by my mother's broken body in the year 2014, did I realise how inappropriate it had been, or no, how completely appropriate, to have given my mother a copy of *Molloy* in the year – what, 1971, 1972? Appropriate precisely because my mother had not remarked on the connection at all. And nor had I. At no point did mother and son mention to each other that they were sharing a book about a mother and son who couldn't communicate. Or is that what literature's for, to talk without talking? To substitute for talking. To escape talking. Rather she said she had been quite enjoying the novel – she offered me that sop – until she came to the part where Molloy talks about his excretory habits, and then she really did not want to read any further, because it was in bad taste and she really couldn't understand why such a talented man as Samuel Beckett evidently was would want to talk about such things. It was vulgar.

I had been disappointed, but perplexed too, because I couldn't recall much talk about excretory habits in *Molloy*, unless you count the passage where Molloy counts his farts, which is madly funny. It was one of the passages that had made me fall in love with the book. But Mother of course did not want these references to the body and its functions. Molloy's farts had come between us, then. There was an unpleasant smell to the conversation. Mother never said a word when someone let off an unpleasant smell in the room. Even when we were young children. Farts couldn't be uttered. It was odd, I thought, squeezing my mother's hand again, and this time there was no response, it was odd that I had never given my father any of my books to read. Never given Dad Beckett. Never given him T. S. Eliot. Never given him Dostoevsky. I never tried to get my father along to White Hart Lane, or to the pub for a pint. Perhaps I sensed my father would not stand in my way. Or I didn't care, one way or another. I did not need my father's consent. I was fine with my father, however sharply we disagreed. It was my mother I had to seduce and never could. Mother was never impressed. Never impressed by a book. Never impressed by a girlfriend. Never impressed by a job, or even a prize. Yet she constantly seemed to invite me to try to impress her, to try to win prizes. I am eager to approve of you, Thomas, she seemed to say, if only you could convince me that you are worthy of approval. I am ready to pray with you, she said that summer, if only you would bend your knee.

'Mum,' I said again, and as I spoke a message buzzed on my phone.

I wouldn't read it. I felt it was wrong for messages to penetrate this scene, as if we were both in church together. How different church would have been in my childhood if there had been mobile phones to take the boredom out of my father's sermons, though it's hard to imagine my parents would have stretched to giving their children mobile phones, even if they had existed in those church-mice days.

I wouldn't read the message.

'Are you awake, Mum?' I repeated. I was worried about the coldness of the hand. Shouldn't it be under the blanket? 'Tom's here.' I tried to warm her, rubbed her fingers. 'Thomas.' Their squishiness was odd. It wasn't normal blood and bone.

My eye strayed round the room. To the left, opposite the bed, there was some kind of bureaucratic regulation on the wall. But the lettering was too small to read in the dim light. Some kind of restriction, or warning. The low table by the armchair was strewn with magazines and chocolate bars. One half eaten. Mother loved chocolate bars, though it seemed unlikely she had done the eating here. My brother-in-law? Would he have left the bar unfinished?

On the other side of the bed was a service trolley, with water in a baby-bottle and various pieces of medical equipment. Those must be the disposable basins, I thought. Grey rectangular trays, like old egg boxes, but bigger, deeper. The drug pump was half hidden under the blanket by her shoulder and fed into her right arm. Presumably. It was good to think she was getting all the painkiller she needed. Then I saw that on the bedside table beside the phone, from which only hours ago she had spoken to my brother, there was a book, and I removed my hand from where it was still holding hers and reached across to see what my mother had been reading. The cover showed a crusader's shield and an ancient sword laid across it, but rather than the historical romance you might have supposed, the antique lettering of the title read, *What To Do When Faith Seems Weak & Victory Lost*. By Kenneth E. Hagin.

Again the phone in my pocket vibrated with an incoming message. I put the book on my lap and pulled out the phone.

'Really sorry about your mum. Things frightening here. Charlie psychotic. Please let me bring him to speak to you. Even ten minutes. When they have got her to sleep. Please, Tom. Need help. Don't know who else to turn to.'

My daughter had texted. 'Poor Gran. Arriving 11 tomorrow. Please send address.'

I sat in the chair and, with my left hand still holding Mother's, turned a few pages of this unexpected book with my right. *What To Do When Faith Seems Weak & Victory Lost*. 'In whom,' read an opening quotation from Corinthians, 'the god of this world hath blinded the minds of them which believe not, lest the light of the glorious gospel of Christ, who is the image of God, should shine upon them.' So much for missing pronouns. And another verse, 'Wherefore take unto you the whole armour of God, that ye may be able to withstand in the evil day, and having done all, to stand.'

I shook my head. I have often wondered whether it wasn't precisely my biblical childhood that gave me my vocation as a linguist; the only way out of madness was to concentrate on the language it was written in. Yet here was my mother on her deathbed in danger of becoming sane. So it seemed. Or at least looking around for props to shore up folly. When faith seems weak. Could Mum's faith really be wavering, with her nametag already nailed on death's door? One of the things that had alarmed me as I approached this visit was the fear that there would be a repeat of my father's deathbed appeal for me to convert. 'I would go to my grave happy,' my father had said, perhaps a week before his death, 'if you would return to the faith, Tommy.' I did not want to go through that again, to have to disappoint the person I had come to comfort. Yet even worse somehow, I now realised, was the thought that my mother might lose her faith, *in extremis*. At the very last moment she might feel she really was nothing other than a decaying, flabby, stinking body. And my presence there, sitting quietly by her bedside, might remind her of all the arguments I had made out for this position, arguments that then seemed so sane to me, playing Scrabble together in her little house four years ago. Suddenly I felt an intense pang of nostalgia for Mother's little house, for its tiny bathroom and treacherously steep staircase. I had felt safe in that house. It was a low-church house, plain and poor and sensible. Safe from my crumbling marriage, safe from the demands of my then girlfriend. Protected. At ease. And what had I given my mother in return? I had sought in every way to undermine her faith, to undermine her house. All at once it seemed crucial that my mother make it through to the end with her faith intact. Four years ago I had had a vague and pious concern that my mother should rediscover the body she had always disparaged and ignored, always subordinated to Christian propriety. Now it seemed essential that she go on ignoring and subordinating her body to the end. Let Christian propriety triumph. The last thing I wanted now was for Mother to tell me I had been right.

Holding her hand, my wrist twisted by the safety rail, I began to dread the mental anguish I might be witness to when she woke up. Certainly my father had been horribly anguished when he had told me he would go happy to his grave if only I would acknowledge the Lord Jesus Christ. I was shaken. Until those very last days Father had always granted me complete liberty of belief. So why did my convictions, or lack of them, have to be at the centre of attention in his dying? Was it that a gesture on my part would have shored up his own faith? Perhaps everyone's belief is challenged with the approach of death. And denial is definitely easier when done together. The more people are Christian, the easier it is for Christians to go to their graves. The more people clap for Tinker Bell, the more Tinker Bell exists. Certainly a marriage can last for eternity, if both partners deny it died a decade ago and hasn't even been decorously embalmed. My mother, I thought, was about to wake in anguish over the last-minute crumbling of her faith and, sitting there by her bed, I would be partly guilty for that pain.

'Mum,' I said. My right hand had dropped the book to return to her forehead. When faith *seems* weak, the title said. Perhaps Mum had been persuaded by that 'seems'. If she had had the foresight to bring the book with her to the hospice, it was because she intended to be so persuaded. Perhaps her wobble had already been drawn into a narrative of temptation and overcoming. Wasn't wobbling part of the story of being faithful? Even Jesus was tempted. Even Our Saviour cried, My God, my God, why hast Thou forsaken me? Mother has gone beyond, I thought.

'Mum,' I repeated. 'I'm so glad I made it here.' I spoke in my softest voice. In the end I just wanted everything to be okay.

My mother snored sharply. Her white nightie, I noticed, was damp with sweat around the neck. Again something gurgled in her throat, pulling the lips deeper into the mouth. The neck tightened to swallow, and the eyes screwed up. She was suffering. Abruptly I stood up, walked out of the room and down the corridor to the bathroom. 'She's in a hospice,' I texted, waiting for the pee to seep through reluctant sphincters. Who cared whether Deborah realised I had been lying before? 'In Grange Road, Claygate. Text when you arrive and I'll come outside for a few minutes.'

Later that night I would be recalling this as the ninth pee since the massage. My fingers were shaking. The pee came in fits and dribbles. The bathroom, clunkily equipped for wheelchairs, was full of depressing requests to respect other users. There was urine on the seat, a puddle on the floor. Reams, I thought, could be written about how people behaved in public lavatories. Reams no one would ever want to read. And I was struck by the thought that after the word 'public' one would never say 'bathroom'. Public bathrooms. Though once one used to say public baths, and even municipal baths.

'Do you remember,' I began, on returning to my mother's room — and again I was impressed to see the plate, MRS MARTHA SANDERS, on the door, and disturbed to smell the cloying smell of cancer as I approached her bed — 'when you used to take us to Derby Baths, Blackpool? And Squires Lane Baths, Finchley? My eyes would weep with the chlorine. Do you remember? They were good times, Mum,' I said.

Mother never joined us in the pool. She did not want to appear in a swimming costume. She didn't want us to see her body. Or maybe she just didn't enjoy pools. I don't know. But she took us to them anyway and dried our ears and gave us oxtail soup from a Thermos. She enjoyed seeing us in pools perhaps. The bodies of her young children. In baths. 'I remember,' I told her, 'my head on your tum while you towelled my hair.'

I was holding my mother's hand again. She was snoring more lightly now. I might as well be talking to myself, I thought. Why was I trying to feel these emotions? As if they were a duty. Sentiment an imperative. Why try to feel warm and sad? Just get up and go. Now the wrinkles at the corners of her lips trembled. Her stomach lifted and fell, the same stomach that fifty years ago had held me to itself, towelling roughly, hurting my ears. Mother was generous, but never gentle. Maybe she just wasn't aware of roughness and gentleness. What is the point of remembering these things? The finger rubbing vigorously in the ear through the towel to make sure all was dry. I wasn't helping her, being here. I wasn't helping myself. Mother was happier when we went into the countryside, I thought. And all at once I recalled something that hadn't seen the mental light for decades. 'You remember, Mum,' I began again, 'that pond called the Figure of Eight? Beyond Leyton Primary School. When you bought me a net to fish minnows and we tried to keep them in an old kitchen sink in the garden?' How tolerant she had been, I thought now, of my pet obsession. Me far more than my brother and sister. I had to have pets. Why was that? The fish, the frogs, the mice, the hamsters, the guinea pigs, the rats, the rabbits, the dogs. All dead now, of course.

Flowers too. At some point, walking in the countryside with Mother, I had started collecting wild flowers, pressing them and taping them in the pages of an exercise book. Bizarre to remember this now. Why had I done that? To please her? Did I hope Mother would be pleased to have a son interested in wild flowers? A son who could knit? Or was I really interested in them? I couldn't recall. Certainly I'm not now. Who gives a thought about wild flowers? But I do remember how quickly they drooped and died. It was astonishing. So much more quickly than daffodils or roses. You picked them and they drooped and died. A matter of seconds. 'You told me,' I said, holding my mother's hand, though I might as well have been talking to the bedpost, 'that everything wild dies at once, when you take it out of its proper world.' Certainly the attempt to create a tiny pond in our Blackpool garden with the help of an old kitchen sink was an abject failure. Barely a day passed before the minnows were upended on the surface, or trapped slimily pale in the weeds. Already the water smelled of death. A low-tide smell. Different from cancer. Different from farts. When the frogs died, their back legs opened wide. They lost their froggy shape. There was no talk of Paradise. They were just matter. Squidgy smelliness. Everything dies; that was the lesson of pets. Everything dies and loses its shape. I didn't say this out loud, in case somehow she might hear. Especially pets stolen from the wild. Yet I was definitely saying it to her, in my head. Shape is life, Mum. The salamanders and that broken-winged blackbird. They died in a flash. Far sooner than a well-bred dog or cat. Lose your place in the world and you lose your shape, your life. Removed from pond or hedgerow, these creatures couldn't give up the ghost fast enough. Why hast Thou forsaken me? Only the mice thrived. White mice in the old vicarage boiler room in Cricklewood. They gnawed through their wooden cages and escaped into a neo-Gothic maze of rotten pipe-lagging. Which clown had sold us thin plywood cages for white mice? They bred and stank of life as powerfully as the minnow-pond had stunk of death. Amazing all the droppings. Till Dad got them exterminated – remember, Mum, while I was off on the Youth Club house party? Dad had the mice exterminated. I never saw their bodies.

'Thomas?'

It was her voice.

'Thomas, is that you?'

Her eyelids were still closed, but trembling. Without her teeth, the voice was a slurred whisper.

'Mum! I just arrived. I'm so glad to be with you.'

'Thomas.' She sighed. 'Of course.' She breathed deeply. 'How silly of me. I am sorry.'

'Don't be.' I squeezed her hand. 'How are you doing?'

'Pain,' she muttered. The head shook from side to side.

'Shall I call the nurse?'

She didn't respond. The mauve blanket had her neatly tucked in almost to the shoulders. Above that, the white nightie was damp with sweat, the head was lumpy and grey. The hair was yellow.

'Thomas!'

Suddenly Mother pulled herself up, wrestled herself upright, the way she had once wrestled herself out of her recliner.

'Thomas!'

Like a child coming out of a nightmare, she forced herself up onto her elbows. Her eyes opened and found mine. She seemed alarmed.

'Mum. I'm so glad I made it.'

Why did I keep saying that?

'If only . . .'

She stopped, staring at me.

'Oh, Thomas, if only . . .'

I stood and leaned across the bed to kiss her. Even as I did so, I felt a text message arrive in my pocket.

'Mum.'

Her mouth opened, to greet, or speak. It was filled with blood. Black blood poured out.

Looking back, you would have to say I moved fast. In a flash I was round the bed and grabbing the grey egg-box basins. Before the second jet rushed out, I had one under her chin and a hand behind her head.

'Mum. Mum. Keep calm. Hang on.' Holding the basin in one hand, I found the buzzer with the other. I pulled it from her hand and pressed.

'Mum.'

Maybe blood was not so bad as the words I had feared.

Her eyes were still fastened on mine. Veiny, bloodshot, but still very blue, very alive, very determined. 'If only.' *In extremis*, my mother was willing something, willing something against the tide. She vomited again. I put down one basin on the bedside table and shifted another under her mouth. The blood was black, and frothy. Now two nurses were in the room with rubber gloves.

'You had better leave for a little while,' they said.

IX

Why did I agree to talk to Deborah and her son Charles in the middle of my mother's agony? It's a question I keep asking myself now, through these difficult nights in the back bedroom of my mother's tiny house. Why did I do that? Who would not feel at once how inappropriate it was? 'I'll go out for a breath of fresh air,' I told the nurse. An expression my father used constantly. 'We could all do with a good breath of fresh air,' my father used to say. As if his clergyman's life were all mustiness. 'Good idea,' the nurse smiled. 'Just ring when you want to come back in.'

Why did I do this? It's not such a tough a question as: Shall I view my mother's corpse? Because there is no dilemma. What has happened has happened. There's nothing that needs deciding before a coffin is sealed, a body burned. But maybe the two issues are not unrelated. And not unrelated either to that other question I had been asking myself a few days before: Why did I agree to go to the conference in Amersfoort, which had nothing to do with my own line of work, an invitation I could easily have turned down or cancelled, when I was falling in love with a fine young woman and was eager to show her my devotion in every way. I could even have used cancelling the conference to further my cause. 'Elsa,' I could have said, 'I am cancelling this interesting and absurdly remunerative conference to spend more time with you.' Why didn't I do that? It would have spared me the anal massage. And why, having arrived in Amersfoort and heard that my mother was sinking fast, didn't I simply stuff my few clothes into my disintegrating Samsonite and head right off at once? Why had I given my talk all the same; not only given it, but actually taken questions afterwards, difficult, finger-in-the-wound questions, lingering so long in my careful responses as to risk missing my plane? And the answer to all these questions can only be my need to be good or, rather, my need to think of myself as good. A man always ready to make his contribution. Only being good, generous, helpful brings me relief. Relief from what? God knows. I have to be good. The problem with Mother's corpse then is that I don't know whether it would be goodness to see it or goodness not to see it. I just don't know. I don't even know why the decision holds any importance for me. And when I say 'it', I refer of course to the person who taught me this obsession and schooled me in this need for goodness or, rather, I refer to her embalmed earthly remains. But how could remains be anything but earthly?

I pushed open the door of the hospice and stepped out into a blowy English night. Deborah and her son were not there. A man was walking his Labrador dog and speaking on his mobile. I consulted my mobile, where the most recent message said. 'Arrived. Whenever you can.' I walked to the gate and looked up and down the road. The air was raw. They were nowhere to be seen.

I had first met Deborah and David at university thirty and more years before. Deborah before David, a posh, coltish PhD student whom I had tried and failed to make a move on. Perhaps it was my second year. She was older. She didn't notice my trying. Her father was some top civil servant, her mother one of those women my parents would have said might as well just go over to Rome now and have done with it. Does anyone use such expressions today? I invited Deborah out and attempted to kiss her on a couple of occasions. I was attracted, I suppose, to a certain brittle flamboyancy she had;

she was bossy and vulnerable together. She seemed to like younger men. But women have always seemed both vulnerable and bossy to me. Perhaps I mean women's bodies. Their shape, skin, smell, voices, eyes; everything about them seems precious and commanding. I'm in thrall. The feeling was especially strong in those days with classy women. This awareness of fragility and authority. I mean those women who constantly perform their being female, who are constantly conscious of the drama of being female in the presence of males, but not necessarily *for* males. They don't interest me now. Elsa is not like that.

Deborah didn't notice my attempts to kiss her. Or she noticed but didn't take me seriously. She collected me. Not unkindly. She had me run errands for her, search out books, take down notes. I was a good note-taker. One of the errands I ran was to David. We became friends as he fell under Deborah's classy spell and eventually moved in with her. I was envious. David's grip on language, on literature, on aesthetics, even politics – and most of all on classy women – was a marvel to me. What did they see in him? He was not handsome. He was a year younger than I was.

A baker's son from Nottingham, David had entirely thrown off his humble origins, first with a scholarship to Rugby, then another to Cambridge. His accent had all but gone. He kept just enough of it to remind people of the distance he had travelled, to remind the class he would spend his life among that he was not quite one of them, though actually rather better than them at representing all they aspired to be: cultured, authoritative, charismatic. And over the years, as I watched Deborah and David have children together, grow older together, but without marrying, without ever being somehow 100 per cent *together*, I sometimes wondered if Deborah hadn't fallen for David precisely in order to seduce this small part of him that he held back, to possess this residual Midlands accent, this pride in not quite finally and utterly capitulating to the class he had for the most part readily capitulated to, or appropriated, so long ago. While, for David, being with a posh lady like Deborah, a real thoroughbred, only intensified his determination to hold that one thing back, as if the nearer he got to his goal of complete absorption into the British moneyed classes, the more powerfully some original and essential part of himself resisted. Or perhaps he chose Deborah precisely because only a really posh lady like her, a lady who constantly performed her feminine poshness, could give him, day by day, the opportunity of showing off his residual baker's boy masculine roughness, his otherwise barely visible distinction from them. David wouldn't marry. He wouldn't bow to imperatives of propriety and dynasty. He wouldn't quite speak in the same accent as theirs. Not quite.

Deborah insisted that she admired him for this. It proved he didn't want her money. She gritted her teeth and tried in every way to make her money work for him. Imperious and anxious, she commanded in every area but the tiny territory he held back. When you saw them together, in whatever wonderful house they had recently bought, for they seemed unable to decide whether it was better to live in town or out, north London or west, or even Paris for a few years, or Provence where they had a second home, you never felt that David was in possession of his domestic space or that he was really at ease there; he was always slightly on the defensive, wrapped in irony and distance. And at the same time you never felt she was entirely satisfied with where she had him, in one splendid property after another, for although she commanded in everything that mattered, and decided herself when to have children and where to send them to school and where to go on holiday and whom to see at the weekends, nevertheless she never made even the slightest gains in the areas David chose to defend. Always on the attack, Deborah was always held at bay.

No doubt it was my perception of David's unease, and his of mine in my very different marriage, that brought us so close together for the period when we both began to have affairs. For a few heady years the exhilaration of betrayal had us constantly eager to be talking to each other, swapping our stories. We were kids truant on the beach, in the pounding surf of new pleasure. Pounding flesh, David laughed. Everything seemed possible. And then, by the same token, as deceit and duplicity became chronic, as it became clear that far from our life's opening up, we had simply exchanged one prison for another more stressful prison, or prisons rather, then the similarity of our situations, instead of bringing us together, began to push us apart. Having cheated on our wives, we couldn't leave them. But we couldn't leave our mistresses, either. And when they left us, we couldn't live without yearning for another. We still loved to meet, to drink, to exchange stories. But now, rather than excitement over anything new, it was the pleasure in meeting the only person with whom you could share your frustration, even humiliation. 'If I believed,' David liked to preface our evenings, muttering the words ruefully as we clinked our glasses, 'that my response were to one who might some day return, etc.', and after taking a first swallow of his beer he would twist his lips in a queer grin. 'Fuckin' inferno, mate.'

But how often do you need to look a shameful secret in the face? Our meetings grew rarer. More and more firmly stuck in our married lives, we were glad when work prised us apart geographically. David and Deborah had gone to Kingston. Upon Thames, of course. My wife and I had returned to her Edinburgh home. Until – and it must have been shortly before that famous Sunday lunch – my separation shifted things between us. At last I had made a real move. I had gone to Spain, left my wife behind, become Emeritus. And even if I didn't quite feel I was in the clear yet, I remember being eager to talk it over with David. Perhaps I had wanted to persuade him to follow suit, to convince him it was possible to come out of a life of duplicity, to start again. In any event, whatever the occasion of my visit to London that time, I had stayed an extra day to see him. But what I imagined would be a meeting in a pub, where all could be told and shared over the proverbial pint, turned out to be a lunch with his children and Deborah at which she announced their imminent, after all these years, marriage. I had separated and David was marrying. On her forthcoming birthday. Her sixtieth.

As we exchanged parting kisses that day, I whispered in her ear, 'Happy, Deb?' And she said, 'Ecstatic.' She had got her man. She had sapped his resistance at last. If I had come out of the Claygate Hospice, then, in the midst of my mother's agony, was it really to assist old friends, to lend a hand in Deborah and David's troubles, or was it rather out of a spirit of *Schadenfreude*: I wanted to know how their lives, their married lives, had gone so spectacularly wrong? Or was it both? I would be good to them *and* enjoy their suffering.

'Tom!' Deborah called. She was hurrying towards me along wet hedges, wearing heels.

'Sorry, this is ridiculous. He's refusing to get out of the car.'

She began speaking yards away, open umbrella tugged about in the chill breeze. Her ankles were slim, brittle.

'Please, go and talk to him. I can't bear it.'

Now she was beside me, in smart cashmere coat and pink scarf. Once again I had eyes pleading with mine, this time in a carefully made-up face.

'Please. It's the white Audi, on this side. Get him to tell you what on earth's going on in his head. I can't bear it.'

I embraced her. 'I'm afraid I only have a few minutes,' I said.

'How's your mother?'

'Bad.'

'I'm sorry.' Deborah sighed. 'Just when David and I are finally happy, the boy goes and does this.'

'What did he do, exactly?'

'I told you, He smashed a chair over his father's head. And he won't say why.'

I walked some fifty yards down Grange Road and found the white Audi with the young man sitting, arms folded, in the passenger seat. Opening the driver's door, I had a strong feeling this was a mistake. I should be concentrating on my mother. On the other hand, these people were old friends. And the nurses had invited me to take time out.

'I've only got a few minutes,' I told Charles, as I sat behind the wheel. 'It's a bit weird, to be honest, your mum wanting me to talk to you so urgently.'

'Isn't it?'

I couldn't judge his mood. He seemed polite but removed. He was a young man from a different generation.

'It's been a while,' I said.

Gazing out of the windscreen, he kept his arms folded.

'When was it? Two summers ago? Eighteen months?'

'You don't have to waste time with small talk, if your mother is so ill.'

He was mocking. I looked around. The car was very clean inside, by my standards.

'So just tell me why you hit your dad. What's it all about? Your mum is frantic.'

'I wish I'd killed him.'

'Come on, Charlie, I'm sure you don't.'

'I fucking well do!'

He turned to me and started shouting. 'I do, and I'm going to.' He brought down a fist on the dashboard. 'I'm going to fucking well kill him.'

I tried not to be impressed. I left a pause. He turned back to the windscreen and folded his arms again.

'What's he done, then?'

'You can guess.'

I thought. 'No, I can't.'

'Yes, you can.'

I thought some more. 'You know, I'm really not sure I can, Charlie.'

'You can.'

Near the hospice I could see that, under her umbrella, Deborah had lit a cigarette. She seemed to be studying the flowerbeds.

'Does it have anything to do with those stories you once sent me?'

Again he turned to me. His face was leaner and older than I remembered.

'Stories? Christ, no.'

'Charlie,' I said. 'Your mum asked me to help, but if you don't tell me what's up, there's not much I can do.'

'There's nothing you can do if I tell you.'

I thought about it, or tried to give him the impression I was thinking about it. I said, 'I suppose I can imagine reasons for being angry with David, but then in the end I can imagine reasons for almost any son being angry with any father. I know my own kids are often angry with me. But why hit him? And why now? Why not years before, or why not some time in the future?'

'Why now?'

'Yes. Why hit him now?'

Charlie had begun to drum his fingers on the dashboard. I watched him. He could easily have refused to get into the car with his mother, I thought, if he really didn't want to talk to me. So at least partly he must want to.

'Why now?' he repeated. His right knee began to bounce up and down. 'Good question.'

'So?'

He rocked his shoulders back and forth, as if to music I wasn't hearing, then asked: 'Why didn't you come to their wedding, Tom?'

The way he used my name shifted something. We were on equal terms.

'I was in South Africa.'

'I don't believe you.'

'I could show you the stamps on my passport.'

'Don't pretend you don't understand. I believe you were in South Africa, but I don't believe that's why you didn't come. You decided not to come to his wedding. Then it so happened there was a trip to South Africa.'

In truth, this was a pretty accurate description of how things had worked out.

'You were Dad's best friend and you didn't come to the wedding.'

I didn't know how to reply. David hadn't insisted I go. The official invitation had come from Deborah. I felt David saw the marriage as a defeat. He didn't want me to be a witness.

'Listen,' I said, 'whatever you think about your father, surely the thing to do now is to get on with your own life. You only damage yourself getting involved in theirs.'

It was advice I'd given my own children any number of times.

Charles folded his arms again.

'I won't talk to anyone who's not straight with me.'

'But why do you suppose . . .'

'I won't, and that's that.'

It was perplexing. For a moment or two I watched him as he gazed through the windscreen to where his mother was smoking under her umbrella. In profile, his face was strong and handsome, a jutting jaw, Roman nose, deep-set eyes. All his mother's.

'Write something about it,' I told him, opening the car door. 'You wrote those stories to tell the world you were gay, right? I thought they were pretty good. So now write about your father. Tell the world what you think of him. Why not? But don't get yourself stuck in gaol for assault. That's just dumb.'

As I shut the door he was shaking his head from side to side, slowly and theatrically.

'So?' Deborah demanded.

'I have to get back.'

'Didn't he tell you anything?'

She was lighting another cigarette and, on impulse, I asked her for one. I'd stopped smoking years ago. It was foolish. She cupped her lighter for me.

'He wouldn't say. Maybe it has to do with your wedding, though.'

'Our wedding?'

'I told him if he had anything to get out of his system to write about it.'

'What?'

'Rather than clobbering people.'

Clobbering was a word I hadn't used in ages.

'But write what?'

'Whatever it is that's eating him.'

Deborah didn't seem convinced. In the fresh air, the tobacco was having a powerful effect.

'I need to be going.'

I leaned forward to brush her cheek.

'Tom,' she said, returning the embrace with unexpected warmth. She held on a little and her body shivered against me. It seemed very deliberate. I was being careful to keep my cigarette from her hair.

'I should really be back with Mum now.'

'Remember?' she said. 'In Wales that time?'

'Deborah Pool,' I protested, 'you're a married woman!'

As I pulled away, a voice behind me yelled, 'Prick!' I turned and Charlie's open hand slapped into my face.

X

The tenth post-massage pee was the worst. I stood, holding the rail handicapped people use to drag themselves out of their wheelchairs onto the pot. Presumably. One is never actually witness to such scenes. Thank heaven. My sister had told me what a nightmare it had been getting Mother onto the toilet when they released her from hospital a week or so after the fall and sent her in an ambulance down to Swanage. She couldn't get herself to the bathroom; she was in too much pain even to stand. Back pain, spine pain. Something was seriously wrong. At the same time she hated to use the bedpan. She felt demeaned by the bedpan, humiliated, I suppose, by the proximity of her own excrement. The water closet whisks your shit away, dilutes your piss in an instant, the bedpan does not. Even if only for a few minutes, before your carer comes to sort you out, you are obliged to lie in close contact with your piss and shit. With your smell. Your corruption.

For some reason that unpleasant word 'corruption' came to my mind in the ground-floor lavatory of the Claygate Hospice, with its paraphernalia for allowing people who are infirm and handicapped not to feel they need be in any closer contact with their excre-ment than the able-bodied who cheerfully flush it away without a glance, as if it had never been, as if piss and shit were just not part of who you are. In the newspapers, corruption means shady payoffs to government officials in foreign countries, but in the Bible, as I recalled – and what did my parents ever read to us as children if not the Bible and its endless spin-offs – corruption meant corruption of the flesh. Sin reaps corruption, and virtue eternal life. As I stood over the loo, my right cheek and my lower abdomen were throbbing in unison. The body is of its nature corrupt. What would the nurses think when they saw the bruise, I wondered? Flowering on my cheek. How could I explain to them that taking ten minutes off from my mother's dying, ostensibly for a breath of fresh air, I had managed to get myself belted in the face by the son of the man who had been my best friend in my philandering days? 'Stop it!' Deborah screamed. 'Prick!' Charlie shouted again. He slapped me hard. 'Coward!'

In the bathroom I soaked paper towels in cold water and held them to my face. Was it puffing up? Could I pretend it was there before, but they hadn't seen it? My abdomen seemed desperately in need of emptying, but no emptying came. Then, exactly as I began to zip up, there was a leak. Infuriating. Now I was damp. Now I would smell. I had been in too much of a hurry to get back to the bedside. For some reason, then, opening my trousers again to sort myself out, I remembered, and this seemed a complete non sequitur, that my sister's one real complaint against my mother as a patient, those three weeks at her home when by all rights Mother should have been in hospital, was that she had refused to watch television or listen to the radio. Mother would not 'while away the time', my sister had complained, with some TV drama or radio comedy. As a result, she thought too much about her illness and became gloomy and anxious. She wasn't cheerful. And what was striking about this comment was that while my mother and my sister were thick as thieves, if I dare use that expression, when it came to giving one's heart to Jesus and going home to glory, so that in this regard their side of the family (sister and mother) were diametrically opposed to our side (my brother and myself), nevertheless I could perfectly well understand my mother's refusal of TV entertainment, her reluctance to 'while away the time', while my sister could not. TV entertainment, aside from the News and Weather, or the occasional detective yarn – Mother always used the word 'yarn', as if storytelling had to do with knitting – was perhaps not a great deal preferable to the bedpan and the excrement, for my mother. A game show, for example. Or the open tumours on her breasts. It had a smell of corruption. Of triviality. Mother refused to be trivial. And I was on her side over this. Where my brother stands on the matter, I have no idea. Though it's true that my brother does set a considerable store by cheerfulness and it was evident that my mother, when communicating with my brother, made a far greater attempt to seem cheerful with him than she did when with myself and my sister. The cheerful person, I thought, frees others from worrying on their behalf. The person chuckling over an old episode of *The Big Bang Theory*, or enthralled by *Breaking Bad*, does not make you feel you need to comfort them over their imminent demise, their embarrassment with a body that is no longer lavender and roses. Was this my sister's problem? Mother's gloominess was a form of demand for sympathy. If Mother *had* actually been gloomy, that is, if it wasn't just my sister's projection. But why did my mother protect my brother, but not my sister or myself? Were we perceived as stronger? Was it because my brother had been so long and so seriously ill as a child? But what on earth was the point of posing all these conundrums, when I had a bruise swelling on my cheek and once again my pee was blocked? Only the gesture of putting my penis back in my pants had made it flow. And what can we say of the person who is trying to be cheerful, trying to allow us not to be worried on their behalf, but isn't really cheerful, understandably so, and actually has every legitimate reason for being worried and having us worry for them? Is that heroism or madness? Or was it, perhaps, that my brother had managed to make my mother feel guilty if she didn't present herself to him as cheerful. If so, how had he managed to do that?

Suddenly, standing in the lavatory – and it was after midnight now – I was aware that I, Thomas Sanders, had come to a complete dead end, a position of utter impasse and ugliness. Every thought was a knot, a snarl. Yet the very extremity of the awfulness, or my awareness of it, brought a small sense of relief. You have hit bottom, I told myself. So just breathe and relax. Forget your mother's dying, even if only for two minutes, and breathe. Untangle yourself. Aren't you a man in love? I could still taste the cigarette on my breath. Breathe deeply for all the time it takes to pee. I coughed. There's no hurry. Fill your chest, drop your shoulders. Remember Elsa. Remember Dr Sharp's exercises. Perhaps the problem had been smoking that cigarette. Could that have had an effect? Anyway, nothing was going to happen in the next few minutes, was it? There wasn't really anything I needed to do, standing here in the lavatory. I was quite safe from attack, safe from disappointment. I wasn't going to die here. And in fact, after a few deep breaths, the flow had actually begun and was even promising, when a message arrived in my pocket. With a sudden happy conviction that this must be Elsa sending a goodnight kiss, I pulled out my Nokia and read. 'Charles won't get in the car. What on earth am I to do?'

I cleared the screen and texted Elsa, 'Think of you constantly. Can't wait to be back.' It wasn't true. I hadn't been thinking of her at all. But I very much wished I had been thinking of her and it seemed the right thing to text.

There was a knock on the bathroom door.

'Are you all right in there?'

'One moment, sorry.'

As I came out, the nurse told me, 'I'm afraid your mother's been sick again.'

'I'll come at once.'

She looked at me hard. The light was low in the corridor and perhaps it wasn't altogether clear that the changed state of my face was the result of a violent blow.

'It might be useful actually,' the nurse now said, 'if you could spend the night with her. So you can call us if it happens again. We can't be in there all the time.'

'I ought to send an email,' I said, 'to my brother, if you have Wi-Fi here. He ought to know what the situation is. He's in the States.'

The nurse said there was Wi-Fi in the visitors' lounge at the end of the corridor. 'Just connect. No password is required.' I went into my mother's room where I had left my bag and computer. Again, on entering, I had the impression I was stepping into a different dimension, a limbo zone between life and death, so that although what was happening in that room, which was what always and inevitably happens, I suppose, in hospice rooms, could only take so long to unfold, nevertheless there was a comforting sensation of timelessness here. Mother was on her back, breathing noisily. I sat down beside her.

'Mum?'

She did not reply.

'Mum, I've left home,' I said. 'I've separated.'

She didn't stir.

'I'm now with a very lovely woman, Elsa. Though I'm afraid she's much younger than me.'

'Why, Señor Sanders,' the shrink asked, 'do you always say you're *afraid* she's younger? Rejoice!'

'I know it's early days, Mum, but I hope sometime to marry her.'

Nothing. The light was dimmer than an hour before. The room felt warmer. Blanket and sheet were perfectly smooth. The nurses must have changed her twice in the time I was away. It was chastening. I picked up my bag and stood to go and email my brother.

Then sat down again. Chaste, chasten, chastise. Somehow those words held me beside my mother. Why? I muttered them out loud. There was some connection. I let go of the bag. Chasten, chastise, chaste. Chased. Mother didn't move. She had vomited blood twice and they had changed her bedclothes twice. The body was corrupt but the nurses kept it clean. With a chastening effort. Then I had it. Or I had something. An incident in childhood. Perhaps it was just a continuation of my thoughts in the bathroom, my bathroom thoughts. I and a friend called Malcolm played a game where we watched each other pee. How old were we? Six? Eight? We had peed into jam jars. In the back garden in Blackpool. Do all kids do that? We wanted to see the colour of our pee. Mother kept a supply of jam jars in the garden shed, for autumn jamming. We left the pee in the jars in the shed. Why? Why not throw it away? I can't recall. I only remember a powerful smell, and my mother's dismay when she discovered it. Who would have thought she went to look at the jam jars in the shed? She opened the jars with their yellow liquid and was distraught. It seemed I had done something terribly wrong, something far worse than the time I stole half-a-crown from her handbag. I couldn't understand it, just associated her anger with the urine smell and the excitement of two boys peeing together. That was transgression, the urine and the smell. Mother yelled and wept. I felt cowed. I can't recall in the end what the punishment was. Perhaps seeing Mother weeping *was* the punishment. Feeling you had hurt her. Did she suppose we were perverted? Gay? The word hardly existed then. Later my friend Malcolm, whose parents were missionaries, was hacked to pieces in Burundi. His whole family were killed. They had refused to renounce their faith. They were cut to pieces with machetes and their mission centre burned to bits. 1965? 1966? My father held a commemoration service for them, throughout which I couldn't stop thinking of the powerful smell of urine in a jam jar in the garden shed. I suppose neither Malcolm nor

I had known that urine smells worse when you leave it in a jar in the shed for a few days. It must have been that smell that upset my mother so much. The smell of our bodies. Our corruption.

'Mum,' I chuckled. 'What a lot of weird thoughts in your old son's head.'

She lay still.

'And in yours too most likely.'

If only, she had cried out.

I picked up *What To Do When Faith Seems Weak* from the bedside table and looked at the chapter headings. Kenneth E. Hagin offered ten steps for having one's prayers answered. This is a practical guide, he said in the preface, to successful prayer. Step one was recognising that your enemy was Satan. Step two was checking whether God had in fact promised to deliver the particular goods you were praying for. Step three was making sure there was nothing in the way you lived that upset God and prevented him from honouring his promises.

I put the book down.

'Do you remember my old friend, David, Mum?' I said. 'David Pool. He came to dinner a couple of times, remember, with his partner Deborah. Can you believe they married recently, after thirty years together? Anyway, it seems his son is going crazy.'

Again I was surprised to find myself talking to my mother like this. As if she were in a position to offer advice. 'He's gay, and he has it in for his father who's always been super-heterosexual. Do you think I should try to help? Deborah asked me to talk to him. After all, you always tried to help.'

This was true. Mother was always helping others. There was always a teenager who was pregnant, a man who believed himself possessed by demons, an elderly lady who could no longer look after herself. During the first AIDS crisis my mother had volunteered to assist sufferers when no one else would go near them – this despite her conviction that AIDS was a scourge sent by God. Throughout the summer I spent in her house, and regardless of her own growing difficulty moving around, she never failed to make her Monday-morning visit to a man with no legs who refused to throw away the lifetime's collection of newspapers and magazines with which he was now slowly walling himself in, or her Thursday-afternoon visit to Mavis who, without in any way suffering from dementia and despite being some five years younger than my mother, had simply ceased, after her sister's death, to look after herself, so that now a dozen or so 'good folks' from the parish had to share the task of doing her washing and cleaning for her.

Mother always had fascinating stories to tell about these people. The legless man, for example, had married a woman twelve years his senior, who complained that her husband was overweight but at the same time fed him a diet of bread, potatoes, fried foods and chocolate. She also told good stories about the people who regularly came to her for 'counselling' and for whom, during that summer, I had to vacate her tiny sitting room while she served them coffee and home-baked cakes. Mother's fruitcake was remarkable. But it had always been like this from earliest childhood. We heard nothing of my parents' early lives, but everything about so-and-so who had been beaten by her husband, and so-and-so whose arthritis had led to her losing her typing job. To be around my mother was to be made constantly aware of people less fortunate than yourself. The refugees in Rwanda, for example, for whom I had knitted those four or five squares of coloured blanket, near-neighbours of the revolutionaries in Burundi who had chopped my friend Malcolm to bits. Had I learned how to knit, I wonder now, to make up for the smell of urine in the garden shed? Was it remotely possible that some of those red-and-yellow squares could have ended up in the hands of those who slaughtered my companion-in-crime?

'Mum,' I said. 'Do you remember Malcolm? The Pearsons? Who died in Africa.'

It was a glorious destiny, my father said, to be a martyr for Christ.

'Would you have preferred that, Mum, to the stink of cancer and the moments when faith seems weak and victory lost?'

I muttered the words in a very low voice, as if there were a danger of her hearing them. She breathed deeply and noisily. Mother had been obsessed, my sister had said, while staying at their house, by the fear that the district nurse would be late coming to dress her weeping tumours and the smell would intensify. 'If only she'd been willing to while away some time with the TV, she would have worried a bit less.'

'No one to help now, Mum,' I said out loud. Unless myself, of course.

If only . . .

Damn. I got to my feet. I had wanted to transmit sympathy to my mother. Instead I felt angry. How many holidays had we gone on with some miserable loser whom my parents were struggling to help? A school friend they offered to foster, when his mother committed suicide and his father turned to drink. A lesbian army sergeant discharged for molesting a private. A jilted young woman on antidepressants. These people were always with us at the seaside, in the Scottish Highlands, the Yorkshire Dales, always ready to raise their voices in prayer after my father read from the Bible when the dinner plates had been cleared away.

My mother would definitely have taken time out from a deathbed to help Deborah and Charlie.

'Mum?'

She lay quite still.

I picked up my bag and walked down to the visitors' lounge, which I now saw was called the Commemoration Room. There were cheap red-foam sofas round the wall, and a counter with kettle and mugs, tea and instant coffee. I made a coffee and, while the computer was firing up, looked at my phone. There was a missed call from my daughter. Apparently at some point I had muted the thing. And beneath that call, so to speak, an unread message. 'He's standing right outside the hospice. I don't know what to do.'

Meantime the computer had booted up and connected itself to the Wi-Fi, but for some reason the Internet wouldn't work. How was it possible, I wondered, that Deborah felt she had the right to insist like this, to bombard me with messages about her unhappy son, who had just slapped me across the face, for God's sake, when my mother was dying? But had I actually told Deborah Mother was dying? I couldn't remember. I must get the truth from the doctors tomorrow morning, I thought. The coffee was bitter, in part because there was no milk and I will not use powder. I hate powder. But then how was it that I myself didn't rebel at Deborah's presumption and tell her to get lost? How the shrink would have chuckled. 'You're a bit of a sucker, Señor Sanders, that's the truth, isn't it?'

'Arrived an hour or so ago,' I typed rapidly to my brother on Outlook, waiting for the Net to connect. ''Fraid I'd hardly started to talk to her when she began vomiting blood. Things don't look good. She's in pain. Tomorrow morning I'll talk to the doctors and we'll see if they have anything up their sleeves.'

Up their sleeves?

'Far from being a sucker,' I told the shrink sharply, 'I've had any number of affairs with an army of beautiful young women.'

'Guaranteeing yourself an ocean of guilt to expiate,' the shrink observed.

'As soon as I've spoken to them, I'll let you know.' I wrapped up the email to my brother, then added, 'What's worrying Sis is that they'll want to move her again for some treatment they can't do here.'

I signed off and clicked Send, but the Net still wasn't working and the email remained unsent. The coffee was undrinkable. My cheek was growing puffier by the minute. I should ask the nurse for an aspirin perhaps. Or ice. I didn't want to look a state at the Berlin conference, the 27th annual gathering of European linguists. But was it likely I would be at the conference? I ought to cancel. It was a shame, though, when I had the inaugural limelight.

I stood up and walked back out to the porch, where, through the glass doors, I saw Charlie.

'What's up?' I opened the door and called to him.

He didn't reply. He was leaning against the railing beside the gate, looking away from me.

'Charlie!'

It was drizzling and chill. All he wore was a short leather jacket. I didn't want to go out and let the door shut behind me, since that would mean ringing the bell again.

'Charlie! For Christ's sake!'

He must have heard. Why stand outside the building where I was if he didn't want to respond when I offered to talk to him? I closed the door and went back to the Commemoration Room, where an elderly man had appeared in pyjamas and was waiting for the kettle to boil.

'Would you like me to make you some tea?' he asked at once.

'If it's better than the coffee,' I laughed. He didn't smile. I asked him if he was spending the night in an armchair too. He shook his head, but now he did smile as if amused by my question. He must have one of the guest rooms my sister had mentioned, I thought. Sitting on the sofa again, I found the computer had managed to send my message to my brother and that no fewer than fourteen emails were now waiting to be read. Scanning the list, I saw Elsa's name. Deborah's, Dr Sharp, the conference organisers in Berlin, an academic publisher, both twins, my wife, an insurance company, no doubt requesting payment, an old girlfriend of a decade and more ago, two names I didn't know or perhaps couldn't remember. As I tried to decide whether to take a quick look at these emails before going back to my mother, another message arrived, from my brother. I clicked at once.

'Coughing up blood not much fun,' he wrote. 'Poor Mum. But by no means fatal. I still wonder if the doctors are not maybe overlooking something that happened when she fell. See if you can arrange for a second opinion. She sounded pretty chirpy on the phone when I spoke to her.'

'Here.' The old man placed a cup of black tea on the low table beside me. Shaking, his wrist was scarred with injection marks. An inmate, I realised. I was being served by the dying.

'Thank you.'

'You're welcome.'

He smiled again, as if he had understood what I was thinking.

'Got yourself a little knock,' he said, observing my cheek. 'How did that happen?'

The truth seemed too complicated.

'I was walking and texting. Ran into a post.'

He shook his head. 'You young folks. Always in a hurry.'

'I'm fifty-seven,' I laughed.

He sighed, as if I'd confirmed what he meant.

'Is it safe to leave my computer here for a few minutes?'

'I'm not going to steal it,' he said. His voice was squeaky. Halfway back to the counter and his own tea, he suddenly sat down on a chair.

I walked back down the corridor, carrying my tea. My hand shakes too, I thought. The man had unnerved me.

'Edward?' my mother asked. 'Edward, is that you?'

I hadn't heard her call his name in decades.

'It's Tom,' I told her. 'I'm back. Good to see you awake, Mum.'

153

She looked lost. She had pulled herself up on her elbows and, through her nightdress, I could see the thick bandage wrapped around her breasts, or what had been her breasts.

'Sorry.' She tried to smile, her bottom lip sucked in over toothless gums. 'How stupid. Did I say Edward?' Her speech was slurred.

'It's okay, don't worry.' I sat on the chair. 'I just went out to get myself a cup of tea. Do you want anything?'

She stared at me.

'Is the nurse coming or not? I'm in pain.'

'Did you call her?'

'Hours ago.'

'Let's call her again.'

I reached for the buzzer that was lying by her hand.

'We mustn't bother her, Thomas.'

'She won't be bothered.'

The fear of bothering someone seemed to have brought her back to herself.

'She'll be upset if we ring twice.'

'No, she won't.'

'I don't want them to think I'm a nuisance.'

'But if you're in pain . . .'

My mother shut her eyes. 'Oh, do what you want,' she said sharply. It was unlike her.

I pressed the buzzer, put it down and took my mother's hand. She pulled it away.

'Mum?'

I sat waiting for the nurse to arrive, sipping the tea, which was no better than the coffee. After a minute or two I became aware that I was looking forward to reading my emails, especially the one from the old girlfriend I hadn't thought of for years. As soon as I recognised this, I felt irritated with myself: why couldn't I just be with my mother and forget everything else? But irritation changed nothing. My computer was calling me. I could feel its pull, a kind of magnetism down the corridor. I was wondering if Deborah had explained anything further in her email. I was wondering if the twins had written to say they were coming. In which case where would they stay? What had Elsa said? And my wife? Could my brother be right that I should ask for a second opinion? What did I know about vomiting blood? Red or black. Only now did I realise I was proud to have been present when she had vomited, proud to have reacted promptly, grabbing the bowl – bowls, rather – and holding them one after another under her mouth, pushing my hand in the grey hair behind her neck. Yellowish-grey. I was proud to have been involved in this tiny way in her agony. Now I was going to spend the night in this room, and perhaps it would happen again and I would help her again and she would register that Thomas was really there at the end and was helping her, unfazed by the smell and the vomit, the corruption, and she would be glad of that and there would be a kind of sad happiness between us, my mother and myself, at the end.

I could bring the computer in here perhaps. Into her room. Even if there was no Wi-Fi, I could read the messages offline. Reply to them here, during the night. Then just walk down the corridor for a few minutes to connect, when I wanted to send them. Why not?

'Did you ring?' The nurse put her head round the door.

'Mum's in pain.'

'Are you feeling bad, Martha?' the nurse asked.

My mother grimaced, screwing her closed eyes.

'I'll go and get something,' the nurse said. 'I won't be a moment, Martha.'

I marvelled at the thought that this was the same nurse who just a few hours before had no idea who Mrs Sanders was, then realised that perhaps the nameplate on the door was actually there for that purpose: each time a nurse opened the door, she had the name there and could address the patient in a friendly way, and I imagined mother approaching the Pearly Gates, and St Peter provided with a nameplate or idiot-card so he could say, 'Welcome, Martha' to someone he didn't know from Adam.

Why does my mind work like this? What is gained?

I sipped my tea. I had imagined the nurse would return immediately, but she didn't.

'The children are coming tomorrow, Mum,' I said. 'The twins as well, maybe.'

She seemed to struggle. At last she said. 'What are you doing here, Thomas?'

'I'm here to be with you.'

'It's night, isn't it? It's dark. When are you going to your hotel?'

'I haven't got a hotel, Mum. I'm spending the night with you. You've been poorly. I'll be here. In the armchair.'

I hadn't said 'poorly' in decades. It was because the nurse had said it earlier, because it was a word that went back to childhood.

She shook her head and kept shaking it, back and forth. I couldn't understand if it was a response to what I'd said, or to her pain.

'Go to your hotel, Thomas.'

'I haven't got a hotel, Mum. You've been sick a couple of times. It's best you have someone here.'

'I don't want you here, Thomas.'

The nurse walked into the room, stripping plastic packaging from a small box. She skirted the bed and went to adjust the drip hanging on the far side.

'I don't want you to see me like this,' my mother insisted.

The nurse was now examining the drug pump in the sheets. I tried to find my mother's eyes. 'It's no problem, Mum. I'm glad to be here.'

Why did I keep on with that mantra? Because she might expect I wouldn't be glad?

Her head was twisting this way and that. It must be serious pain. 'This will have you comfortable, Martha,' the nurse said brightly.

'You should go to your hotel now, Thomas,' Mother said. Her speech was slurred but stern, as if talking to a small boy. A boy who had peed in a jar. 'It's late now.'

I exchanged glances with the nurse, indicating I would like to speak to her outside. At which point she noticed my cheek. I saw the sudden narrowing of the eyes. As soon as she came round the bed, I got up and followed her into the corridor. She pulled the door to.

'How did you get that?' she asked. As I told her the same story I'd told the old man in the Commemoration Room, I was aware of the irony that nothing could be less like me than this man who blundered into lamp posts while sending text messages. 'You heard what Mum said,' I hurried on, 'about not wanting me to see her in such bad shape. What should I do?'

The nurse frowned, still staring at my cheek. I had the impression she was confirming for herself that it could not be the consequence of a collision with a lamp post.

'The morphine will make her sleep,' she said. 'She won't know you're there. It would be useful if you stayed. We have two other critical patients, so it's going to be a busy night. Meantime, I'll go and get some disinfectant for that wound.'

'Thank you,' I told her. 'I'll just sit quietly in the shadows then.' Glancing up as I said this, I saw Charlie was standing at the end of the corridor, near the Commemoration Room.

'On the other hand,' the nurse was saying, 'I suppose you have to decide whether you want to respect her wishes.'

Charlie had folded his arms and was gazing down the corridor.

'I'd appreciate your advice, Nurse,' I said. 'What do you think?'

I was hoping she hadn't seen Charlie, hoping I wouldn't have to explain about Charlie and confess that he had been responsible for my puffed-up face.

'There's also the problem of whether to book a flight or not,' I said.

A buzzer sounded and a light began to flash over a door halfway down the corridor. Turning towards it, the nurse must have seen Charlie, who hadn't budged. But now another nurse appeared from one of the doors quite near to him.

'I have a major conference in Berlin,' I said, 'the day after tomorrow. So I need to know . . .'

My voice faltered. The second nurse had exchanged words with Charlie, who was nodding in my direction.

'It's my son,' I said.

The nurse beside me seemed lost for a moment. She was still holding the packaging of the drug she had given my mother.

'One thing at a time,' she said. 'Let's get through tonight first.' She frowned. 'I suppose, if you're sure your mother is the kind of person who would be upset by your seeing her so ill, perhaps you should respect her wishes. It's up to you.'

'But where would I stay? I haven't got a hotel. I don't have a car here.'

She turned to watch her fellow nurse disappear in the door where the emergency call light was flashing.

'My son,' I said, seeing the objection before she did, 'is in a tiny bedsit with his girlfriend.'

The nurse had begun to move off. 'I can give you one of our guest rooms. That way, we can call you if she takes a bad turn.' She smiled more kindly. 'Just let me know when you've decided, Mr Sanders.'

'Thomas,' I said.

She smiled.

I went back into Mother's room to find she was snoring lightly, almost healthily, though still with a grimace of pain knitted into the forehead. I looked around at the dimly lit space, breathed its smell, and now it seemed to me I very much wanted to spend the night there with her, in this warm nest, ready to help, if help was needed. I imagined myself dozing through the small hours, or communing quietly with my mother, trying to remember the good times, maybe, the country walks, fishing for newts, looking for unusual wild flowers. Or even the evenings, decades later, playing Scrabble when she put her feet up and took her shoes off and kept on saying, 'I wonder' to herself over the little rack of letters she had, 'I wonder, I just wonder.' How her feet smelled in their nylon stockings when she took her shoes off! Stronger than the cancer smell, come to think of it. Mother had never worried about my smelling her feet. Perhaps she wasn't aware they smelled. Children have sensitive noses for their parents' smells. I had seen that with my own children. Yes, now that she had forbidden me to stay, I found I very much wanted to stay and sit with her. Yearned to. My computer with its fourteen unread emails had lost all allure. On the other hand, I knew Mother had meant it when she said she didn't want me to see her in that state. She didn't want me to associate this broken, stinking, vomiting body with her, Martha Sanders, on her way home to glory. I bent down to kiss her. The eyelids puckered.

'Mum.'

You could feel she was still there, in this body. Or rather you could feel this body was still alive.

I let my lips press on the old skin, very aware of what I was doing, as if being observed. Then I realised there was somebody behind me. Charlie. He was in the doorway, staring. I turned and hurried him out into the corridor. I didn't want him to see my mother, in that state.

'What in God's name are you doing here? You're soaked.'

I began to walk back down the corridor to the Commemoration Room. He walked beside me without answering. On our left, one of the nurses appeared with a basket of dirty sheets.

'I said you were my son.'

'How funny.'

In the Commemoration Room the old man was gone. I went to my computer, where the screen was in standby.

'You can make yourself a coffee, if you like. Or tea.'

'I'd rather have a Coke,' he said. He went to a machine I hadn't noticed in the far corner of the room, dispensing cold drinks and snacks.

'Want one?'

'Why not?' I thought it might sharpen me up.

As I lifted the computer on my lap, it occurred to me that it was a mistake perhaps not to stay with mother. Whether she liked it or not, she needed me. In the end, I had only left the room because of Charlie. I hadn't actually decided to leave. Then it also occurred to me that almost every decision I take I quickly regret having taken, with the result that not only do I always feel I have taken the wrong decision, but also that I haven't really taken a decision at all. Or not altogether.

And Elsa? The thought presented itself with surprising urgency. Have you really taken a decision over Elsa? If so, why ask your sister not to mention her to the kids?

'Here,' Charles said, putting a can of Coke in my hand.

I clicked on Elsa's email and saw a long paragraph in Spanish. About her sister. Something had happened between her sister and her mother. As my eye moved across the paragraph I became aware of Charlie looking over my shoulder.

'*Mi amor*,' the email finished.

I closed it.

'Don't mind me,' Charlie said. 'I no speak no dago.'

I turned on him. 'What are you doing here, Charlie? You didn't want to talk to me, so why not just go home? Your mother is worried sick.'

Charlie leaned back so sharply his head clunked against the wall behind the sofa. It was quite a knock, but it didn't seem to bother him. He stretched out his long legs, shut his eyes, raised the Coke can to his chin and sipped. Along the corridor another buzzer sounded and I heard the nurses calling to each other. Suddenly, all I wanted to do was read my emails and go to bed, hopefully get some sleep before the early-morning meeting with the doctors.

'Call your mum and get her to come and pick you up.'

'I'm sorry about the bruise, Tom,' he said.

I looked at him. He seemed a picture of youthful health.

'You don't sound sorry.'

'Sometimes I feel so angry I don't know what I'm doing.'

'You need help, Charlie. You need to see an expert. I can't understand why your mother wanted you to talk to me, of all people.'

'I can,' he said.

It sounded like a bait. I opened Elsa's email again. Her sister had finally told her mother she was pregnant. This was an ongoing saga. There had been a heated argument. 'At least it takes the spotlight off us, Tommy.' Elsa still hadn't told her family about me. But why should we hurry to tell our families? To hell with families.

'Is your mum dying?' Charlie asked.

'Seems so,' I told him. 'Just you can never tell how long these things will take.'

Without intending to, I managed to sound as though I had considerable experience in such matters.

'How does it feel?'

He was still sprawled in the same position, head back on the wall, face upturned, eyes closed.

'Feel? I don't know. I haven't had time to feel anything.'

But just saying these words, I experienced a sudden rush of emotion. I had to put the computer to one side. 'I feel sorry for her,' I said quietly. 'I wish she didn't have to go through this. I wish she didn't have to suffer.'

After two or three sips of Coke he asked, 'Were you close?'

I hesitated. 'In some ways. In others, we were poles apart.'

'But she had a good life, didn't she?' Charlie insisted. 'I mean, from what I heard from Mum. She's old now. She had a normal marriage and everything. They didn't leave each other or make each other unhappy.'

I had no real answer to these questions. What is a normal marriage? On the other hand, trying to answer them seemed the best way to deal with Charlie.

'My dad died thirty years ago,' I said. 'She's been alone since then.'

Saying this, I sensed a connection somewhere; a thought was pushing to become conscious.

'She never had anyone else afterwards?' Charlie seemed genuinely interested.

'I think there were a couple of offers. One guy in particular. Worked on the stock exchange. A Dutch bloke. But she wanted to live with the memory of my father.'

'Noble,' Charlie said at once.

I looked at him. His position hadn't changed, but his face had relaxed a little. My emotion of a few moments before was receding too.

'I mean, unusual – romantic,' the boy elaborated. 'These days.'

'I suppose so.'

I tried to remember what the story had been around this rather wealthy Dutch man. Or was he Danish? They had met through the Church of course.

'I guess she would have felt guilty if she had started something with someone else.'

Again a dark wing brushed by. There was a thought out there.

Charlie sat up, drained his Coke, put the can on the floor and reached across me for the computer. 'Can I show you something?' he asked. 'On Facebook?'

Since he seemed to be cheering up, I let him go ahead. Moments later we were scrolling down photos of his parents' wedding on his mother's Facebook page. David had worn a bow tie. A turquoise bow tie. His long hair was tied back in a ponytail. He had always kept his hair long. His glasses had thick turquoise frames. His big beard was unusually neat above his barrel chest. It was a strange mix of formality and burly flamboyance.

'Mum wearing white was a kind of joke,' Charlie observed.

There were more pictures of the couple raising glasses, intertwining arms and champagne cups. David had a glazed look; Deborah was gleaming. I was glad I hadn't gone. One picture showed the whole family. The newly-weds embraced, Charlie had his arm round his mother from the other side. The other two children crouched in front.

'He doesn't deserve her,' Charlie said flatly.

'Nobody deserves anybody, Charlie,' I told him. 'They've been together thirty years. Get a life.'

'You left your wife after thirty years, didn't you?'

'Charlie, for Christ's sake. I'm tired. I'm going to bed.'

I snapped the laptop shut and stood up. Charlie got to his feet too. He was tense again. The photos had worked him up.

'You should have stopped it,' he said.

'Stopped what?'

Again there was the sound of a buzzer along the corridor. I turned but couldn't see where the light was flashing.

'The wedding.' Now he was emphatic. 'You should have stopped the wedding.'

'Why on earth would I have wanted to do that?'

Rather than answer, he glared. He looked wild.

'Charlie, if you so much as touch me, I'll call the police. Is that clear?'

'Even if I'm your son?'

'Enough. I'm tired.'

'You didn't have any trouble telling my parents I was gay.'

I pulled my old Nokia from my pocket, pressed for recent calls and phoned Deborah.

'Mum wanted me to speak to you because she said you knew Dad better than anyone.'

This was unexpected. 'Years ago, maybe.'

Charlie's face changed again.

'I definitely will kill him, you know. I feel I will.'

The phone rang, but Deborah didn't answer. How was it possible that she had left her seriously disturbed son with a friend whose mother was at death's door?

'Why don't you tell her what kind of man my father is?'

I wanted to be shot of him.

'Your mum's not answering, okay? But it's really time you went now, Charlie. Let's do this, I'll call a cab and you go home in it. But my advice is that you leave the family, go and live somewhere else, and keep as far away from your parents' relationship as possible. Whatever they think of each other is what suits them. Your father is a brilliant publisher and a fantastic man. The heart and soul of every party. Your mum loves him. Everyone loves him. Leave them alone.'

'Actually, I live with my boyfriend,' Charlie answered.

This was a surprise.

'So why don't you just be happy with him?'

As I spoke I was looking around for where I had seen a notice-board with useful phone numbers. In reception? I stepped out of the Commemoration Room, with Charlie following. Down the main corridor a red light was flashing over a door to the right.

I remember a fleeting anxiety that the nurses might not have seen it: somebody was in trouble, and no one was going to help. Remembering this now, I realise I am ridiculous, quite ridiculous. But I wasn't wrong about the useful numbers. They were on the same small noticeboard that was advertising the Christmas party. I called a minicab.

'I haven't got any money,' Charlie objected.

'I'll give you some.' I, who hate paying for my own cabs, was now longing to pay for his. Then I remembered I had only my cards and some euros. I couldn't give him cards.

'Damn.' I explained I had no cash. 'Your mother can pay when you arrive.'

'What if she isn't home?'

He was relishing my unease.

'It's nearly two, why wouldn't she be home?'

'Maybe she's gone to see Dad.'

This was exasperating. I closed the call exactly as a voice answered. At the same moment an elderly woman in a dressing gown appeared from the main corridor and shuffled towards the Commemoration Room, leaning on a stick.

'Call your boyfriend. Perhaps he can come and get you.'

Charlie shook his head. He looked hard at me. 'I couldn't believe it when I found out you'd told them. I was furious, but in the end you did me a favour.'

'Call your boyfriend. I'm going back to my mother. At a push, you could always spend the night on the sofa in there.' I nodded to the Commemoration Room.

'Drinking tea with moribund insomniacs?'

It was exactly the kind of thing his father would have said.

'You don't have to talk to anyone.'

'While you sit with your mother?'

'That's right.'

Once again I found myself lying. I wouldn't be sitting with Mother. But it was too complicated to explain. Then if I mentioned a guest room, who was to say Charlie wouldn't want to join me there? He seemed to need my company, while I needed to be alone, with my thoughts and with the pain in my abdomen that had now become a deep scalding from bladder through to groin. Yet the thought that I was lying again upset me. Another person wouldn't have lied. 'The person I'd like to be,' I'd told the shrink, 'does not lie.' 'So don't,' she said.

Charlie was watching me. 'Let me have your computer,' he said.

'What?'

'Lend me your computer for the night, so I have something to do.'

'No.'

He sighed. He looked around the reception area as if there was something he might have forgotten, then turned to me again.

'I thought they'd be incredibly upset and disappointed. With me being gay. Instead they converted the top floor of the house into a separate flat for myself and Stephen.'

'Great parents,' I told him. 'There you are. And now you want to ruin their lives.'

The boy swayed on his feet, hands thrust in his pockets.

'Thinking about it, you could probably walk home from here, right? It can't be more than a few miles.'

'Stephen is away,' he said. 'On a training course.' He looked out of the window. 'And I don't have an umbrella.'

I felt a powerful urge to walk away, but was worried he might follow me. Should I offer my sister's umbrella? Where had I left it?

'You say I'm ruining their lives,' he went on. 'But don't you want me to tell you why I hit Dad?'

'Charlie, I asked you that in the car and you wouldn't answer. Now I want to sit for a while with Mum. You can tell me tomorrow, if it will help, but not now.'

As if we were bargaining over something, he said, 'If you let me have the computer, I'll just sit in the room here for the night and surf and maybe write something.'

'Charlie, I'm not giving you my computer.'

'Why not? You're not going to be using it while you sit with your mum, are you?'

'Because not.'

'You don't want me reading your emails?'

'Among other things.'

Charlie laughed. 'I read your emails ages ago.'

'I beg your pardon.'

He grinned, 'I read your emails to Dad. That's why I sent you those stories. I felt I knew you pretty well.'

'You read my emails to your father?'

'I cracked his email password. Years ago. It wasn't hard.'

This felt considerably worse than a slap in the face, and certainly more dangerous. At the same time there was a large part of me that just did not want to deal with it right now. Making a gesture I hadn't expected to, I raised both arms to the boy's shoulders.

'Charlie, as one human being to another, let me have these moments with my mum; today, tomorrow, whatever. Do me this favour. Then we can have a long talk.'

I gave him a small, friendly push and headed off down the corridor.

XI

This is still the same day in which I enjoyed a man putting his finger into my anus.

That thought crossed my mind in the sleepless dead of night. Or if not the same day, calendar-wise, at least the same twenty-four hours. The other doctors hurt you because they were in a conflicted state, the Californian physiotherapist had said. What a nice man he was, so at ease with himself and with others. They wanted to be good doctors and arrive at a correct diagnosis, but they didn't want to do what it took: put their fingers in your anus. They found it distasteful. They didn't want to give their whole selves to this act, willingly. They put their fingers in your anus, but unwillingly, the way a man might carry a dead rat, touching only its tail, through rubber gloves, arm fully extended, rigid with disgust, face averted. They looked away and stopped their noses, mentally at least, as they put a finger in your anus, to perform their diagnosis.

The American physiotherapist hadn't actually said all of this, but at some point during the night, in the guest room of the Claygate Hospice, I began to elaborate this train of thought, I imagined him saying it and I began to conjure up – really to see – the disgust of doctors exploring anuses, and also my mother's disgust at dealing with her weeping tumours. Mum didn't want to face them. She turned her head away from her own breast. But who would want to face such things? Would I want to see the state my mother's body is really in?

On leaving Charles, I had gone into Mother's room again to say goodnight. All the doors along the corridor were open now, so that a nurse walking up and down in a low glow of night lights could see at a glance the condition her patients were in. Not unlike air hostesses, I thought, on intercontinental flights, walking up and down the aisles to check on their sleeping passengers. So even from the door I could see the pain on my mother's face as she slept. 'Mother is falling into death,' I muttered, surprising myself with this odd expression. Ninety-nine per cent of the time the brain churns clichés, then all of a sudden something new. Mother is falling into death. The words seemed to come from a dream. The dream of falling is always a dream of falling into death, till waking's safe hands catch you *in extremis*. How often have you thought you must die in dreams, then you wake up? But this would not happen for Mother now. The dream was reality.

Her forehead creased as I approached. It was painful to look at her in this state. Painful to smell her. But it would also be painful to leave her, painful to let that smell go. I sat down and took her hand, which now had an extraordinarily leathery feel to it. At once I felt sorry for her hand, sorry for her knitted forehead, sorry for her sunken mouth, sorry for her bruised cheeks, and at the same time I reminded myself that Mother didn't want me to be here, seeing these things and feeling this sorrow for her. She didn't want me to witness this. For her, this hand and face and mouth were not *her*, not the real Martha Sanders, née Crawford, who, on the contrary, was outward-bound for Paradise on a flight that had departed some time ago, was already cruising above empty deserts while angelic hostesses watched over her; and my father, needless to say, was already preparing to greet her at the pearly arrival gate – claygate, pearlgate – already practising his dance steps, though Dad had never danced a single step on earth, nor Mum for that matter. Never, never danced a single step, that I knew of.

Why, I wondered, gazing at my mother's tense and suffering face, did my mother and father have this idea of dancing in Paradise, when they had never danced in London or Leeds or Liverpool or Manchester, all places where they could have danced any time they wanted? Dancing was popular in the North of England where they had lived in the early years of their marriage, and hardly unheard of in north London in their more mature days. Why was dancing okay in the above and beyond, but not in the here and now? Dancing is a supremely physical thing. Bodies moving around each other in space to the rhythmical beat of music. My mother and father wanted to do a supremely physical thing, but without the encumbrance of their bodies. The heavenly music was never mentioned. Psalms? Canticles? The trumpets of the Revelation? How bizarre. And how lovely it was to dance with Elsa, I thought, and to dance *for* Elsa, in my small flat on Calle Abel. I hadn't danced for a decade till I met Elsa. Now I danced for her in the evening with exhibitionist abandon, and she found old favourites on YouTube and laughed and held me in her arms and danced with me.

This happy thought immediately drew a shadow with it. All at once I felt threatened, sitting by my mother's bed, by something hidden in that happiness. It was the same shadow, I realised, that had threatened me when Charlie had asked about my mother's never remarrying. 'Noble,' Charlie had said, when I told him I thought my mother would have felt guilty if she had started something with somebody else after my father's death. Suddenly I had a powerful impression of darkness coming over me, of being drawn into darkness, which was also the dark pain in my belly and the grim pain I was watching knitted in my mother's forehead. You can't start anything new after the death of your marriage. That was the knowledge the darkness brought. Mother knew she couldn't start anything with another man after Father died. It was forbidden. A man who has abandoned his wife of thirty years is not allowed to enjoy new happiness. He does not deserve it. Not while his wife still suffers. Or at least he cannot go to his new happiness wholeheartedly. He is held back by his wife's misery. That was surely what my mother must have told herself after Father's death, since of course she believed him to be alive in another dimension, not dead at all; she believed him to be watching over her from Paradise, as I have often thought my wife is watching over me somehow, from some kind of unhappy Purgatory.

'In your head you have not really left her, Señor Sanders,' the shrink observed. 'That is the truth.'

Dad was waiting for Mum in Paradise. So how could she love someone else? How could she go on living even? She might as well have been burned with him on his pyre. Suttee made sense. You think of your love for Elsa as idyllic, I told myself, sitting by my mother's deathbed, trying to understand why she had remained faithful to Father even after he was dead, even when a wealthy Danish businessman whose friendship she very much enjoyed made a generous proposal; but this idyll is no more believable, no more congruous than the image of your father and mother pirouetting in Paradise. It's a delusion. The idea, I suddenly thought, of Thomas Sanders beginning again, dancing again, with a woman thirty years his junior, is complete folly. Now the shadow really was on me. It is meaningless, Thomas, it is futureless. If Thomas was a doubter, it was because Thomas wasn't stupid. Thomas wanted the truth. And the truth right now is your mother falling into death, her face knitted in pain; the truth is your ruined marriage, your unhappy wife, your thirty years raising children. These are the truths that count, that smell, that have body. David did the right thing, I realised now, agreeing to marry Deborah after thirty years' resistance. What else could he do? Leave her? Marrying was the right and honourable and only thing for my friend to do – an acknowledgement of reality, an acceptance of who he was. I should have gone to the wedding. The affairs David and I talked about, Charlie, in those emails you read, were absurd. Not really him. Not really me. We had affairs that seemed wonderful at the time, but they weren't us. Not really. They were diversions. Mother didn't start again after Father because it wouldn't have been her. It wasn't me to be with Elsa, as all my affairs hadn't been me but the work of the devil. Charlie had discovered the devil in his father's email. There was no other word for it. It had turned his head.

And there was no other word but despair for the state of mind I was falling into now. The whole love story with Elsa is ridiculous, I muttered. You're ridiculous, Tom Sanders. I shook my head from side to side and, as I did so, my mother also became agitated. Her head jerked a little, first to one side, then the other. They were sudden spasmodic movements this way and that, as if the head itself were trying to escape some pain coming from the neck, desperate to escape an ominous rumbling and gurgling that had begun somewhere beneath the bedclothes. The head wanted to twist itself off its own body, to look away from its own corruption. Without hesitating, I got to my feet and reached for the buzzer on the bedside table where faith seemed weak and the victory lost, in the shape of Kenneth E. Hagin's odious book, and rang for the nurse. I did not want my mother to wake and see me seeing her in this state.

While my mother vomited and the nurses cleaned her up – we were well into the early hours now – I took the key they had given me and climbed the stairs at the end of the corridor to the guest room. No sooner was I on the stairs than I wondered whether perhaps Charlie had been watching as I left my mother's room and, if so, whether he would have the gall to walk the length of the corridor and try to follow me. What exactly did the boy want, I wondered at the top of the stairs, trying to remember whether the nurse had said the door on the right or the door on the left? I didn't want to wake someone up or scare them. He was young, good-looking, well educated, well placed for what they call a successful life. Being gay is hardly an obstacle these days. Why didn't he get on with it? Why was he allowing himself to be held back by his parents' problems? Are my own children similarly held back, I wondered, choosing the door on the left and inserting the key as quietly as possible? It did not seem to me they were. I chose the left-hand door at random, if only to avoid being forced to go back downstairs to where the nurses were mopping up black blood and changing sheets for the third time in a matter of hours. Not to mention the risk of being seen by Charlie again. Had any of my children tried to hit me? They had not. They had criticised me. From time to time they had seemed cold. They were sympathetic to their mother and responded to her suffering. But no one had been raising their fists. Though it was true they did not know about Elsa yet.

The key turned. I was in luck. The door opened on a spare narrow room with single bed and en-suite, as they say, bathroom. You would never say en-suite toilet. A stale smell. The pink eiderdown had a dusty look. The room was too hot. It needed air. I went to the window, but it wouldn't open. It must be locked. Not a mechanism I had seen before. Or was I just too stupid to understand, at two in the morning? Too tired to cotton on, as Mother would have said.

In pain, I sat on the bed. There were emails to read, but not now, I thought. I needed to sleep. Though how I would sleep if I couldn't open the window wasn't clear. 'When these moods are on you, Señor Sanders,' the shrink had said, 'just remember they will pass. However painful, they will pass.' It is interesting how unhelpful this advice is, despite its evident wisdom. One knows perfectly well the mood will pass, yet when one is in the mood and under that black cloud, one is in it and under it. It was the same when one had wished one's wife dead. One knew it was folly to wish one's wife dead, one knew one would regret it, and yet one wished it. When you are in a dark place you really are in a dark place, that's the truth of the matter, whatever a shrink may say. Dark places are dark. And even if I get out of this darkness, I thought, sitting on the bed, I will only fall back into it again. Even if I get back to Elsa from this trip, and already she seemed immeasurably further away than she had been that morning, or even this evening on the telephone, even if I get back to Elsa and we make love in my small apartment above the bus stop on Calle Abel and dance again and everything is wonderful, all the same I will fall back into this dark mood, if only because the very intensity of being happy with Elsa, happy around Elsa, reminds me of my failure to be happy with my wife, and above all reminds me that since my wife is not happy, I also am not supposed to be happy. If I wasn't happy with Elsa, I wouldn't feel this intense unhappiness of knowing that I'm not supposed to be happy. Happiness calls to unhappiness. For me. I had noticed that the twins in particular seemed uneasy when I had told them I was perfectly happy these days. For sure, putting 'perfectly' together with 'happy' has to be a provocation. All my children change the subject, if ever I suggest to them that I did the right thing striking out on my own (I don't say, abandoning your mother), I did the right thing thinking of my own well-being. 'How much time do you suppose you have left, Señor Sanders, at your age, for taking a major decision like this?' That was a direct hit on the shrink's part. The one that sank the *Bismarck*. 'How much time do you think you have now?' Pushing sixty, as you are. Lying down on the bed, it occurred to me for the first time that perhaps my mother had not started a relationship with someone else after my father's death for fear of upsetting us children. For fear of upsetting me! Or for fear that such a move would alter the image we children had of her and hence, by reflection, the image she had of herself. Was that possible?

This was a new thought, a new question. And though the idea itself was disturbing, its very newness encouraged me. With surprising energy I jumped to my feet and went round the bed back to the window, to see if I couldn't figure out the opening mechanism. 'Cotton on', as I recall, is one of those expressions no one quite knows the origin of. Not only was the room stale and dusty, but the air was suffocatingly hot. I would never sleep in this situation. So my mother, I thought, studying the window, trapped in the identity she had projected for her children, the puritan evangelical identity she had constructed alongside my father, would not have been able to accept the Danish businessman's proposal, even had she wanted to.

Did she want to, though?

The handle, I finally realised, had a small keyhole at its pivotal point. That was it. A lock. I looked along the window ledge for a key, but there was none, only one of those tags dry cleaners leave on your shirt. Complete with broken staple. It must be an extremely small key, I thought. I looked underneath the empty glass vase on the bedside table, which was where my mother would doubtless have left it. Mother always hid things under vases. Or in them. I turned the vase upside down and some flakes of potpourri drifted onto the carpet. The radiator was beneath the window, belting out heat, and this I did manage to turn off, forcing a miserably stiff valve to budge with burning fingers. Still, a hermetically sealed room was not going to cool in ten minutes. Charlie wanted to cause havoc, I thought, still looking around for the key, so as to nail everyone to their responsibilities; he wanted an end to all ambiguity. But why did his parents' ambiguity bother him, if it didn't bother his older brother and sister? Or his parents themselves, for that matter. Charlie had read his father's emails – not just those to me, no doubt, but those to his various mistresses. That must have been upsetting. But that was a long time ago. Why react now? Because they had married? Unmarried for thirty years, Deborah and David had finally married. They had insisted they were precisely the people they had always said they were, to the world and to him. Why couldn't Charlie run with that?

I decided to look all round the room for the key to the window, where the rain was running down glossy black panes, promising a freshness that was becoming more and more tantalising. Like the rich man looking up from hell and asking Lazarus to dip a finger in cool water and wet his tongue. No, not like that at all. I looked in the bathroom cabinet, the dresser, the drawers to the bedside table, the cupboard under the TV. I turned on the TV and fumbled for the Mute command when the volume exploded. Where was it? Damn! Bodies writhing in a discotheque. Got it. The bodies fell silent. Surprisingly close to how I would conjure hell, I thought. Perhaps they dance in hell as well as heaven. No key anywhere. Charlie should have been delighted about that decision, delighted they were marrying. It was a sign their troubled period was over, wasn't it? There were times when I had dreamed of some symbolic remarriage with my wife, some solemn ceremony of re-dedication, of the kind various friends of ours had staged with varying degrees of credibility. Charlie's mother and father had accepted there was no reality outside their relationship, all the rest was the merest diversion, merest parenthesis, and so they had decided to make that relationship even more real and evident in the holy institution of marriage. What could the boy possibly object to? Deborah and David were marrying and declaring themselves settled and happy, declaring their relationship sacred. Those affairs you read about, Charlie, they were saying, may have seemed important, but actually they were meaningless. You needn't bother yourself about them. That was the message their marrying sent out. The affairs were a sort of bizarre vagary, a temporary physical need. That's what I should tell Charlie, when next we talked. You should be in seventh heaven your parents have married. Another of my mother's expressions. No doubt Mother thought of yielding to the Danish businessman as the merest physical need, the crass need for physical comfort, physical presence. How important was that, beside a spiritual project carried forward for a lifetime, beside a voice that was always in her head, my father's voice?

He had been quite insistent though, I recalled now, this Danish businessman. Was his name Freddy? Something basic, coarse even. He had been a rather coarse, but cheerful man. Red-faced. Very Danish. As I imagine the Danish to be. And very insistent. He had bought flowers and wine and concert tickets. He had taken Mother to hear Ravel and Rimsky Korsakov at the Royal Festival Hall. Perhaps he just looked coarse and red-faced but was actually quite cultured. Certainly he had wooed in a traditional way. Had he asked Mother to dance, I wondered? Most likely he had. He was a Christian of the old school, stalwart and undoubting, but by no means a puritan. Was my mother hard-pressed by Freddy, I wondered? Did she toy with the idea? Or did she know from the start it was the merest vagary? She would never have exchanged future dancing in Paradise with some slow waltz in Golders Green or Swiss Cottage.

So what was actually left for my mother after my father died, I suddenly asked myself now, giving up on the key hunt and lying down on the bed again to flick through the muted TV channels? She had been fifty-eight at the time. Only a year older than myself and my wife now. Only two years older than David was, when he married Deborah on her sixtieth birthday. Did David choose sixty because there is no life after that number? 'Time is running out,' the shrink observed. What was left for my mother when my father died, if the idea of a second partner was unthinkable, if Freddy had to be sent away because too assiduous, bearer of too many flowers, too much wine? Please dance with me, Martha? Please hold me. Mother showed him the door, in homage to a future dance beyond St Peter at the final gate. St Peter with the keys I couldn't find.

'I will never have any man but you,' my wife had said on signing the separation papers.

Damn.

What was left for Mother? To be useful, of course! Useful to my sister with her handicapped child. My sister, whose childhood bedroom, I suddenly recalled, had had exactly the same flowery pink wallpaper as this room, exactly the same pink eiderdown. Pretty comfortable actually. My sister had done everything to keep her severely handicapped child alive, despite murmurings from the doctors that they might 'let her go'; and hence, as the child grew larger and ever more unmanageable, physically unmanageable, because unable to walk and unable to control her sphincters front and back, my sister had been in need of exactly the kind of help my mother was able to offer on my father's death. Physical support. Moral support. So that my mother's decision not to remarry after my father's death must have been, it occurred to me now, at least in purely practical terms, quite a boon for my sister and her husband, my brother-in-law, who was working all hours to keep a small business afloat; though at the same time, as I recall, my sister, the only child of the three who shared my parents' religious fervour, was actually quite taken with Freddy, pronounced him charming – the Great Dane, I seem to remember her calling him – and had appeared quite happy at the prospect of a second marriage. My sister needed my mother, but found her Florence Nightingale visits, she told me, when the child was ill, or when my sister herself had put her back out, burdensome. 'Mother takes over,' she would say. 'She helps of course, but she takes over too. It's burdensome.' Yet both sister and mother agreed it would have been an absolute disgrace to 'let the child go'. A horrid euphemism for murder, my sister said. Did my sister really use the word 'euphemism'? I can't hear it in her mouth.

Yet I remember her expressing this idea. 'As if all that counted,' she would say, and now I can hear her voice, 'was our own *personal* happiness.' She stressed personal, as if there were other kinds of impersonal happiness.

My sister found my mother burdensome, but shared her Christian rhetoric. Inside, she said, the child was like any other child. Inside, she had a beautiful soul. She wasn't just a twisted malfunctioning body. Or not even. She was the beautiful childlike soul inside the body. Nothing else. She deserved life as much as the next person. That child is my niece, I thought. We are talking about my niece. Though the thing one most needs in order to live like the next person – the thing that most makes life a pleasure, whoever you are – is, of course, a healthy, functional body. So why not let the young soul put on her dancing shoes and go skipping off to Paradise? Instead of trapping her down here in a wheelchair, as if there were no afterlife?

'Why are Christians so damn inconsistent?' I announced out loud in the suffocating guest room of the Claygate Hospice, my head turned to the dark panes of the window and the promise of rainy freshness on the other side? Christians talked so much about the afterlife, then made a virtue of clinging to this one. One hated to be out in the rain, but one yearned to open the window and let a little rain in. 'Even the dogs can see,' my sister said, and she had had any number of dogs over the years, 'even the dogs can see Suzy is a child like any other, that's why they play with her and lick her face.' The child – my niece – was in her early thirties now. The dogs, I thought, didn't have to lug Suzy's twelve stone about the house, or clean her shit. What a chore! Every shit that girl had done for thirty years had had to be cleaned. By my sister. What a labour of love! How could someone like my sister, I saw this clearly now, ever condone a man who had let his handicapped marriage go, let his wife go, his family die, and had struck out on his own with a woman thirty years his junior – a woman actually younger, come to think of it, than my sister's handicapped child, my niece, who was not her body, but normal inside like Elsa, perhaps more normal than Elsa, and who deserved to live as much as Elsa did. You are doing it for her body, my sister would say, will say tomorrow perhaps, meaning her *young* body of course. Doing things for a body is wrong, when even a dog can smell out a soul and try to lick it through the eyes. Even more wrong when the body is young and attractive. But did the child – I mean my niece – also deserve to die, I wondered, in the sense of deserve to be spared life? If one could deserve to live, surely one could also deserve to be spared living. How much fun was this life charade, twisting this way and that incontinent on the carpet as three big dogs, one of them similarly incontinent, licked your face?

Suddenly I felt an intense yearning to have my sister meet Elsa. My mother too. To have my mother meet and know and *like* Elsa, to have her, them, acknowledge – this was never going to happen – that Elsa was a wonderful person, not just a beautiful body, though of course at first glance a lithe, beautiful body, a beautiful and beautifully mobile face, are exactly what people tend to notice of Elsa – bright eyes, dark curls, friendly smile; certainly that was what I first noticed. Speaking of which, I had now zapped my way through to a TV channel where two people were making love in generous, even lavish fashion. Bodies. Beautiful bodies. Moving lithely around and against each other in strenuous pleasure. But now they broke off – as, alas, they always must when it's not pornography – because afraid, it seemed, of discovery.

Should I unmute the volume, I wondered, to find out what was going on in this TV drama? I started to watch more carefully. Sometimes it's fun trying to guess what's going on from a silent screen, rather than hearing the actors actually say it. The lovers were in a room upstairs and someone had entered the house downstairs. Unexpectedly. An intruder. It was a rather luxurious house. Or somebody had been in the house, which they had supposed empty, all along. It hardly matters if you guess wrong. The two seemed frightened now, frantic even. They'd gone from ecstasy to terror in a matter of seconds. I knew the feeling. Footsteps were approaching. How I could be sure, with the volume off, I don't know, but I was. Footsteps were approaching and discovery was imminent for the lovers. Discovery of their illicit love, presumably.

Why on earth was I watching TV, I wondered, while my mother was dying downstairs? Why on earth was I enjoying the sight of this young woman's body, in particular a charming flurry of nipples as she pulled a protective sheet around her? Madness. The man was older, I thought. Not as old as Thomas Sanders, though. Was this his son approaching, perhaps? Up the thickly carpeted stairs. His footsteps were right outside the door now – mute or no mute. It was Charlie come to discover David with a young mistress. What on earth was I doing watching this stuff while my mother was vomiting blood? If they showed more of the lovemaking, I might even masturbate, I thought. She seemed a nice woman. Though I doubted they would. Show more, I mean. And hadn't I stopped masturbating since Elsa came into my life? Hadn't I simply stopped, from one day to the next, even glancing at pornography? If Charlie really had read through my emails to his father, he would know that we had occasionally exchanged links to pleasurable items of pornography, invariably heterosexual, invariably involving beautiful women, taking pleasure in love, in sex. In their bodies, no less. At least they seemed to be taking pleasure. There was a period when videos like that had been an obsession. Charlie would know. A mental obsession about beautiful loving bodies, showing affection and taking pleasure. Appearing to. Pornography has to be condemned, of course, and it wasn't really me, it wasn't like me, Thomas Sanders, to be looking at it. I had always felt it wasn't. And yet . . .

On the TV the girl was now hiding under the bedclothes, her lover was behind the door. Waiting. They felt threatened. Volume or no volume, this wasn't a bedroom comedy. Horror, more like. The handle of the door began to move. Or was it possible that on the contrary it was exactly me, precisely me, to be thinking of pornography and masturbation while my mother lay dying in a room below? Though if she had permitted her son to spend the night beside her, to look after her, such things would never have crossed my mind. I would have been sitting beside her bed thinking of her, trying to meet her every need. If I had been allowed to be beside Mother – on the TV the handle of the bedroom door was fully depressed now – allowed to feel sorry for her rough hands and sorry for her cancerous breasts and sorry for her sunken, toothless mouth and furrowed brow, deeply furrowed, then I would have done so. I would not have been whiling away my time watching a pretty woman's body as she committed adultery on TV; I wouldn't be admiring the curve in her back and relishing her shy smile, though now there was a close-up of her frightened eyes gleaming in the dark beneath the bedclothes as the door at last, and very slowly, swung open and in the bathroom of the Claygate Hospice guest room my mobile began to trill.

Immediately forgetting the TV drama, I jumped off the bed and dashed to the bathroom, which was painted in the same pink almost as the bedroom wallpaper, the same pink as my sister's bedroom wallpaper in adolescence. I had left my mobile on the glass shelf above the sink and, since I always keep the vibration option activated, not only was the phone trilling, but the shelf was buzzing and rattling and all the more so because, as I realised now, switching on the bathroom light in its pink shade, I had left the room keys beside the phone on the glass surface. I picked up the phone before it got to the third trill, and saw, as I did so, that the third key on the key ring, tiny as it was, must be the key for opening the bedroom window, the key I had spent a good fifteen minutes hunting for.

'Tom.'

'Deborah.'

I felt pleased, stupid, agitated.

'I just saw you'd called. I'd turned the volume off.'

As Deborah spoke, I went back through the bedroom to try the key on the window and saw, reflected in the black glass, that some seriously unpleasant stuff was under way on the television.

'Is everything okay, Tom?'

The key turned easily, the handle clicked down and a rush of cold, damp air completely changed the feeling in the room.

'What time is it?' I asked with a sleepiness I didn't feel; I was pretending I needed to keep my voice low out of respect for someone else. Wasn't I supposed to be on the recliner with Mother?

'Sorry, were you sleeping? It's, hang on, two twenty-five. I just saw you'd called. Is everything okay?'

Explaining to Deborah that I had called her because I hadn't been able to get rid of Charlie – he was sleeping, I said, on the sofa in the Commemoration Room – I turned away from the window and saw that the pretty adulteress had been stabbed to death. At once I felt a twinge of sadness for the girl, as if I had known her, as if this weren't just the merest TV drama, as if her death were partly my fault, for having left the room at the crucial moment when the intruder burst in.

'You mean he is still there?' Deborah asked.

'I think so.'

'That's odd. I was sure I heard him come upstairs just a short while ago.'

'I'm in my mother's room,' I lied, keeping my voice low. It seemed the best way to avoid a long conversation.

'Could you check?' she asked. 'I was sure I heard him come back.'

Why didn't *she* check? I fumed, but said I would. To keep things short. Thank God I hadn't undressed. I took the keys and headed for the stairs. Hopefully, I could see whether Charlie was there from the end of the corridor. Or halfway down, at a pinch.

'Did you get any more out of him?' Deborah enquired. 'I was thinking of seeing if I could get him on tranquillisers tomorrow.'

'Only that he was furious about your marriage.'

'But that's silly,' her voice squealed. 'Charlie was thrilled by the marriage. He had a whale of a time at the wedding!'

'Perhaps it was his boyfriend you heard coming back to the flat,' I said. I was at the bottom of the stairs now.

'His what?'

'The guy he lives with. Is it Stephen? Charlie was saying how you'd given him the upstairs as a flat.'

'But, Tom,' Deborah sounded reproachful, 'how on earth did you get the idea he was a boyfriend? Stephen's just a room-mate.'

I was walking down the corridor now. Either side, door after door, larval figures were lying on their beds in a tangle of drips and tubes. To the left, one door was pulled to, the nurses' voices urgent behind. At the end of the corridor the Commemoration Room was dimmed. I would have to go all the way.

'You didn't really think Charlie was gay?' Deborah asked.

'I did, yes,' I said. 'In any event, he's not here.' I had reached the glass screen now and could see inside. 'He's gone.'

'You really thought he was gay!' Deborah was chuckling. 'I must say, I have sometimes wondered if Stephen might be.'

She seemed cheered by my mistake. Supposed mistake. I had the feeling she'd been drinking. I felt cheered that at least Charlie was gone. At least I could grieve on my own. Suddenly I wanted to grieve. I wanted to get my teeth into grieving. Like thick bread.

'By the way, how is your face?'

'My cheek's puffed up.'

'You poor thing.'

'I told them I'd walked into a lamp post, texting.'

'Told who?'

'Whom,' I corrected.

'Tom!' she squealed. 'You never change!'

'The nurses here. I mean, I went out of the building looking perfectly normal, and came back like I'd been through the mill. I had to say something.'

'Hope you're mum wasn't upset.'

'Mum is beyond upsetting. In fact you'll have to let me get back to her now.'

'Do give her my love, if you can,' Deborah said. 'Charlie must have got a cab. It was so sweet of you to talk to him. He has a kind of obsession about you, for some reason. I mean he's always mentioning you. That's why I thought you might be able to help. Perhaps you have. You never know.'

'Goodnight, Deborah.'

'Is that you, Edward?'

I had stopped at my mother's door. She was on her back, properly cleaned up again, the muscles on her face working away as before, lips muttering. Then she said very clearly, 'Is that you, dearest?'

I took a couple of steps into the room.

'I sent Thomas away. I don't want the boy to see me in this state.'

I stood still.

'Edwaaard?' Her voice dragged the name into a moan. 'I want to come to you tonight. Let me come to you, Edward. I have asked the Lord to take me tonight. Tonight.'

My mother raised herself on her elbows and tried to shout.

'Dear Lord, take me now! Please take me.'

XII

Even by my standards, it was a bad night I spent in the guest room of the Claygate Hospice. There were twitches, sudden visions, old voices, echoes, giddiness. At one point I know I caught myself humming the baptismal hymn. *In token that thou shalt not flinch.* Why was I humming the baptismal hymn, I wondered, the night of Mother's agony? Why not *Abide with me, fast falls the eventide*? In some strange state between sleep and panic I saw turbulent seas frothing with sewage. I saw a cattle-ship foundering and animals sliding about the deck, bellowing to be free. I saw a grasshopper push its way out through the eyes of a toad. I heard drumming hooves and my own heart humming, *We print the cross upon thee here, and stamp thee His alone*. Until finally a voice woke me from my sleeplessness. An imperative cut the air of the Claygate Hospice. Get up, Tom Sanders. It's time to get up.

So I got up. Who knows why one wakes when one does, why one imagines a voice has spoken? Extraordinarily, I didn't need to go to the bathroom. It was shortly before seven. Showering, I had no idea whether I had slept or not. Yet I felt good now. I felt that yesterday could be showered away, that my pains could only improve. Perhaps I *had* slept. The cattle-ship was a dream, it must have been, the animals bellowing as they thrashed in sewage. A nightmare. Perhaps the organism is simply kick-started by another day, regardless of whether or how you've slept.

At once I was eager to get down to Mother. Her veto has lapsed now, I thought. Mother hadn't wanted me to sit beside her through the night, to face the night's demons with her, but she would be happy to see me now. She would be feeling better and we could talk a little. The morning was always a good time to talk to Mother. I would come downstairs to find her in her recliner, Bible or prayer book in hand. I'm speaking about that summer, of course. In Mother's tiny Hounslow house the stairs were actually in the sitting room, so I would see her from above, over the banister, her grey hair bowed in prayer, or reading the Collect for the Day. One felt surrounded by prayerfulness in the early morning at Mother's house, before she started humming. Before the cuckoo cuckooed eight.

In the kitchen, breakfast was already laid. The cereal was on the table. The Brazil nuts. The milk in a china milk jug. The toast rack, the tea cosy. These were the kind of objects my mother surrounded herself with. Milk jugs, tea cosies, toast racks, serviette rings, cuckoo clocks. And in the morning one could talk easily of humdrum things. I would ask her if she had slept well and she would say, So-so, which meant she had hardly slept at all, and she would ask me how I had slept and I would say I had slept fine, thank you, and she would say, Oh, in a surprised voice, Oh, I was afraid you hadn't, Thomas, meaning she had heard my trips to the bathroom in the night – how many? five, six? – but she would never push the point, and I would never explain that I was perfectly capable of going to the bathroom six times in the night and still sleeping fine, and all in all there was a feeling of truce in the air and prayerful calm. In that long summer we spent together four years ago.

At the Claygate Hospice I hurried downstairs somehow convinced that we were going to have a pleasant chat, a cup of tea, even cereal.

As in Hounslow. Perhaps I would ask for her thoughts about David and Deborah and Charlie. If Mother and I could never talk about our own woes, we were always good at talking about other people's, about the legless man with his house packed with newspapers, and the helpless Mavis who staged her small domestic disasters so as to have people come and help. Mother was a woman of considerable experience and when she kept off religion she was perceptive and generous. Perhaps, I thought, pushing swing doors at the bottom of the stairs, she would offer some useful insight into Charlie's mad behaviour.

As I approached her room, a nurse came out. Not the same nurse as yesterday. This was a small woman in her early sixties, calmly deliberate, birdlike. Like a pecking bird.

'How is she?'

'You are Thomas?' the nurse asked.

I said I was. She had noticed my puffed-up cheek. 'Your mother's quiet now. She's sleeping.' Each thing she said seemed to be a little peck.

'I'll sit with her.'

Then, because she didn't move, didn't peck, I asked, 'Do you have any idea, well . . .'

She cocked her head to one side, opened an eye.

'I'm supposed to be at a conference tomorrow. I should tell them if I'm not coming.'

Now the eye narrowed. She had an air of preserved youthfulness, curly hair set in a honey perm, smile lines hovering round her mouth. She was still, but very ready to move.

'The doctors will be coming soon and you can ask them. But no one ever really knows, Mr Sanders.'

'I realise that.'

She watched me with unsettling intentness. Eventually she said, 'I have only nursed your mother for two days, Mr Sanders, but I wanted to tell you, I feel I have been in the presence of someone extraordinary. Your mother is an extraordinary person.'

I was taken aback. 'Mum is definitely a special person,' I said.

'I never knew anyone radiate so much . . .' the nurse hesitated, at a loss, 'godliness.' She smiled. 'All the staff have felt it.'

Again her eyes searched mine, but I couldn't think what to say.

Seconds later the nurse had moved away and I had already pushed open the door of Mother's room when I heard my name again.

'Thomas?'

She had turned back.

'Yes?'

'It's always difficult for the nursing staff to know what to say to relatives.'

'I can imagine.'

'Your mother mentioned you are very successful in your line of work. She's proud of you.'

I found a wan smile.

'But it's also true that many people do regret not having made some time, at the end. You know.'

We were a few feet apart in the corridor. Behind me the breakfast trolley was advancing. Two young Asian women were fussing with trays and drinks.

'It is kind of you to say that,' I told her. And I made up my mind. 'I certainly won't be leaving,' I said, 'while Mum is in a critical state.'

Now I felt good. This was the right thing. I would inform the conference organisers mid-morning.

'Of course you must do as you feel is best,' she said, more cautiously. She frowned and turned away again. She had slim ankles, I noticed. There was a nice quickness to them as she hurried away.

In her room, Mother was exactly as she had been the night before. The Lord had not taken her. On the other hand, she was hardly up for a cup of tea, either. What on earth had I been thinking of? All my life people have been telling me what a remarkable woman my mother is. More remarkable than her children. That was always the implication. And I remembered now, sitting down beside her again, and again taking her hand over the bed's guardrail, that one of those people had been the Great Dane, Freddy, or perhaps it was Franz. 'Your mother's face shines,' he had told me once. After twenty years in London he still had a slight accent. 'With God's goodness,' he said. I think my sister was there too. I think he actually took my sister's hand in his as he said this. That's how I recall it. Certainly his ruddy face shone as he spoke the words. He really did want to marry her. Perhaps he had hoped we would speak well of him to her. Perhaps my sister did speak well of him. The marriage would have made us rich. Freddy had cash. Or Franz. Mother's hand in mine was cold now, soggy somehow. It didn't respond to squeezing. 'Your mother is the personification of loving kindness,' the lesbian army sergeant had told me. Later she was discharged for sexual harassment.

Yet even this remarkable mother of mine did not have her prayers answered. The Lord had not taken her when she wanted to be taken. Kenneth E. Hagin would know the reason. She hadn't checked perhaps whether this was one of the requests God has pledged to grant. 'Let me die tonight!' She hadn't made sure there wasn't some sin or imperfection in her life that inhibited God's generosity. However saintly the world thought you were, you never really knew where you stood with God. Not until the threshold was crossed.

Holding my mother's hand, shortly after seven o'clock – I shook my head when the breakfast ladies offered cereals and scrambled eggs – it came home to me that this had been the focus of all my parents' teaching and all my childhood education: death is the supreme moment of truth. All life looks forward to death, and only death gives meaning to life. In a way there is no life, or has been no life, until death confirms it.

So you live in expectation of the decisive moment, the great and final selection; everything you do is done in view of that, in view of death. That is the Christian life. Everything is good or evil; everything tenses to this or that verdict, at death, when every past action is weighed in the balance. Isn't that madness? And before the irrevocable judgement, before that single split-second dividing past and future, time and eternity, you can never really be sure where you stand, whether you are among the saved or the damned. Yet this one thing that you cannot know is the very thing you need to know if you are to have any peace of mind. You cannot have peace of mind. That was the vision of life our parents taught us. Mother was now inches from the great divide.

'Good morning, sir.'

I turned to find two young women at the door. Both tall, both handsome. One in particular, slightly ahead of the other – blonde fringe, pale lipstick, bright eyes – was extremely pretty. The other was darker, frowning at something on her phone.

Who were these women so early in the morning? They did not look like the girls in need that Mother was always helping. Fellow members of her church congregation, perhaps? Fellow helpers of Mavis and the legless collector of newspapers? Coming into the room, the blonde woman, who I now saw had a ponytail, walked quickly round me, took the patient's medical reports from the folder at the foot of the bed and asked me if I would mind leaving the room for a few minutes.

Responding to my surprise, the other woman smiled and said, 'Doctors don't wear white coats at the hospice, Mr Sanders. We try to keep things homely.'

After their rounds, they granted me an interview at a table in the Commemoration Room. They really were two very handsome women. Unsettled, I put my hands on the table and tried to stick to the script I had prepared. My sister and I were extremely worried, I told them, that there would be some attempt to move my mother.

This had happened before, as they probably knew. Last week, in fact. Perhaps to a hospital for further treatment, I said, or for diagnostic tests, perhaps even to my sister's house. The whole family, I told the two women, was very much against this. I tried to sound firm, emphatic. I did not want to let my sister down, or my brother-in-law, or indeed poor Mother herself. And I began to list all the reasons why such a move really would not be a good idea: Mother was incontinent and bedridden; she couldn't stand, let alone walk; she was in pain; then she was very happy with the nursing here. She felt well looked after and cared for.

As I spoke, the doctors watched me patiently, while in some distant part of my consciousness I was aware that ten years ago I would have been tempted to throw my cap at one of them.

'Mr Sanders, if I may.' The darker of the two women raised a hand as if to call a halt to an audition that had become embarrassing. 'Mr Sanders, there is no question of moving your mother.' She stretched her lips, sighed, looked straight into my eyes: 'Martha is . . . on her way,' she said.

I stared at her.

'Your mother is *on her way*, Mr Sanders.'

'She has been bringing up blood all night,' the blonde doctor put in. 'There has been a major haemorrhage.'

For some reason I didn't believe what I was hearing.

'There is nothing we can do now but try to make her comfortable.'

'Ah,' I said.

'A doctor has to be wary about making predictions,' the darker woman took over. She hesitated. 'However, I am sure you will want to take this last opportunity to be with her.'

As I stood too, the blonde said, 'You have hurt your cheek. Perhaps you should ask one of the nurses for some medication.'

'Thank you,' I said curtly. 'You have been extremely helpful.'

*

I hadn't been in my mother's room half an hour when the clergyman arrived. I had texted my sister and told her to email my brother. I had texted my son, my daughter, the twins. I had texted Elsa and suddenly felt anxious because she was far away. Perhaps she was slipping away from me. There would be a family gathering around my mother's deathbed and Elsa would not be part of it. Elsa could never really be part, I found myself thinking, of what suddenly seemed to me the core of my life. My mother's death. That was the truth. David had done absolutely the right thing at the end of the day, I decided, in marrying Deborah. Why wasn't Charlie happy with the arrangement? What if, even now, I went back to my wife? My children would be delighted. Why not please them? It would be better for Elsa too, when all was said and done. What was the future for Elsa with a man pushing sixty? The best thing I could do for Elsa, I thought, was go back to my wife.

The curtains were open this morning and bright light was falling on puddles in the patio, showing the birdbath I had seen on my brother-in-law's iPad. It was a beautiful day, a day to be walking in the country, gathering wild flowers perhaps, or inspecting ponds for newts and minnows, or just strolling along the river at Marble Hill. How often did we do that, Mother and I, that summer? Stroll along the Thames at Marble Hill. 'This is so unlike you, Mum,' I cried out loud, 'to be in bed still at nine and gone! You're getting lazy, love.' I laughed and for a moment it did seem a smile might have stirred the greyness of her face.

'Mum?'

I was standing over her. Her breath rasped. We would never speak to each other again, I realised. Mum was on her way. Perhaps I need not call the conference organisers after all. Then I remembered something my father had said a few days before the end. 'I am taking an earlier train, Tommy,' he had said. 'Think of it that way.' My father liked to call me Tommy. Something my mother never did. 'An earlier train.' Now Mother was aboard too.

I went to the bathroom, peed, freely and abundantly – apparently I was in great shape – and when I came back a clergyman was by her bed.

He was a tall man, of athletic build, wearing all his robes. They were the same robes – the black cassock, the white surplice – my father had worn to church, though not, I think, to visit the sick. At once I knew this man was pleased with his robes, pleased with himself and his solemn role.

'Good morning, Thomas.'

The clergyman stretched out his hand. He knew my name. He was the vicar at my mother's church, he said. My mother had been his finest lay preacher, for many years. He had learned so much from her. It was an extraordinary help, he said, for a young clergyman, to have a woman of my mother's experience, my mother's charisma, in the congregation. She was a very remarkable woman, he said. And he told me his name – Patrick perhaps it was, or Philip, or Peter – a name I at once and very deliberately forgot. I didn't want to know his name. I felt angry. There was so little time left for me to be alone with my mother now – soon my sister would arrive, my children, my uncle – and this young clergyman was taking that time away, that precious last time alone with Mother. He imagined I would be pleased to hear my mother had been a great help to his ministry, pleased to know how highly he valued her. I didn't give a damn. I refused his hand and sat down by the bed.

How had the clergyman known, I wondered then, as he turned towards my mother, to hurry here this morning? To Claygate. Had my sister told him? Last night perhaps. Or the hospice staff? Or had my mother warned the hospice staff that they should call the clergyman on his mobile, when they felt the time had come. The Reverend had brought a little leather case with him, which no doubt held the communion cup, a case exactly like the case my father took to give bread and wine to the sick thirty and more years ago. This is happening now, I thought. Your mother's death. This is the moment we all must pass.

I was sitting on one side of the bed, holding my mother's cold hand, and the clergyman stood on the other. The Reverend Peter or Philip or Patrick. First he stood in a kind of trance, head bowed, lips muttering prayers to himself, then he opened his eyes and stretched out a robed arm to place his hand on her forehead. He held it there for a while, a large pink healthy hand. Not as if he were checking for fever, but more as though he were transmitting something, some spirituality or otherworldliness, that came, as it were, with the job, with the freshly laundered robes. He was gazing at Mother intensely, his hand on her forehead, while her breathing rasped and her fingers were ice. Then, slowly shaking his well-groomed head, the clergyman whispered, 'How beautiful!'

I could have killed him.

'How beautiful,' he breathed again, as if in awe, over my dying mother.

And a third time, 'How beautiful!'

I was furious, and my fingers closed very hard on my mother's hand, which didn't respond in any way. Had he said the words for my benefit? I felt he had. I felt it was pure exhibitionism. I can see your mother's beauty, this clergyman was telling me, the beauty of a saintly soul at the gates of Paradise, while you, Thomas Sanders, the doubter, see only the gross corruption of the body. But I didn't believe he saw anything of the kind. It was a script in his head, long before he reached the Claygate Hospice. It was what one says over the stalwart Christian on her deathbed. Mother looked awful. She was mottled and flabby and grey and swollen and sunken and veiny and waxy and she smelled. She smelled of cancer. My mother was not beautiful.

Again the Reverend Philip or Peter or Patrick breathed, 'How beautiful', and again my anger boiled, and now I wanted to challenge him and to demand where he saw beauty when I saw only lips I felt sorry for, eyes I felt sorry for, a grey nose that had lost all shape, a gaping mouth, great flabby ears, a flabby neck. I felt sorry for Mother's nose and ears and mouth and neck, I felt sorry – terribly sorry – that she was reduced to this. It was a mockery to talk of beauty.

I wanted to challenge the clergyman. But then I remembered that the Reverend Phil or Pat or Pete was there because my mother wanted him there. He was creating the atmosphere my mother had wanted him to create, sustaining the beliefs my mother had given her life for. My mother did not want me to be beside her while she vomited blood in the night, she was afraid I would catch some sign of desperation perhaps, she was afraid my scepticism would be confirmed by some weakness of hers, or might even corrupt her, my scepticism would actually bring about the weakness in her that it sought for its own confirmation; she had not wanted me, her son, but she very much did want this upright man in his freshly laundered robes to come and see the beauty of her soul on the brink of departure, to confirm the faith, to print the cross a last time on her brow. *In token that thou shalt not flinch.* At death's door. One says 'death's door'. And only yesterday, seeing Kenneth E. Hagin's book by her bed, hadn't I myself very much hoped that Mother would not lose her faith, the faith I felt was folly? Hadn't I hoped, almost prayed, that she would not flinch, would not fall at the final fence? I didn't want that. Surely it was quite enough to die, without having to fear that one's whole life had been lived in a foolish, self-denying, bigoted error. I should be delighted with this clergyman; I should be delighted with this theatre of salvation. The Reverend Pat played his part pretty well. He had it off pat.

But I wasn't delighted and couldn't be. This posturing seemed grotesque. It inhibited the kind of tenderness I had hoped could be shared in these moments. I see things you do not see, the Reverend was telling me. There was something complacent, even triumphant about the man. He was younger than me, but he had the robes. He had the communion chalice. And I wondered if my mother had discussed her sons with him. Her unchristian sons. Very likely she had. She had worked as a lay preacher in this man's parish for many years. She had told Philip or Peter or Patrick that her two sons had disappointed her. They had fallen away from the faith. She grieved over them. I see things it is not given to you to see, this clergyman was telling me. In your mother. I see her beauty. You are not one of the Lord's chosen people. I am closer to your mother than you are, Thomas, because I share and confirm her faith. You are excluded. You are here because of kinship only. Because you are a son. You are not close to her in any other way. You are holding her hand, but her hand is cold and dead. Her hand is dead meat. I see the beautiful soul flutter in her face.

'Dear Martha,' the Reverend announced as if suddenly in touch with her. 'Dear Sister in Christ.' He raised his voice to pulpit volume, perhaps because she was hard of hearing these days, or as if saying things more loudly might make them more true. He was calling on a cloud of witnesses.

'Martha, today you will be with our Lord in Paradise.'

I had my head bent, at the bedside. I couldn't look at him. And I wondered if he would interpret this bent head as my participating in his prayer, if he would think perhaps he had scored that small success, persuaded Martha's recalcitrant son to bow his head in prayer? Over her dying body. And immediately I wanted to tell him that it wasn't like that, that I had bowed my head because I couldn't bear to look at him. I didn't want any contact with him. Over my dead body.

'I envy you, Martha, Sister in Christ,' he repeated. 'Today you will be with the angels in Paradise. Today you will see your beloved Edward once again.'

I kept my head lowered. On what authority did Mr Pip Clergyman pronounce these words, I wondered? Wasn't he jumping the gun? Wasn't the decisive moment still ahead for my mother, the moment at the Great Divide when all is won or all is lost? Not far ahead, true, but still ahead, Reverend Pete. It isn't given for us to know.

All the same, we must have faith. I have never understood this conundrum. You are ordered to believe and told you cannot know and, what's more, must never pretend to know, or even ask. But must believe.

What kind of mindset is that?

And wasn't it amazing in the twenty-first century in Claygate, south-west London, that an athletic young man in fancy dress was pronouncing this nonsense over the broken body of my mother, her arm with its sophisticated drip and hi-tech drug pump, her head raised on the manoeuvrable hospice bed to prevent her drowning in vomit? And wasn't it extraordinary that many people would find this performance less grotesque than the Dutch lady physiotherapists exploring each other's anuses for therapeutic purposes?

But Mother had wanted the Reverend Pat or Pete to be here. Or Phil. I had to keep telling myself that. He was *invited*. And now it occurred to me that she had foreseen I would witness this moment. She had known I would hear the Reverend's blessing. And she had wanted that too. Mother had thought this scene might draw me to salvation, perhaps. This demonstration of confident Christianity on the brink of eternity. It wasn't beyond my mother to have planned such a thing. Her death would be an example to me. This last blessing was a sermon.

'Today, dear Martha, you will be among the angelic hosts.'

Her breath caught in her throat. Her chest lifted an instant. I glanced up as the Reverend spoke. Pain flickered on her cheeks. He prayed on. And on. I felt trapped now. I would have liked to leave the room, to leave him to it. At the same time, I felt bound to stay and protect my mother from this man, from the man she had wanted to be here and who was absolutely on her side. The man she had brought along to show me what a Christian death should be like. I wanted to protect her from him.

'Dearest Martha,' the Reverend Paddy said in his pulpit voice. He imagined she was hearing him, I realised, the same way Christians imagine God is hearing them when they pray. He thought she had responded, she had moved her lips.

'Remember not, Lord, our sister's iniquities, nor the iniquities of our forefathers.'

He was reading from a book now. His voice had that special drone of the clergyman reading the prayer book's quaint syntax. Then it changed again. A brusque declaration.

'O Lord, save Thy servant!'

'Which putteth her trust in thee,' came the response.

It was my sister's voice. My sister was right behind me. I hadn't realised. Far from theatrical, she sounded perfectly calm and matter-of-fact.

'O Lord, hear our prayers!'

'And let our cry come unto thee,' my sister answered softly. She had come into the room without my hearing.

Head bowed, I was caught now between the two voices, the boom of the Reverend Pete's voice and my sister's faithful echo. I was trapped in their performance. Versicle and response. It was pure theatre. They are called versicles, I think. I felt so angry. With them, and with myself. With them, for taking over the stage like this; with myself, for my impotence, my not understanding how to be myself in this unexpected situation. And it seemed impossible to me that they shouldn't be aware of this, the Reverend and my sister; if they could see the beauty of my mother's soul preparing for Paradise, why couldn't they see the anger boiling beneath her son's bent head and knotted shoulders? Get up and leave them to it, I thought. But I knew I wouldn't. I wouldn't leave my mother alone with this preposterous Reverend. This ham actor. And my sister was obviously in tune with the man. No doubt he believed in his part. He believed his own hamming. I was afraid of the anger I felt now. It seemed to have escaped the immediate circumstances and blown up out of all proportion. Like Charlie's anger yesterday. I would hit someone. I would make an exhibition of myself. 'Don't make an exhibition of yourself, Thomas.' Mother speaking.

'Almighty God,' the Reverend droned, 'with whom do live the spirits of just men made perfect, after they are delivered from their earthly prisons.'

It was a long prayer, blowing over my head now, a rich rain of old words that teemed down on my seething mind. Mother is full of doubts, mate, I wanted to object to the Reverend Pippo. Did you know that? Look at the book on her bedside table, if you will. Why do you think she is reading that stuff?

Behind me, my sister said, Amen, in exactly the voice she might have used to say, Pass the sugar. I loved her for that. And I wanted to grab *When Faith Seems Weak* and wave it under the clergy-man's nose and tell him my mother had doubted at the end; at the end she was plunged in doubt, like doubting Thomas, and the rea-son she doubted was that when it came down to it, this stuff was all nonsense, arrant nonsense. What's more, it was stealing these last moments of my mother's life away, this last chance for some kind of serene relationship, as it had stolen away – truth be told – almost all normal relationships in our family from as early as I could recall. It was sick.

But I did not jump up and object, and I did not grab Kenneth E. Hagin's book and wave it under the clergyman's nose. Mother would not have wanted me to. And deep down I did not want to think she had doubted in any serious way. Far better, then, to act as if she hadn't doubted at all. Better to hide the truth. That was the conclusion one always seemed to arrive at in our family. Better to keep quiet. I wanted to scream, and did not.

'Wash her soul, we pray thee, in the blood of that immaculate lamb.'

The voice harped on. My mind fastened on this paradox I had heard so often. Washing things in blood. My mother and father loved this nutty idea. The idea of washing in the very liquid that stains worst. The bodily fluid. But Mother wanted this mumbo-jumbo of immaculate lambs, I thought. There was no point in protesting. Wash her soul, we pray thee, in the urine of that immaculate lamb. Can you imagine? The dung of that immaculate lamb. If the blood is sacred, why not the piss, why not the shit? Not only did I not object to this nonsense, but I actually kept my head bowed, as if in prayer, as if in assent. How many times, I remembered as the Reverend's voice droned on, how many times had I pretended to pray as a child? Worse still as an adolescent. How many times had I hidden in prayer, taken refuge in the theatre of prayer, refuge from their coercive prayers in the posturing of my fake prayer? But your praying was always fake, I suddenly realised. And at the same time I remembered how once, playing Scrabble, in a stroke of luck and genius, Mother had added 'immacul' – all her seven letters – to 'ate', reaching out in the process to the Triple Word Score on the left-hand side of the board. And I remembered how, seeing that, and congratulating her, I had known the game was lost, and I wanted to burst out laughing now and cover Mother's poor face with kisses and tell her how much I loved the way she had really, really wanted to win at Scrabble, the same way little children really want to win at games, she was so competitive, while I, in the end, could never care tuppence about Scrabble, even though it was a game of words, and words were supposed to be my thing. I never gave a damn about a Triple Letter Score.

Then the clergyman was gone and I was exhausted. I hadn't even raised my head to say goodbye to him; he was outside in the corridor speaking in low tones to my sister. Tears were running down my cheeks; the whole affair, the clergyman's visit, had shattered me – why hadn't he given Mother the communion; was she beyond it already, or were the last rites a high-church thing he had thought better of, in my sister's low-church presence? – and as soon as he was really gone and my sister came back into the room, I stood and embraced her and held her tight, and I was trembling, as if I hadn't seen her for years.

Pulling away, my sister said, 'Well, this is it, Bro. We have it to do.'

XIII

The notice on the wall opposite Mother's bed said, 'Visitors are warned that all doors, including patio doors, will be closed and locked before 10 p.m. in order that the security system can be turned on for the night.' In the event, I was out of the Claygate Hospice well before that hour. My son drove me to Heathrow, where at airport Security they again questioned me over Dr Sharp's anal-massage tool. At the boarding gate I spoke on the phone to David. During the flight I rewrote the presentation I was to give in Berlin, a task I then completed in poor light at the hotel in Görlitzerstrasse. So it was only towards midnight, laying my head on the pillow after a sweet exchange of messages with Elsa, that I began to sense the enormity of the mistake I had made: I should have sat a while with Mother, after she had gone.

Absurd ideas passed through my mind in my Berlin hotel room that night – the night after the night in the hospice: the duty to protect the soul in the moment it leaves the body, the duty of a son towards his dead mother and her departing spirit. I knew these ideas were mad; nevertheless they carried enormous weight as I lay in my German hotel bed covered by a quilt I feared would soon become oppressively hot. 'All our emotions are an accident of evolution,' my son had explained, as we drove through heavy traffic to Heathrow. An unforeseen consequence, he thought, of the opposable thumb and the growing human ability to manipulate the world. On becoming able to shape things, primitive man had been faced with the need to make pondered decisions: *whether* to shape something, *how* to shape it. I said I was sorry, but I had lost him. I didn't understand. The need for decision-making early on in modern man's evolution had fostered thought, he said, and speculation: if I shape a thing this way, that result will follow. And this habit of speculation had got mixed up with man's animal instincts, to produce complex emotions of a kind animals didn't experience. 'But in evolutionary terms,' he concluded, 'we actually have no need for all these mixed-up feelings. They're really no use to anyone, Dad.'

Was he trying to help me, I wondered?

'So all our sorrows are meaningless?' I asked him. 'Not to mention the joys.'

'Well,' he hesitated, 'not to the person feeling those emotions, of course. They mean something, to you.'

Five hours later, in the hotel on Görlitzerstrasse, I realised that because I had not sat beside my mother's corpse for the hour or so after her death – or maybe just a few minutes would have been enough – I would have to go back to London as soon as my inaugural address was over. I could not stay for the rest of the conference. Of course I had been looking forward to getting back to Elsa, I needed Elsa, Elsa was the future, I was only happy, I only felt myself – my new self, that is – when I was with Elsa; instead I would have to go back to London, back to the past.

Lying in bed in that four-star German hotel, I imagined myself already in London again and sitting beside my mother's corpse, wherever it was, wherever they were keeping her, and saying sorry to her for not having sat beside her at the crucial moment when the body died and the soul must take flight to meet its Maker. And all this despite my rather brilliant – I say it myself – rewriting of the Berlin conference, my inaugural address, I mean, on the flight from Heathrow to Tegel, in the wake of all that had passed through my head that long day of my mother's dying, above all my sudden understanding of the reasons why I had begun to hum the hymn, the baptismal hymn, *In token that thou shalt not blush, to glory in His name.*

'We have it to do,' my sister said when the odious Reverend Paddy was gone.

I understood at once what my sister meant: dying was a job, a kind of test or exam even, and we had to get on with it. Mum had to get on with it. The 'we' included my mother. My sister did not seem unhappy with the prospect. It's always good to roll up your sleeves and get a job done.

'We're here now, Mum,' she told my mother, who showed no sign of response. Occasionally her forehead tensed, as if to suggest she too was doing her bit, or her breast lifted sharply with a deeper breath, as if the work were harder than she had imagined.

'Do you like that clergyman?' I asked my sister after a while.

She was sitting on the other side of the bed, holding Mother's other hand, and this positioning suddenly seemed to me emblematic of the relationship between my sister and myself. We only really met through my mother and, when we did so, my sister was invariably on one side and I invariably on the other. From the moment I had lost my faith, in my mid-teens, or rather the moment I openly declared, in my late teens, that I had no faith, my mother had not wanted my sister and me to meet much, had not wanted me, I think, to contaminate her, for my mother doubtless viewed my sister as the weaker of the two, the one most likely to give way.

'The guy annoyed me,' I told her. 'He seemed fake.'

'Oh,' she said, 'Patrick' – or perhaps she said Peter, or Philip – 'is okay. It's just he's high-church. You know what they're like. They have to put on a show.' She smiled as if at another's forgivable foibles.

I asked why on earth Mum had started going to a high-church place in her eighties, and my sister explained that this had happened around the time Mum had given up driving. It was her only church within walking distance.

'He's all right,' my sister repeated. 'Just a bit full of himself. He's young.'

Mid-forties, I thought. Mid-forties was young for my sister and myself now. We were forgiving people because they were in their mid-forties.

Uncle Harry arrived. My mother's brother. He walked with a stick. He had recently lost his wife. No sooner had he seen the state Mother was in than he began to cry. 'Are you going too, Martha?' he asked. He bent over her. His voice quavered softly. 'Are you leaving me, my dear?' He shook his head from side to side. 'She was quite talkative yesterday,' he protested. 'We had a good talk yesterday, didn't we, Martha?'

The old man's tears seemed to stiffen my sister's resolve to do her quiet duty by my mother, to stay calm and see her through without a fuss. There was a remarkable steadfastness, I thought, on my sister's face. Perhaps I had underestimated her. Somewhere between grimness and ecstasy. And it occurred to me I really had no idea what my mother meant, for my sister, or what Mother's dying would mean for her. Perhaps I had no idea what it meant for me.

I gave my chair to Uncle Harry and went out to get a coffee. In the Commemoration Room there was a tin with home-made cake. Free for everyone. How English. I turned the phone on and at once a message arrived from my wife, to say the twins couldn't come because they had a bike race at the weekend; they'd been training for this bike race for months, and what if my mother didn't actually die? What had they said in their email then, I wondered? I still hadn't looked. There was another message from Deborah, to ask if

Charlie was here at the hospice. He had got up and gone out, she wrote, without speaking to her. I didn't reply.

While I was drinking my coffee, my daughter arrived with her man. They were parked illegally, she said; they needed to know where they could park properly. For some reason, unexpectedly, I was absolutely overjoyed to see my daughter, whom I hadn't seen for quite a while. I felt a sudden injection of energy, or as if I were briefly released from the duty of darker thoughts. I gave suggestions to her man for the car, though really I had no idea where he could park; I embraced her, took her by the shoulders, looked her in the eyes. I could feel her young body was full of emotion – 'Poor Granny,' she muttered – and at once I led her down the corridor to my mother's room, feeling, for reasons I couldn't explain, oddly proud: proud of my mother's dying, proud of the work my sister was doing to see her on her way, proud above all of my daughter – our daughter, my wife's and my own – who had appeared like this from her own distant life when drama called. We were a family.

Towards midday my son arrived. My older son. He was tense from the long drive, but came directly to the sickroom. He stood over my mother, tall and blond, and took her hand and greeted her. He said he regretted not coming earlier. His voice was quiet and earnest and very adult. His wife had also come and she stood discreetly behind him. She looked very dark and beautiful. This discreet respectfulness suited her, I thought. I had never seen her like this. I felt proud of both of them. Then my brother-in-law also came in, my sister's husband. He had taken the dogs for a long run in Richmond Park, he explained, so that they could then be left in the van for a while. Everybody in the room agreed how hard it was to park around here. But not impossible. If you were patient. My brother-in-law showed my daughter's man photos of the dogs on his iPad. Photos taken in Richmond Park, he said, an hour before. He loved photographing the dogs and they loved being photographed, he said. They loved the attention. They even stayed still while you took the snap. They understood.

My uncle's son arrived – my cousin, that is – who had been staying with my uncle for a while to see him through his bereavement, the loss of his wife, who was my cousin's mother of course, my aunt, and now the old man was facing a second bereavement, the loss of his sister, my mother. My cousin shook his head and said he had just picked up his second parking ticket in three days. My uncle spoke to my son and described himself as the last man standing. 'The last of the Mohicans,' he said. 'Cheer up, Dad,' my cousin told him.

The brisk nurse brought more chairs. She asked me if we would appreciate a visit from the hospice chaplain. I said no. A clergyman had already been and prayed with Mother, I explained, as if every death required one, but one was enough. Then I took a bathroom break and couldn't decide whether things down there were really getting better or I was just getting used to their awfulness. You need fresh underwear, I told myself.

The hours passed. I had my place at Mother's side again. I wanted everybody to be silent now, but I knew it would be pointless to make that request. Perhaps offensive. My sister and her husband told the others the story of my mother's fall on the stairs and the harrowing weeks that followed, the impossibility of looking after her in their house, her unwillingness to watch television, the difficulty getting her to the bathroom. I could see my sister was ready to feel guilty for not having kept Mother at home to the end and was fighting this guilt by reminding us all how impossible it had been, something none of us doubted for one moment. My son explained that a fall often dislodges a tumour, speeding up a cancer and precipitating events. My daughter remembered that Granny was the only person who had never forgotten her birthday. 'She never missed sending a card and present. Never, never, never.'

As she spoke, the tears began to roll, but she was smiling too. My son laughed and said it was true, 'Gran never forgot', and my cousin, Uncle Harry's son, agreed. Auntie Martha had never forgotten his birthday. 'She really was a stickler for detail,' my uncle said. 'Though the presents she sent,' my son observed, 'were often things like illustrated Bible stories.' 'All in a good cause,' my sister's husband said robustly. 'Remember that holiday when she made us go to Sunday school,' my daughter smiled now. 'The twins went crazy.' It was at that moment that I suddenly understood why I had *In token* on the brain.

There were nine of us, then my sister's elder daughter arrived, and so we were ten. The nurses helped us to arrange more and more chairs around my mother's bed. At a squeeze, there was just room. Everyone greeted my mother on arrival and touched her hand perhaps and shivered at its coldness, and shook their heads at her complexion, if complexion it could be called. There was a sense of occasion. Then they talked softly among themselves, as if there were any danger of waking her up. In particular, my uncle recalled how when their mother, my grandmother, had died very young, Martha, in her early teens, had taken over the care of her two younger brothers. 'So that she was almost like a second mother to me,' my uncle said, his voice breaking up again. And he started saying that their mother, my grandmother, who had died of a burst appendix, was a wonderfully lively woman, a great dancer and dresser, a great hostess, and what a loss it had been to the family, and to Martha in particular perhaps, when she died. A great dancer, I thought. Why had no one ever told me this before? My grandmother danced and my mother did not. Why? Because Mother had had to mother her mother's younger sons perhaps? She didn't have an adolescence. I had never thought of this.

There were ten of us seated round the bed, all turned towards the dying woman, but talking sideways among ourselves, or face to face across the bed, talking – though I wasn't talking at all – about the person on the bed, mother sister grandmother aunt, who was now excluded, yet still the centre of everything. Occasionally the nurse came in and checked her drips and drug pump and felt her pulse and went out again, and I realised that the reason I was humming the baptismal hymn, silently now, was that this had been Mother's supreme gesture in my regard. My parents' supreme gesture towards each of their children had been exactly this: to print the cross upon our brows. To stamp us for His own.

Rather bizarrely, as the minutes passed and my mother went on with her dying, I began to imagine my own baptism service. Babies should be baptised at the earliest possible age, my father always insisted. They should be brought to church, Father said, to receive the sign of the cross absolutely the first Sunday of their lives, or if not the first, the second; and if not the second, then very definitely the third, which was a kind of last-ditch. How extraordinary that these conversations should be so present now, beside my dying mother. This would have been in Manchester, 1956, in a church soon to be demolished, when they discovered dry rot had eaten up the foundations. The structure was unsafe. Baptism was an outward manifestation of inward grace, my father would say in his baptismal sermon. Father loved these vaguely intellectual, vaguely mysterious formulations. It seemed the church might fall down on us all at any minute. And he loved to take tiny babies in his robed arms in the midst of his congregation – his folk, he called them – gathered around the font. Years later, as a choirboy, I would watch him as he reached out to anxious mothers to take their babies and welcome them into the Church. The more a baby yelled and squirmed, the more my father enjoyed it. The sacrament, he said in his baptismal sermon, redeems the child from his original sin; God grants his ordained clergymen the power to transmit this grace. And the grace is transmitted, my father said, even if the clergyman himself is not in a state of grace. My father would always emphasise this, as if to suggest that no one need enquire into his character to check the efficacy of the ceremony; as an ordained Anglican clergyman, all he need do was take the child in his arms, speak the formula, make the sign with the holy water and the original sin would be washed away. One hundred per cent guaranteed. The automatic nature of the transaction seemed to be part of my father's pleasure in it. It was a trick that could not fail.

And perhaps my father's happiness in administering the sacrament did transmit itself to the squalling child, for as my mother never failed to observe over the lunch table afterwards, passing the Yorkshire pud perhaps, or the Brussels sprouts, to one of the lonely spinsters or bereaved unfortunates who were always invited to the Sanders' Sunday lunches, no sooner had my father dipped his finger in the water of the font and made the sign of the cross upon the infant's downy brow than the child would fall silent, would cease to squall and squirm, apparently awed by the echo of Father's voice in the musty church and the cool splash of the water from the old stone font. But my father said this was the redemptive inward grace that automatically followed the outward sign. The child subsided in beatitude.

So very likely, that is how it was for me: the congregation gathered themselves together round the font in the back corner of a damp neo-Gothic nave, my mother handed me over, wrapped in a white blanket, and my father fervently intoned the prayer-book prayers he knew by heart:

'Grant, O merciful God, that all carnal affections may die in him and that all things belonging to the spirit may live and grow in him.'

All carnal affections were to die! In a child of ten days old. All spiritual things were to flourish. Outward and inward, inward and outward. My father loved that opposition. The inward was always superior. The outward never more than a sign, or husk.

'Grant, O Lord, that he may have power and strength to triumph against the devil and the world and the flesh.'

So from the earliest age, I thought, sitting by my mother's bed while my uncle was now explaining how his wife had passed away quite suddenly, while watching *Come Dancing*, my sister, my brother and I had been introduced into a world of ferocious opposites where the inward must always triumph over the outward, the spirit over the flesh, God over the devil. And while for other babies these prayers were the merest formal mumblings, no sooner heard than forgotten, or perhaps never even really heard – the watery cross washed off in the bathtub that same evening, to the tune maybe of 'Baa Baa Black Sheep' or 'Old MacDonald', while a happy mother lathered her child under the armpits and between the legs, and the child wriggled in delight for the sheer pleasure of mummy's soapy hand on those delicate parts – in our house this wasn't the case. In our house baptismal words and water sank into infant skin like acid. We blazon, we print, we stamp, we seal. All the long morning of my mother's dying I was silently humming the baptismal hymn, repeatedly imagining my mother passing my tiny body to my father, and my father dipping me down towards the font, as I would later see him doing with scores of other babies, and signing my forehead with the sign of the cross, grafting the Old Adam – Father loved these mysterious formulas – into the body of Christ's Church, introducing me, in short, into a world where desire and will would always be in conflict.

My parents had generated their children, I reflected, watching Mother's chest rise very slightly, and very slightly fall, not out of carnal desire, not for their own benefit and certainly not for our ours, but to be soldiers for Christ, Christ's quarrel to maintain; to be servants of the project that had united them ever since they met in missionary college. They were a couple with a mission. In a way, the mission was the relationship. My sister – I was exchanging glances with her across my mother's body – was unequivocally a soldier for Christ. Beneath his banner manfully. My sister loved the soldierly rhetoric. She saw no problem with a woman being manful. Firm at thy post remain. My sister was happy with the militant Christian life my parents prospected for her. She had remained firm beside her handicapped child. My brother and I were deserters. The men of the family were not manful. We had not fought the good fight. We had not stayed at our posts. The baptismal hymn, I thought, whose tune I had always loved to sing – even as a choirboy I relished the fricatives of *thou shalt not flinch* – was a grotesque prison of rhyme and rhythm, a grotesque appropriation of minds too young to understand the spell they were falling under. And as midday passed and my mother drew each breath with a little more labour than the one before, it occurred to me I now had the subject for a much better conference in Berlin: archaism as entrapment. Mother's dying had given me a much better idea for the conference that she was preventing me from going to.

A nurse tapped my shoulder. 'Mr Sanders, there is somebody in the foyer to see you.'

We ate lunch in the Green Man in two shifts. First my sister, her husband and daughter, together with Uncle Harry, then, when they came back, myself, the two children with their two partners, and my cousin. Needless to say, the person in the foyer was Charlie. He was fretting in a dark duffel coat, hands thrust in his pockets, and even before I got close he was telling me not to worry, he would not keep me.

'Phone this number,' he said and placed a folded yellow Post-it in my hand.

'Why, who is it?'

Charlie shook his head. He pushed his hands back in his pockets, glaring at me. Then turned to go.

'You know,' I called after him, 'your mum says you're not gay.'

'I know,' he replied over his shoulder. 'Think about it.'

Returning to my mother's room, I decided it really was imperative now to call the conference organisers in Berlin. However, the phone number was on my computer, which was in my bag upstairs; also this idea of picking apart the baptismal hymn in the inaugural address of a major international conference on linguistics and rhetoric was exhilarating. It had cheered me up. The call could wait another hour or two.

'Why don't you guys go and eat something?' I told my sister and her husband. And I added, 'We'll hold the fort.' Another of Mum's expressions.

An hour later, in the pub, my cousin started to tell my children and their partners what it was like to live in Belfast. I hadn't planned to drink at all, but while my son and I were parking his car, the others had already got in a pint of Pride and an order of gammon and chips for everyone. The city was deeply divided, my cousin was explaining to my daughter as I lifted my glass, but at the same time life was actually very normal and even dull. As he spoke I watched my children, whom I hadn't properly spoken to for some months. I hadn't spoken to anyone in the family for many months. It was a sort of permanent truce, my cousin was saying. My daughter sat with her hands linked over her partner's wrist. He was a large, beefy boy with forthright opinions, immediately asking my cousin about the Protestant parades. Shouldn't they be banned? At a break in the conversation I told the story my mother had always told, that when as a child the family visited her grandfather's farm in County Longford, on Sunday morning, as the Protestants headed for their church at one end of the village and the Catholics for theirs at the other, the men and women of differing denominations would spit on the ground as they passed each other. In all other circumstances, and this was the thing that always fascinated my mother, people were perfectly polite to each other. Only religion divided them. I laughed and saw my son turn to his partner across the table and whisper something into the softness of her neck. And his young wife smiled happily as he whispered and nudged her cheek to brush against his lips. They are in love, I thought, as the gammon steak arrived.

No one mentioned my mother as we ate. Nor did my children mention their mother or ask me awkward questions about my present life. This was the advantage, I thought, of having my cousin with us, talking about how well Belfast was served with parks and public transport. My mother and the Christian ethos she passed on to me, I thought, slicing the pink gammon, had certainly delayed my leaving their mother, my wife. And the children too; the children had also delayed my going. Or rather, not the children themselves, they hadn't done anything, but the idea I had of the children as creatures to be protected at all costs had made it seem important to remain firm at my post, manfully, for as long as possible, a great cross stamped on my brow. David, I thought, had manfully opted for remaining at his post, his cross, when he finally decided to marry Deborah after all those years. Perhaps he did it for the children, even though they were grown-up. Who knows? Perhaps he sensed how Charlie disapproved of his philandering. Or he worried that his son's sexual orientation was to do with his own constant unfaithfulness. David was constant in his inconstancy, I smiled to myself. But he had definitely done the right thing, I thought now, when he decided to remain at his post and marry Deborah. That was the only decision that made sense. In my own case, though, it had been precisely my children's romances that made it impossible to remain. One stays in a loveless relationship for one's children, and then one's children's love relationships remind one what love is. And it becomes impossible. Unless of course one could love one's wife again. 'Señor Sanders,' my shrink lit another menthol cigarette, *'por favor!'*

'Earth to Dad?'

It was my daughter.

'Thinking of Gran?' my son asked sympathetically.

There seemed no point in not saying yes. At the same time an inner voice ordered me, Phone Elsa. You must speak to Elsa at the earliest possible opportunity. That a love should be. Excusing myself for needing a pee, which for once I didn't, I walked round the bar towards the bathroom and phoned from an alcove.

'Elsa, I love you.'

The signal was surprisingly good. She was in the university canteen. 'Tommy! I love you too.'

My daughter-in-law crossed the bar on her way to the bathroom and saw me phoning in the alcove. She smiled.

'When I'm away from you I feel scared.'

A beep told me someone else was trying to call.

'But scared of what?' Elsa asked.

'I don't know. That it's not real somehow. Us.'

'You're just upset about your mother, Tommy.'

'I'll have to cancel the conference in Berlin,' I told her. 'I should have done it already.'

'Do you want me to do it for you? Just give me a number or email.'

Suddenly, my cousin came running round the bar, phone in hand. 'She's going!' he said. 'We have to get back.' His father had called, Uncle Harry. 'The nurses say this is it.' I closed the call.

It was two-thirty. Mother died towards five. Sitting down by her bed again, I felt dazed from the pint of Pride and the hurriedly eaten gammon steak. Mother's breathing had slackened. Her face had smoothed. Her body lay absolutely still. Her pulse was fading, the nurse said. It was there, but fading. Likewise the winter light, filtering in from the patio. It bled from the room. Through the window the birdbath faded from pink to grey. The conversation dwindled, like embers greying. Occasionally it sparked. Someone said a word or two. The food in the pub had been pretty good, hadn't it? I hope the dogs aren't taking the van apart. Then the silence came deeper than before.

Sensing the drama of the end, people had started to lean forward from their seats to catch the sound of Mother's breathing as it came and went, now faint, now stronger again, but always fainter still when again it fell away, fainter and fainter as her forehead became smoother and smoother. Everyone in the room was focused on this breathing. Everyone was leaning forward from his or her seat. I needed to go to the bathroom and did not go. I needed to phone the conference organisers and did not phone. Every ten minutes or so the nurse came in, a new nurse now, young and plain and neutral; she threaded her way through the chairs, bent over my mother a moment, felt her pulse, looked at us all leaning slightly forward from our chairs, listening for the next breath, smiled faintly and went out again.

My son sat stiller than I imagined he ever could. The tip of my daughter's tongue poked between her lips, as it had when she did her homework as a child. I was profoundly glad my children had come. I felt comforted by their presence. I was relieved they hadn't asked anything about my present life. I was relieved they hadn't seen my mother vomit, hadn't heard her speaking without her false teeth. Messages vibrated on my phone, but I did not check them. I would have been ashamed to check them, ashamed to be seen to be checking text messages while my mother really was dying now, before my eyes. Not that I didn't feel an urge to check them, but the shame that would have followed stopped me. Uncle Harry's head was tilted to one side, cocked like an old dog's waiting for a caress, or a command that wouldn't come. An occasional tear rolled down his grey cheek, but he did not speak. No one spoke. From time to time my sister's eyes met mine across our mother's expiring body, or rather across the mauve blanket that was covering that body. She raised her eyebrows and sighed, communicating I wasn't sure what. She seemed solemn but also unworried, untroubled. Mother is holding our attention for the last time, Bro; was that what she was saying? Just stay firm at your post, Bro. Manfully. Just a little longer. Then, perhaps the second or third time my sister looked at me like this, I relaxed. It was quite a sudden thing. I breathed deeply and all at once felt the muscles relax, in my face and jaw, in my shoulders and thighs. There was a definite letting go. It was my old sis did this for me, I realised, with her calm, oddly businesslike presence, her sense that we were doing a job together. I relaxed with her into my mother's dying. In token, stopped stamping and printing and blazoning the baptismal cross in my brain. I stopped worrying about the conference. You can go now, Mum, I thought. We're beside you.

So, for almost two hours, we focused on Martha Sanders's dying. I cannot recall ever being with people, family particularly, thus quietly focused, enchanted even by the phenomenon of fading breath. And now it did seem there was something beautiful in the room; not Mother, not us, but this twilight togetherness of the living and the dying, these long suspensions between one breath and another. The long silences. Sometimes it seemed impossible another breath could come after such long silence. But come it did, with the faintest rising of the mauve blanket. And every breath of hers was an awareness we all shared, a shared relief in her still breathing and a shared disappointment of drama deferred. As when a parting must happen, yet is unthinkable. You say goodbye, but turn back. You breathe again. And my sister gently shook her head, shook her pink permed hair, with its faint green highlights, and looked at me with a knowing wonderment in her eyes, communicating something I could never have put in words, and I for my part found myself thinking how natural all this was, yes, how *natural*, simple, simply physical, and anyway utterly unlike the tormented spiritual battle my parents had always prospected. Mother was dying simply, physically, naturally dying. Without melodrama. No angels or demons were tussling over her immortal soul. An old lady was nearing her end. In Claygate Hospice. Her clay at the open gate. A dying animal. Breathing her last. Mum is breathing her last, I muttered. The old expression made sense, intensely. Lastness was in the hospice air. Mum was breathing it. We all were. And this calmness we shared, the calmness of Mother's dying, had entirely stilled my need to go to the bathroom, stilled it or frozen it, anyway made it bearable, as we all sat in the near-darkness now, waiting and waiting for the next soft breath that didn't come and still didn't come and perhaps would never come again, it seemed; and then the nurse walked into the room, threaded her way between the chairs, raised mother's wrist, paused, held the limp wrist, feeling and waiting, still paused, face intent, lips pursed, and said, 'She's gone.'

Then the light was on and people were on their feet, and now I badly needed to get to the bathroom, really badly. It was three hours since the beer. I would kiss my mother goodbye, after I had been. 'Can you speak, mate?' David had texted. I pulled my phone out in the loo. 'Call when you're free,' Deborah had texted. 'Do you know where the spare set of keys is?' Elsa had texted. 'I'm locked out.' And standing over the bowl then, phone in my left hand, it occurred to me I could still make it to Berlin tonight. It was only fiveish. I could still make it. And I wondered, Why should I let them down, since Mum was gone now? There was nothing I could do for her. It was almost as if she had timed it on purpose so that I could go to Berlin after all and talk about the baptismal hymn. She didn't want to disturb, didn't want to force me to cancel. Mother's old obsession with never disturbing. I smiled. A disturbing obsession. Certainly it would be a major disturbance for the organisers, if I cancelled now, I thought. Two hundred people were expected. It was the inaugural address, a plenary session. I too have an obsession with never disturbing. Why should I disappoint them, I wondered, when it was all done and dusted here, when Mother had explicitly appointed my brother-in-law as the executor of her will, explicitly preferred the manful Christian who was always at his post to the agnostic son so often absent? Why shouldn't I go to Berlin, when the person handling all the practical details would be my sister, obviously? Even if I stayed, was it likely my sister would defer to me in practical matters like the washing and dressing of Mother's body? And if I was going to cancel, shouldn't I have done so hours before? Stepping out of the loo, I felt purposeful and liberated.

In the corridor my son was coming towards me. 'I guess we'll be off now, Dad,' he said. His wife had to be up at the crack of dawn, he explained, for her own nursing work. They had a long drive ahead of them. 'Take me to Heathrow,' I told him. 'It's on your way, isn't it? More or less?' Only in the car did it occur to me I had not kissed the corpse. I had not bent over her dear dead face and kissed it goodbye. I had not said anything to her dead body or touched her in any way. 'Spare set with Raul in number 6,' I texted Elsa. 'Mum died at 5.' Checking her iPad, my son's wife told me Lufthansa had a flight at seven-thirty. We bought a ticket online as my son negotiated heavy traffic on the M4. 'All our emotions are an accident of evolution,' he said.

PART TWO

XIV

One of the by-products of human language development, I told the 27th annual gathering of European linguists in Berlin the morning after my mother died, was a heightened awareness of mental activity and consequently a flattering illusion of inner presence and power. Whatever the external reality, we all have the impression that we can think what we wish.

If this was not quite what members of the Society of European Linguists were used to hearing, at least it had made them sit up. It was nine-thirty and the auditorium was packed.

Whereas the truth was, I went on, savouring an excellent PA system, that language was above all an appropriation of the mind on the part of the community. 'We could think, if you like,' I told my fellow linguists, 'of first-language acquisition as a form of baptism, a welcoming into the community, a token of belonging and a cross one has to bear.'

'By all means take a good long look,' I had told the Security lady at Heathrow the evening before. 'In another year or so, these will be all the rage.'

She held the anal-massage tool at arm's length, as if she expected it to smell.

'And what does it do for you, sir?'

My mobile had begun to trill.

'Eases tension,' I said.

'With respect, sir,' the lady handed the instrument back, 'you're not the best advertisement for the product.'

She had seen my hand shake as I fumbled and dropped the phone.

'Because I haven't started using it yet,' I told her. 'Wait until you see me next time.'

She smiled. 'Good luck, sir.'

Deborah asked, 'How's your mother?'

'She died, Deb.'

I was walking through the Duty Free store.

'My God, I'm sorry,' Deborah said.

'At the end it was very peaceful. With all the family round the bed. Like something out of Dickens.'

Was it because there had been so many people at the bedside that it had seemed okay for me to dash off? If I had been there alone, I surely wouldn't have done that.

'I'm glad.' She hesitated. 'Tom, I just called to ask if you'd seen Charlie. The police came to talk to him; it seems they'd given him an appointment, but he didn't show. He isn't answering his phone.'

I told her Charlie had dropped by at the hospice and given me a phone number to ring; immediately Deborah asked what number that was. Whose? Could I give it to her? I fished the Post-it from my back pocket, then changed my mind.

'Sorry, I can't find it right now, Deb. I must have put it in my bag or something. I'll text you later.'

In the departure lounge, snacking at Caffè Nero, I found myself enjoying the thought that I hadn't had to cancel my conference, as if this was an important personal victory, and at the same time a little perturbed by the odd feeling that Mother hadn't actually died either, that the whole dying scene had been a dream; nothing had happened; or as if only my cancelling the conference would have made her death real. Then once again the phone was ringing and this time David's voice asked, 'All right, mate?' which was how David always began phone conversations. 'Condolences over your mum. Debbie just told me.'

'*Que sera, sera,*' I said.

'I read that as cautious optimism,' he observed.

I laughed.

'Aside from which?' he asked. 'It's been a while, hasn't it?'

'Oh, I'm fine,' I told him. 'More than fine.'

'Reaping the fruits of legal laceration?'

'Yep. I'm deliriously happy, if you want to know, Dave, with a charming young lady. But tell me about married life.'

'Way-ay-ayt a minute!' David cried. 'Do I hear crowing on the other end of this line?'

'Cawing,' I confessed. 'I was hoping for a pint, to debrief.'

'Pretty?'

'Beautiful.'

'Hmm, intelligent? Creative, perceptive and, of course, sensitive?'

This was an old routine.

'Are you still in hospital, Dave? How are you doing?'

The PA announced our flight was ready to board. I had to gather my stuff, and the phone left my ear a moment.

'Would be good to see you,' he was saying.

I told him my situation. We could speak after the conference tomorrow.

'That was quick.'

'What?'

'Deathbed to Departures in nine minutes.'

'Not much point hanging around,' I said.

'After the horse has bolted.'

'The chickens hatched.'

'Joking aside, mate,' David said, 'My sympathy.'

'I guess it hasn't sunk in,' I told him. 'But this is a big conference. Society of European Linguists. Inaugural address. Proper money, if nothing else.'

'What else could there be?' he laughed and said he was hoping to be discharged the following morning. 'I'm afraid young Charlie doesn't play Queensberry. He really crocked me up.'

'So your lady wife told me.'

I was feeling in my pockets for my passport.

'Enough of the wife stuff, Tommy. Speaking of *whom*, however' – David knew I was a stickler for 'whom' – 'the dear creature told me Charlie had given you a mysterious number to call.'

'Plus a whack round the chops.'

'Ah. She didn't mention that. Is it bad?'

'Not pretty. He seemed determined to get me involved in your, er, shit.'

'Faeces. Yep, delicately put, Tom. Listen, you couldn't tell me what the number was, could you?'

I hesitated.

'I'd have to look through my bag. I'll text it later.'

'Sure.'

'About Charlie, though. You should get him to a psychiatrist.'

'Couldn't agree more. I've been surfing eBay for straitjackets.'

I laughed.

'To be serious, though, Tommy boy, did you get any idea what his problem is exactly?'

'I thought you would have fathomed that.'

'Sort of yes-and-no-*ish*. I was just interested to hear what you made of it.'

'Well, he seemed upset about your history of extracurricular activities.'

'I'm afraid the boy's been a bit of a nosy parker.'

'He said he'd read some of our old emails.'

'A serious breach of privacy.'

As we spoke I was having a minor passport panic, searching back and forth between the pockets of my jacket, the pockets of my coat and the endless zipped compartments of my disintegrating Samsonite.

'Odd,' Dave was saying, 'when you think how generous we've been, giving him the upstairs flat and everything to share with his little "friend".'

'What I thought was strange, Dave, was that he's so worried about the past now, even after you've made his mother an honest woman, so to speak.'

'He and his ingratitude can go to hell,' David said flatly.

The passport was in the back pocket of my trousers. I felt relieved, but had absolutely no recollection of having put it there.

'You know Deborah told me he wasn't gay.'

'Her reasoning is that if one day the boy should change his mind, it might be better if no one ever knew. Denial, in case the truth changes.'

I shuffled along in the queue, shifting my bag over the floor with my foot.

'Lots of debriefing on both sides,' I said lamely.

'You were always very forgiving to your own little spies, as I recall,' he observed.

'They were rather younger than Charlie, Dave.'

'Still.'

'Maybe I was grateful they forced things to a head.'

I showed my passport.

'Tom, for Christ's sake. A spy is a spy. You would never have separated if they hadn't blown the gaff. Am I right, or am I right?'

'Hard to call.'

The thought that my destiny, and Elsa's, had depended entirely on the twins reading a few text messages was depressing.

'Listen, old mate, whatever number my miserable offspring may or may not have given you, you're not going to call it, right?'

I was walking down the tunnel to the aircraft.

'To be honest, Dave, I haven't had a second to think about it.'

'Spot on, so let me think for you. Don't. And don't give it to Deborah, either. In fact, that most of all. Don't give it to Deborah.'

'Course not.'

'It's a shame, actually, you mentioned his giving you a number at all.'

'Wasn't thinking,' I agreed. 'It's been a heavy day. Woke with a puffed-up face. Mum died. My old peeing problem has returned.'

'Ah, sorry to hear that,' Dave said. 'Punishment for porking Miss Perfect, I suppose.'

'Could be.'

'It'll pass.'

'Everything passes.'

'That optimism again.'

There was the usual huddle of passengers at the plane door. To end the call on a positive note, I said, 'By the way, Dave, about your marrying.'

'Yeeees?'

'Seeing Deb yesterday, I was thinking: you really did the right thing, staying in there. In the end, if you weren't going to split up . . .'

'We might as well go the whole hog.'

'As my dear mother always used to say. Anyway, I feel bad not having made it to the wedding. Sorry about that.'

Entering the plane, phone pressed to my ear, I was suddenly very aware I only had the flight and then a couple of hours in the hotel to rewrite my talk and prepare a decent PowerPoint. If I was going to rewrite it, that is. And in a way, if I was going to Berlin, it was partly because the day beside my dying mother had given me such an electrically eccentric idea to present there.

'Well,' Dave was saying, 'it seemed the right decision at the time. Y'know. Speaking of which, or whom, how's your own other half? Ex-half. I must say, I rather miss the dear girl.'

I said I really didn't know how my wife was. We rarely communicated.

'Thirty years together and you don't know how she is?'

'It's called separation, Dave.'

'Sounds like cruelty to me.'

'You have to be cruel to be cruel, as someone we know once said.'

David chuckled. 'Let's have a pint soonest, Tombolino.' He coughed and lowered his voice. 'I need you to give me skin, mate. Things are dire, to be honest. This stuff with Charlie has completely thrown me.'

'Will do, Dave.'

Sitting down, I inserted earplugs, brought out my notebook and began work on the talk. Since I had managed to get an aisle seat towards the back of the plane there would be no problem going to the bathroom as often as I wished. For the next two hours, then, while the attendants went through all the pre-flight rigmarole and trolleys of refreshments rattled up and down the aisle, I worked away furiously without ever once thinking about my mother, or about David and Deborah and Charlie, or about my wife, my children, my separation, or even about Elsa. 'Language,' I scribbled off the top of my head, 'has always been fascinated by everything that came before language, everything that lies beyond it, always eager to imagine and possess that unimaginable space, to describe it as brutal and crude, or as noble and sublime – in short, to feel superior or servile. And being supposedly close to that no-language experience, early language is alternatively seen as primitive or pure, the howl or the hallelujah. So archaism suggests a contact with a more intense, natural, spontaneous world. Life was nobler when people said "thou", not "you".'

Earplugs snuggly in place, cruising at 30,000 feet over the North Sea, only hours after my mother breathed her last, I scribbled down these questionable ideas in a notebook and found, as the seatbelts sign came on for our descent, that I had not gone to the bathroom once. I rejoiced. Only later, when my head hit the pillow in Görlitzerstrasse, did I realise I was in the wrong place, the wrong country. I shouldn't have come. I hadn't even kissed my mother goodbye. Why do I never get a single call right?

It was past midnight. I got up and paced back and forth, barefoot on four-star carpeting, between polished black desk and polished black bathroom door. If I didn't sleep, of course, I would make a hash of my talk tomorrow and there would have been no point in my coming at all. So the thing to do, surely, was to give all my attention to the talk until it was over, then head straight back to England to right the wrong I had done by leaving the corpse in such a hurry. Then perhaps I could take one or two key decisions for the future, about Elsa, about my family. My mother's death, it appeared, and it seemed barely credible that she was gone, had altered the landscape; as if my life to date, without my being remotely aware of it, had leaned against my mother, like a shed against a wall, and now it would have to stand alone without this hidden support, though in what way my mother of all people could have been supporting me, living far away as she was, rarely seen and never agreed with, I could not have said. Or as if my existence, at some very deep level, had been anchored by my mother and now was at the mercy of the tide, in need of a new harbour, a new direction; or had been imprisoned by my mother and was now free at last.

It seemed there was no end to 'as if's' and analogies.

Then, at some point during that night in the German hotel, my third night away from Elsa, lying awake in the dark, I became intensely aware that fifty-seven years ago my infant unbaptised naked body had actually physically emerged from my mother's flesh.

This might seem self-evident – what else does the word 'Mother' mean? – yet amazingly I had never actually visualised this defining event until the night after my mother's death and my thought-lessly rapid desertion of her body, a moment when I really should have lingered, should have stayed with her, at least for a few min-utes, perhaps an hour. And what I visualised now – fidgeting under the unpleasantly heavy quilt – was my infant body emerging from Mother's body, not as she had been in 1956, but as she was on the bed of the Claygate Hospice fifty-seven years later. My flesh emerg-ing from Mum's cadaverous flesh. Her breathing her last at the very moment my newborn lips let out their first plaintive yell.

For some time, then, unable to sleep, I couldn't get this grotesque image out of my mind, or the strange, stupefied emotion that came with it, as if the fact of flesh giving birth to flesh were a matter of huge significance that I had never really taken on board, and this despite having witnessed the birth of my own children. I recalled my vivid dreams of the night before, in the guest room of the Claygate Hospice: a grasshopper pushing out of the eye of a toad, bellow-ing cattle spilling into breakers from a storm-tossed ship. Are our dreams also accidents of evolution, I wanted to ask my son? How self-assured he had seemed, how knowledgeable! Fifty-seven years ago I had emerged from my mother's belly, her last child. Days later, as if to keep me bound to her, I had been baptised with the sign of the cross. Why a grasshopper from a toad? Why through the eye? Twenty-five years after that, my father had performed the ceremony that bound me to my wife. This time the token was a ring slipped onto my finger. Outward sign of inward fetters. Those whom God hath brought together, let no man put asunder.

These disquieting thoughts raced through my head in the Görlitzerstrasse hotel on the night after my mother's death, and this despite all my efforts to concentrate on my inaugural conference speech the following morning. At some point towards dawn, waiting to pee and observing myself in the bathroom mirror, I imagined that words themselves were insects in cerebral slime, thoughts were maggots crawling in my brain. The slimy grey matter of my brain was crawling with noisy word-insects and fat white thought-maggots. Only minutes later, it seemed the alarm was waking me at seven-thirty to give me time to go over my conference paper at breakfast. I took a shower and felt surprisingly resilient and good to go.

XV

The conference in Berlin could not have been more different from the conference in Amersfoort. In Amersfoort a group of people had got together to see how they could help other people who suffered from Chronic Pelvic Pain Syndrome. They told embarrassing personal stories or they put themselves on the line, allowing their own pelvic floor to be explored through the anus, or exploring the pelvic floor of others, through the anus. A lot of rubber gloves were used, a lot of lubricant. Participants came away with a heightened awareness of their flesh. They were in the quick of life, groping into blood and bone. At that conference I had but a small walk-on part, as one who has suffered and survived, apparently. And all was paid for by the participants themselves, who wished to improve the service they were offering to their clients.

The 27th Annual Conference of the Society of European Linguists was funded by the European Community. Its participants were all salaried professors from European universities. They delivered papers in order to publish them in the conference proceedings, so as to accumulate points that would improve their chances of promotion, increasing their salaries and hence their pensions. They talked about the semantics of unaccusatives, about metonymy and metaphor in the evolution of phrasal verbs, about datives versus nominatives in early Icelandic, about comparative auxiliary distribution in Germanic and Romance languages.

In short, nothing could have been further from the world of the Amersfoort conference, or indeed from the Claygate Hospice where my mother had vomited blood and breathed her last. I was back in my normal environment. All the same, there was no doubt in my mind that it was because I had spent such a large part of my life in the abstractions of diachronic and synchronic linguistics that I had ended up with the kind of abdominal condition that required anal massage – or at least Dr Sharp thought it did. It was the abstracted, cerebral, mental space I moved in that had left my body so dramatically uncared for. Add to that a marriage which neither partner wished to admit wasn't working, and you have the perfect pathogenic situation: a live, flesh-and-blood human male, full of spit and spunk, who has been ordered from the earliest age to put aside all carnal affections, even though he knows he cannot put them aside, and to cultivate all things of the spirit, even though he never really believed there was any such thing as the spirit. 'Spirit is an invented word to cover an invented space,' I told my colleagues at the 27th conference of European Linguists. 'Beginning as the innocuous *spiritus* breath, something absolutely verifiable and physical, observable at any deathbed, for example, or at any childbirth, the word morphed into the metaphysical, vaguely archaic *spirit*: a hypothesis, a hope, a nothing.'

Why had this happened, I asked? To satisfy a craving for profundity, but also for separation from the contingent world, something that went hand-in-hand with the enhanced inwardness that language had produced. An accident of evolution. You evolved language to make the species more efficient and ended up with something you absolutely hadn't bargained for – this nonsense of the spirit, this nonsense of renunciation of carnal affection, angels, devils, whatever. 'The role allotted to archaism then,' I confidently declared – and I don't doubt my academic colleagues were quite astonished to hear me making such unsubstantiated and impassioned claims – 'was that of providing the illusion of a more profound and meaningful space where quite simply there was none.'

At this point I projected the first verse of the great baptismal hymn on a PowerPoint slide, typed in Victorian Gothic to get people in the mood. I would have sung it too, had I had the nerve:

> *In token that thou shalt not fear*
> *Christ crucified to own,*
> *We print the cross upon thee here,*
> *And stamp thee His alone.*

As a child singing this hymn, I confessed to my learned audience, I had had no idea what a token was, or what 'in token' meant. Sometimes perhaps I had got 'token' mixed up with 'totem', which was not as unreasonable as it sounds; the whole dynamic of the text was one of substitution: as a sign of something I want to occur in an invisible world, I draw a symbol in the visible world, a cross on a newborn's forehead, and to this sign – and, indeed, to this whole murky apparatus of appropriation – archaisms cluster and attach themselves like iron filings around a magnet.

'The mystification of baptism, and indeed of all religious ceremonies,' I told the European Linguists, 'is only made possible by language, preferably old language. In fact as the hymn progresses, the simple outward sign of the baptismal cross is surrounded by expressions whose exact referents largely elude us: 'to glory in His name'; 'to blazon on thy front'; 'to sit thee down on high'. What do these things mean? Archaisms,' I suggested to my colleagues, 'create gravity where there is only wishful thinking, nouns where there are only adjectives. Even to call it thinking was wishful.'

I was aware, as I began this talk in the plush lecture hall of the Friedrich Schlegel Conference Centre, Berlin, that I had not had the proper time to prepare it, and that very likely it would come across as superficial and forced. I was aware that three-quarters of my audience were not themselves native speakers of English – perhaps five-sixths, to be more accurate – and hence might not grasp the nuances of the baptismal hymn. I was aware too that many colleagues would have their laptops open and would hardly be listening to what I was saying, since while it is always politic to be present at these conferences, there is no real onus on anyone to pay attention. And the more I got into my subject, focusing on the relation between archaism and belonging, archaism and coercion, the more I was aware that I had simply fallen into the trap of ranting about my own personal issues, while at the same time, oddly, actually avoiding these issues, in that I was ranting rather than confronting them.

Hence it was somewhat to my surprise when, at the end of this mad sermon, I received three whole minutes of solid and enthusiastic applause. Two or three of my colleagues actually stood up, shook the dust off their baggy sweaters and applauded. What exactly I had said at the end of it all I wasn't even sure myself, and had the whole talk been read back to me, I would very likely have winced. Yet it had gone down well with a qualified audience, perhaps more for its entertainment value than any academic worth, or for the pleasure of having seen a colleague expose his own weaknesses so embarrassingly. In any event, the morning's chairman stood and beamed and declared that never had the relevance of linguists in the modern world been more forcibly put. He even offered me his hand, something I can't recall happening at a conference before. I sat down in a sweat.

In bed the night before, in the Görlitzerstrasse, I had promised myself I would leave the conference and return to England as soon as my talk was over. But even as the applause died down, it was evident that I could not do this. I could not simply stand up and go. It was one of those situations where all four speakers of the morning session were sitting on the podium together, and would take questions together at the end of the session. If I wasn't to be extremely rude, I must stay put and listen to three other talks, each half an hour long, then make some kind of contribution to the debate at the end. I should have foreseen this. Already the next speaker was being introduced in the usual fulsome fashion: this milestone publication, that prize, the other prestigious appointment, etc., etc.

So I would leave the conference at lunchtime, I decided. Officially, of course, I was supposed to be here the full two days, listening to my colleagues' papers and offering my penny's worth in the discussions, particularly the final round table. An inaugural speaker is expected to make himself available. That's why he is well paid. Then there would be the conference dinner. My flight to Madrid was not until the morning after that. But staying two days was out of the question. I had to get back to London. As soon as this morning's session was over, I would invent some excuse.

The present speaker, meanwhile, a feisty eighty-year-old in bright-red pullover and grey tie, was discussing hieroglyphs in Mesopotamian cultures. Each culture in the Euphrates valley borrowed freely from the others, he said, as far as languages and writing systems were concerned, over a period of many centuries. He wore spectacles on a string that he kept putting on and taking off. I could get Elsa to phone me, I thought, when we were all at lunch together, and pretend I was being called away for some family emergency. The question was – the speaker removed his spectacles to look at the audience – did writers of hieroglyphs distinguish between signs that were new and signs that were old, and did they introduce old signs among the new for certain rhetorical effects that went beyond the symbol's immediate referent? What excuse, I wondered, would be most credible? For example, the elderly speaker replaced his spectacles, after the Mesopotamians moved from carving in stone to carving in clay, a process that rather altered the shape of certain glyphs, did they occasionally resurrect the shapes of the older glyphs in the way a writer in later centuries might deploy an archaism? I could hardly, I thought, say that my mother had died yesterday, since then people would wonder why I was here at all. Who is it sets off to a conference the very second his mother has died?

The talk on Mesopotamia was actually more interesting than I had expected, though it was crazy, I thought now, that my colleague's PowerPoint slides showed only old photographs of the archaeologists and linguists who had found and deciphered the Mesopotamian glyphs decades before, many of them the speaker's own teachers and colleagues. Why not show the glyphs themselves, and the difference between the old and the new? These photographs are ridiculous, I thought, twisting my neck to look at the screen behind the podium. They were all men, all old, all bearded. What were the students who had been co-opted for the occasion supposed to make of this? For of course to give the impression that the conference was well attended and had aroused lively interest, something the sponsors would want to be reassured of in a perfunctory kind of way, a number of students – most of them young, most of them women, as in all liberal-arts courses these days – had been diverted from their regular university classes and were sitting patiently at the back of the auditorium. What were these young women supposed to think, I wondered, of a set of PowerPoint slides showing black-and-white photographs of ageing male linguists with beards and pipes? Why not show the glyphs? These slides were themselves a kind of archaism, I suddenly realised, lending a romantic and chauvinist aura to a period of research and discovery long over. What could the young female students conclude, but that there was no place for them in the worlds of archaeology and linguistics; and what excuse should I give my hosts, who to tell the truth had welcomed me very warmly, for leaving the conference when it had barely begun? Elsa would call, I would respond at table, sitting beside my colleagues in the conference-hall refectory. Andreas Leitner, the chairman of the European Society, a nice, avuncular, rather sleazy fellow, had specifically asked me to have lunch with him. Elsa would hang up, as I had told her to. We had done this before. And I would continue to speak to the silent phone, as if in urgent conversation with someone requesting my immediate departure. Leitner would look at me, raising a bushy eyebrow. But for what reason? I didn't want to invent an illness for one of the children, if only out of fear that such lies might bring bad luck. Did I really fear that? I don't know. Bringing in the children just seemed beyond the pale.

Mr Mesopotamia, meanwhile, had sat down amid tepid applause and now a petite young woman, Elsa's age maybe, or not much older, was talking about a corpus linguistics project which involved counting the archaisms in *Don Quixote* and in translations of *Don Quixote* in a dozen languages, including Russian and Mandarin Chinese. One day you sit beside your dying mother in a state of great emotional intensity, I thought, and the next you are obliged to listen to this kind of silliness.

What excuse could I give for leaving the conference?

Sitting behind the podium, while this young woman in a white blouse and green cardigan showed batteries of statistics on the mean distribution of archaisms in Czech and Japanese translations of *Don Quixote*, I began to feel seriously trapped. This happens to me all too often at conferences, as it happened to me as a child in church listening to my father's sermons. One feels one has lost control of the present moment, that life is slipping away.

Automatically, I did what I always do in these circumstances: I pretended to take notes. As a child in church I pretended to pray, and as an adult at conferences I pretend to take notes. There you are.

'*Dear Elsa,*' I wrote. Each sheet of notepaper had the logo of the Society of European Linguists in the centre at the top. '*I have been* *remembering when we first kissed at that seedy bar off Calle Mayor. What a strange evening it was! First the casual meeting on the stairs by the library, then the beer in the open market. My idea. Then my surprise when you suggested we move on to La Latina. Or rather, you said, If we're going to have a drink, we should go somewhere nice next time. And I said, Why not go now? And you looked at your watch and thought a bit and then said, Okay. A couple of hours later, halfway down the steps into the metro, I proposed a whisky. Because you'd said earlier you'd never drunk whisky. You said okay. And right at the moment that you drained your first whisky, I kissed you. I had been meaning to kiss you for a long time of course, but I also thought of this meaning to kiss you as an aberration that any sensible man my age would soon get over. I did everything to suppress that urge to kiss, yet still found, despite myself, that I really did mean to kiss you. I had come to think of you, I suppose, over the two or three years we had known each other, as somehow, possibly, the <u>right</u> person, though any relation-ship between us seemed improbable and even incongruous. Yet I felt that. Impossible, incongruous, but right. Then that evening there was a growing warmth – no doubt the alcohol helped – and I kissed you. And you returned the kiss with a heat I couldn't have expected. Madly, it seemed to me. Not your usual composed self, Elsa! Our lips touched and you were transformed. You sprang into life. And between kisses, as we decided to walk one metro stop across the park – remember? – you began to say that this should never have happened. This is a disaster, you said. We should never have allowed this to happen. You were distraught. We kissed passionately in the street, like teenagers, and between kisses you said, I am not the kind of person who does these things. I can't do this. And I said, You are doing it, Elsa. Rather well, actually. You laughed. We sat on a bench in the park and you were on my knees, things got pretty wild, and then again you said you couldn't do this, it wasn't you, and what if people recognised us? And I said, I want to marry you, Elsa. I actually said that, didn't I? Minutes after the first* *kiss. You laughed. I repeated, Elsa, I really believe you are the person I should marry; and you said I was mad, or very bad, or both, and the whole thing was a catastrophe and you had better be getting home. So we walked to the metro and now your boyfriend started calling you. From Barcelona. He called, you didn't answer, but he kept calling. He called you every evening at bedtime, you said. It was a long-distance relationship of canonical phone calls, regular as clockwork. Liturgical even. He needed to know you had got home safely. You always said goodnight to each other. But only once you were safely home. You were upset, thinking you were not the kind of person who did this sort of thing. You could never hurt anyone, you said. But again we stopped in the park to kiss on another bench and, because it was getting cold now, you let me put my jacket round your shoulders and that was how your phone ended up in my jacket pocket. Then no sooner had you climbed into the metro just before midnight, having categorically refused to come home with me – you just didn't do that kind of thing – than of course the phone started ringing again in my jacket pocket and, when I pulled it out, the screen showed it was your boyfriend. If I had known where you lived, this would have been the perfect excuse to come and see you and bring you the phone and perhaps start kissing again in more comfortable surroundings. But I didn't know where you lived, and I couldn't phone you now because you didn't have your phone. I went home and wrote you an email. But you didn't reply. You weren't online. I couldn't understand why not – it seemed the obvious thing, having lost your phone – and the phone kept ringing and I thought I couldn't turn it off, because then your boyfriend would think you had turned it off so as not to speak to him, while if I left it on, he might just think you'd lost it or put it on silent. I tried to put it on silent myself, but it was not a phone I was familiar with and I couldn't figure it out and didn't want to tamper, so in the end I put the phone in an oven glove in a Tupperware box in the fridge, so as not to have to hear it ringing all night. I remember thinking there was a person who was very upset because of what we had done together, or who would be upset if he knew, but I couldn't feel bad about what we had done; and towards six when I woke and checked the email, you had come online, you couldn't sleep, and you said to meet you immediately, as soon as possible, because if you didn't respond to his calls, he would tell your mother – probably he had already told your mother; his family was friends with your family, and if your mother couldn't contact you, she would immediately call the police, because she too had to speak to you at least once a day and had to feel you were always on the other end of the phone ready to speak to her. I realised there was a whole life, your life, that I had stumbled into and upset. I thought you would never leave that life for me, and I went out and took the metro and found you at Atocha, looking exhausted and fraught, and I gave you the phone almost without a word, certainly without a kiss. You emailed to say you regretted it all, because nothing could ever come of it, and we must act as if nothing had happened, and I said I was immensely glad that what had happened had happened and that I had meant every word I said, but that I would do exactly as you wished. I promised never to mention it again and you wrote back a single word.* Gracias.

Having overrun her time by almost ten minutes, the young lady colleague had now stepped down, and an older female professor in a maroon tailleur had gone to the lectern and was asking the question: When does grammatical correctness become archaism – for example, in the affirmations 'It is I', 'It is he', and so on, as against the present received usage, 'It's me', 'It's him'?

I sat up on hearing this, since the question was an interesting one: when is the old, the correct, the proper, perceived as out of date, as not really correct or proper any more, or too proper; why and what to do about it? The way to develop the argument, I immediately felt, was to show how, as soon as a usage acquires the status of a rule, a propriety, it is at risk of being perceived as old-fashioned, as resisting life, resisting change. Instead, the colleague went on to catalogue examples of correct usages now lapsing into disuse, and she too had a battery of statistics gleaned from a corpus of some ten million words of discursive texts.

I looked at the audience; a number of the students had left, others were whispering together, others still were busy with their phones, though some did seem to be taking serious notes. And I looked at my colleagues, most of whom had long learned to assume an air of professional interest at these occasions, whether out of a genuine sense of duty and respect to the speaker or the merest calculation of personal convenience, I couldn't have said. Perhaps some of them really were interested.

I took it all in at a glance, saw the clock at the back of the room inching towards midday, then went back to my notepad and wondered why on earth I was writing like this to Elsa, on paper, by hand, when no one mails paper to anyone these days. Let alone handwritten. Handwritten letters on paper are as archaic as the assertion 'It is I'. Everything I had written here to Elsa was true and it was rather wonderful to remember it, but it was also true that after Elsa changed her mind and fired her boyfriend and came to live with me, I found there was a part of myself that had always thought she had been right, that this shouldn't have happened between us. I was too old. The future was impossible. People would be highly critical. My children would be shocked. Elsa herself would regret it. I was forcing my ageing body on her, I thought. My decay. My corruption. Things might be fine today, but what about in ten years? We should never have done this.

The happier I was with Elsa – and I was very happy, quietly, calmly happy in a way that was entirely new to me – the more frequently these negative thoughts presented themselves. Now the sudden return of the old peeing problem confirmed all misgivings. Elsa, this is hard, but you must leave me. That is what I ought to be writing to her. I ought to be explaining to this young woman that I didn't have the energy, the vitality, to carry through this relationship. Yet on scribbling down a letter absolutely off the top of my head, while my colleague rather tediously considered the relationship between archaism and syntactical correctness – and it seemed astonishing to me that she didn't field the case of 'whom' (perhaps I could mention it myself, I thought, in the discussion afterwards; perhaps I could offer the classic example 'for whom the bell tolls', where archaism and memento mori are superimposed, as if archaisms *were* mementi mori, of a kind) – on scribbling down a few thoughts, to take my mind off the vast waste of life that every conference is (why had it seemed so important for me to come?), instead of telling Elsa we should split up, I had been writing a love letter, remembering the excitement, the wonder, the huge rush of positive emotion that evening when we first kissed and the barriers fell away between us. We moved from being strangers who happened to meet from time to time to man and woman arm-in-arm. Lovers. I felt Elsa and I were lovers the moment we kissed. At once I said, I could marry you, Elsa, no, I *want* to marry you, and you said we should never have done this, then kissed me all the more passionately, as if something tremendously urgent were at stake, something that just had to be done. That a love should be.

I sat now, at the conference, needing to go to the bathroom, with my pen poised, wondering how I might continue this letter to Elsa, all the time trying to look as if I were taking notes about my colleague's talk on grammatical correctness and archaism. Had something really changed between Elsa and myself over the last forty-eight hours? With my mother's death? Unable to answer that question or go on with the letter, I suddenly had the very strong sensation that I was two people. That was the only way to describe my state of mind. I was two people: one going one way, one another; one in love with Elsa, determined to make this young Spanish woman my destiny, and one still attached to family and children, wife and mother, and my position in that world of family and mother and wife. Which was also the world of my work, of course, in the sense that the colleagues in my field knew about my family, and my family knew about my work, but neither the one nor the other knew about Elsa. And each separate 'I' was attached to a place: the Elsa 'I' to Madrid, where I was now Emeritus Professor, and the other family 'I' to almost everywhere else – all the many cities we had lived in through the years – and of course, to Edinburgh, to London, to Mother. Mother was a place, I suddenly thought, as much as a person. Mother was a planet. A clay planet. She had gravity. But it was not a gravity that included Elsa. Elsa was a comet. A shooting star. It had been a mockery, I thought, to have pronounced Elsa's name in Mother's presence, when Mother was not only unconscious but never likely to become conscious again. It was like a comet passing unseen on a night of thick cloud cover.

The present speaker had now fallen into the error of disparaging and regretting the new usages that had replaced the old, showing an obvious preference for more syntactically elaborate periods and an emotional, and perhaps class, attachment to the supposedly 'correct'. Correct syntax, she said, tended to attract a greater lexical richness. This was a state of affairs she evidently felt was positive, even morally positive. Which amounted, I felt, to a complete misunderstanding of the dynamic that fuses syntax and vocabulary in language. Nothing could be less rich than a dusty embalming of elaborate syntax in the Anglican hymnal. But how could two selves become one, I wondered, still unable to continue this letter, which most likely I would tear up as soon as the conference session was over.

How do two selves become one? I wrote on the same piece of paper, immediately under the word *Gracias. You were two selves, Elsa, when you kissed me passionately, then said it was a disaster. But after that month of silence, when I supposed the romance was over, you showed me*

245

how two can become one. Simple. One self kills the other. You fired your boyfriend, came to my apartment and we made love. He was upset. You were upset. It was a death. But you did it of your own free will. I never asked you to. And from the moment you had done it, you never looked back. So why am I looking back, I wondered? Why do I find it so difficult to go forward? Was it perhaps – I remembered another of Mother's favourite expressions – that I had feet of clay? I wanted to go forward but my feet were stuck in the ground, clay in clay. Or perhaps the ballast in my older life was simply too great; it generated a crippling gravity. It was the ballast made David decide to marry the woman he had already lived with for thirty years, always saying that she was not his woman. Those thirty years with Deborah were David, even if not the whole David. So he killed the other David and married Deborah. But not with the same joy that Elsa killed her other self and turned to me. *Elsa,* I wrote, *you fill my life with joy . . .*

My effusion was interrupted by applause. The syntactically correct lady in the maroon tailleur sat down with an archaic smile. The chair asked the audience for questions. There was a fidgety silence. People were getting hungry. Following a routine etiquette in these cases, the chair framed a question himself to be put to all of us. Most of the words we use, he said, are more or less old. Would any of us care to comment on why some remain current for hundreds of years while others become archaisms, and others again simply fall into disuse and do not have a second life of any kind, not even in Scrabble?

He smiled and said, 'Professor Sanders?', throwing the ball to his inaugural speaker, as good manners demanded.

'I can't answer that question,' I told him. My head was elsewhere. 'There are a thousand reasons why one thing supplants another. Arguably, behind it all there is a dynamic that requires there be a constant process of death and renewal. Perhaps more interesting would be to wonder about the tensions that occur in people's behaviour when those linguistic changes take place: why some people resist change and others lap it up; why someone is happy to say "bathroom" while another will stand firm by "toilet" till his dying day; why one person enthusiastically embraces the use of "impact" as a verb while another refuses and will never, ever form a sentence in which one thing impacts on another.'

As I said this, the chairman smiled and raised a hand and said, 'That's me!' and the audience laughed.

'Perhaps the whole process of linguistic change,' I wound up, 'has the hidden function of allowing people to make clear their attitude to change in general.'

We were still discussing this forty minutes later over lunch, when Elsa phoned me in response to my text message. I excused myself for answering the phone in their presence, assumed an alarmed expression, pushed my seat back and went between the tables towards the door of the canteen, as if seeking a quiet place to talk. In fact Elsa had already rung off. Back at the table, I said I would have to leave at once. My mother had just been taken to hospital. She had been seriously ill for some time, I explained. Quite likely this was the end.

Andreas Leitner, bearded and affable, chewing pork, was upset. 'Of course, you must go at once.' He swallowed. 'Let me get someone to check when your next flight is, while you finish your meal.' But I said I preferred to go absolutely at once, rather than losing any precious time. I didn't want to arrive and find my mother had already passed away. I would go and get my things from the hotel and take a taxi straight to Tegel, to be on the first flight available. Otherwise I might hate myself later.

'But this is such a shame, Tom.' He wiped his mouth and stood up, took my hand. 'It's been so good seeing you again. You're always so full of ideas.'

Walking back to the hotel, I felt that he was right and it really was rather a shame; it had been a genuine pleasure talking to Leitner, who was one of those cautious, politically astute academics who nevertheless appreciate the more maverick and kamikaze members of the fraternity when they come across them. The meat had been surprisingly good too, and I had left most of it on my plate. Fairly sure no one from the conference would be following, I stopped at a café and ordered a goulash and a glass of wine. Waiting for the food, I phoned Elsa.

'Mission accomplished,' I laughed.

'I don't suppose any of them will know, will they?' Elsa worried.

'Hardly,' I said. 'Mum isn't the kind of person whose death gets into the papers.'

I realised then that it had made me feel close to Mother again, using her as an excuse for one last time. And not just as an excuse, of course, since I really was going to see her. It was urgent.

'Is she still at the hospice?' Elsa asked.

'I don't know.' My wine arrived. 'Actually, I imagine not, since they'll need the beds, I'm sure. I doubt they have a proper morgue there. She'll have been taken to the undertaker's.'

'Are you sure you need to go, Tom?'

Perhaps just a little sip of wine before the food arrived.

'I just feel I left things unfinished, in the hurry to get to the conference. You know? It was stupid. I should have cancelled. In the end, I hate conferences. I can't understand why I bothered.'

'What matters is that you were there while she was alive.'

'We didn't really have a conversation, though. I arrived just too late. It seems she'd been having ordinary conversations right up to a couple of hours before. Even on the phone.'

'But she knew you were there.'

'Yes.'

I deserved another sip. It felt like I hadn't breathed for forty-eight hours.

'I'm sure that was the important thing, Tom. For her to know you were there. That was a big comfort. When will the funeral be?'

I said I had no idea. Probably in a few days. My brother-in-law was arranging it.

'Do you have anything major to do before then?'

'A couple of lessons. An article to write.'

'You could get someone else to do the lessons, and stay in London till it's over. You could work from there.'

It was generous advice.

'Tell me about your sister,' I said.

She chuckled. Her mother had reacted rather better than expected to the news of this baby, though she didn't seem to want to hear about the father at all. 'As if the business of there being a man involved was completely irrelevant.'

Elsa's mother had divorced three times. We talked about her family, until the goulash arrived and I rang off and ordered a second glass of wine. Eating with appetite, I felt immensely encouraged by the conversation with Elsa, almost back to where I'd been before the conference at Amersfoort, a happy man who'd had the good luck to meet the perfect woman rather late in life. I downed the second glass of wine, and now it occurred to me that perhaps the best thing would have been to stay at the conference, which wasn't so dire as I had feared, and return to Madrid on my scheduled flight. I could have spent the night with Elsa, which always meant sleeping well, and the following lunchtime there was my weekly appointment with the shrink, who no doubt would have had much to say about my volatile state of mind these last forty-eight hours. Instead I had made this dramatic gesture of returning to my mother's deathbed when she was already dead.

The sun was bright in the broad Berlin streets. I enjoyed the walk back to Görlitzerstrasse. The wine had given me a buzz. The air felt chill and sharp. Perhaps it was going to snow. Life is good, I thought. On arrival at the hotel I went straight up to my room, without stopping in reception, and lay on the bed. The room was freshly clean and, with the sunshine through lace curtains, it looked nicer than I had thought yesterday evening. I had been tense and too busy with my PowerPoint. Now I noticed a comfortable armchair in blue leather and a competent painting of a frozen lake under leaden skies, with ducks flying low over the ice. Closing my eyes, I fell at once into a deep sleep and dreamed the phone was ringing. I mean, I dreamed a ringing phone had woken me up. But it was not a phone I knew. First, I had to find where it was in the room and then I had some trouble actually answering it. I didn't know which button to press. In the end I missed the call and was just falling asleep again, in my dream of course, when it rang a second time. This time I picked it up at once, and at once the line was open. I didn't need to press anything. Hello, I said. Tom Sanders here. There was an electronic silence of beeps and scratches, which I found threatening. I felt I had been caught out and was about to be accused of something terribly compromising. Then, very loudly, my mother said, 'Hello, Thomas dear, it's Mum!' It was her brightest, most cheerful, let's-all-be-jolly-together voice, and I woke with a start.

It was five o'clock. I had slept two-and-a-half hours. Presumably the hotel hadn't been warned I was cutting my stay short, otherwise someone would have come up to check the room. I felt groggy and surprised by the intensity of the dream. 'Hello, Thomas!' It was exactly Mum's voice. She had called me. There would be a crumble in the oven, farmhouse cream in the fridge. I took a shower, then wearing the white bathrobe they always give you in these places, I opened my computer and sat down to check my email and book a flight. It was already twenty-four hours since Mother died, I thought, waiting for the machine to boot up. I wondered what would have happened to her body in that period. How did it while away the time? I could have phoned my sister and asked her, but I didn't. For some reason I didn't want to speak to my sister.

Checking my email, I found that with what had arrived today and what I hadn't managed to look at yesterday, there were now twenty-nine messages demanding my attention.

I wrote to Elsa at once, telling her how wonderful it had been to speak to her on the phone and how every time I heard her voice I felt more deeply in love with her. The problem, if I left for the airport now, I thought, would be that very likely I would run into one or another of the conference speakers in reception, since we were all staying in this same hotel. Then they would see I hadn't departed in haste to my mother's deathbed, as I'd said I would. Probably the best thing, then, would be to check out very early the following morning – say, six-thirtyish – when there was no danger of running into anyone. My brother had written saying he had heard from my sister that Mother had died peacefully in the afternoon. No doubt, he said, she felt she had struggled enough. He was glad, he wrote, that he had managed to speak to her while she was still compos mentis, only the evening before. On the phone. I replied asking him when he planned to arrive for the funeral? If he was already on his way, would he like to go and see the body with me?

I then opened Dr Sharp's message. He had been concerned, he said, about the state of mind he had left me in at Schiphol. Had I made my plane? How was my mother? It had been generous of me, he said, in the circumstances, to go ahead with the talk to the physiotherapists. If I used the wand, he warned, I should be careful. 'Read the attachments I'm sending with this email, which will explain the correct amount of pressure to apply,' he finished, 'and feel free to call me any time.' There was a number in California. But now I saw a new message had arrived; it was a reply from my brother already. He had no plans to come to the funeral, he said. He couldn't really see the point of making long transcontinental trips for funerals. But even if he did come, he said, he certainly wouldn't be going to see Mum's body, thank you very much. The coffin would be quite enough.

I felt rather shocked by this – brought up in my tracks, as Mother would have said. Perhaps language constantly renews itself, I thought then, so that we can identify a whole series of sayings that were special to our parents' generation, then feel nostalgic using them ourselves from time to time. Whoopsy-daisy. Feet of clay. Almost like seeing old photographs. And I wondered if someone would take a photograph of the body. Of Mother dead. Should I do that perhaps, when I went to visit her? What struck me was not just my brother's not wishing to see the body, but his absolute certainty that he didn't want to see it. I really should leave for Tegel as early as possible tomorrow morning, I decided. I should look for a flight now.

'I'm surprised you don't want to come to the funeral,' I wrote to my brother. 'I mean, I know it's a long haul, but it's Mum's funeral, for heaven's sake. I think you should come.'

I didn't usually write in these urgent tones to my brother. He was an older brother. I wasn't in the habit of telling him what I thought he should do. He would reply at once, I thought, and I got up to make myself a coffee to clear my head. There was a tartan mini-pack of Scottish shortbreads. How strange to be reminded of Scotland, and hence of my Scottish wife. How was I going to have dinner, I wondered, if I didn't want to risk going out through reception? And if I ordered food in my room and it came out that I had done that, what would they think of me? But why did I care what they thought of me?

My brother hadn't replied. I logged into my bank account and paid the insurance premium that was pending, then opened the message from the old girlfriend that had so intrigued me yesterday, but had somehow lost all interest today. 'Was in Camden Market, this afternoon,' she wrote, 'and had to pop into the pub for a pee. Suddenly remembered we had had lunch there once. The Lock Tavern. It was a lovely memory.'

How nice. How nice it was to get friendly messages from old lovers. Should I reply? This was very likely the girl I had been with when Charlie read my email correspondence with David. Maybe. Hard to remember the chronology of those who were never part of your official life. Like dreams. David and I always exchanged jokey, sexually explicit remarks in our emails. No doubt it had been disturbing for Charlie to read them, to think of his father, who lived and slept with his mother, talking so flippantly about the way this or that woman did or did not do oral sex. Why had we insisted on that infantile correspondence, I wondered now, over three or four long years? I could go back in my email account, presumably, and find those emails, if I wanted to. I had no desire to. Why would I do that? We were trying, I suppose, to find some way of making light of those impulses that were pushing us to abandon our partners. We were trying to pretend that the absolute necessity of some new relationship was merely a sexual drive, merely a fleshly impulse. We weren't suppressing the flesh, but we were pretending it was *only* flesh, not important, while continuing with the old relationship, which was the spiritual thing, the inward thing, hence the superior thing. Plus, of course, the old relationship was above all the *practical* thing, the thing that made social and economic sense, the thing that didn't hurt anyone but ourselves. That was why our emails had to be so sexual, so scornful of love, so pornographic. So infantile. I had explained all this some time ago to the shrink. Or rather, while I had talked about the past, the shrink had encouraged me to see it all in this light: a wilful denial of the need for love. 'What is all this about?' my wife demanded when the twins told her about the text messages. Pornography is a denial of the need for love. That seems obvious now. 'Nothing,' I told her. 'A stupid erotic game. Nothing else.' So I betrayed my girlfriend of the time, not unlike St Peter, perhaps, when they put him under pressure and he denied Our Lord three times. What an analogy! But of course this was exactly what my wife wanted to hear. It was nothing. It was an erotic game. Her husband had feet of clay. And what Deborah had wanted to believe, no doubt, if anyone had ever told her anything about David. Her man was caving in to some meaningless cravings of the flesh. Carnal affections. Pornography is not the enemy of respectability, I thought. Rather its secret ally. 'You had your Mexican poncho,' I wrote to this girlfriend of some years ago. 'And England won the Ashes while we drained our beers.' A world of respectable ordered lives could hardly exist without pornography, without affairs.

But what did any of this have to do with Mother, or the business in hand, my getting back to London to see her body? Nobody was more respectable than Mother, I thought, no one more willing to hear a respectable lie rather than a painful truth. I opened the two emails from the twins, sent almost simultaneously. No doubt their mother had told them to write to me and they had. 'Dad, how's Granny? We have a big race tomorrow. We've been training for it for months. Give us some news. Tell us if we should come right afterwards.' 'Dad, sorry we can't come right now because of this race, but tell Granny we love her and we'll come soon.' 'Kids,' I wrote to both in one email, 'I'm afraid your gran passed away yesterday afternoon. You shouldn't worry about not coming, because I don't think you could have made it in time, and anyway she wasn't conscious at the end. Your brother and sister were there. She died very peacefully. Let me know if you will be able to come to the funeral. It would be good if we were all together.'

Of course this news, I thought, would now go straight to my wife. When I communicated with the twins, it often felt as if in fact I were communicating with my wife, but at a remove. I wondered sometimes if both of us didn't find some consolation in this communication, as if it testified to an old affection between us. But I also wondered whether it was right to put this burden on the twins. And, in this particular instance, whether it was right to exclude my wife from an event like this, my mother's death, when she had been part of the family for so long. So without having planned to write to my wife at all – on the contrary, I had supposed I would already be in England and heading for the undertaker's, or a morgue somewhere – I now found myself writing quite a long email to my wife, possibly the longest email I had written to her since the day we signed the separation papers. 'It was great the children came,' I wrote. 'They both behaved wonderfully, I felt proud of them. Mother died peacefully surrounded by the people she loved. Not a bad way to go.'

Rereading this, I was struck by the fact that I had again used the word my brother said my sister had used, when describing the death: 'peacefully'. Peaceful is the word that collocates with dying when you want to express reassurance. Or to reassure yourself, per-haps. But reassure yourself of what? That dying is not so bad? That the dead person didn't suffer too much? What is too much? Did Mother really feel peaceful? Certainly she hadn't the night before. 'If only,' she had shouted. When faith seems weak and victory lost. 'Take me tonight, Lord.' Mother was only peaceful the follow-ing day because the battle was already over. 'She is on her way, Mr Sanders.' She was already gone, was what they meant. She had lost so much blood, and was so full of drugs, that the wildest, most tormented, cocaine-snorting fanatic would have been peaceful. Mother had been a fanatic of course, in her respectable way. She was certainly tormented. So should I change what I had written to my wife, I wondered? Should I tell my wife that my mother had died doubting her Christianity? This would lead me back to the long complicity between myself and my wife against my family's faith. My wife and I had always felt superior to my mother, my father, my sister and my brother-in-law because they were born-again

Christians, ingenuous and evangelical. Barbarians really. Should I tell my wife about my mother's need at the end for props, in the form of Kenneth E. Hagin's book about why God doesn't always answer your prayers? My wife would feel gratified by this reminder of our old complicity. A couple is a couple in part because of the enemies they share. Certainly this was the case with my mother and father, who were a couple against the World, the Flesh and the Devil. In token that thou too shalt strive. My wife would feel gratified and say, If you're over for the funeral, Tom, why not come up to Edinburgh for a day? Yes, writing that my mother's death had not been a peaceful one would almost certainly lead to an invitation to go up to Edinburgh to see my wife. Would that be such a bad thing? Travelling back with the twins, perhaps, after the funeral, on the fast train from King's Cross, always assuming they actually came to the funeral. I looked at the word 'peaceful' on the screen – she died peacefully – and thought how unflaggingly and shamelessly we yearn for the reassuring narrative. The narrative that allows us to bury the whole damn thing and get on with life. It can only make sense. And in the end, after the tormented night, there *had* been an extraordinary atmosphere of peace around Mother's deathbed those last two hours when she was breathing her last.

Sitting at the window in the Görlitzerstrasse, looking out at bare branches, parked cars, tidy Teutonic façades, I went back in my mind to the feeling in the room when Mother was dying, to the bodies of my son and daughter, their partners, my sister and brother-in-law, their daughter, my uncle, his son, my cousin, all leaning slightly forward on their seats, listening for something that would soon be something no more, listening for an absence that would confirm a departure we all knew had already occurred. Was that peaceful? Certainly it was calm, and resigned. There was a feeling of truce. There were battles set aside. There was a baseline affection for each other. Something had been allowed to emerge that is always there, but that we don't often express: our tenderness towards others, and towards ourselves, because mortal.

That was it. What we had all shared, during those last two quiet hours as my mother slipped away, was the intense awareness of being mortal, fleshly, animals. That was where the tenderness came from. Being dying animals together. With feet of clay. It was important that no one had said anything. The silence had made the awareness possible. Our silent awareness of the breath that was going. Our shared attention to dying. Then the absence. The last breath gone and our not knowing it was the last breath. A rising intensity of animal awareness and expectation. Smelling death, perhaps. My son and my daughter who came into this world from my semen leaning forward on their seats, breathless, listening for another breath from my mother who brought me into this world from her belly, between her thighs, then the nurse coming in and lifting the wrist and the swollen arm, making her announcement, and immediately an explosion of action. Immediately haste and movement and fretfulness. The last hours had been peaceful, but apparently it was a peacefulness that yearned to end and explode in action, in denial of dying. Life is always a denial of dying perhaps. I had stood up and hurried to the bathroom and recovered my suitcase from the guest room and, without even realising what I was doing, abandoned Mum's poor body right at the climactic moment when the soul flies to heaven to meet its Maker. Animals stay by their loved one's bodies, I thought. Even if only to lick their fur for a while. You fled to Berlin to give the Inaugural Address at the 27th Annual Conference of European Linguists. Knowing that these conferences are all much of a muchness. As Mum would have said.

I sent the email to my wife unchanged and immediately started to hunt for flights back to the UK. There was one at 8.40 a.m. I could make it, I thought, but for some reason I couldn't bring myself to buy the ticket.

Confused, I went to the bathroom to pee. Why wasn't I buying the ticket, when I felt so intensely I should go back and see Mother again? 'Hello, Thomas,' she had called in my dream. She had phoned! 'It's Mum,' she said. The voice was cheerful. She was cheerful because she thought I was going back to see her. So why didn't I book the ticket? This confusion was alarming. I should call the shrink, I thought. From our very first meeting, the shrink had made a point of telling me I could always call her in a crisis. 'Don't hesitate to phone me, Señor Sanders,' the shrink said. And whenever she saw I was going through a bad patch she reminded me, 'Don't hesitate to phone me, if it all gets too much, Señor Sanders.'

I should call her.

Yet I never had called the shrink. I did not want to appear weak. It seemed like an enormous collapse on my part to have gone to a shrink in the first place. To have sat down in a shrink's office and wept and formulated the bizarre phrase '*Que haya un amor*'. How strange to unburden oneself in a foreign language. Surely that was humiliation enough. I didn't want to become the kind of guy who has to phone his shrink at the drop of a hat, as my mother would have said. The kind of guy who needs to have his hand held. I don't want to give the shrink that satisfaction, I thought, that power over me. Though why I should think of my relationship with the shrink in these terms, I don't know. For example, if I phoned the shrink now, she would advise me against going back to London to see my mother's body. She would see it as another manifestation of an indoctrinated guilt, as she did when I kept going back to see my wife after having left home, making long and tiring flights from Madrid to Edinburgh for weekends that could not have been more depressing. 'Why do you keep doing things that you have no desire to do, Señor Sanders?' she would say. Although actually I did desire to go back and see Mother and spend a few minutes with her body. It wasn't remotely comparable to going back to see my wife. Nothing could be said to be *starting again* from going to see my mother. Could it? She was dead. How could anything start again? Why haven't you bought the ticket then, the shrink would ask? Why have you phoned me? You have phoned me because you know I will advise you not to go. That was true. And since I knew that would be her advice, there was clearly no point in phoning her.

I moved the computer to the bedside table where the phone was – it was extraordinary my brother hadn't responded to my message, since I know he checks his email every waking hour – opened the email from Dr Sharp again and dialled his number in California. What time was it now in California? I had no idea. Early in the morning.

'Mark Sharp.' It was his voice. I have it on my computer in fifty-five relaxation sessions.

'This is Tom – Tom Sanders,' I said. 'Am I disturbing?'

Lifting my eyes, I saw the frozen lake in paint and the three ducks flying low across it, looking for some water to land on perhaps? It really was a rather fine painting, for a hotel room.

'Tom! I've been thinking about you! How's it going? How is your mother?'

I told the doctor that my mother had died, but that I had at least got to see her, and when he started to offer his condolences, I said thanks, but that was not what I was calling him for. 'The fact is I'm just about to use your wand for the first time; I was wondering if you had any advice to offer.'

'Ah. Okay.' The doctor seemed surprised. 'Have you read the articles I sent? About trigger points and calibrating the pressure you apply?'

I said I had.

'And you have the videos with Tom Ingram's instructions, right? On the pen-drive.'

I said I did.

'Well, there's really not much I would want to add to that,' Dr Sharp said.

I had the impression he was drinking something as he spoke. Perhaps it was breakfast time.

'Are you still flared up,' he asked, 'after the massage?'

I said I was, a bit. I'd had a bad couple of days.

There was a silence on the line, which was a little odd, considering what a loquacious man Dr Sharp was. Calling California from a four-star German hotel was not going to be cheap.

'I just thought there might be some crucial piece of personal advice you could offer,' I told him, my eyes fixed on the three ducks in search of a spot to land. At least they had company.

'Tom,' Dr Sharp sighed. 'The thing is not to imagine it will solve things from one moment to the next. Maybe we made a mistake when we decided to call it a wand. You know? It's not magic. Use it slowly and very gently, otherwise you'll make things worse. You've got a lot of tension stored up in there. Be kind to yourself. Don't try to hit a home run.'

'Got you.'

The nice thing about the painting was the way it caught the last rays of sun over the wintry scene, with the ducks flying through a pinkish dusk, looking for somewhere to spend the night. An odd mix of beauty and anxiety.

'So, did you tell your mother about your separation?'

'I decided against.'

'I'm sure that was wise,' he said.

'She died peacefully with the family all around.'

'That's good,' he said.

I said thanks, I would be in touch to let him know how I got on with the wand, and hung up.

So was I going to take tomorrow morning's early flight, or not?

I pulled the wand from its plastic bag, which also included a pack of ten thin rubber gloves. The idea was to stretch the middle finger of the glove over the ball at the top of the wand, pull it down the shaft, then tie it off beyond the plastic ring that prevented the thing from disappearing up your butt. All of which I did. What was missing was some lubricant. I went into the bathroom, where there were the usual pots of hand cream. Would that work? I feared it wouldn't, but opened a pot anyway and smeared the runny white cream on the rubber. Apparently I had decided to go ahead with this wand experiment, come what may. Yet another of Mother's expressions. Come hell or high water. I hadn't realised how many I used. I plumped up two pillows so that I could half sit, half lie on the bed, then decided perhaps I really should read the article Dr Sharp had sent me and at least open the video on the pen-drive and check out the first lesson. I got up again to fetch the computer, which was on the desk. Outside, snowflakes had begun to fall into the tidy German street.

The article was more complex than I had imagined. There was a long preamble about myofascial muscle tissue, the formation of trigger points, their referral of pain to remote points of the body, such that a trigger point embedded in the muscle of the abdomen could be responsible for a pain in the perineum or testicles. Why was that? Why did life have to be so complicated? Then a long section on the proper technique for releasing the tension that these trigger points supposedly stored and blocked. Was it all nonsense? Could it be that Dr Sharp was a quack? I felt impatient. Toggling to my email, I noticed new messages from my wife and Deborah, among others. I didn't want to open them and so went back to Dr Sharp's article. The key was to use the wand only to meet the pain, but no more than that. At least initially. Just go to greet the pain, Dr Sharp's article said, then stop. Or rather, then hold it there for two minutes. What exactly did he mean by that? Were meeting the pain and greeting the pain the same thing? Can you greet something for two minutes? There was the slight problem that since I had already smeared the rubber glove covering the tip of the wand with hand cream, I was having to hold it in the air with my left hand to prevent it from smearing the sheets. Fed up with this, I now got off the bed and managed to hook the snorkel part of the wand over the bedside lamp in such a way that the creamy bit wasn't touching anything. I then removed my jeans and underwear, ready for the adventure.

Why was I doing this stuff, instead of booking the flight?

Back on the bed, I opened my wife's email.

'Thanks for yours, Tom. It's good to think of the kids being there. It's an important experience for them, and I'm glad it was so peaceful. I would have come myself, but feared I would not be welcome. I have written messages of condolence to your brother and sister. I hope that's okay with you. Let me know if you want me to come to the funeral, though I don't suppose you will. You seem so determined to throw everything away. Anyhow, the twins want to come. They adored Gran. Just let me know when it is and I'll put them on the train. Your loving ex.'

I scanned this through a first time, very rapidly, skipping here and there, as I always do with my wife's emails, in much the same way, I suppose, that you open a package you fear might be hiding some kind of booby trap. Then, having checked it was safe, as it were, I read it again carefully, at which point I realised that actually it wasn't safe at all. Precisely its reasonableness, its air of placid, nostalgic hurt, made this brief email extremely dangerous.

Deciding not to respond, or not at once, I turned to the window, where snow was falling thickly and steadily through yellow lamplight. It looked rather beautiful and very calm and I watched it for a couple of minutes, as if granted a truce. It was the slow steadiness of the falling flakes that did it, the feeling that they were simply doing what any snowflake has to do, falling: without enthusiasm, without protest. The ice on the lake where the ducks were flying also communicated a sense of calm and truce. Something had been stopped, arrested, though it was hard to see where the ducks would be able to stop, if they didn't want to land on the ice. Were the ducks calm? I felt they were. They were calm despite their predicament, flying over this broad expanse of ice. Then, turning back to the window and the snow, I was reminded of the calm in my mother's room in the hours before she died. Mother was falling into death, the way every mortal animal must at some point fall, and every fleeting snowflake. It was a movement beyond conflict, beyond the aberration of metaphysical battles won and lost, of faith weak or strong. All of a sudden you let go and bowed to the old imperatives of gravity and death. It was so easy. Everything is easy, I thought, in the end. It's before the end that's hard.

Meantime, on my computer screen Tom Ingram was sitting on a blue sofa holding the yellow wand between the fingers of two raised hands. I clicked Play and he began to talk. Even on the video he conveyed the sense of a man entirely at ease. Not a professional broadcaster or a publicity man, simply a good honest fellow at ease with himself and his technical competence and perfectly happy to appear on a video about anal massage. 'Today we're going to start you off on the wand,' he said and was obviously talking not just to camera but to an audience, presumably at Dr Sharp's San Diego clinic. At once I wished I was there, at the clinic with the other sufferers, listening to this wonderful man. 'Nothing spectacular,' he said, 'nothing life-changing. We're just going to get used to inserting the wand in the anus and taking it out again, without doing ourselves any harm.' He leaned back on the sofa, lifted his knees and showed how to position the wand against the dark perineal seam of his jeans. All this with a quiet laconic dignity that hypnotised me, as I was also hypnotised, looking up again, by the falling snow. It seemed I wanted to be hypnotised.

It was now 7 p.m. Should I order dinner or try the wand first? I could hardly have the thing hanging over the lampshade when they brought up a tray of schnitzel. Undecided, it occurred to me I should check the weather forecast. Heavy snow. That was worrying. I found the Tegel website. What if they were cancelling flights? Nothing. Tegel's website said nothing about the weather. Was that encouraging? I should definitely buy my ticket now. 'What happens to a body,' I typed into Google, 'after death and before burial?' This to find out where Mother was up to, so to speak. But glancing through the sites that popped up – *Our dear Auntie Lilah exhumed after fifteen years, YouTube, 4.27 minutes* – I decided to investigate no further. All I wanted to do was to see Mother for a few moments, half an hour maybe, touch her forehead perhaps, say goodbye, maybe apologise for having rushed off to a stupid conference when she was going to meet her Maker. Though why my mother should be interested in an apology from me, if she was waltzing her way through Gloryland, was hard to say; and if she wasn't, she would be none the wiser. I toggled back to the email and opened Deborah's. 'Tom,' she had written, 'something terrible has happened. Dave took some pills. He's in coma. If you can, please come.'

I took the wand from the bedside lamp, peeled off the creamy rubber glove and chucked it in the bin, dressed, packed my bag, wand included, then hurried down to reception, where I checked out and paid my extras in full view of various speakers from the 27th Annual Conference of the Society of European Linguists, who were sipping what looked to me like *Weissbier* in the busy hotel bar.

XVI

I realise now that I couldn't, as I first thought, have received that email from my sister, the one that listed her expenses on Mother's behalf and introduced the unexpected embalming, while at the hotel on the Görlitzerstrasse. It must have been in the Ibis at Tegel. And not the evening I checked in there, after finding there were no places on the last flight to Heathrow. A courtesy bus had driven us through a sprawl of airport wasteland to this miserably prefabricated dormitory. Convinced it would be another sleepless night, I hadn't seen the point in spending more. Not the evening, then, when I arrived at the Ibis, at once a mythical bird and a miserable hotel chain, nor the following morning, when ten inches of snow had caused the suspension of all flights in and out of the airport, so that having gone down early for breakfast, I realised there was no point in checking out in a hurry. No, I must have got my sister's email towards midday, shortly before being forced to vacate the room if I wasn't planning to stay another night. Hence one of the reasons I responded to my sister so rapidly would have been the need to shut down my laptop and check out of the hotel.

I had booked myself onto a Lufthansa flight due to leave at 11 a.m., but it was repeatedly rescheduled as the morning passed and the snow disruptions got worse. My old friend David was in a coma. Outside, the world was absolutely white. On checking into the Ibis the evening before, I had phoned Deborah, who told me David had come home from the hospital in the morning and taken the pills that afternoon in his room, where he had gone for a nap. She had called him to come down for his tea towards five and gone to peep at his door when he didn't reply. From this I deduced that they now slept in separate rooms. He was lying on his back, fully dressed with his hands folded on his stomach. And I mustn't imagine it was a suicide attempt, she protested, because they had just had a really lovely lunch together and downed a bottle of Sauvignon. He hadn't left a letter or anything. It was just that his frustration with insomnia had led him to overdo it.

'And Charlie?'

Charlie had gone off to stay with Stephen at his parents' place in Cornwall, she said.

'But how did he react to the news?'

'I haven't told him.'

This seemed extraordinary.

'He would think it was his fault,' Deborah's voice became shrill. 'He'd be terribly upset.' If David came out of the coma, she thought, before next weekend, there'd be no need to tell the boy at all.

When I asked what the doctors were saying, she said they weren't being very communicative. He was in the West Middlesex again, she said. Intensive care.

On putting the phone down, I looked through my pockets and wallet and the various compartments of my old Samsonite bag and finally found the Post-it Charlie had given me, stuck to the back of my Barclays Connect. It was disquieting that I couldn't remember having put it in such a very particular place. David's veto had surely lapsed now, I felt. If anything, I owed it to my old friend to try to find out what was going on. I called the number three times, but only got the answering service. 'My name is Tom

Sanders,' I said. 'I'm a friend of David Pool's. I wanted to talk to you about him.'

Snowed in at the Ibis, I had spent a night much like the two previous nights, and finally flew out of Tegel towards evening the next day, knowing now that if I wanted to see Mother I would have to see her embalmed, and that if I wanted to see David I would have to see him in coma. Things had moved fast while I was at the 27th Annual Conference of the European Society of Linguists.

Landing at Heathrow, I had only to take the Piccadilly Line a few stops to East Hounslow, then walk for fifteen minutes to arrive at my mother's house at the bottom of a small suburban cul-de-sac. It was snowing again, but without the conviction and solemnity of the German snow. These were ice flakes in a gusty wind. Mother kept her spare key, as I recalled, in a plastic pill-container pushed down the side of the big earthenware bowl in the middle of her front patio. In the summer this was a place for geraniums, but right now it was coated in a thin rime of snow. I put my bag down by the door, crouched beside the bowl and got my hands dirty, thrusting cold fingers into the earth at various points around the rim. I knew that the neighbour to the left, Christine, would also have a spare key. Her light was shining between the cracks in heavy curtains. She was the person my mother had turned to after her fall, when the pain got too much and she realised she wouldn't be able to go on in the house. But for some reason I didn't want anyone to know I was here. Ferreting in the earth for the key, I couldn't help thinking of exhuming bodies. There was no analogy really, but seeing the dirt under my fingernails on this icy Hounslow evening, I thought of it anyway. *Our dear Auntie Lilah . . .*

A white plastic tube surfaced: Haliborange Vitamin C chewable tablets, the same more or less that Mother had given us as children, though in those days you sucked rather than chewed. The key was a little rusty, but it turned the lock. Inside, everything was as she had left it, except for a small pile of post that had accumulated on the doormat, in particular five editions of the *Church of England Weekly*. I went to the kitchen to wash my hands and found dirty dishes in the sink and a fridge full of sour milk and decomposing greens. The cuckoo clock had stopped. Its two iron pinecones had descended almost to the floor. I reached up, took the other end of the chains and pulled them down. The cones climbed up to the little wooden house. At once the clock began to tick and, even before I could turn away, the door squeaked open and its tiny yellow bird whistled out. Cuckoo! I had always hated Mother's cuckoo clock. So why had I wound it up?

The following morning I took stock. I had come back to see Mother and, in so doing, complete a filial duty that hadn't been performed when it should have been. But in the meantime Mother's body had been embalmed, transformed, which somehow altered the nature of my mission. Rather than feeling I had to see her urgently, I now found myself wondering whether I should be seeing her at all – seeing the corpse at all, I mean – since embalming was the last thing she would have wanted. Her sick and suffering body had been removed from me. The ritual I had imagined performing was no longer possible. Now there was the mockery of her looking very much her old self, in pale-blue tailleur and matching bonnet. Did I want to be a party to that?

To kill time, I sat on the sofa where I had sat so often during the summer of four years ago, looking across to the recliner where Mother had been more or less a permanent fixture when she wasn't cooking shepherd's pies and crumbles. It was a clunky thing with golden-brown upholstery. I hadn't really noticed it when my mother was there in it. She had monopolised my attention. Only now she was gone did I see how ugly it was. The whole house, without my mother's presence, was drab, and oddly heterogeneous. The surfaces were gathering dust.

Laptop on my knees, I exchanged emails with my brother, who was still resisting the idea of coming to the funeral. For the moment I did not write to the children, who did not write to me. I did not write to my wife. My ex-wife. I knelt for hours studying the books in the small revolving bookcase under the stairs. It was a mahogany thing, at least I think it was mahogany, that had once been at my grandfather's house, and then at the vicarage where we grew up. On one side were children's books from fifty years before. *The Water Babies. Tales of the Riverside.* I mean the editions were fifty years old. And fifty years ago I had knelt by this same bookcase and looked at these same books. On another side were yarns, as Mother called them, Biggles and Buchan and Sir Walter Scott and Robert Louis Stevenson. Again fifty years old. They were the books Mother had read aloud to us when we were ten or twelve. *Kidnapped. Biggles Flies South.* Safe books – *The Thirty-Nine Steps* – with war heroes and no sex. It was curious that she had kept them there, in their place in the revolving bookcase, even after moving out of the vicarage when my father died. They must have been taken off their shelves for the move, then carefully replaced in the same order, after the revolving bookcase was safely transferred from the spacious Victorian lounge where it had looked at home among drapes and draughts, to this miniature modern dwelling where a two-bar electric fire was topped by an illuminated plastic screen that vaguely recalled flames rising and flickering.

There were still cakes in the larder. I ate the last slices of a lemon sponge, cutting mould off one exposed surface. You could see Mother had made it herself from the way the icing was smeared on with a kitchen knife. From the mantelpiece above the fire, my father's photo smiled at the room in black-and-white. I had hardly noticed him here when my mother was around. Now she was gone, he seemed to have taken over. He was wearing his robes and leaning forward, arms folded, on a wooden lectern, smiling generously towards some congregation, some gathering of people happy to listen to him and make him the centre of their attention. Every time I entered and left the room I felt compelled to look at my father. If the room had any anchor now, or animating principle – in the absence of my mother – it was Father, in his white surplice and black cassock leaning persuasively over the top of his lectern. At the bottom of the photo, resting against the frame, Mother had placed a piece of white card with these words:

> *Death hides –*
> *But it cannot divide*
> *Thou art but on*
> *Christ's other side.*
> *Thou with Christ*
> *And Christ with me*
> *And so together*
> *Still are we.*

I ate the lemon cake and looked at Dad's photo. You could see he was still in his forties here, because he had hair. And he wasn't wearing bifocals. He seemed full of life and enthusiasm. It was odd, I thought, that the main photo Mum had preserved of him showed him in his public role, not in a moment of intimacy. Dad was a natural preacher; he would have been so, whatever he believed in. When he was preaching he was more seductive, perhaps, than in their private life. Was that true? Halfway up the stairs to the bedroom there was one of his favourite texts on a plaque:

> *But they that wait upon the LORD*
> *shall renew their strength;*
> *they shall mount up with wings as eagles;*

they shall run, and not be weary;
they shall walk, and not faint.

My father had loved these powerful affirmations of religious optimism. But he had also loved the powerful words on the Churchill jug Mother preserved behind the glass door of the polished cabinet opposite the electric fire. 'I have nothing to offer but blood, toil, tears and sweat,' Churchill was saying and, on the other side of the jug, beneath a Spitfire in flight, 'Never in the field of human conflict was so much owed by so many to so few.'

My father loved powerful rhetoric of all kinds, and in his sermons strived in every way to reproduce a powerful rhetoric of his own. He lived in words, powerful words of praise and prayers and supplication. He loved preaching. He loved pronouncing the blessing at the end of evensong: 'Now unto Him who is able to keep you from stumbling and without stain . . .' He would raise his robed arms like angels' wings and lift his face to heaven.

And because Father lived in words, he lived on in them too. Under the television was a box of audio cassettes. His sermons. Mother still had an ancient stereo unit with a cassette player. She perpetuated an old enchantment, listening to her dead husband's sermons. Though never in my presence, as I recall. Never once had I caught my mother listening to them. She did not want that to happen. Perhaps she feared I would mock him. I would break the spell. There was a cassette in the player now.

In the afternoon I went to the West Middlesex and found Deborah on the sixth floor. She was sitting beside David's bed reading the *Daily Telegraph* and *The Lady*. He was out of intensive care, but still heavily tubed up. 'We're supposed to keep talking to him,' she said. The next few days would be critical. 'Tom's here, Dave!' she announced in a loud voice. 'He's come all the way from Madrid to

271

keep you company!' She spoke as though he were suffering from deafness, or dementia. David was on his back, his greying hair in a ponytail, face blank and uncharacteristically peaceful. 'Can you talk to him a bit while I take a break?' Deborah asked. 'We're supposed to recall positive memories and speak in a gung-ho voice.'

So for the second time in a few days I was sitting beside a hospital bed with a person who was altogether out of it. I put my mouth close to his ear. 'Are you there, Dave, old mate?'

My old friend's expression was distant and calm. His skin still smelled faintly of his beloved nicotine. 'You'll have to wake up, if you want a fag,' I told him. I watched and wondered. I wondered what on earth I could say that might penetrate a mind that had wanted to be dead. 'Remember that girl,' I tried, 'you shagged in the Odeon in Richmond. With the piercings. Who drove you crazy for a year and more?'

Nothing.

'"Cunt-struck," you said.'

I waited. It was strange noticing the quite different emotions of seeing Mother dying one day and David in a coma the next. With Mother I had been overwhelmed. Now I was absolutely cool. I had nothing to say. After a while Charlie appeared at the door. He smiled in a quiet kind of way. 'Talk to him about cricket,' he said. 'Dad loves cricket.' He spoke like the most loving of sons.

I used the buses to go to the West Middlesex. Two red buses, with a wintry connection in Isleworth. At the bus stop going home I exchanged messages with Elsa. 'Miss dancing with you, Beauty.' 'Miss cooking with you.' My fingers were numbed. I needed gloves. Elsa phoned, but neither of us were great talkers on the phone. I found myself inventing tasks to explain my stay, when actually I couldn't even begin to explain it to myself and she wasn't asking for explanations anyway. On the bus two Asian men were glued to a small box producing mournful Asian music.

'This is a 281 to Hounslow Bus Station,' a female voice warned. I told Elsa about Dave. He had been a close friend, I said. Years ago.

'It's strange, but his wife doesn't seem too troubled with the situation.'

'She'll be in shock,' Elsa said.

'She's talking about spending whatever it takes to nurse him back to health.'

'Good for her. Did you go to see your mother?'

'Not yet.'

'Just do whatever you're comfortable with, Tom.'

But I couldn't feel comfortable in Mother's house. It felt so cold and poky. I found little meal packages she had prepared for herself, in the freezer compartment of the fridge. Moussaka. Chicken curry. Cauliflower cheese. They were the same recipes she had fed me with, overfed me, that summer four years ago. You are eating her remains, I thought.

I defrosted the packages in the microwave. There was a frozen gooseberry tart for dessert. I was overfeeding myself. I would get fat. When Mother did the dishes she never rinsed, just washed in soapy water, then dried things at once with ancient tea-towels. Washing up now, I left the cold tap running and rinsed everything thoroughly. When the freezer was empty, it would be empty and I would be free to eat other things.

One question was where to sleep. At the front of the house was Mother's room, with the same double bed my parents had slept in decades before at the vicarage. This was the room she gave us when I visited with my wife. It was warm and cosy. But first I would have to strip the bed, which still had the sheets she had slept in.

In the bathroom there was the device she'd had installed to be sure to be able to climb out of the tub after she had taken a bath. It was a sort of seat with a crank. There was something medieval about it. A plaque on the wall above the toilet bowl said, *This Toilet is twinned with a latrine at latitude* 22.92730 *longitude* 90.15011 *Aghailjhara, Bangladesh, Asia*. There was a photo of a thin brown boy grinning from the door of a primitive outside loo, and the name of a charity. Mother always gave her tithe, even on a modest pension.

When you sat on the toilet a plaque on the door opposite read.

> *I am here*
> *Where He placed me*
> *For His purpose*
> *Under His training*
> *In His service*
> *For His time*.

When my mother was in the toilet – the bathroom, that is – she wouldn't answer if you called her. You might let yourself in the front door and call her and, when she didn't answer, you assumed she was out. You thought nothing of it. Then, with a sudden 'cooee', she appeared. She had been in the bathroom. A person urinating or defecating, or simply the other side of a toilet door, didn't exist for my mother, wasn't part of this world. 'Hello, Thomas dear,' she would call downstairs in her most cheery voice. 'You're back.' But the person who was really back was Mother, back from the bath-room dimension where she didn't exist.

I slept in the back bedroom beside the toilet. It was colder. It was also the only room without a text on the wall. This was where I had slept that famous summer. Looking out of the window, beyond the small yard, I could see a British Telecom depot where large yellow vans came and went at all hours. Long after midnight or in the early dawn they revved up and set off on their journeys, presumably to fix some communications failure. Sometimes the drivers called to each other, slamming doors, laughing, speaking in loud voices on their mobiles.

Mother had used the room as a study. There was a narrow bed against one wall and a desk against the other, with barely space for a chair between the two. There were papers on the desk. She had been preparing a Bible Study. Her big old Bible was still open on the table. The passage under discussion was Paul's first letter to the Corinthians: 'When I was a child, I spake as a child, I understood as a child, I thought as a child: but when I became a man, I put away childish things. For now we see through a glass, darkly; but then face to face: now I know in part; but then shall I know even as also I am known.'

I set up my computer on the desk and emailed the shrink to cancel our Friday appointments until further notice. Doing this, I felt as one who has ceased to take a powerful medicine and fears what the consequences might be. I was in free fall. What does St Paul mean, I wondered, by 'then we shall see face to face?' See whom face to face? Who is it that one normally sees through a glass darkly? More or less everybody. Wives, husbands. Lovers. Children. Myself even. Perhaps glass meant mirror. And when was it that one would see these people *face to face*? Surely not after death, when there would be no body and hence presumably no face. Are there mirrors in Paradise?

I felt a sudden yearning to go and confront Mother, to challenge her, in her coffin, face to face. What did St Paul mean, Mum? I would demand. But beside the yearning was revulsion. The last thing I wanted was to confront my mother. Her embalmed face. And behind the yearning and the revulsion, a profound indifference.

Under St Paul's verses Mother had written, 'Praise the Lord!' Her handwriting was shaky but emphatic. I turned the paper over and picked up the pen beside it, the same pen she had been using, an ancient brushed-steel Sheaffer. Very likely it was the same pen my father had used, and already old-fashioned when he used it. A pen of thirty or forty years ago. Father always wrote with Sheaffers. I removed the cap and tried the nib. After a lick and a couple of strokes, it produced a thin line of blue-black ink. And I wrote:

> *Mother's corpse. This is what I keep thinking about.*
> *Should I view it?*
> *Why can't I decide?*

XVII

I have been writing here at Mother's desk with Father's pen for nine days. Writing and listening to the cuckoo clock. I will keep writing until I go to see Mother, to view the corpse and have done with it, or until I am certain in my mind I am not going. But what if I don't go, yet never reach the certainty that I am not going? Will I stop writing after the funeral, the cremation, when the corpse is no more? Or am I condemned to thinking about this for ever?

Thinking about what exactly? What *exactly* am I thinking about? And when I write: 'In the Görlitzerstrasse I thought this' or 'In the hospice bathroom I remembered that', is it really true? Can I really remember all those thoughts, and when and where I thought them? What substance does it all have? And why am I not in Madrid with Elsa, sleeping and waking and *living* with beautiful, beautiful Elsa?

Returning from the West Middlesex, I got off the bus a stop before I normally would, to go to the undertaker's. It was closed. It was Saturday afternoon. A notice said, 'Mourners wishing to view their loved one's body should phone the number below to make an appointment.' I felt relieved. It was like those situations where, not having said thank you or sorry at the right moment, it begins to seem pointless ever saying sorry at all. Or thank you. It's too late. A sense of impossibility grows and, with it, the need to deny that there ever was any need to say thank you or sorry in the first place. Or as if viewing the body were like asking to see Mother in the bathroom, making an appointment to view Mother in the toilet. She hadn't wanted to be embalmed. She believed the body was mere clay, to be flushed away with no great consequence when her soul flew up from the latrine for ever. If I went to see her, to view her, she wouldn't respond. The way she never responded from the toilet. She wouldn't be there for me. Even if I apologised, she couldn't absolve me. This wasn't like the moment on the death-bed, I told myself. The moment the breathing stopped. When I should have stayed. That moment can never come back. On the other hand, at that crucial moment I had badly needed to go to the bathroom. It had been urgent, painful. I had been resisting for hours – the hours of her dying – resisting manfully, firm at my post; I had needed to go. And then of course as soon as I stood over the bowl, there were messages to be read on my phone. There was the conference. Mother wasn't interested, I thought, in my seeing this embalmed travesty. It wouldn't be like Thomas pushing fingers in Christ's open wounds. There was nothing I needed to be convinced of.

On the other hand, she had phoned me. 'Hello, Thomas, it's Mum!' Pulling out my phone, I tapped in the number of the undertaker, called it and immediately cancelled the call. I had the number now.

'You *must* come to the funeral,' I emailed my brother. I used italics. 'We've got to be *together* at a moment like this.' My brother replied that he was tired. He had a lot on, he said. Mum was dead. He had spent a little time with her in summer. He would like to see me, he said, but winter was not a good moment to travel. 'There's been a lot of snow, hasn't there?'

'You *have* to come,' I wrote. 'It's Mother's funeral. Let's stand together this one last time, *brothers and sister together*.'

As soon as I had sent this message I wondered where all this urgent rhetoric had come from. I was sounding like my father. I was sounding like a Churchill jug.

When my brother didn't reply, I wrote, 'Have you ever thought how little Mother spoke of Father, despite remaining faithful to him, as it were, all those years? I mean, when you said Dad had been to a shrink, do you think it was possible he did that because he wanted to leave her, or he was attracted to someone else? Or he wanted to leave the Church maybe, which would have been a disaster for her. I mean, why else would Dad have been in so much trouble he had to see a shrink? And why did Mum never talk about this?'

My brother replied at once. He said Dad had always had niggles with his nerves, and there were a million reasons for going to see a shrink. You didn't need to be having a crisis of faith, or a pretty parishioner on the side. The parents were crazy with their religion, but they'd been pretty happy at the end, he thought. It was just a drag Dad had died so young. He was reading a book, my brother went on, which he couldn't recommend highly enough, on the neural transmission of information through the brain. 'We are all one hundred per cent predetermined,' he wrote. 'Free will is an illusion.'

As the wintry days passed and I walked back and forth on the pavement by Hounslow railway station, without ever going into the undertaker's and without calling the number I had stored on my mobile, eating Mother's frozen meals, walking along the river where I had walked with Mother but also, and perhaps more often, with my wife, I became strangely and frantically concerned that my brother should be at the funeral, that brother and sister should embrace each other and that there should be some shared sense of occasion, a recognition between the three of us – brother sister brother – that this major thing had happened in our lives: Mother was dead.

Where these emotions were coming from I had no idea, and at the same time, as if superimposed over them, an old fantasy returned. I would go back to my wife and we would look each other in the eye and then very deliberately, and by mutual unspoken accord, we would slap each other hard across the face. Not just one slap, but repeated slaps, across the face, and we would go on slapping and slapping hard across the face for as long as it took to feel that old scores had been settled and deep hurts repaid. They would be angry slaps, but also loving slaps. Why was I suddenly thinking of this again? Why couldn't I focus on Elsa?

I looked in the mirror at where Charlie's bruise had all but faded. If my brother and sister had been here now, I thought, at Mother's house, and if we had gone together to see her body, embalmed or otherwise, at the undertaker's opposite Hounslow railway station, all would have been well. I felt sure of that, in the way I often find that I am absolutely sure of the nature of some experience – some wonderfully cathartic experience – I know I cannot have. I would have gone to the undertaker's when my brother and sister wanted to go, stayed as long as my brother and sister wanted to stay, made the same gestures my brother and sister saw fit to make. They could decide everything, as far as I was concerned. All would have been easy if we had gone together, as brothers and sister, to say goodbye to Mother. But that wasn't going to happen. As my sister saw it, Mother was already in heaven. She wasn't there to be viewed. As my brother saw it, she was dead. And corpse-viewing was morbid.

I was in between. Torn between.

I phoned my sister and asked her to phone my brother and encourage him, in the warmest possible way, to come to the funeral. 'I already have, Bro,' she said. He had replied that he was thinking about it and would give a definitive response as soon as we had a date for the ceremony. Why hadn't he replied like that to me, I wondered? And how could he say free will didn't exist, and then talk about giving a definitive response when we had a date?

'What are we supposed to do about the bills that have arrived at the house?' I asked. There was a bill for the Wi-Fi, which I was making heavy use of. Another for a Waitrose delivery.

'Oh, you're in the *house*!' my sister said. She hadn't realised. She'd thought I was calling from Madrid. Apparently I hadn't told her I'd returned to London. Was that possible? She was delighted, because my presence there would save her a journey she had been putting off for days. I had to look for a life-insurance policy, she told me; it should be in one of the files beside the desk in the back bedroom. And I should check a point on the bathroom ceiling that might be leaking from the tank in the loft. In which case a plumber would have to be called.

'Did you go to see the body, then?' she asked

'Not yet,' I said.

'Uncle Harry goes every day. Maybe you could go together.'

'Don't you have any idea when the funeral will be?' I asked.

Her hubby, my sister said, was working on it. The problem was a logjam for the cremation.

'Logjam?'

But now my sister asked, 'So what are you actually doing there, Bro? In Mum's house?'

There were people I had to see in London, I said, about a project I'd been invited to get involved in. I put the phone down and stared at my father, smiling from behind his lectern. Without thinking, I went to the old stereo beneath the television, turned it on and pressed down the clunky button to play.

' . . . was a child, I spake as a child, I understood as a child, I thought as a child: but when I became . . .'

Dad was reading from the Bible. The moment I heard his voice, my father's voice – the very instant I caught the first cadence that was recognisably his, last heard thirty years before, on his deathbed – I hit the Stop button. I needed to go to the bathroom there and then. I made for the stairs.

Mother, I thought, peeing, must have been checking out some old sermon of father's for her Bible Study. Quite likely she had referenced the whole collection. Boxes and boxes of tapes. She had found an old sermon on Corinthians. Perhaps she repeated his very words when speaking to her study group. Perhaps repeating his words, she felt close to him. To her dead husband. On Christ's other side. Thirty years after his death, Mother and Father were still a team. Yet Father had gone to a shrink.

The Bangladeshi boy smiled from the twinned toilet in Aghailjhara. How do you pronounce that? My pee came slowly. Was I ever going to use Dr Sharp's wand? A strange game had been played between my mother and myself that long summer together four years ago. Vis-à-vis the bathroom. Since I had to pee often at night, and she too, perhaps because of the drugs she was taking, had to get up three or four times, there was the question whether to flush or not on every occasion that one peed. The flush was loud. The house was tiny and poorly insulated. We would both be waking each other up all night long. So we didn't. Didn't flush. Out of courtesy. However, this meant that towards morning the loo, the one loo, was rank with stale urine. And we both experienced this rankness, this shared corruption. Our two bodily fluids mixed together. Yet neither of us could mention it, Mother because she just did not mention these things, and I out of respect for her, being her son.

So this strange, sad intimacy formed between us, behind the surface cheerfulness that was always such a heroic achievement on my mother's part. At one point, wishing to alleviate the situation, but also to prevent my mother from feeling sorry for me, something I found depressing and even strangely offensive, as if manhood itself were at stake, I decided to look for some sort of container I might pee into through the night, so as not to have to slip out of the door of the bedroom into the space at the top of the stairs, where a board creaked beneath the carpet, and then into the bathroom, whose door would only close if you clicked it rather loudly. If you didn't close it and click it, it swung wide open of its own accord. It wouldn't stay ajar. This meant that on those rare occasions when both of us headed for the bathroom at the same time, one of the two of us would risk being seen by the other in the toilet. Which was unthinkable.

So I looked for something I could pee into through the night, then empty in the morning when Mother had already gone downstairs to make her morning tea and read the Bible and pray in the recliner by the revolving bookcase, that prayerful moment, when all was serene and the body's irksome nagging in delicious remission. And the only thing I could find, in the cabinet above the fridge, beside the cuckoo clock, because I mustn't take anything that would be too obvious, was a pint mug. What a pint beer mug, evidently stolen from a pub, was doing in the kitchen of someone who would never darken the door, as she would have put it, of a licensed bar, I have no idea. Perhaps my brother had stolen it. I must ask him. As an adolescent, my brother was the kind of person who might well come home with a pub ashtray in his pocket or a pint glass in his hand. In any event, I took this mug upstairs every night, giving the impression I wanted to have some water by my bed, then peed into it two or three times as required, until it was nearly full, so that although it never quite got me through the night, it did reduce the number of trips I made; and in the morning, when Mother wasn't around, I filled it with water from the bath tap and emptied this water in the loo. Perhaps two or three times. This seemed hygiene enough. Nobody had to drink out of it. Until one day, for reasons I can't recall, I had emptied the glass but not yet washed it – perhaps the cuckoo cuckooed, to call me down to breakfast – and left it in this state in the back bedroom, forgetting it there when I went out. So that Mother, who always liked to show her generosity by coming into the room and putting things in order, found the anomalous pint mug and took it downstairs and washed it with dish soap, though without rinsing of course. Which meant she must have smelled its smell and realised I had peed in it. She said nothing, but after that I could not bring myself to take the pint mug upstairs again.

Why not? It was so *childish*. When I was a child, I spake as a child. There was a kind of enchantment with my mother that prevented very much from being said. As there was a kind of spell with my wife that had prevented something quite different from being said. With my wife, one could have talked of peeing problems till the cows came home, but one could never mention the dire state our relationship had fallen into, the possibility that perhaps we should call it a day. Call it a day was Mother's expression. Likewise, till the cows come home. However, in both cases – mother and wife – it was precisely the unsaid things that made the bond between us so strong, so dense with emotion. As if my mother and I knew each other above all in the smell of nocturnal urine, while my wife and I knew each other most intimately in the stink of my betrayals. And winding up this pee, which I had hurried upstairs for after hearing just a half dozen words of my father's voice reading from the Bible on an ancient cassette, it occurred to me that finding that peed-in beer mug that morning four years ago, my mother would very likely have connected it with the time she had found the jam jar with its stinking pee in the outhouse in Blackpool fifty years before – is there anything that sets off memory more than smell? – and so would very likely have remembered how she had yelled at me that day and wept, and said if I went on like this I would bring her down with grey hairs to the grave, an expression she always used whenever one of her children did something seriously beyond the pale; and how contrite on that occasion her good little bad boy had been, to the point of offering to learn how to knit squares of blankets for black people dying in Rwanda. Did Mother smile then, remembering that? Or did she frown? Did she think life had been worth living? And had she perhaps gone on to recall how my accomplice in crime on that occasion, my friend Malcolm, had been martyred with his entire family, in Burundi a year or so after that incident, cut to pieces because they had refused to renounce their Christian God for whatever other gods were on offer in West Africa and, remembering that, did she long for such a death herself, a glorious, martyr's death as opposed to the slow malodorous decay of cancer?

In any event, sleeping in the small back bedroom these last ten days, getting up in the night far too often, it has been impossible for me not to remember that old nocturnal intimacy with my mother, and its melancholy urinary tang. And on more than one occasion during these nights I have allowed myself to imagine I can hear Mother's uneven breathing as she sleeps, fitfully, in her old bedroom. Or worse than that, when there was no breathing to be heard, allowed myself to imagine her lying in silent wakefulness, listening to the uneven flow of her son's pee in the bathroom. Yes, standing in the bathroom in the middle of the night, I sometimes imagine my mother is not in her coffin at the undertaker's at all. She is in the room behind me, feeling sorry for me as I pee. Nothing is more irksome than the thought of my mother feeling sorry for me. Even in her coffin, Mother will be feeling sorry for me, because I am not a Christian and not going to heaven. It's crazy.

Having escaped my father's voice and hurried upstairs to the latrine, I now went straight into the back bedroom, removed the plastic bag with Dr Sharp's wand and took it into my mother's bedroom, where there was more space to put the computer on the bed and watch the video in which my enviable namesake Tom Ingram explains how to tackle anal self-massage. I fired up the computer, pulled a rubber glove over the wand and tied it off beyond the stopper that prevented the thing disappearing up your back passage. There was the problem of lubrication again. Had I seen Vaseline in the bathroom cabinet? Indeed I had. True, the tube had all the appearance of being a dozen years old, but I can't imagine that Vaseline has a sell-by date.

I smeared the Vaseline on the wand and had just removed jeans and underwear, and lain down on the flowery eiderdown over Mother's bed, when the phone rang. Not my mobile, which I had kept beside me, but the landline downstairs beside the television and the stereo system with my father's voice. I hurried downstairs in stockinged feet with no trousers or underwear and, being in a hurry to get to the phone before it stopped ringing, managed to slip. The staircase at my mother's house is desperately steep and covered what's more with a thick-pile carpet that encourages the foot to slip forward, unless placed firmly and deliberately on the flat of each stair. It was the accident we had always feared would happen to my mother. We had marvelled that in thirty years it hadn't happened, she had never fallen. For a while we told ourselves we had been wrong to imagine she would fall, we had been too fearful – the mount-up-with-wings-as-eagles text was working miracles, my brother-in-law joked – and then she did fall and it was the end.

I fell. My foot slipped away from me, my backside hit the steep stairs and in a flash I was at the bottom, clattering into the wooden railing where the staircase turned left into the sitting room. For a moment or two I was in a daze. The phone must have stopped ringing at some point, because now it started again and I found myself crawling over to it, rather than getting to my feet.

Had I found the life-insurance document, my sister asked?

I said I had.

Had I checked the damp on the bathroom ceiling, she asked?

I said there was none.

The funeral would be the 20th, she said. Her hub had just sorted it. At 2 p.m. We needed to work out how many people were coming, and who was going to sleep where.

I climbed back up to Mother's bedroom, on my feet now, relieved that I did not seem to have hurt myself seriously. Lying down where Mother had lain in the days after her fall, I shifted aside Dr Sharp's wand and assorted paraphernalia, found my phone, opened the recently called numbers and phoned the number Charlie had given me.

'Hello, I'm sorry to disturb you, but I'm a friend of David Pool's. I left a message on your answer service a few days ago.'

'I'm sorry, sir, I think you have the wrong number. This is the Hounslow Funeral Parlour.'

I closed the call, closed my eyes and fell into a deep sleep.

XVIII

'Excuse me, I'm looking for David Poole.'

I was at David's bedside when a shadow at the door made me look up. It was a woman in her late twenties perhaps, small, buxom, with long, straight brown hair framing a round face, a snub nose, a generous mouth.

'I'm looking for David Poole,' she repeated.

'You've found him.'

I was sitting between David and the door. She came in a little way. When she saw his face she stopped. There was tape on his nose, a tube in the nostrils.

'Is his wife here?'

I looked at my watch. 'She'll be taking over at four.'

The woman stepped round me and crouched down. She was wearing a grey wool coat, unbuttoned, a roll-necked sweater and jeans.

'Davy,' she whispered.

She put a hand on his cheek.

I could see the fullness of her thighs as she crouched.

'What happened?'

'He took some pills.'

As I spoke, a nurse passed the door, talking. The woman started and got to her feet. She stood looking down at him, her mouth trembling, then again crouched down and caressed his cheek. 'Oh, Davy.' Her shoulders began to shake. In a single rapid movement she turned and hurried out.

Then I went to the undertaker's to see Mother at last. That same afternoon, returning from the hospital. Time was running out. The funeral was on Saturday. Just as I was crossing the High Street from the station, a young couple went in ahead of me. A couple with two young children, one in a stroller. The door opened and closed. It was a dark glass door that you couldn't quite see through. I had finally decided to go in and see my mother face to face. To confront my mother, in her blue tailleur and the bonnet with the peacock brooch. But I should wait, surely, I thought, until this other family came out. I didn't want to be in there with others. With crying children.

I peered through the smoked glass. The fact is I hadn't phoned to book a viewing. Somehow my calling the undertaker by accident, when I had thought I was calling the number Charlie had given me, had made it more difficult for me to phone again afterwards. In any event, the only way I was ever going to see Mother, I realised, would not be by appointment, but on impulse, rushing into the undertaker's from the street. Hello, Mum. It's Tom!

I paced up and down in the High Street, waiting for the young family to come out. Traffic was heavy, the pavement busy, and two young women in scarves and bubble jackets were asking people to sign up for some dentist's deal, where you could have your teeth whitened cut-price. No, thank you, I said every time I paced past them. They had set up a small stand with before-and-after photos. My teeth are white enough, I said.

After five minutes an elderly man using an umbrella as a walking stick also stopped at the dark glass door. He rang, and it opened for him. You had to ring. I hadn't noticed that. How many stiffs could they have in there, I wondered? The place didn't look much bigger than my mother's house. Or did they keep the corpses elsewhere, in a refrigerated warehouse, and only bring them when people made appointments? In which case, I might not find her even if I went in.

I retired to Costa Coffee across the street. The day was blowy and spitting rain, but I sat outside anyway. To keep watch on the undertaker's door. Surely if they only brought the corpses when people made arrangements to view them, I would have seen a coffin arriving from time to time, I thought. Or departing. And so far I had seen no sign of a hearse.

Over my coffee, staring at the dark glass door of the undertaker's, I remembered that Mother loved stopping for a cappuccino when she was out doing her shopping, or visiting the folk she helped – 'folk' was her word – but Costa hadn't arrived on the High Street until she was already too ill to get out. All the coffee places round here are hopeless, she would say, but she went to them anyway. Mother was always on the lookout for small pleasures that could not be construed as sinful.

Now the door opened and the young father appeared with his two small children, but without the mother. The mother had stayed no doubt because it was a parent of hers who had died. She wanted to be alone in her grief. I stared at the glass door as it swung to and realised that there must be a service entrance at the back. Of course. If only to bring the coffins in the first place, and then load them into the hearse for the final journey. Quite suddenly I was afflicted by the impression that Mother wasn't really dead. She can't be. Or she was dead, but alive too. She was alive in her coffin, in the undertaker's.

I needed a pee. I drained my coffee, gathered the crumbs of my cinnamon twist and stood up. For a moment I thought I might use the bathroom in Costa, but decided against. The urge was merely psychological. I need to get this behind me, I thought. As I crossed the High Street, the glass door swung open and the old man with the umbrella came out arm-in-arm with the young mother. Apparently the two were together. They had made an appointment to see the same corpse and arrived separately from their separate homes. Now they were chatting happily. Seeing the dear departed had cheered them up.

The coast was clear and I could have gone in, or at least rung the bell. Instead I hurried past the dark glass and turned right off the High Street, then right again. Sure enough there was a narrow access street lined with garage doors. A hearse was parked tight against the right-hand wall.

I waited at the corner of the street. The wind was chill, but I had my hat and scarf. The need to go to the bathroom wasn't going away, but it wasn't getting worse, either. I thought again of my mother turning up at this rather downbeat undertaker's to negotiate the terms of her body's disposal. Had she shopped around? And I remembered that when Father died, it had fallen to me, as the only child on the spot, to identify an undertaker's and take her there. And when the man started talking about rose trees and plaques in the crematorium garden, it had been me who said, Put him in the river, Mum, where he liked to row. Put Dad in the river. And she had said: Perhaps you're right, Tom. Dad loved the river.

The food in the freezer was running out. I would need to do a spot of shopping myself soon. I walked back to Mother's house via the Barclays cash dispenser and Tesco's, bought fresh salad, fresh fruit, fresh vegetables, fresh cheese, fresh meat, dumped the lot on the kitchen table, saluted my father's photo in the living room, mounted the steep stairs as an eagle, visited the latrine, nodded to Bangladesh, went into Mother's bedroom and prepared to use Dr Sharp's anal-massage wand. As I pulled the rubber glove over the shaft, the expression 'arming a harpoon' came to mind. From *Moby-Dick* perhaps. How do you arm a harpoon?

But nothing would distract me this time. I lay down on the bed and turned off my phone. Then turned it on again and phoned the shrink in Madrid. Her phone was off. I didn't leave a message on her answer service. You didn't really want to speak to her, I told myself. You are relieved she didn't answer. I turned the phone off again. My computer was in the back room. I got up and went to fetch it. Perhaps what I should really have bought was a fresh tube of Vaseline, but this thought would neither distract nor delay me. Otherwise there would be no end. I took off my jeans and underwear, then once again lay down on Mother's eiderdown. You should change the sheets, I told myself. No. I tied the rubber glove off beyond the stopper, smeared it with ten-year-old unguent, raised and spread my knees, carefully sited the wand where it had to be sited and prepared to plant it in my fundament.

Every muscle in my body tightened to resist intrusion, to resist this strange snorkel affair, Dr Sharp's harpoon. 'Savour that resistance,' Tom Ingram laconically suggested. I had his chinless face onscreen. 'Don't fight it.'

I pressed gently. All at once the wand was as if sucked upwards into the viscera. It seemed to happen of its own accord. The Vaseline had done its job and, with only the slightest pressure, the wand was in. Downstairs the cuckoo clock cuckooed. I burst out laughing. It was nothing, Mum. It was a joke.

'We're not going to do any exploring or massaging,' Tom went on. 'Not today. We're just going to insert the wand, leave it in place for a minute or two, then very carefully withdraw it.'

Feeling pleased with myself, I disobeyed orders and wiggled the wand a little from side to side. This was muscle that had never been touched before. Against orders, I wiggled the wand a bit more. Everything was tender, but not exactly sore. I pulled and pushed and manipulated the wand between my legs so that the ball inside pressed here and there. The wand was a gearstick shifting in my innards. It saved my life, the Portuguese paediatrician told the Dutch lady physiotherapists. Perhaps I could release the clutch and get moving,

I thought. I wondered how the handsome man had spent the night after the talk. Do not try to hit a home-run, Dr Sharp had warned. I pushed down gently on the wand's handle and again it seemed to move of its own accord. Just a hint of resistance, then it popped out. It wasn't even dirty. Pulling my jeans back on, I felt surprisingly relaxed. Perhaps I had done something right at last. Taking the computer into the back bedroom, I immediately fired off an email to my sister.

'Sis,' I wrote, 'if it's one of those funerals where the nearest and dearest are invited to stand up and say a few words about the deceased, I'd really like the chance to do that.'

I then went downstairs, ate a heavy lunch and slept all afternoon.

I had sent this email to my sister on Monday, but received no reply for almost forty-eight hours. On the Tuesday, checking to see that I really had sent it, I was surprised to find I had used the word 'deceased'. Eventually, Wednesday evening, I got a reply, not from my sister, but from my brother-in-law, executor of course of my mother's last will and testament. 'Mum specifically said she didn't want any eulogies at her funeral,' he said, and went on to explain that the ceremony would be officiated by the vicar of St Peter and St Paul, Hounslow, who had been informed of my mother's wishes. 'As you know,' my brother-in-law concluded, 'Mum wrote the funeral programme herself, and my son-in-law, who's a whizz with these things, is getting it printed out with photos, and so on. Hopefully it will look very posh, for a proper sending-off.'

'What I'd planned to say,' I responded at once, 'was not exactly a eulogy.'

My brother-in-law did not reply. He had a business to run, of course.

Each morning, now, I spent half an hour with Dr Sharp's wand. It seemed important to do the deed on Mother's bed. Or at least not inappropriate. Perhaps it was a kind of *un*-baptism, I thought, or *un*-birth even. I put the computer on the bedspread beside me and had Tom Ingram talk me through the explorations of my pelvic floor. His twangy, laconic voice was an adrenalin-damper of the first order. 'We're just managing our insides with a stick,' he said. 'The same way you might use a stick to scratch your back. It's boring, ordinary stuff.'

And yet it was mysterious. Eyes closed, moving the wand fraction by fraction across the muscle behind the abdomen, it seemed I was exploring the dark side of the moon, or the deep inside of myself. Every slight shift of pressure might trigger a pain that was also, obscurely, an emotion. Oceans of fearfulness were frozen here. Sunken hulks of guilt. Did I really feel better afterwards? Did I pee more easily? I wasn't sure. I wasn't sure it mattered. Actually, I wasn't sure anything had happened at all, except my having finally decided to do something I thought I never would. This in itself cheered me up.

At lunch with Deborah in the hospital canteen, she said that Charlie had split up with his friend Stephen and come back down to his old room in the main house. 'It's such a relief that he's himself again,' she said. 'He speaks very highly of you,' she went on. 'Says he's eternally grateful.'

'For what?'

'Whatever you said helped him.'

It was curious, watching Deborah in the humdrum bustle of an NHS canteen. She wore her class about her like a sci-fi deflector-shield. Her table was a protected environment, absolutely distinct from the hubbub all around. She lifted her eyes to mine, batting long lashes. 'And I'm sure you're helping David too, you know.'

As far as I could see, my friend was utterly remote in his barbiturate coma.

I ate fresh food now. Fruit and salad and fresh meat. I sat up writing late into the night. The Telecom trucks came and went. I had the mad idea that when I had written all this down, I would give it to Elsa. And with that gift, all indecision would end.

'I'm writing something for you,' I told her, 'something you won't want to read.'

'I can't wait till you're back, Tommy,' Elsa said. 'It's been such a long time.'

'I'll arrive Friday a.m.,' my brother wrote now. He hadn't written for three days. He would fly from LA to Heathrow and would return immediately after the funeral, Saturday evening.

'That's crazy! You won't even be here forty-eight hours. Come Thursday, stay at least till Monday.'

He had booked the flights, my brother replied. He had a lot on and did not like being away from the family. 'I presume there is somewhere to sleep.'

I spent an hour on Booking.com and eventually settled on the Ibis in Hounslow. I was in an Ibis phase. A room for the twins, a room for my daughter and her man, a room for my brother and myself. My sister's family could have Mother's house. It was the usual Sanders split.

'I'll pay,' I told my brother.

'Ibis?' he wrote. 'How appropriate.'

'Why so?'

'Didn't the Egyptians stuff ibises and place them on guard outside tombs?

'How could a stuffed bird guard anything?' I objected. At the same time I felt I should have chosen a more expensive place. I was still trying to save money. I should have set us up in a four-star suite in Richmond with champagne beside the Jacuzzi.

'I've put the twins on the train.'

It was hardly necessary for my wife to phone to tell me this. The twins could perfectly well have called themselves or sent a text. It was the first time we had spoken since the separation. She sounded perfectly relaxed.

'I'm looking forward to seeing them,' I said. 'I'll be at the station.'

She asked me how I was, and I told her about David's attempted suicide.

'Poor Deborah, she waits all those years to marry and this is how he celebrates.'

Then she said if I felt like it, I could always travel back with the twins on the train to Edinburgh. I could stay a night or two and fly to Madrid from there. There were a couple of things we really ought to discuss.

It was the invitation I had foreseen.

'We could have dinner with the boys. They'd be thrilled.'

'We'll see,' I said.

There was a brief pause, then my wife sighed. 'Listen, Tom, about your mum, I just thought I should tell you I've forgiven her. May she rest in peace.'

I was thrown.

'Forgiven her for what?'

There was another sigh. 'The horrible things she wrote to me after you went.'

I knew nothing of this.

'Anyway, I hope the funeral goes okay. It will be good for the boys to have the experience, I suppose.'

As she said this there was the beep of another phone call arriving and when I closed the conversation, extremely unsettled by what she had told me, I found a number that looked familiar and dialled it at once.

'I'm the person who came to the hospital the other day,' the voice said quietly. 'You're Tom, aren't you? Can we meet?'

'Do you have a name?'

'I will when we meet.'

I explained that I was on my way to pick up my children from King's Cross. 'I'm afraid Saturday is my mother's funeral.'

'I'm so sorry.'

'There's no need to be. She lived to a ripe old age.'

I had been wondering when I would use that expression.

'Perhaps we should speak on the phone,' I suggested.

She hesitated. 'I don't think I'm up to talking on the phone.'

I gave her my mother's address.

'But you'll be there with your family.'

'My sons today, the tribe tomorrow.'

The hour I now had before setting off to Euston to pick up the twins was actually my last chance to see Mother, before being constantly in other people's company until the coffin lid was screwed down on Saturday morning. But instead of phoning the undertaker's, I found myself looking up the website of St Peter and St Paul, Hounslow, as if checking out a conference centre where I was to speak, even though of course I had been told I must not speak on this occasion.

The heart of Christ in the heart of Hounslow, read the slogan. The site had the same feel as the noticeboard in the porch of my father's church forty years ago. Wednesday Coffee Mornings, Friday Prayer Evenings, The Praise & Joy Service every third Sunday of the month. After service, my father, in his robes, would stand in the porch to shake people's hands as they left, rather as an air hostess says goodbye to those disembarking her flight. And when I appeared from the nave and passed him, to get out at last into the fresh air, we would exchange a glance that had a strange complicity and embarrassment, as if we both knew, but must not say, that this was all theatre, that our real lives were at home, in the kitchen, at the dinner table. Or as if he both envied my youth and freedom and feared for me too. I had not remembered this exchange of glances with my father for many years. We both sensed, I suppose, that I would soon be leaving not just the building, but the Church and the faith in the broadest sense, and this understanding somehow brought us closer in a way it did not with my mother. I came down the two steps from the nave into the porch and looked at my father in his robes and he smiled at me with a sad smile that meant, I love you, Thomas, and will not oppose you.

Did my father go to his shrink about me, I wondered?

St Peter and St Paul was a busy church. On the home page photos came and went every few seconds, beneath eight drop-down menus. On a page entitled *The End of Life*, I read, 'Making plans for your death and funeral will be a source of much comfort to those whom you leave.' That depends on the plans, I thought, and I wondered what my wife could have written to my mother, to get an unpleasant response in return. Just the thought of my mother writing in anger seemed so improbable. It wasn't her. And if my wife had written about our separation, why hadn't Mother spoken about it to me? What was the point of my protecting her from the news, if she already knew? Unless Mother was protecting me from the knowledge that I hadn't been able to protect her.

If only, she cried.

Then, clicking on a bright-red button with the word NEWS, I was suddenly looking into my mother's eyes. Or she was looking into mine. *Lay Preacher Martha Sanders Goes Home to Heaven*. We were face to face. It was a recent photo that showed all the toll her disease had taken; still, Mum's eyes were smiling hard. 'If Martha Sanders was not a saint, I don't know who is or ever will be,' the article began. Had I married my wife, I wondered, because she was one of the few people who never succumbed to the myth of my mother's saintliness?

XIX

From the moment I saw the twins detach themselves from the crowd in King's Cross Station, I was drawn into an atmosphere that was wonderfully familiar. We hugged warmly. They had missed me. We hugged again. They liked my hair shaved pretty much to zero. I liked everything about them, their meatiness and bounce. We laughed. They wanted to go immediately to Tottenham Court Road, where they hoped to buy some gadgetry that would accelerate their game console. They were excited to be in town, excited to be on the Underground. I was excited to be with them. I was a father. And I remembered my pleasure when their older brother and sister had arrived at the hospice, the pleasure of seeing strong grown-up children. 'You are throwing all that away,' my wife protested.

'Someone's got a girlfriend.' Mark staged a yawn when Matt kept sending text messages. 'What a bore!'

'Someone's jealous,' Matt responded.

In a pub off Goodge Street they ordered quantities of food. I asked them about their bike race and they explained it had been rained off. Across the table I was overwhelmed by their loud laughter. They had a youth and health quite different from Elsa's, but that made me think of Elsa. It made me think that to tell them about Elsa would somehow mean the end of my fatherhood. Would it? 'The problem,' I remember the shrink remarking, 'is not not-telling them. Why should you tell anyone about your private life, Señor Sanders? Your private life is yours. The problem is not telling them when you feel you should tell them.' But the shrink's voice was fading now. Perhaps I will not go back to Madrid at all, I thought. I will stay in the UK and be a father.

'By the way, there's someone I might have to see later,' I said. 'A woman who was a friend of a friend who's seriously ill. Remember David Pool.'

'It's cool,' the boys interrupted. 'We've got plenty to do.'

They wanted to know what time the funeral was, and whether they could make it to Twickenham for the rugby game afterwards. England–Scotland. It was less than a mile away. Talking it over, I said it would depend on whether or not they came along after the service, to the cremation. They were perfectly free not to come. The main thing was the funeral, not the committal.

'You'd better see if there are still tickets, though.'

I couldn't remember ever having used the word 'committal' before. I must have learned it from Father.

The two fell silent. The twins had always distinguished themselves from each other in all kinds of ways – dress, posture, hair – but all the same there was an intense oneness about them; they emitted the same aura.

'We'll come,' Mark said. 'We've come to see Gran off.'

I felt heartened.

'By the way, can we actually see her, Dad?'

'See her body?'

They nodded.

'You can,' I said. 'Actually, we could go together.' I looked from one to the other. 'Are you sure you really want to, though?'

'Mum said it was the thing to do.'

'It's up to you, really.'

'The truth is we feel bad we didn't come when she was dying.'

I smiled. 'There's no need to feel bad. But if you do want to see her, we'll have to phone for an appointment.'

They hesitated.

'We'll do it,' Matt said. 'We'd like to see her again.'

'Her body,' I reminded them. 'It's not her.'

'Is it frightening?'

'She's been embalmed,' I told them.

Matt wasn't convinced. 'Which means?'

'Which means she's been made to look like she always was.'

'We'll do it,' Mark said.

'You're sure? Shall I phone?'

'Yes.'

'When? When would you like to go?'

They seemed to consult together, without speaking.

'This afternoon.' Matt grinned. 'Get it over with.'

'Okay.'

They listened while I pulled out my old Nokia and phoned at once, from the pub.

'Good afternoon. It's Tom Sanders here, son of Martha Sanders who's in your care. We would like to come to' – I hesitated – 'to view the body. This afternoon.'

'Four o'clock,' I told the boys.

They ate quietly for a while and I asked them how their mother was.

'Fine,' they both said. 'Mum's fine.'

When we got back to Mother's house towards three-thirty, the woman I had seen at the hospital was sitting on the doorstep, smoking. She wore the same jeans and grey coat.

At the gate, Mark leaned across to whisper in my ear. 'Cute.'

Twenty minutes later we all walked together to the undertaker's, rang the bell and I left the twins there. As we walked away, the woman remarked, 'They seemed anxious.'

'It's their first dead body,' I told her.

Her name was Mary Hammond. But at first it seemed she wanted to know all about me, rather than vice versa.

'David never stopped talking about you. He felt it was an omen when you left your wife. He'd thought you never would. And you live in Madrid now?'

'That's right.'

'It must be fantastic.'

'It's far away,' I said.

On automatic pilot, I crossed the road to the bus stop; we could go to Marble Hill and the river, I thought. As we spoke, my boys were viewing Mother's corpse.

Mary Hammond asked me if I was happy.

I said it was not an easy question to answer, when your mother had just died.

'But are you seeing someone? In Madrid.'

'David didn't mention that?'

'No.'

'Sure, I'm seeing someone. We've just moved in together.'

'That's great.'

As we stepped off the bus, the day was dull and cold. We crossed the road and set off across the park towards the river.

'Tell me how you met David,' I asked.

'That's a bit of an issue. You must promise not to tell anyone.'

I promised.

'It was through his son, Charlie.'

'You know Charlie?'

'I went out with Charlie. Briefly.'

'But you're older.'

'Three years. Just. Charlie went to school with my little brother, that's how I met him. We went out for a month or two.'

'But isn't he gay?'

She laughed. 'He is and he isn't.'

I tried to calculate. David must have had Charlie in his early thirties. Which made the age difference between himself and Mary just a little less than that between myself and Elsa.

'You went from son to father?'

She shook her head. 'With Charlie, it was a sort of fun friendship. It wasn't anything really. We didn't do anything. With Dave, it was electric. We knew that we loved each other instantly. Only it wasn't a great way to start, I suppose. That's why we've been so secretive.'

'But Charlie knows. He gave me your phone number.'

She stopped and grabbed my wrist.

'Charlie mentioned me? To you?'

'Not exactly. He gave me a number and told me to call it, and it was yours.'

She thought about this for a moment and we started to walk again.

'The fact is, that's not my regular number. He must have found some messages on David's phone, but not my name. We had rules about that. No names on the phone.' She frowned. 'I nearly jumped out my skin when you called, because I never use that phone for anything except to speak to Dave. It has a special ring for him and another for anyone else, but no one else had ever called. Afterwards I phoned him at once to find out what was going on. I had no idea anything had happened. And of course he didn't reply. He hadn't told me anything.'

I tried to understand. 'When did you last speak to him? You knew he'd been in hospital?'

'Of course! We spoke a dozen times a day. He called me right after the accident. I knew he was going to be out of it for a few days, after a bad fall like that. Obviously it would have been tricky to visit him in hospital. We were going to meet the evening he was discharged.'

Her voice faltered.

'He never said anything about being desperate or taking his life.'

We had reached the river now and the water was moving sluggishly at low tide. We sat on a bench dedicated to the loving memory of someone who had enjoyed walking here, and once again I thought that what I should have done was to stand beside my sons as they viewed Mother's corpse. We should have seen her together. Why did I allow events to capture me like this? My friend's melodrama was his business, not mine.

They had met in David's house, she said now, three years ago. At the time she had just been awarded a PhD place in the States, but understood at once that she would never go. She wanted to be with him as much as possible.

'Life changed completely. In a matter of days. It was crazy. We did crazy things.'

I waited. Mother was laid out in her bonnet and blue tailleur, and my boys were standing beside her.

'He was married, of course. And he was Charlie's father. But you could see the marriage had died ages ago. I hardly even thought of it. David said we just had to believe, and it would work out for us.'

This didn't sound like something David would ever have said. I wondered if he had told her he was married, which of course he hadn't been at the time, or whether she had simply assumed he must be.

Mary talked about the holidays they had taken together. Cornwall, Scotland. They were youthful, inexpensive holidays, camping and hiking, not the four-star hotels Deborah preferred. They had surfed in the Atlantic on Sennen beach. They had walked the length of the Ridgeway. It wasn't the David I knew at all.

'He changed. He kept saying, I'm changed, I've finally changed! He didn't smoke when he was with me. He didn't drink.'

'Didn't drink!'

He had lost weight, she said. They had rented a flat for her. In Richmond. So they could spend nights together.

'I didn't understand how he could wangle this, being married. He said his wife barely noticed where he was or what he was up to.'

She began to describe a cycling trip in Holland. Imagining David cycling was beyond me. Mary was not his type of woman. David went for tall, sassy women in smart skirts and heels, with smart accents, women his own age, or not much younger, with a place in society and forceful opinions and other well-established relationships. Mary was a generous, earnest young woman, well built, round-faced, with a frank, wide mouth and full lips. Ready to begin life.

'Did he introduce you to his friends?'

'He wanted me to meet you, but you were always abroad.'

'It didn't get claustrophobic, just you two?'

She hesitated. 'Not claustrophobic. Just that I wanted things to move on. I wanted to tell people I was in love.'

'You put pressure on him.'

'He put pressure on himself! The problem was always that we'd met through Charlie. He didn't see how we could get round that. Then I was ill for a while. Last spring. I had stomach pains. They did all sorts of tests and never found out what it was. For two or three months. I was feverish and weak. Dave was fantastic. He did everything for me.'

'David's a wonderful guy.'

Mary twisted her neck from side to side as though trying to release a stiffness. 'When he told me you'd left your wife, I took it as a sign. I think he saw your lives as parallel. He said, If Tom has left his wife, anything can happen. He kept saying, Let's go to Madrid and visit Tom.'

I sat staring at the river. I liked Mary, but what was I supposed to say to her? That there had been no fall. That David lied to her systematically? And to everyone else.

305

'Didn't you tell anybody at all?'

'A couple of friends. But no one who mattered.'

'And you're sure Charlie doesn't know?'

She shrugged. 'I see him now and then at my brother's. I'd have noticed if there was a change.'

'And your brother doesn't know?'

'No.'

I thought about it. Why had Charlie asked me to get in touch with this woman? What was it supposed to lead to? A justification for his assault on his father? While marrying my mother, my father is still playing around with other women, promising to marry them even. Was I supposed to tell Deborah? Why didn't he tell her himself? Or was I supposed to tell Mary that David had finally married the woman who had never been his wife, while pursuing this relationship with her? So that she would then leave him alone? Did everybody think that if nothing was ever officially declared, it could all be reversed and denied and no damage done?

Mary leaned forward, elbows on her knees and chin on two white fists. She spoke in a flat voice: 'Sometimes I felt I didn't really exist. And now he's at death's door and no one understands why I'm grieving.'

I couldn't find anything to say.

'I'm usually a happy person,' she said.

Out on the river there was a solitary rower sculling swiftly upstream, occasionally resting his oars to twist around and see where he was going. The conversation had completely emptied me. My sons had seen Mum and I hadn't been with them.

'You said it was your mother's funeral tomorrow? Maybe I'll come along. No one asks why you're crying at a funeral.'

'Feel free,' I told her. 'St Peter and St Paul, Hounslow. Two o'clock.'

Her shoulders trembled. She put her face in her hands. 'I can't,' she muttered. 'I just can't.'

I waited.

'I can't let go of him. I can't believe he did this. I keep thinking it must be my fault.'

'It's not your fault.'

'We were so happy! And there were no obstacles, not really. Who cares how we met? His wife is rich. There was no money problem. She'd lost all interest in him.'

I hesitated, then said quietly, 'I don't know about that.'

Mary's eyes were red. 'Okay. But even if she did care and it mattered to her – even if it really mattered, I mean – why did we have to suffer instead of her?'

'That's a good point.'

'And his children are grown-up. They aren't babies. They aren't even adolescents.' She found a pack of tissues in her bag.

'There are children,' I said, 'who decide to stay children. Or whose parents want them to. For whatever reasons.'

'Charlie,' she said.

We looked at the brown water tugging at an anchored rowing boat. Three ducks were hunkering down in an eddy by the near bank.

'Why did he do it? Why would anyone try to kill themselves when they are with someone they love?'

She turned and leaned against me and I put an arm round her.

'We could have been so happy. We could even now, if he got better.'

I sensed she wanted some encouragement from me.

'If I had an ounce of courage, I'd go and tell them all to fuck off and leave him to me and I'll nurse him. They should just all fuck off, his wife and his children. Then he'd come round.'

'David wasn't well,' I said.

She blew her nose and pulled back a little.

'When do you think he'll wake up? What are the doctors saying?'

'The doctors aren't saying anything.'

We walked back across the park and stood at opposite bus stops for a while, she to go to Richmond, me to Hounslow. Aware of each other across the busy road, there was that slight embarrassment of not knowing whether to make eye contact and, if so, what face to wear. I looked to the right towards the park, but as my bus appeared I turned to say goodbye and found her staring at me. She wore a bewildered expression, as if she'd only just realised something that hadn't occurred to her before. I tried to smile and for one split second imagined Elsa in her place. Only on arriving home did I realise I hadn't been to the bathroom for two hours and more.

'Gran looked pretty cheerful,' Matt said as soon as I was through the door.

The twins were watching television, with bowls of ice-cream on their knees.

'Like she always did.' He was texting as he spoke.

'It wasn't scary at all,' Mark said. 'Just a bit weird.'

'Like a film,' Matt said.

I said, 'That's great.'

'Oh, Mum phoned. She said you're coming back on the train with us. That's fantastic, Dad.'

XX

'You look awful,' my brother told me at Arrivals. Later he asked my daughter's boyfriend, 'Which of us is older, hey? Try and guess. Try and guess. It's a three-year difference. Come on. Who's the older brother?'

'Tom,' the boy said at once.

'Wrong! And I'm just off the fucking plane!' He grinned at me. 'Nine hours' lag!'

'You're in form,' I said.

When we went up to our room at the Ibis, I again felt ashamed I hadn't found anything better. As we let ourselves into a tiny double there was a distinct smell of sewage. Furious, I ran down four flights of stairs to confront the receptionist. 'We can't possibly accept this,' I shouted.

He was an affable young Pakistani. 'No problem, sir,' he said. 'We have plenty of rooms.'

Once in the new room, my brother slept until mid-afternoon. My daughter and her boyfriend went into town with the twins to buy clothes. To make up for my miserliness in the choice of the hotel, I offered the whole family dinner at a Thai restaurant in Twickenham. 'You don't want to be cooking for twelve,' I told my sister.

'You're being very generous these days, Bro,' she observed.

Over spring rolls and Soave, at the end of three tables strung together, my brother-in-law told a story about the problems a Christian community in Gillingham had run into, when one of their members raised another from the dead. 'They couldn't get the registry office to revoke the Death Certificate,' he laughed. 'Please let's not talk nonsense,' my brother said brusquely. The twins were sniggering. 'Did you go to see her in the end?' my sister asked me quietly, as if appreciating that I wouldn't want the others to overhear. 'The boys went,' I told her. Then as the noise level swelled, making it possible to whisper to one's neighbour, I admitted to my sister that I had been feeling extremely bad about not having sat with Mother for a while after she finally expired. 'I just feel I should have stayed,' I said. 'I feel I let her down.' There was a hail of laughter now, because my daughter's boyfriend was challenging my brother to a game that involved flipping up beer mats from the table edge and catching them as they spun in the air. 'I didn't stay, either,' my sister said easily. 'Mum would never have wanted us to.' 'At least over dinner you could stop texting,' Mark complained. 'Matt has got a girlfriend,' he told the whole table. 'Be sure that you're the lucky one,' my brother told him. 'Old cynic!' my sister laughed. She had always called my brother an old cynic.

Later, when we had retired to our Ibis room, my brother asked me what on earth was wrong with me. 'I thought you had a beautiful new woman,' he said. 'Shouldn't you be in seventh heaven? You look like you're expecting to be arrested any minute.'

I told him about David. About Deborah and Charlie. About my conversation with Mary. My brother lay under his white quilt chuckling and shaking his head. 'Someone should put a stake through that guy's heart,' he said, 'before he does any more damage.'

'Why do I keep feeling I have to go and see Mother's body?' I asked him.

'Morbid curiosity,' he replied at once. 'She's there, so you think you have to see her. But you don't have to and it's not really her, and because you still have half an ounce of sense in your skull, you don't go.' He turned over to sleep. 'Unless it's some genetic thing,' he added, 'programmed a million years ago.'

'Almost all cultures have wakes,' I told him. 'Or some kind of ritual, being together around the body.'

'For Christ's sake, Tommy,' he said. 'Cheer the fuck up!'

The twins had gone to hear a band in Putney. Towards midnight a text message arrived from Mary. 'Managed to get in the ward and sit with him. I think I will go mad.'

I decided not to reply.

'Bob is bringing the programmes,' my brother-in-law said.

We were at Mother's house again, mid-morning. Saturday. A huge wreath of yellow roses was lying on the kitchen table. My brother and I were to contribute fifty pounds each. She had chosen yellow roses rather than lilies, my sister said, because lilies were so melancholy. 'Heartily agree,' my brother said. 'Those white lilies do make everything feel so awfully funereal.'

'Idiot,' my sister smiled. She wanted to take the roses home with her, she said, when it was over. It was silly spending all that money and leaving them to rot in the crematorium.

'Embalm 'em,' my brother proposed. 'Let's have 'em last for ever!'

There was coffee and Viennese chocolate biscuits, served on Mother's old trolley. Its wheels laboured in the thick carpet. The twins were imitating the cuckoo. A small dog tore back and forth between sitting room and kitchen. A text from my wife read: 'Since you're coming up with the boys this evening, any chance you could get me a new laptop? Mine's clapped out. Anything that works. I never have any idea what to get.'

My daughter's boyfriend was telling the twins the Scottish rugby team didn't have a ghost of a chance. Uncle Harry arrived with my cousin, and my brother-in-law began to tell us who would be riding in which car. It seemed natural that he should play master of ceremonies. I put my coat back on and walked up the High Road. I called Elsa, but her phone was off. Was that odd on a Saturday morning? I stopped at the newsagent's, asked for a pack of Marlboro and a lighter, then went into Dixons and bought a mid-range Toshiba with a pale-pink case. Why on earth are you doing this, Señor Sanders, I imagined the shrink's voice, as if you were still her husband?

I crossed the High Road, ordered a cappuccino at Costa, took it outside and nearly fainted after the third puff of Marlboro. Then, seeing a young man at the door to the undertaker's, I jumped to my feet and rushed into the road. A motorcyclist braked and shouted. I slipped through the dark glass door as it was closing.

'Mr Carrington?' a voice was saying. 'This way, please.'

There was a very tight little space and a reception desk, low wall-lighting and low music of a New Age variety, flutes and running water. At first glance, it was not unlike a doctor's surgery, except for a heavy use of dark-green marble, white lilies on a low table and large black-and-white photos of horse-drawn hearses. Quite determined now, I waited. There were murmurs from another room, then a blonde woman in her forties appeared wearing a dark-red skirt and jacket.

'Sorry, I popped in on the wake of the other gentleman,' I explained. 'I would like to see Mrs Sanders. I'm her son.'

The woman consulted a timetable on her desktop. 'We were expecting you yesterday,' she said. She sat down at her desk and adjusted her spectacles. 'So many people have been to pay homage to your mother, Mr Sanders. She must have been very popular.'

'She was well known in the church,' I said.

'However, I'm afraid your mother's coffin has already been sealed.'

She looked at me from slightly narrowed eyes. I didn't know what to say.

'Let me just go and see if there's anything we can do, Mr Sanders.'

Perhaps I smiled, or tried to. The woman pushed back her chair and slipped out of the door behind. A message arrived in my pocket, but I ignored it. Low voices came from the back room. Then a loud thud. And with that thud I realised I had left the Toshiba in a Dixons plastic bag beside my seat on the pavement outside Costa Coffee.

I banged out of the door and again raced across the High Road. This time a horn sounded. The bag wasn't there. I stood staring. How long had I been away? Five minutes? Yet another message arrived and I pulled my phone out.

'Dad, can you get some H3 batteries please?'

'Sir,' a voice interrupted. It was the young French girl who had served me. 'Sir, your bag.'

Only a few minutes later did I check the other message. It was from Deborah.

'He's woken up, Tom. It's a miracle.'

Entering the church of St Peter and St Paul for my mother's funeral, it seemed to me time ended here. Having failed either to view her body or decide not to view it, I might as well be cremated with her. Had I really agreed to travel north to Edinburgh as soon as the cremation was over? Would I ever get on a plane to Madrid? To Elsa. Both these journeys seemed the stuff of fantasy. From the moment the Californian physiotherapist had slipped his subtle finger into my anus at the hotel in Amersfoort, I had fallen under a spell. The time spent in my mother's house had been an enchantment. A coma. Across west London a soft drizzle had begun to fall. Planes descended on Heathrow in thick cloud. I too was proceeding on automatic pilot, guided by others. Under the flight path, the church was packed. At the top of the aisle, two trestles awaited my mother's coffin.

A miracle, Deborah had texted. I had read her message on the street, carrying the box with my wife's new computer and a pack of H3 Duracells for the twins. Presumably it was Mary who had woken David up. Woken him to what? To his wife's declaring it a miracle. Your beloved mistress brings you back to life, only for your wife to repossess you and rejoice. Entering Mother's house, I had felt a powerful urge to vomit.

In the sitting room my sister's son-in-law had just brought freshly printed copies of the funeral programme, which my brother-in-law was declaring 'mighty spiffy'. He turned the pages back and forth with evident satisfaction.

'A very superior publication,' my brother agreed. He too turned the pages. 'Only it doesn't say anything about a funeral.'

'Mum didn't want us to use the word,' my sister said. 'She wanted it to be a service of thanksgiving.'

There were plates of sandwiches on the low table between recliner and sofa. A dozen people crowded round. 'Going Home to Glory' the programme was titled: 'A Service of Celebration and Thanksgiving for the Life of Martha Florence Sanders'. A round photo showed Mother in half profile, face tilted to the sky, full of energy and hope.

'Who chose the picture?' I asked.

'She did,' my sister said.

I went upstairs to dress. My dark suit from the Berlin inaugural address was hanging in the wardrobe in her bedroom. I should never have gone to Berlin, I thought. Together with a white shirt. Should I wear a tie? It had been sheer lunacy to set out for the airport the second her breathing stopped. I couldn't decide. The shirt wasn't freshly cleaned, but clean enough.

I stood barefoot in my mother's bedroom, unable to decide about the tie, unable to shake off the reflection that my inaugural address to the 27th Annual Conference of European Linguists had been fatal. Without that conference, I would surely have sat with Mother for a few minutes after her death. I would have protected her in the crucial moments when the soul abandons the body. She would have acknowledged my presence. In some way. Or I would have imagined her acknowledging it. In short, I would have taken leave of my mother properly, then flown back to Madrid and Elsa and sanity. If I hadn't gone to Berlin to deliver that talk, driven by an inflated idea of my own importance, a childish excitement about my own feverish ideas, I wouldn't be hovering here now, unable to decide whether to wear a tie or not. Mother always insisted I wear a tie to church, I remembered. Not wearing a tie had been a first significant step towards emancipation and independence. How old was I, the day I finally walked into church without a tie? Sixteen, seventeen? But why was I thinking about such trivia?

What settled it was seeing an old tie of Father's in the top drawer of Mother's dresser. I pulled out the top drawer of the dresser, quite at random, and for some reason, thirty years after his death and cremation and the scattering of his ashes from Kew Bridge, there was a tie of Father's neatly folded among Mother's underwear and stockings. Dark blue with silver crests. Seduced by a sense of inevitability, I wrapped it round my neck. If I couldn't give my heart to Jesus, I could at least wear a tie. Downstairs, I noticed my brother was entirely himself in a grey tweed jacket over a smart black polo neck. Who – whom – would David choose, I wondered, now he had woken up again? Or would he just make a better job of topping himself, when he found he couldn't?

Programme in hand, my brother-in-law was reminding us of the timing. D-Day minus fifteen. D-Day minus ten. He consulted the digital display on his iPhone. The cars, the coffin, the seating, the reception, the cremation. The day was out of my hands. 'I will get the first available flight,' I had texted Elsa, making no reference to the train to Edinburgh. 'If you want to stay another day or two with your family, feel free,' she replied.

'The cars!' Mark and Matt shouted.

Mother's cul-de-sac was in the form of a T. The three big cars had trouble turning, the hearse in particular. It manoeuvred back and forth. Standing at the front door, I glimpsed the coffin through gleaming glass. It seemed too large, too polished, and quite unconnected with the exhausted body I had abandoned on the hospice bed. I stared. I felt intensely that we should be moving towards it, to greet it in some way, to pay our respects, but nobody moved. We watched together from the doorstep as the hearse inched backwards and forwards and the coffin slowly turned through a hundred and eighty degrees, like some object on a revolving display. You follow none of your instincts, I thought. Dad's tie felt tight. Anal massage had not saved my life. I hurried back into the house for a last pee and instead found myself vomiting. I vomited my breakfast. At least this was something new, I reflected, drinking from the tap to freshen my mouth. It just wasn't Tom Sanders to throw up his cereal.

One thing I hadn't foreseen was that the undertaker would walk in front of the hearse in his dress suit, all the way from Mother's house to SS Peter and Paul Parish Church, a distance of perhaps half a mile. In the car immediately behind, I began to wish I too was walking ahead of the hearse, or beside the coffin. I needed to move.

'Who will carry the coffin into church?' I asked my sister.

'The undertaker's men,' she said.

Then she added that the undertaker's secretary had asked whether any of us wanted to help with the bearing, but her husband had thought no, and at once I yearned to carry the coffin, to feel its harsh weight on my shoulder. If I couldn't view Mother, at least I could carry her. Bear her. One says 'bear' when it comes to coffins. As with children. Bear a coffin, bear a child. Bear the brunt.

Then my sister asked, lightly but seriously, if I and my brother were planning to cry at the funeral.

We were sitting three on the seat, looking forward beyond the driver to the hearse, which was now slowing traffic on the High Street. Faces tried to look into our car as we slid by.

'Planning to cry? I've nothing scheduled,' my brother joked.

'I'm determined not to,' my sister told us. She didn't want to make an exhibition of herself, she said, and be in a state for the reception afterwards. 'Mum wouldn't have wanted us to,' she added.

'I always cry at funerals,' I said.

My brother made to ruffle the hair I no longer had. 'Tearful Tommy!' he laughed. 'Feet of clay!'

The hearse proceeded up the High Street with exasperating slowness. My brother was making quips about the undertaker now, his Dickensian demeanour under that tall top hat. So reassuring to be back in the UK, he said. Settling into the back seat, I opened my mother's programme:

Welcome, dear friends.

The text was in italics.

Thank you for coming and joining in; what I desire, above all things, is that this should be a service of celebration – not of my life and achievements, but of the wonderful Lord, who has been my strength and stay, all my life.

It was her voice. Mother was going to conduct her own funeral. I hadn't quite grasped this till now.

I have always loved the words of Jacob who, after a long and chequered life, could say as he blessed his grandchildren, 'The God who has been my shepherd all my life to this day, the Angel who has delivered me from all harm, bless the boys.' The Lord has certainly been my shepherd, saved me, blessed me, guided and delivered me. I heartily recommend my dear Saviour to you.

Martha Sanders.

Bless the boys! I suddenly felt alert. Why the boys, and not the children? I couldn't remember the details of Jacob's story, but felt at once that this blessing was intended for my brother and myself, the unbelievers. Mother was dead, but still making this appeal, still playing her hand.

In something of a daze, I climbed out of the car and followed my sister and brother across a patch of grass, into a porch and up the aisle of the nave. I had expected that we would walk behind the coffin, but it seemed that it was to be brought after us. The canonical moments for showing grief had been edited out of the event, together with the word 'funeral'. *What I desire, above all things, is that this should be a service of celebration.*

Inside, the church was petite Victorian Gothic, dank and twee, but generously festooned with flowers. The congregation murmured as we passed. These people knew Mother well, they had heard her preach on many occasions, but had never seen her children. Or not her boys. The rebellious boys. They knew Mother's charisma, but not the cross she had to bear.

With the coffin trestles to our left, we filed into a very short front pew, truncated by a thick stone buttress. Our places had been decided for us: my brother at the end against the buttress; myself beside him; we were trapped there, quarantined perhaps, by my sister, to my left; then next to her, beside the aisle and closest to the coffin, my brother-in-law. 'Because he has to go up front to read the lesson,' my sister whispered.

In the pew behind us were Uncle Harry and his son. But again the place by the aisle, close to the coffin, went to my sister's son, my nephew; he too was to give a reading. My sister's family, who shared Mother's evangelical convictions, would be active in the service. This had all been agreed months ago. Her boys, more accustomed to public speaking, would play no part. We had been blessed. We must keep mum.

Waiting for the coffin, my brother turned round and joked with our cousin, Uncle Harry's son, immediately behind him. I stared about me at the familiar trappings of an Anglican church and the less familiar paraphernalia of high-church ceremony: lighted candles, a crucifix. I hadn't been in a church in decades. Suddenly the old aura was upon me. The organ struck up, sombre.

It was the funeral march. I turned and there she was. The wooden box was swaying on the shoulders of six coffin-bearers, six men I didn't know from Adam to carry my mother, who was dead, embalmed against her will, but also conducting the service that brought us all together. I had failed to view her, failed to make up my mind. Indeed, no sooner had the coffin been lowered on its trestles than a dog-collared lady with a breathy voice began reading out Mother's welcome. 'The God who has been my shepherd all my life to this day, the Angel who has delivered me from all harm, bless the boys.' I had failed to understand how I should behave towards my mother's embalmed body. Over the yellow roses heaped on the polished wood, I saw my children in the front pew on the other side of the nave. My daughter was trying to catch my eye.

Pink and blond, the Reverend Pip or Paddy or Pete now popped up from his seat in the chancel and announced the hymn. *Thine be the glory, risen, conquering Son.* As in the Claygate Hospice, this incongruous man was there to execute my mother's wishes, to confirm her version of events 100 per cent. She was in Paradise; she was sitting at God's right hand. As at the Claygate Hospice, I was electrified in pure opposition, but could do nothing, say nothing, bound and gagged by the person who refused to be grieved.

On our feet now, my brother turned to share my programme. He had contrived to lose his. The hymn was printed over a faded close-up of Mother singing from a hymn sheet. She was singing with us. As the organ launched into the tune, I opened my mouth to sing, but nothing came. I couldn't. My brother, on the contrary, immediately found a strong, even fruity voice. *Endless is the victory*, he sang, *Thou o'er death hast won*. He was enouncing the words with great energy and apparent satisfaction. I opened my mouth again, but again nothing came out. Dad's tie was choking me. *Angels in bright raiment*, my brother sang, *rolled the stone away*. I was surprised by his polished performance. I had expected my brother to remain silent – he had never wanted to come to the funeral, had he? he was a declared atheist – and here he was, projecting his hymn-singing voice like a pro, even vying with the Reverend Pat, who stood immediately above us on the chancel steps, in voluminous robes, his ruddy complexion glowing with complacency. *Kept the folded grave clothes where thy body lay*, my brother sang. Was it participation, I wondered, moving the programme a little closer for him to read, or irony? He was pronouncing his t's and d's with exaggerated emphasis. Or is irony the only participation possible in certain situations? If one isn't to walk out. Husbands and wives. Doctors exploring anuses. I don't want to be here, but if I have to, I'll ironise. *Lo! Jesus meets us*, my brother sang, *risen from the tomb*. Was it my impression, or had he really pronounced the b? The hymn was a clutter of crazy archaisms, as the twee church was an agglomeration of tired architectural gestures from centuries before, Norman arches, stone crosses, stained windows. *Lovingly He greets us*, my brother sang, *scatters fear and gloom*. Did gloom have a b too? Not a trace of a smile crossed my brother's chiselled face. I should do as he does, I thought. I should join in and enjoy the awfulness, the awfulness Mother loved. I opened my mouth, but still no sound would come. Then my hand was shaking so much my brother had to raise his, to steady the programme between us. His voice rose even louder: *Let the Church with gladness, hymns of triumph sing.*

Suddenly I was aware that someone in the crowd behind was watching me, watching intently, observing my posture, spying on my emotional state, my failure to join in the singing. Was that possible? Had Elsa come, without saying a word? Or more likely my wife. Or Charlie even. How had Charlie reacted to David's waking? Or Mother from her coffin; Mother still willing me to change my mind, reaching for a Triple Word Score. If only, Thomas. Instinctively, I turned towards her. The coffin was huge. She had swelled in death. And over the gleaming wood, in the pew beyond, I once again met my daughter's steady eyes.

Unsettled, I turned back to the programme. To my left my sister was singing softly and deliberately. It wasn't in her plans to cry. Beyond her, her husband's voice was powerful and full of faith. He was so solid. To my right my brother soldiered on. *Death hath lost its sting*, he sang. *Safe through Jordan to thy home above.* Then all at once he was struggling. Suddenly, my brother's voice wavered. It was getting to him. Mother was dead in her box and we were rhyming tomb and gloom.

I pulled myself together. It seemed important that my brother not cave in, not lose his caustic poise. I opened my mouth for the final lines, and this time the words came loud and clear. *No more we doubt Thee,* I sang, *glorious Prince of life.* Immediately his voice grew stronger too. We even gave the last refrain some real oomph. *Thine be the glory. Endless is the vict'rrry.* The ghost of a smile crossed my brother's lips and we both sat down, exhausted. I needed to go to the bathroom. In my pocket a text buzzed. I had forgotten to turn off the phone.

My brother-in-law now read about Lazarus raised from the dead. In the programme Mother had titled the lesson *DO YOU BELIEVE THIS?* (John 11, 12–27). 'Do you believe this?' the big man boomed. He dropped his voice and smiled. 'Actually, I should apologise to Mum, our dear Martha, because I'm going to read from the Contemporary English Version. She preferred King James, of course. But I'm not a boffin, and what matters most is understanding.'

So, after all that had been said about obeying Mother's wishes, I thought, my brother-in-law was doing as he saw fit. He was being himself. As my sister had seen fit to have her embalmed. If you believed strongly enough, you could allow yourself a certain latitude. If your faith was rock-solid, you didn't need the archaisms. I felt a sniff of envy for my brother-in-law. He had replaced my brother and myself as the legitimate son, the executor of Mother's will, and I realised that whenever I hear the question, Do you believe?, I automatically answer, No. No, I really don't.

Do you believe in your love for Elsa?

A man by the name of Lazarus was sick in the village of Bethany. He had two sisters, Mary and Martha. This was the same Mary who later poured perfume on the Lord's head and wiped his feet with her hair.

How odd, I thought, that Mother was called Martha and I had so recently met a woman called Mary. Had she poured perfume on David's head, to wake him from his coma? Or wiped his feet with her hair?

The sisters sent a message to the Lord and told him that his good friend Lazarus was sick. When Jesus heard this, he said, 'His sickness won't end in death. It will bring glory to God and his Son.'

Glory again. This constant repetition of words with no concrete referent. What could omnipotence care, in the end, what impotence happened to think of it?

Jesus loved Martha and her sister and brother. But he stayed where he was for two more days. Then he said to his disciples, 'Now we will go back to Judea.'

'Teacher,' they said, 'the people there want to stone you to death! Why do you want to go back?'

This had to be the right question. Why go looking for trouble after you've deliberately let slip the chance to say goodbye to your friend?

Jesus answered, 'Aren't there twelve hours in each day? If you walk during the day, you will have light from the sun, and you won't stumble. But if you walk during the night, you will stumble, because you don't have any light.'

I must have missed a few lines here, trying to fathom what on earth this was about. What did it mean, walking in the light, walking in the dark? Mother is dead, I thought then, and you are trying to work out what day and night have to do with the dangers of being stoned to death. But now I heard my name.

Thomas, whose nickname was 'Twin,' said to the other disciples, 'Come on. Let's go, so we can die with him.'

Thomas. Mother had chosen a passage with Martha and Thomas. Why was he called twin? Because he was double in some way? My brother leaned to me and whispered. 'Ever the catastrophist.'

When Jesus got to Bethany, he found that Lazarus had already been in the tomb four days. When Martha heard that Jesus had arrived, she went out to meet him. 'Lord, if you had been here, my brother would not have died. Yet even now I know that God will do anything you ask.'

Jesus told her, 'Your brother will live again!'

Martha answered, 'I know that he will be raised to life on the last day, when all the dead are raised.'

Jesus then said, 'I am the one who raises the dead to life! Everyone who has faith in me will live, even if they die. And everyone who lives because of faith in me will never really die. Do you believe this?'

'Yes, Lord!' she replied. 'I believe that you are Christ, the Son of God. You are the one we hoped would come into the world.'

My brother-in-law stopped. That was it! He closed the book. Just when I had begun to relax and enjoy the story, begun to look forward to the moment where Jesus tells the family to roll away the stone and Martha protests, *Lord, he stinketh*. I remembered that line from my choirboy days. Though no doubt it would be 'smells bad' or something similarly lame in this modern version. 'I'm not afraid of the dying,' Mother had said, 'but cancer just smells so bad.'

'Do you believe this?'

My brother-in-law raised his head to repeat Mother's challenge, before returning to his seat. It was obvious she had meant the question for her sons. She had trapped us in church one last time for the final confrontation. Do you believe, Tom? 'Yes, Lord!' The affirmation was Martha's, my mother's. She imagined the words ringing out as she went to meet her Maker. Meantime, Lazarus would have to live and die again, as David would have to choose between his wife and mistress and suicide. Happy as Larry, I had told my sister in their stinking van. After the funeral, I thought, I must rush to the West Middlesex and confront David. That was the way forward. Neither Edinburgh nor Madrid, but my old friend, David.

Choose Mary, I would tell him.

No, choose Deborah.

We were on our feet for the next hymn. 'An old favourite,' the Reverend Pip announced, *'Just as I am, without one plea*. Composed,' he informed the congregation, 'in 1835 by Charlotte Elliot, but with a last verse' – here the Reverend paused and smiled indulgently – 'with a last verse written by Martha herself.'

Mum was rewriting the hymns. And only now did I realise there was a choir. How had I contrived not to notice? A dozen or so men and women, none under fifty, standing in the stalls, holding their hymnbooks on opened palms.

> *Just as I am, and waiting not*
> *To rid my soul of one dark blot*
> *To thee, whose blood can cleanse each spot*
> *O Lamb of God, I come, I come.*

I was singing together with my brother now. I was smiling at the inanity of it. Perhaps this was the verse I should have used for my address to the European linguists. It was too stupid. And I was wild with frustration. When was I ever going to grieve? To get my teeth into grief? First I had missed the moment beside my mother's breathless body, then the viewing at the undertaker's, now even the funeral was to be turned into farce, grief bottled up in rhyming babble because Mother needed to believe there was no cause for grief. Like someone who will not blow their nose because they cannot concede the existence of colds. Grief was thickening in me like catarrh. Even Jesus wept, didn't he? Wept for Lazarus, before raising him from the dead. Jesus wept. But Mother had stopped her son-in-law before we got to that verse.

> *Here for a season, then above,*
> *O Lamb of God, I come, I come.*

My son, I remembered, had once asked me for a CD by the heavy-metal band Lamb of God, for a birthday present. *Burn the Priest*, it was called. But now we had arrived at the verse Mother wrote:

Just as I am, old, tired and frail,
To see Thy face beyond the veil,
I climb on still, though steep the hill
O Lamb of God, I come, I come.

I stopped singing and wept. How near, how very near Mother had come to saying the truth. That she was in trouble. That faith was weak and victory lost. But this dangerous truth had to be quarantined in the safe house of dogma and doggerel. My shoulders shook. Mother lived all her life imprisoned in the stanzas of *Ancient & Modern*. They were the veil that prevented us from meeting face to face.

We sat while my nephew read a poem. One stands and sits like a marionette in church. Up down, up down. Moved by wires. My sister's son, this was. I couldn't follow his words. He's a handsome young man. Blond again. I was aware of the pink face of the priest, watching me with sublime condescension, pitying the breakdown of the unbeliever. I was aware that my nephew read well, but clearly felt a certain embarrassment with what he was reading. Another text message arrived in my pocket. *Trustfully treading Your path,* my nephew wound up. *The only one that leads to life – to You.*

Now that I had started weeping, I couldn't stop. I saw no cause to stop. I wept for Mother and I wept against her. My sister leaned her lips to my ear.

'Everything will be all right, Tommy,' she said.

My brother gave no sign of having noticed. He seemed more rigid than ever, frozen in a trance of irony. And as yet another message arrived in my pocket, I thought that my brother and sister had put me in a position where I would have to weep for all three of us. I would have to howl.

'Dear Martha didn't want a eulogy,' the Reverend Pip or Pat began his sermon. 'But she's jolly well going to get one.' He chuckled. 'She will just have to listen up in heaven and grit her saintly teeth.'

There were titters, from the pews behind. I sobbed.

Since when was 'listen up' standard English?

'It's understandable,' the Reverend Pat conceded, 'that members of Martha's family will lament her passing, but essentially, for our Christian family, this is a happy day, a day of celebration.'

The man had no idea of the anger he was stirring. I bowed my head, always with the feeling I was being observed. Someone was pitying, criticising, someone who knew I had failed to view my mother's body, or failed to decide whether to view it. But I had no intention of stopping my tears now. I needed to pee. The Reverend Pete was explaining how Mother helped him with his sermons. '"The Lord has laid out so many rich foods," she would tell me. "All you have to do is choose which you are going to serve up each day."'

I kept my eyes closed, my face in my hands. No doubt this was how Mum felt about guests who came to lunch. What should she serve them? Macaroni cheese, or lamb cutlet, or chicken salad. In the end she had a pretty limited repertoire. And what would I serve up, I suddenly asked myself, if by some miracle they were to let me say a word here, or if I had the courage to vault the pew and wrestle the microphone from Reverend Pip. This is a funeral, I would shout. Mother is dead. That's how I would begin. Then I would say, Mother was always generous. Which was true. I would say she always remembered birthdays. I would say she never complained if you didn't phone for a while. Which is a special form of generosity. I would say that when Mother finally learned to stop preaching to her children, it had actually been pretty good to sit down and have a sherry with her or polish off a rhubarb crumble together, very likely discussing the latest follies of the Church of England Synod. Women clergymen, gay bishops. Of course it was Mother who taught me how to lie; it was Mother's need to believe I was good that taught me all my shiftiness. But I would have spared the good folks that. If my sister and brother-in-law, in league with the Reverend Pete of course, or Puck perhaps, had given me a fraction of the credit they afforded to this son of God, who let a friend die so that He could impress the world by bringing him back to life, I would not have troubled the congregation with my personal gripes on this solemn occasion. I wouldn't have mentioned Mother's invariably dismissive opinions of my girlfriends. Or the fact that she thought yoga the work of the devil, and AIDS a scourge from God to prick gay pride. Skip that. We learned to enjoy a few good times together, I would have told the good Christian souls, without insisting on our differences. We learned, almost, to be mother and son. And on her headstone, if she had chosen to have a headstone, I would have put: Her Christmas cards always arrived early.

It was over. My eulogy had more or less matched the Reverend's in time. I had shut him out. We were jerked to our feet for the last hymn. *Tell out my soul, the greatness of the Lord!* I wouldn't even try to sing. *Unnumbered blessings give my spirit voice.* My brother sang it. I didn't. Enough irony. Irony is corrosive, of the ironist more than the target. I must tell my brother that. *Unnumbered* was awful. Irony was a way of living with a situation you really should refuse to live with. Unnumbered inanities. Back to the Trouble and Strife, David would sigh, after discussing mistresses over three or four pints. Back to the Queen of Unreason. I must tell my brother to stop getting through with irony, before the irony gets through him. *Proud hearts and stubborn wills are put to flight,* he sang. From a proud heart, I thought, from a stubborn will.

Suddenly I took his hand. I switched the programme to my left hand and took my brother's left in my right. At once he squeezed it with intense warmth. His grip was firm and manly. After a moment

I switched the programme back and took my sister's right hand with my left. She was singing steadily, guardedly. She too seized my hand with great warmth. She too squeezed it, affectionately, immediately. And now it occurred to me I could drop Mother's programme and take both my brother's hand and my sister's, one on each side, all three siblings holding hands in grief. But it was impossible. I couldn't just let Mother's programme fall to the floor while we were still singing her last hymn. *Tell out, my soul, the greatness of the Lord, to children's children and for evermore!*

It was over. The moment was gone. As we filed out of the pew, the coffin was triumphant under its pile of flowers. Invulnerable. Mother was safe inside. I turned away. Walking down the aisle, I searched the congregation. Who had been watching me? There wasn't a face I knew. Not Mary or Deborah or Charles. Why on earth would they have come, with all they had on their plate today? Not my wife, or Elsa. Everybody was staring at the one tearful face, the one person who had made an exhibition of himself. I knew none of them. In the drizzle outside the porch I took the phone from my pocket and called my shrink. The screen told me there were four messages. I had only registered receiving three. I ignored them and called Madrid. Not Elsa, but the shrink. The phone rang and rang. People milled around in the drizzle: *Ha llamado el número seis ocho cinco . . .* began the answering service. I closed the call and texted: '*Estoy en dificultades, doctora, necesito consejos inmediatos.*'

I also needed the bathroom. My children had come to me, all four of them. Tears call for comfort. We embraced. It was fine to have them here. But I didn't want to be crying now. I wanted to pee. Meantime, people were making for the Church Hall. Since the cremation couldn't take place till four-thirty, there was now to be a reception in the Church Hall. To kill the ninety minutes' wait. I asked an elderly lady where the bathrooms were, then read my messages, leaning on the wall behind the bowl.

'Had a bad dream, Tom. Could you call?'

'I'd be grateful if you could come and comfort my mother. No doubt you knew all along I had given my father no more than he deserved.'

'Tom, which room shall I make up for you? Looking forward to seeing you. The boys are thrilled you're coming. Hugs.'

'Tom, old mate, St Pete just rattled his keys at me and sent me back to mayhem. Any chance you could get over here and give me skin?'

I peed and washed my face in cold water. Someone turned the handle to get in. For the second time. A long church service can push the oldies to the limit. Just the crematorium now, I thought, just the flames.

The hall was a buzz of voices. There were long tables and food. The Lord has laid out so many rich foods. Salmon sandwiches, vols-au-vent, fruit salad. Had Mother chosen these too? It seemed terribly unlike Elsa to ask me to phone because of a bad dream. A man shook my hand and began to tell me he had known my father, who had helped him greatly. My parents were saints, he said. He appeared to be in his late sixties. They were sitting at God's right hand. I reached for a piece of quiche and found I had no appetite. 'You will get quite a welcome yourself when you join them,' he laughed. 'You are a lucky man to have had such a mother and father.' I listened with a piece of quiche in my hand and no desire to eat it, as previously I had held a hymn sheet with no desire to sing. The important thing is to do what you want to do, the shrink will say. But what possible advice can a shrink offer someone who has lost all desire? Someone who isn't anyone at all – or two someones cancelling each other out. Thomas, whose nickname was Twin. The quiche in my hand seemed to be cancelling out anything I might have said to this man who was trying to be kind to me. My father had helped him to make important choices at a crucial moment in his life, he was explaining, a moment when he could easily have taken a wrong turn. He spoke with a full plate in his hand. I noticed a roast-beef sandwich. The woman nodding vigorously beside him must be his wife. Not wanting to, I took a bite of quiche, if only to have some excuse for not responding. A more elderly woman joined the conversation, leaning on a stick. 'The Lord will wipe away your tears,' she said. 'Your grief will pass.' 'England will wipe out the Scots,' a voice behind was saying emphatically. My daughter's boyfriend. 'Want to bet?' My phone was ringing. My mouth was full of quiche. My knees felt weak. Then somebody pushed a book into my hand. *Prayers that Rout Demons* by John Eckhardt. He had borrowed it from Martha, but she had died before he could return it. Taking the book, I put down the quiche and pulled the phone from my pocket. It was the shrink's number. I rejected the call. I am beyond advice. But what was I supposed to do with John Eckhardt, I wondered? Take him to the cremation? Then across the room a voice shouted. 'Piss Christ! It's the "Piss Christ"!'

XXI

The voice was my brother's and it broke the spell. He shouted the words at the top of his voice. 'Piss Christ!' There was something of a kerfuffle, if not exactly mayhem. Only later would I appreciate how it began. My brother and sister had come over to the church hall together, surrounded by a murmur of condolences. In the hall, while I was in the bathroom trying to pee and reading my texts, the Reverend Pat, Bible in hand and still in full liturgical regalia, had come to say a word to my sister, who had introduced him to my brother who, typically, had passed some remark about not under-standing why no one had arranged for a firework display, to give our thanksgiving a bit of a crackle. 'Not a bad idea!' the Reverend had indulgently replied and had begun to say to my sister, as if she were the only interested party, that the church grounds did seem to him the obvious and appropriate home for my mother's ashes, when my brother spotted the photograph that the Reverend Pip had pasted, or taped, to the back cover of his Bible. It showed a yellowish crucifix looming in a strangely smeared, intensely orange atmosphere, as though in a murky flame-lit smoke.

Then, while my sister was saying she couldn't honestly recall my mother having said anything as to where her ashes were to be scattered – it was the one thing she didn't appear to have thought of – my brother asked the Reverend Pete if he was aware that this was a photo by the controversial American photographer, Andres Serrano. The Reverend said he did know, but said it in such a distracted fashion, still evidently focused on the question of whether my mother's ashes should be dug into the roses climbing the east wall or simply dispersed on the lawn, that my brother was convinced he did not know. Was he aware what the photo was called, my brother pressed the Reverend, who didn't reply, as my sister was saying it would be a month at least before the crematorium handed over the ashes, though heaven only knew what they did with them all that time. How could it take so long? Did he realise why the image had that strangely lemony-orange colour, my brother insisted, still holding the Reverend's Bible – and it was quite a large Bible, a handsome, priestly Bible – in his hand, staring at the image of a traditionally crucified Christ apparently suspended in this murky cellophane orange. 'I find it very beautiful,' the Reverend Pete confided, entirely failing to catch the dangerous edge in my brother's voice. He liked to surround himself, the Reverend Pat or Pip said, with images of Our Lord's passion. 'By the way, it was good to hear you in such fine voice,' he added appreciatively to my brother. 'You have a fine singing voice.

That was what did it, my brother later told me.

'The orange is the photographer's urine,' he said.

The Reverend said it was always heartening when relatives of the deceased found solace in the hymns and prayers. Not to mention the sermon, he laughed. He really was a cretin, my brother later observed. And in the same loud, plummy, hymn-singing voice that the clergyman had just been congratulating, he, my brother, announced, 'This photo is called the "Piss Christ". It is a blasphemous image.'

The Reverend was finally lost for words.

'Bro,' my sister said.

Three or four people had gathered round, whether to pay their respects to the mourners or to share the glow of the clergyman's charisma wasn't clear. Devotional imagery had always been important to him, the Reverend began to say.

'It's the "Piss Christ",' my brother suddenly shouted, as if inviting the whole room into the conversation, the hungry Christian soldiers with their vols-au-vent. The Reverend made to take the Bible from my brother's hand, but he raised his arm above his head to show it to the crowd. 'It's the "Piss Christ". *Ecce Homo*.'

I hurried across the room to him with my copy of *Prayers that Rout Demons*. Others had stepped in, asking my brother to please keep his voice down. To please not blaspheme. 'This cretin is complimenting me on my fine voice,' my brother told me loudly. Again he spoke in plummy tones. 'He can't distinguish between devotion and taking the piss. He has Christ crucified in piss on his Bible. He can't tell a Christ from a Piss Christ. I hate singing hymns,' my brother shouted at the Reverend Pip. 'Hymns are cretinous.'

As I joined the group, I felt a message arrive in my pocket. The Reverend was mouthing something inaudible. His face had lost its rosiness.

'Clergymen are cretins,' my brother was saying, 'when they're not criminals.'

'Please, Bro,' my sister begged.

'Mr Sanders,' one of the elders put in. 'Out of respect for your mother . . .'

'Dad was a clergyman,' I said.

'So I know the territory,' my brother laughed. 'At least my mother could tell a Christ from a Piss Christ,' he rounded on the elder.

Making a huge attempt to get control of the situation, speaking in a far louder voice than was necessary, my sister said to me, 'Tom, the Reverend was just saying that the east wall of the church with the little rose garden would be the perfect place for Mum's ashes. Shall we go and take a look?'

'Quite a few of the senior church folk have been scattered there,' the Reverend said, recovering his voice.

My brother was shaking his head savagely.

I said, 'No. That's not going to happen.'

My sister's eyes pleaded solidarity.

'Mother said I was to scatter her ashes.'

Only as I spoke these words did I finally realise the nature of Mother's concession. Out of love for me, pity for me, Mother had granted me this one filial duty, to be performed when she was already beyond contamination. I could scatter her ashes.

'There was nothing in the will.' My brother-in-law had arrived on the scene.

'It would still be a suitable place,' the Reverend said, 'whoever does the scattering. It would be good to keep Martha here at the St Peter and St Paul.'

'Piss Christ,' my brother muttered.

'Mother told me four years ago,' I said, 'that it would be my duty to scatter the ashes.' I spoke with sudden firmness. 'And I have not yet decided where I will put them,' I told the Reverend. There was a moment's quiet. My sister had understood. My brother was shaking his head. Five minutes later, climbing into the car to the crematorium, I read the message, '*Que haya un amor*, Señor Sanders.'

I don't know at what point I discovered that the coffin would not actually be committed to the flames during the brief ceremony at the crematorium. Perhaps I mentioned in the car what a profound effect it had had on me years ago when the curtains parted and Father's coffin had slid into the furnace. Perhaps, saying this, I was actually seeking to dampen down the flames as my brother went on muttering, 'Cretin, Piss Christ', and my brother-in-law, who was travelling with us now, rather peremptorily asked could he refrain please from blaspheming, and my brother replied that it wasn't his fault if the cretinous clergyman had an image of Jesus drowned in piss on his Bible. He was deeply shocked, my brother said in his plummiest voice.

'What struck me more than anything,' I said, 'was when the coffin slid away and you could distantly hear the flames roar and you knew your father's face had gone for ever.'

'Tommy!' my brother said quietly, and my sister said, 'Don't worry, Bro, they don't do that any more.'

'Don't do what?'

I hadn't grasped what she meant.

They had realised, my sister explained, that the knowledge the coffin was actually going into the flames, then the sight of the smoke when you left the crematorium, was upsetting; it was more than some people could bear, my sister said. So these days they burned the body sometime later – at night, usually.

There was a silence in the car as we took this in. Not only had Mother been embalmed, sanitised for public viewing, in such a way that had made viewing impossible, but now she wasn't actually to be burned while we were present. We were not to be close to her at that final moment. Her body would slide into the flames late at night, as we drank beer perhaps, or took a shower, or simply slept.

'So why,' my brother enquired, 'are we going to the crematorium?'

There was silence.

'To recover the expensive roses?'

'It's a ceremony,' my sister said patiently.

All our childhood my brother had teased my sister, and invariably my sister would lose her temper. Not now. Now my sister would not cry and she would not lose her temper. She had grown up.

'Ah,' my brother said, 'a ceremony. Prayers? Hymns? Magic spells?'

336

'They read out the Committal,' my brother-in-law said.

'Dust to dust?'

'Right.'

'That's something to look forward to then.'

'Bro!' my sister protested. 'You're amazing.'

Que haya un amor, I was thinking. The shrink's only advice was my own weird plea of that first meeting so long ago. That a love should be. Closing my eyes in the funeral car as we followed Mother's hearse along Mortlake Road, I imagined the words stretching out into the empty future, a slender bridge reaching through flames and mayhem. *Que haya un amor*.

Forasmuch as it has pleased Almighty God, began the Reverend Pete, *to take unto Himself the soul of our dear sister here departed* – there were only a dozen of us in the crematorium chapel – *we therefore commit her body* – again I was sandwiched between my brother and sister, as if this were the only order possible for us – *to be consumed by fire*. Again the children were on the other side of the aisle. A*shes to ashes, dust to dust*. I looked up and saw the Reverend Pete sprinkling holy water on the coffin as he spoke, something my low-church mother would never have wanted. But Mother was dead, she couldn't react. *In sure and certain hope*, the Reverend droned on, *of* – 'Piss Christ,' my brother muttered – *resurrection to eternal life* – Did the holy water prevent the flames from consuming the soul? Did 'sure' shore up 'certain' and 'certain' bolster 'sure' – *through our Lord Jesus Christ, who shall change our vile body that it may be like to His glorious body, according to the mighty working whereby He is able to subdue all things to Himself.*

The Reverend Pete clearly enjoyed intoning these solemn prayers. As had my father, in his time. The crucifix in urine was the divinity in the vile body, I thought. Incarnation. The Reverend Pip was right that the photo had a certain beauty. It was not an ugly thing. And what was wrong with pee, in the end? Perhaps that's what the photographer meant. The body isn't vile. Pee is beautiful. Absurdly, I imagined myself peeing on Mother's coffin, but not in disrespect. In the intimacy of shared mortality, the intimacy of those difficult nights four years ago when we didn't flush.

O Merciful God, the Reverend proceeded.

The pee in the outhouse was a gift of intimacy, I thought. It's curious how the past – one's own past, at least – is never past. I imagined a crucifix in that jar Malcolm and I had peed into. It was a gift Mother returned, when she breathed her last and her family leaned in close to breathe it with her. Only mortals can be intimate, I told myself in Mortlake Crematorium as the Reverend Pete shook his holy-water sprinkler again. We are not vile at all. That a love should be. 'Piss Christ,' my brother muttered. *In whom whosoever believeth shall live, though he die*, the Reverend Pat read. Elsa's body, in particular, was not vile. *And whosoever liveth and believeth in Him*, the Reverend pursued this monstrous paradox, *shall not die, eternally.*

I'm going.

We were half sitting, half kneeling, but now I stood up.

'Let's go,' I whispered to my brother. I took his hand.

'I have to go to the bathroom,' I muttered to my sister. She didn't object. She sat back to let me pass. My brother followed, his hand still in mine. 'Piss Christ,' he said. Audibly. We walked out. Two cab drivers were chatting under umbrellas at the crematorium gate. During the ride my brother kept his eyes closed. We had walked out of Mother's committal. I had left the twins behind. 'I knew I shouldn't have come,' my brother finally said. 'I shouldn't have come, Tommy.' 'I'll pick up the tab for the taxi,' I told him. 'That a love should be,' I texted David. 'Figure it out for yourself.'

'I'm at Heathrow,' I told Elsa later. 'What was the dream?'

'Oh, nothing.' She sounded tired.

'I've got a flight at seven-thirty.'

There was a brief silence.

'It must have been something.'

She half laughed.

'It frightened me. It was so vivid.'

I waited. My brother was bringing pints of Bombardier from the bar.

'I was at the beach with my family. We were at the water's edge, but nobody wanted to swim because the surf was so high. The waves were enormous.'

She paused.

'We were all laughing, and my sister had her baby in her arms. It was already born.'

My brother put the pints on the table.

'Then I saw there was someone way out in the sea, on the waves, floating, not even swimming.'

She stopped.

'Me.'

'Yes. I knew it was you at once. I didn't know what to do. I tried to go to you, but the others pulled me back. They were shouting, He's already dead. Can't you see, he's already dead?'

'Just a dream,' I told her. 'We should be landing at ten-fifty. Bubbly in the freezer for midnight.'

'To vile bodies,' my brother raised his glass.

EPILOGUE

In early June of the following year, on our first trip to London, Elsa and I met my sister at Vauxhall railway station. It was a weekday. After hurried introductions, we all took the train to Richmond, where Elsa got off to do some shopping, while my sister and I stayed on a stop further to St Margaret's, whence we walked to Marble Hill Park, crossed the broad grass lawns to the river and ordered ourselves cappuccinos in the cafeteria. As soon as we were settled, my sister opened the zip of the large shopping bag she was carrying and pulled out a tall black cardboard cylinder, perhaps twice the size good whisky comes in. The weather was bright and we were sitting outside with young mothers and their children, pensioners, amorous couples. There was a general hum of contentment. My sister placed the cylinder on the table between us and sipped her coffee as I fiddled with the lid. It was difficult to see how it opened. My sister explained something the lady in the crematorium had said to her: that you had to be careful with your nails because the seal was tight. In fact I had already torn a nail.

'Damn!'

'I hope,' my sister eventually said, watching me carefully as the lid finally came loose, 'that you're not going to get emotional, Tom.'

I was taken aback.

'Because I couldn't handle it,' she said.

She explained that Uncle Harry had begged her to join him at a hospice memorial service for those who had died the previous November. And some people had simply howled. After a while she had had to get up and go.

I assured my sister that I had done my crying at the funeral and expected this little event to be a breeze. 'A nice day out,' I said. 'No worries.' We finished our coffees and walked to the landing stage.

'Mum hated the water,' my brother had emailed me the day before, 'except for baptisms, of course.'

'She let Dad row her on the Thames,' I replied.

'Only because she was in love.'

Later he wrote, 'I suppose she's more likely to rejoin him in the river than in Paradise.'

The boatman untied a skiff and pushed us off. My sister sat in the stern with the tiller and I rowed us out into the stream, then along with the ebb tide down towards Richmond. After a few hundred yards I shipped the oars, removed the lid again and looked inside.

'It seems an awful lot, if we're really ninety-eight per cent water.'

'Because of the coffin,' my sister said. 'It's mostly wood ash.'

I held the cylinder over the side and began to tip it up. A grey grit slid out and spread in a slick on the water. I hadn't realised it would float. It looked dirty on the glassy surface of the river, as if we were polluting. I glanced round to see if anyone was watching, and rowed on a few strokes. Then I emptied the rest. This time I held the cylinder with my right hand and let the ash fall through the fingers of my left. It took about a minute. I dipped my hand in the river to wash the ash off, then rowed on to Richmond, where we picked up Elsa at the bottom of the steps by the bridge. She had bought avocado wraps and cold Corona. She and my sister clinked bottles and munched as I rowed back to Marble Hill. Fortunately, the tide was turning, the water was slack and there was a steady breeze to keep me cool. Sitting in the stern together, my sister and Elsa seemed to be getting on fine. There was no embarrassment between them as we rowed across the water where Mother's ashes must still be floating, or had sunk perhaps. In any event, I saw no trace of them. The slick had gone. Afterwards, Elsa and I drank the last Corona in the cab back to our hotel, where we made love on starched sheets, before heading out to enjoy the town.

FOR THE CHILDREN OF SAWREY
FROM
OLD MR. BUNNY

Frederick Warne has a continuing commitment to reproduce Beatrix Potter's exquisite watercolours to the highest possible standard. In 1993 and 1994, taking advantage of the latest advances in printing technology and expertise, entirely new film was made from her original book illustrations. The drawings are now reproduced with a quality and a degree of authenticity never before attainable in print.

FREDERICK WARNE

Published by the Penguin Group
27 Wrights Lane, London W8 5TZ, England
Penguin Books USA Inc., 375 Hudson Street, New York, N.Y. 10014, USA
Penguin Books Australia Ltd, Ringwood, Victoria, Australia
Penguin Books Canada Ltd, 10 Alcorn Avenue, Toronto, Ontario, Canada M4V 3B2
Penguin Books (N.Z.) Ltd, 182-190 Wairau Road, Auckland 10, New Zealand

Penguin Books Ltd, Registered Offices: Harmondsworth, Middlesex, England

First published 1904 by Frederick Warne
This edition with new reproductions of Beatrix Potter's book illustrations first published 1997

Colour reproduction by
Saxon Photolitho Ltd, Norwich
Printed and bound in Great Britain by
William Clowes Limited, Beccles and London

THE TALE OF
BENJAMIN BUNNY

❋

BY BEATRIX POTTER

FREDERICK WARNE

ONE morning a little rabbit sat on a bank.
He pricked his ears and listened to the
trit-trot, trit-trot of a pony.

A gig was coming along the road; it was
driven by Mr. McGregor, and beside him sat
Mrs. McGregor in her best bonnet.

AS soon as they had passed, little Benjamin
Bunny slid down into the road, and set off—
with a hop, skip and a jump—to call upon
his relations, who lived in the wood at the
back of Mr. McGregor's garden.

THAT wood was full of rabbit holes; and in
the neatest sandiest hole of all, lived
Benjamin's aunt and his cousins—Flopsy,
Mopsy, Cotton-tail and Peter.

Old Mrs. Rabbit was a widow; she earned
her living by knitting rabbit-wool mittens and
muffetees (I once bought a pair at a bazaar).

She also sold
herbs, and
rosemary tea,
and rabbit-
tobacco
(which is
what *we* call
lavender).

LITTLE Benjamin did not very much want
to see his Aunt.

He came round the back of the fir-tree, and
nearly tumbled upon the top of his Cousin
Peter.

PETER was sitting by himself. He looked poorly, and was dressed in a red cotton pocket-handkerchief.

"Peter,"—said little Benjamin, in a whisper—"who has got your clothes?"

PETER replied—"The scarecrow in Mr. McGregor's garden," and described how he had been chased about the garden, and had dropped his shoes and coat.

Little Benjamin sat down beside his cousin, and assured him that Mr. McGregor had gone out in a gig, and Mrs. McGregor also; and certainly for the day, because she was wearing her best bonnet.

PETER said he hoped that it would rain.

At this point, old Mrs. Rabbit's voice was heard inside the rabbit hole, calling— "Cotton-tail! Cotton-tail! fetch some more camomile!"

Peter said he thought he might feel better if he went for a walk.

THEY went away hand in hand, and got upon the flat top of the wall at the bottom of the wood. From here they looked down into Mr. McGregor's garden. Peter's coat and shoes were plainly to be seen upon the scarecrow, topped with an old tam-o-shanter of Mr. McGregor's.

LITTLE Benjamin said, "It spoils people's clothes to squeeze under a gate; the proper way to get in, is to climb down a pear tree."

Peter fell down head first; but it was of no consequence, as the bed below was newly raked and quite soft.

IT had been sown with lettuces.
  They left a great many odd little foot-marks
all over the bed, especially little Benjamin,
who was wearing clogs.

LITTLE Benjamin said that the first thing to be done was to get back Peter's clothes, in order that they might be able to use the pocket-handkerchief.

They took them off the scarecrow. There had been rain during the night; there was water in the shoes, and the coat was somewhat shrunk.

Benjamin tried on the tam-o-shanter, but it was too big for him.

THEN he suggested that they should fill the pocket handkerchief with onions, as a little present for his Aunt.

Peter did not seem to be enjoying himself; he kept hearing noises.

BENJAMIN, on the contrary, was perfectly at home, and ate a lettuce leaf. He said that he was in the habit of coming to the garden with his father to get lettuces for their Sunday dinner.

(The name of little Benjamin's papa was old Mr. Benjamin Bunny.)

The lettuces certainly were very fine.

PETER did not eat anything; he said he should like to go home. Presently he dropped half the onions.

LITTLE Benjamin said that it was not possible to get back up the pear-tree, with a load of vegetables. He led the way boldly towards the other end of the garden. They went along a little walk on planks, under a sunny red brick wall.

The mice sat on their door steps cracking cherry-stones, they winked at Peter Rabbit and little Benjamin Bunny.

Presently Peter let the pocket-handkerchief go again.

THEY got amongst flower-pots, and frames and tubs; Peter heard noises worse than ever, his eyes were as big as lolly-pops!

He was a step or two in front of his cousin, when he suddenly stopped.

THIS is what those little rabbits saw round that corner!

Little Benjamin took one look, and then, in half a minute less than no time, he hid himself and Peter and the onions underneath a large basket. . . .

THE cat got up and stretched herself, and came and sniffed at the basket.

Perhaps she liked the smell of onions!

Anyway, she sat down upon the top of the basket.

She sat there for *five hours*.

*   *   *   *   *

I cannot draw you a picture of Peter and Benjamin underneath the basket, because it was quite dark, and because the smell of onions was fearful; it made Peter Rabbit and little Benjamin cry.

The sun got round behind the wood, and it was quite late in the afternoon; but still the cat sat upon the basket.

AT length
there was a
pitter-patter,
pitter-patter,
and some
bits of
mortar fell
from the
wall above.
The cat
looked up
and saw old
Mr. Benjamin
Bunny prancing
along the top of the
wall of the upper terrace.

He was smoking a pipe of rabbit-tobacco, and had a little switch in his hand.

He was looking for his son.

OLD Mr. Bunny had no opinion whatever of cats.

He took a tremendous jump off the top of the wall on to the top of the cat, and cuffed it off the basket, and kicked it into the greenhouse, scratching off a handful of fur.

The cat was too much surprised to scratch back.

WHEN old Mr. Bunny had driven the cat into the green-house, he locked the door.

Then he came back to the basket and took out his son Benjamin by the ears, and whipped him with the little switch.

Then he took out his nephew Peter.

Then he took out the handkerchief of onions, and marched out of the garden.

WHEN Mr. McGregor returned about half an hour later, he observed several things which perplexed him.

It looked as though some person had been walking all over the garden in a pair of clogs —only the foot-marks were too ridiculously little!

Also he could not understand how the cat could have managed to shut herself up *inside* the green-house, locking the door upon the *outside*.

WHEN Peter got home, his mother forgave him, because she was so glad to see that he had found his shoes and coat. Cotton-tail and Peter folded up the pocket-handkerchief, and old Mrs. Rabbit strung up the onions and hung them from the kitchen ceiling, with the bunches of herbs and the rabbit-tobacco.